Professor Bernard Knight, CBE, became a Home
Office pathologist in 1965 and was appointed Professor
of Forensic Pathology, University of Wales College of
Medicine, in 1980. During his forty-year career with the
Home Office, he performed over 25,000 autopsies and
was involved in many high profile cases.

Bernard Knight is the author of twenty-three novels,
a biography and numerous popular and academic
non-fiction books. *Crowner Royal* is the thirteenth novel
in the Crowner John Series.

You are welcome to visit his website at
www.bernardknight.homestead.com

Also by Bernard Knight

CROWNER ROYAL

Bernard Knight

POCKET
BOOKS

LONDON • NEW YORK • TORONTO • SYDNEY

First published in Great Britain by Simon & Schuster UK Ltd, 2009
This edition published by Pocket Books, 2009
An imprint of Simon & Schuster UK Ltd
A CBS COMPANY

1 3 5 7 9 10 8 6 4 2

Simon & Schuster UK Ltd
1st Floor
222 Gray's Inn Road
London WC1X 8HB

www.simonandschuster.co.uk

Simon & Schuster Australia
Sydney

A CIP catalogue record for this book is
available from the British Library

ISBN: 978-1-84739-328-9

Typeset by Rowland Phototypesetting Ltd,
Bury St Edmunds, Suffolk

Printed and bound in Great Britain by CPI Cox & Wyman,
Reading, Berkshire RG1 8EX

AUTHOR'S NOTE

In the twelfth century, the vital Exchequer of the Royal Council (the *Curia Regis*), which governed England, gradually moved from the old Saxon capital of Winchester to London. It was housed in the Palace of Westminster, which was also the main residence of the king – though when in England, the kings (especially Henry II and John) spent much of their time away from Westminster, progressing around the countryside with their huge court retinues.

William the Conqueror had first resided in the Great Tower (later known as the 'Tower of London'), which he built to dominate the city, but he later moved into Edward the Confessor's old palace at Westminster, depicted in the Bayeux Tapestry – though like most monarchs until John, he spent little time in England. His son William Rufus began rebuilding the palace and his huge Westminster Hall, dating from 1097–9, was the largest in Europe and is still in use today. For centuries, the rest of the palace grew piecemeal around it, several times being devastated by fire, which eventually caused Henry VIII to abandon it as a royal residence and move to the nearby Palace of White Hall. The present huge edifice which houses Parliament, was the result of almost total rebuilding after the fire of 1834, Westminster Hall being virtually the sole survivor of the Norman structure, together with the crypt of St Stephen's Chapel, which was the first home of the House of Commons.

The palace was only yards from the Confessor's great abbey, between it and the river. In those days, before the Thames was confined within embankments, it was much wider and shallower, being fordable at low tide just above the palace at Horseferry. The whole area was marshy, often flooded, so Westminster was built on a gravel bank, known as Thorney Island because it was covered in brambles. A number of streams drained the marshes, such as the Tyburn, which formed the southern boundary of the Westminster settlement.

A small town grew up around the abbey and palace, which was less than two miles from the walled city of London. From Westminster, a country road passed through the village of Charing and along the Strand, past the New Temple of the Knights Templar to Ludgate, just across the Holbourn stream, later called the Fleet.

The exact topography of Westminster in the twelfth century is not precisely known, but archaeologists are still discovering traces, such as those found between 1991 and 1998 during excavations for the extension of the Jubilee Underground line. In addition to the many clerks, court officials and tradesmen who lived there, some of the Ministers of State had town houses, though others lived in the palace itself.

What is clear is the economic and political divide that existed between Westminster and the city, as it does to this day. The former was an administrative and monastic centre, whilst the fiercely independent city was the commercial hub of England, with the competition and jealousies between them never far below the surface. In the Middle Ages, the city was sometimes for, and sometimes against, the reigning monarch, as when they supported King Stephen against Empress Matilda or the barons against King John.

Relations with government were not always easy: the city demanded the right to appoint its own mayor in 1193, and in 1194 they did not accept the imposition of the coroner system, their two sheriffs carrying out these functions in the city and the county of Middlesex. At a distance of over 800 years, it is unclear how the jurisdiction of the Coroner of the Verge, around which this Crowner John story revolves, clashed with these other entrenched interests, but it seems likely that he did not have an easy time.

The Coroner of the Verge dealt with all cases within a twelve-mile radius of the court, wherever that might be on its frequent procession around England. Later, this office became known as 'The Coroner to the Royal Household', which in very recent times came into the public eye in relation to the controversial inquest into the death of Princess Diana.

One of the problems of writing a long series of historical novels, of which this is the thirteenth, is that regular readers will have become familiar with the background and the main characters and may become impatient with repeated explanations in each book. On the other hand, new readers need to be 'brought up to speed' to appreciate some of the historical aspects, so a Glossary is offered with an explanation of the medieval terms used, especially relating to the functions of the coroner, one of the oldest legal offices in England.

Any attempt to use 'olde worlde' dialogue in a novel of this early period would be as inaccurate as it would be futile, for in the late twelfth century, most people would have spoken Early Middle English, quite incomprehensible to us today. The ruling classes would have used

Norman-French, while the language of the Church and virtually all writing was Latin. Few people could read and write, literacy being virtually confined to the few people who were clerics in holy orders. Only a minority of these clerics were ordained (bishops, priests and deacons), most being in 'minor orders', unable to celebrate mass, take confessions and give absolutions. These were clerks, lectors, sub-deacons and door-keepers and there were even more 'lay brothers' who performed the menial work of religious institutions.

All the names of characters in the book are authentic, who are either actual historical persons or taken from the court rolls of the period. The only money in circulation would have been the silver penny, apart from a few foreign gold coins known as 'bezants'. The average wage of a working man was about two pence per day and coins were cut into halves and quarters for small purchases. A 'pound' was 240 pence (100p) and a 'mark' 160 pence (66p), but these were nominal accounting terms, not actual currency.

maps

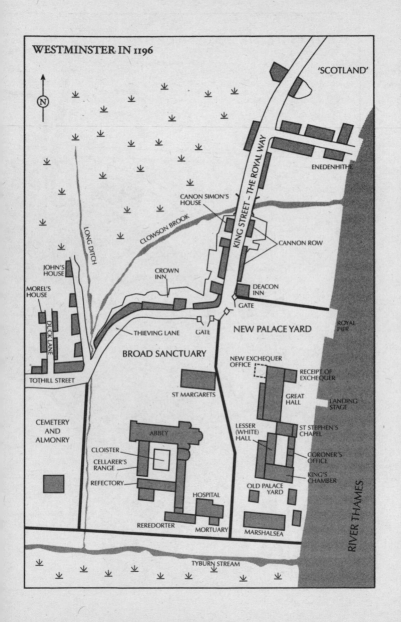

WESTMINSTER IN 1196

'SCOTLAND'

N

KING STREET – THE ROYAL WAY

ENEDENHITHE

CANON SIMON'S HOUSE

CLOWSON BROOK

LONG DITCH

CANNON ROW

JOHN'S HOUSE

CROWN INN

MOREL'S HOUSE

DECK LANE

DEACON INN

GATE

ROYAL PIER

THIEVING LANE

GATE

NEW PALACE YARD

TOTHILL STREET

BROAD SANCTUARY

NEW EXCHEQUER OFFICE

RECEIPT OF EXCHEQUER

ST MARGARETS

GREAT HALL

LANDING STAGE

CEMETERY AND ALMONRY

ABBEY

LESSER (WHITE) HALL

ST STEPHEN'S CHAPEL

CLOISTER

CORONER'S OFFICE

CELLARER'S RANGE

KING'S CHAMBER

REFECTORY

OLD PALACE YARD

HOSPITAL

REREDORTER

MORTUARY

MARSHALSEA

RIVER THAMES

TYBURN STREAM

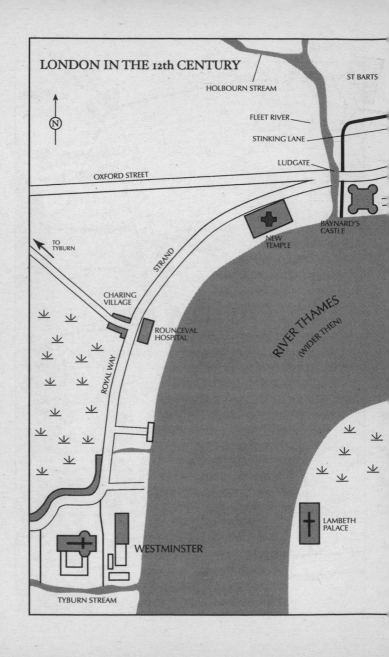

LONDON IN THE 12th CENTURY

N

HOLBOURN STREAM

ST BARTS

FLEET RIVER

STINKING LANE

LUDGATE

OXFORD STREET

BAYNARD'S CASTLE

NEW TEMPLE

TO TYBURN

STRAND

CHARING VILLAGE

ROUNCEVAL HOSPITAL

RIVER THAMES
(WIDER THEN)

ROYAL WAY

LAMBETH PALACE

WESTMINSTER

TYBURN STREAM

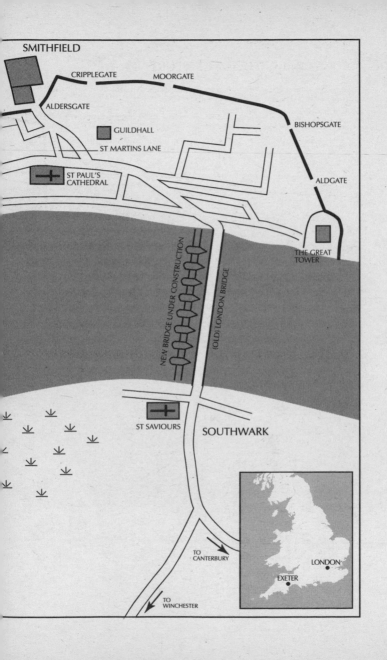

GLOSSARY

ABJURING THE REALM

A criminal or fugitive gaining sanctuary in a church, had forty days grace in which to confess to the coroner and then abjure the realm, that is, leave England, never to return. France was the usual destination, but Wales and Scotland could also be used.

He had to dress in a sackcloth and carry a crude wooden cross to a port nominated by the coroner. He had to take the first ship to leave for abroad and if none was available, he had to wade out up to his knees in every tide to show his willingness to leave. Many abjurers absconded *en route* and became outlaws; others were killed by the angry families of their victims.

ALE

A weak drink brewed before the advent of hops. The name derived from an 'ale' which was a village celebration, where much drinking took place, often held in the churchyard. The words 'wassail' and 'bridal' derive from this.

BAILEY
Originally the defended area around a castle keep, as in 'motte and bailey' but later applied to the yard of a dwelling.

BALDRIC
A diagonal strap over the right shoulder, joined back and front to the belt, to carry the weight of a sword.

BARON
A lord who was a 'tenant-in-chief,' holding his land directly from the king, who owned the whole country. A 'Baron of the Exchequer' came to mean a judge of the royal courts, not connected with the actual Exchequer.

BOTTLER
Servant who attends to the supply of drink, later known as a 'butler'.

CANON
A senior priest in a cathedral, deriving his living from the grant of a parish or land providing an income.

COIF
A close fitting helmet of felt or linen, worn by either sex and tied with tapes under the chin.

COVER-CHIEF
From the Norman-French 'couvre-chef', a linen or silk cloth that covered a lady's head, the ends hanging down the back and over the bust, usually secured by a head-band. In Saxon times, it was called a 'head-rail'.

CURIA REGIS
The Royal Council, composed of major barons, judges and bishops, who advise the king.

COB
A building material made from clay, lime, ferns, dung, etc (also see 'wattle and daub')

COG
The common sea-going sailing vessel of the Middle Ages, derived from the Viking longship, but much broader and higher, with a single mast and square sail. There was no rudder, but a steering oar on the 'steerboard' side.

CONSTABLE
Several meanings, either the custodian of a castle, but also applied to a watchman who patrolled the streets.

CORONER
Though there are a couple of mentions of a coroner in late Saxon times, the office really began in September 1194, when the royal justices at their session in Rochester, Kent, proclaimed Article Twenty, which in a single sentence launched a system that has survived for over 800 years.

They said '*In every county of the King's realm shall be elected three knights and one clerk, to keep the pleas of the Crown.*'

The reason for the establishment of coroners were mainly financial; the aim was to sweep as much money as possible into the royal Exchequer. Richard the Lionheart was a spendthrift, using huge sums to finance his expedition to the Third Crusade in 1189 and for his wars against the French. Kidnapped on his way home from Palestine, he was held for well over a year in prisons in Austria and Germany and a huge ransom was needed to free him. To raise this money, his Chief Justiciar, Hubert Walter, who was also Archbishop of Canterbury, introduced many measures to extort money from the population of England.

Hubert revived the office of coroner, which was intended to raise money by a variety of means, relating to the administration of the law. One of these was the investigation of all deaths which were not obviously natural, as well as into serious assaults, rapes, house fires, discovery of buried treasure, wrecks of the sea and catches of the royal fish (whales and sturgeon). Coroners also took confessions from criminals seeking sanctuary in churches, organised abjurations of the realm (q.v.), attended executions and ordeals (q.v.) and trial by battle.

As the Normans had inherited a multiple system of county and manorial courts from the Saxons, the coroner also worked to sweep lucrative business into the royal courts. This gave him the title of 'Keeper of the Pleas of the Crown', from the original Latin of which (*custos placitorum coronas*) the word 'coroner' is derived.

It was difficult to find knights willing to take on the job, as it was unpaid and the appointee had to have a large private income of at least twenty pounds a year. This was supposed to make him immune from corruption, which was common amongst the sheriffs. Indeed, another reason for the introduction of coroners was to keep a check on the sheriffs, who were the king's representatives in each county ('shire-reeve').

CRESPINES
Nets, sometimes of gold or silver thread, which confined plaited coils of hair worn at the sides of ladies' heads.

DESTRIER
A large war-horse, capable of carrying an armoured knight.

EXCHEQUER
The financial organ of English government, where all taxes were received in coin twice-yearly from the sheriffs. The calculations were performed with counters on a large table spread with a chequered cloth to assist accounting, which gave rise to the name.

FARM
The taxes from a county, collected in coin on behalf of the sheriff and taken by him personally every six months to the Exchequer in Winchester and later Westminster. The sum to be raised was fixed annually by the Exchequer and if the sheriff could raise more, he could keep the excess, which made the office of sheriff much sought after.

FLUMMERY
A blancmange-like soft dessert made by straining boiled oatmeal and flavouring with fruit and honey.

FRUMENTY
A dish of wheat boiled in milk with sugar and spices such as cinnamon. Meat such as venison could be added.

HOSE
Long stockings, usually single-legged, secured by laces to an underbelt. Worn under the tunic and sometimes having a leather sole in place of a shoe.

HUNDRED
An administrative sub-division of a county.

MARSHALSEA
Originally the province of the Marshal, who was responsible for all horses and transport for the royal entourage. It was then applied to the marshal's court, where offences concerning the king's servants were heard. It contained a prison and the later meaning was confined to this.

MASLIN BREAD
A coarse loaf of wheat and rye.

MAZER
A drinking vessel originally made from maple wood.

ORDEAL
An ancient ritual intended to reveal guilt or innocence. The subject of the enquiry, in the presence of the coroner and a priest, had to submit to painful procedures, such as walking barefoot over nine red-hot ploughshares, taking a stone from the bottom of a vat of boiling water or licking a red-hot iron. If the affected part had healed well after three days he was adjudged innocent. Women were tied up and thrown into deep water – if they floated, they were guilty!

The ordeal was abolished by the Vatican in 1215.

OSTLER
A servant who attends to the care and stabling of horses.

OUTREMER
Literally 'the land beyond the sea' referring to the Christian kingdoms in and around the Holy Land.

PALFREY
A small horse for riding, especially used by ladies.

PELISSE
An outer garment worn by both men and women, with a fur lining for winter wear. The fur could be sable, rabbit, cat, marten etc.

POTAGE
Soup or stew.

PRECENTOR
A senior monk or priest in a cathedral or abbey, who organised the choral services and music as well as the library and archives.

PRESENTMENT
At coroner's inquests, a corpse was presumed to be Norman, unless the locals could prove 'Englishry' by presenting evidence of identity by the family. If they could not, a 'murdrum' fine was imposed by the coroner, on the assumption that Normans were murdered by the Saxons they had conquered in 1066. Murdrum fines became a cynical device to extort money, persisting for several hundred years after the Conquest, by which time it was virtually impossible to differentiate between the races.

PROCTOR
A senior priest or monk responsible for discipline in an abbey or cathedral. He had lay servants to carry out his orders.

POSSET
A drink made from hot spiced milk curdled with wine and sweetened with sugar or honey.

REREDORTER
Literally 'behind the dorter' (the dormitory of an abbey or priory). The reredorter was the lavatory block, almost always built over running water.

ROUNCEY
A general purpose horse, used for riding or as a packhorse.

RUSH LAMP
Illumination given by a lighted reed standing in a small pot of animal fat, as candles were expensive.

SCAPULAR
The black tabard-like garment worn over the white habit of a Cistercian monk, or the black habit of the Augustinians.

SCRIP
A pouch carried on a man's belt.

SECONDARY
A young man aspiring to become a priest when he reached the minimum age of twenty-four. Secondaries assisted canons and their vicars in their cathedral duties.

SERGEANT (or SERJEANT)
Several meanings, either a legal/administrative officer in a Hundred or a military rank of a senior man-at-arms. A serjeant-at-law was a barrister.

SURCOAT
An outer garment worn over the tunic, often open in front.

TIRE-WOMAN
A female attendant on a lady of substance.

TORC
A heavy necklace, originally solid gold or twisted strands, Celtic in origin.

TRENCHER
A thick slice of stale bread, used as a plate on the scrubbed boards of a table, to absorb the juices of the food. Often given to beggars or the dogs at the end of the meal.

TUNIC
The usual wear for men, a long garment belted at the waist, the length often denoting the wearer's status. Working men usually wore a short tunic over breeches.

SHINGLES
Roof covering of thin wooden tiles, in place of the usual thatch.

WATTLE AND DAUB
A building material plastered over woven hazel panels between house-frames to form lanels. Usually made from clay, horsehair, straw and even manure (q.v. 'cob').

WIMPLE
A cloth of linen or silk, pinned at each temple, framing a lady's face and covering the throat.

CHAPTER ONE

In which Crowner John loses a corpse

'Not half as good as Mary's, but it will have to do us for now,' grunted John de Wolfe, looking down into a wooden bowl in which a few lumps of meat floated in a pallid stew. Across the small table, Gwyn of Polruan was already slurping his food from a horn spoon, alternately dipping a hunk of barley bread into the liquid.

'It's not too bad, Crowner! At least it's piping hot, though I don't know that we need that on a day like this.'

He stopped eating momentarily to take a deep swallow from a quart pot of ale and wipe the sweat from his brow with the back of his hand. It was just past noon and the sun was at its highest, pouring down its stifling radiance on the lower valley of the Thames.

'I wonder what my wife's doing now?' he added pensively. 'Pouring better ale than this for her customers in the Bush, no doubt!'

His comment emphasised the nostalgic mood that both men were in at that moment. Though they were sitting in a relatively decent house in Westminster, their thoughts were a couple of hundred miles away. Sir John was contemplating his old dog in Exeter, his mistress in Dawlish and his former mistress now decamped back to her home in South Wales. Given the food situation, he also had thoughts to spare for his excellent cook Mary, who had once been another of his paramours. The only person for whom he had no nostalgia was his wife Matilda, who was sulking in self-imposed exile in a Devonshire convent.

'Still, I'm glad we're out of that bloody palace,' persisted the big Cornishman. 'The airs and graces of that lot got right up my nose!'

John grunted, his favourite form of response. 'Thomas seems to enjoy it, though he always loved being with all those damned clerks and priests. But I agree, it's easier being in our own dwelling.' He had rented the cottage to get away from the stifling atmosphere of the palace staff quarters where they had spent the first week.

They finished up their stew and waited for Osanna to waddle in and take away their bowls to the kitchen hut in the backyard. The wife of their obsequious landlord Aedwulf, Osanna was an immensely fat woman who did the cooking, washing and perfunctory cleaning of the house in Long Ditch.

As they sat on their stools in expectation of the next course, John went over yet again in his mind the events of the past two months. He was not all that happy with what had taken place, but he consoled himself with the thought that he had had no choice. As a knight of the Crown, he had little option but to obey orders – especially when they came directly from the mouth of his king! For more than eighteen months, he had been the coroner for Devon, but Richard the Lionheart in his wisdom had recently decided that he needed a coroner dedicated to the English court, similar to the one that existed in his Normandy capital of Rouen. Given the past association of de Wolfe with the king and his chief minister Hubert Walter, John had been the obvious choice, so now here he was in Westminster, like it or not.

The move had coincided with an upheaval in his private life, as his mistress Nesta had despaired of any future for them together and gone home to Wales to get married. His surly wife Matilda, equally exasperated by his infidelities, had once again taken herself to a nunnery and this time seemed determined to stay there. To round off the situation, he had resumed his affair with an old flame, Hilda of Dawlish, though distance now seemed to have frustrated this particular liaison.

Gwyn's deep voice broke through his reverie.

'We could do with a couple of good murders or a rape to cheer us up, Crowner!' he boomed, only half in jest. 'Too damned quiet in this holy village.'

He was referring to the small town of Westminster, which was a unique enclave ruled by the abbot, William Postard. Though geographically part of the county of Middlesex, it lay outside its jurisdiction on both religious and political grounds, as it contained both the great abbey of Edward the Confessor and the Royal Palace, the residence of the Norman kings since William the Conqueror had moved out of the Great Tower.

De Wolfe grunted his agreement, as the caseload so far had been derisory compared with the number they had dealt with across the large county of Devon. He wondered again why the king had been so insistent on having a 'Coroner of the Verge', when there seemed so little business for him.

Osanna came in with a platter containing a boiled salmon, which the two men looked at with resignation. It was Tuesday, not a Friday fish day and they had already had salmon twice in the past week. The fish was so plentiful in the Thames and its tributaries that it appeared on the menu with depressing regularity.

However, they were hungry and there were buttered carrots and onions to go with it, as well as more fresh bread.

'I've got eels for tomorrow, you'll like those!' she announced cheerfully, ignoring the glowering look from the coroner. Her accented English was strange after the West Country dialect, but he understood her well enough to be depressed by the prospect of yet another meal dredged from the river.

'A nice leg of mutton or a joint of beef wouldn't come amiss!' grumbled Gwyn, as he filtered the last of his stew through the luxuriant ginger moustache that hung down both sides of his mouth, the colour matching the unruly mop of hair on his head. The Cornishman was huge, both in height and width, with a prominent red nose and pair of twinkling blue eyes.

His colouring was in marked contrast to that of his lean master, who though as tall as Gwyn, exuded blackness, from the jet of his long, swept-back hair to the stubble on his gaunt cheeks. Heavy eyebrows of the same hue overhung deep-set eyes, between which was a hooked nose that gave him the menacing appearance of a predatory hawk. To complete this sombre appearance, his long tunics and surcoats were always black or grey. In campaigns in Ireland, France and the Holy Land, the troops had known him as 'Black John', though this was partly from the grim moods that could assail him when things went wrong.

When they had finished their meal, the two men buckled on their sword belts and left their rented house, one of several two-storey thatched cottages facing a muddy channel known as the Long Ditch, which drained into a stream called the Clowson Brook. At the southern end, the track joined the ominously named Thieving Lane, which curved around the landward side of the abbey towards the river. Here the main gates to the abbey and the palace stood together, at the point where King Street formed the start of the 'Royal Way' which led along the river towards the bustling city of London, almost two miles away.

The great church of Edward the Confessor loomed above them on their right as they walked slowly towards the palace, where government administration was now largely centred, having been gradually transferred from the Saxon capital of Winchester. The heat was intense and dust lifted from the road as they walked. They took care to keep clear of the central stone-edged gully which was filled with a drying slurry of sewage and rubbish, now stinking in the summer sun.

The north side of the lane was lined with small houses and cottages, built either of planks or wattle-and-daub, mostly with roofs of thatch or wooden shingles. One or two better dwellings were stone-built, with tiled roofs which were less hazardous than straw or reeds, which had caused many disastrous town fires.

The heat was keeping some people indoors, but many remained on the streets. The busiest time was the early morning market, when people were out buying their food for the day, but there were still some haggling at the stalls that sold a whole range of goods. Handcarts and barrows trundled up and down and Gwyn and the coroner had to stand aside as a flock of goats were driven past on their way to the water meadows that lay beyond Tothill Street.

It was little more than a five-minute walk from their door to the palace and it was with some relief that they passed through the arched gate into New Palace Yard, where a sentry struck the butt of his pike on the ground in salute to the king's coroner.

The palace was a rambling collection of buildings of various types and ages, the major feature being the huge hall built almost a century ago by the Conqueror's son, William Rufus. Behind and to the sides of that, an extensive collection of stone and wooden buildings had sprung up without much attempt at organised planning. More buildings, stables and houses lay behind the hall, including another hall, a chapel and a large block which formed the king's accommodation. This was largely unused, as Richard the Lionheart had spent barely a few months in the country during the whole of his reign, preferring to be across the Channel in Normandy or his homeland of Aquitaine. At the farther end, a wall and then the Tyburn stream demarcated the palace precinct from the marshy pastures beyond.

The coroner and his officer walked down the landward side past the great hall and turned into a small doorway in a two-storeyed stone building that housed the Chancery clerks. A gloomy corridor gave immediate relief from the heat; they pushed past worried-looking clerics clutching rolls of parchment as they scuttled between various offices.

'I'm starting to get the hang of this place at last,' muttered Gwyn. 'For the first couple of weeks, I didn't know where the bloody hell I was!'

He turned left at a junction in the passageway, walking with a sailor's roll, a legacy of his youth as a fisherman. De Wolfe loped alongside him with characteristic long strides like the forbidding animal whose name he bore.

'It's very different from Rougemont,' he agreed, thinking with some nostalgia of Exeter Castle where his brother-in-law, the former sheriff, had grudgingly allotted them an attic room in the gatehouse.

Another dozen yards brought them to another junction, but here a flight of stone stairs rose to the upper level. At the top, another corridor abruptly changed from stone to timber construction as they entered an older part of the palace. Clumping across the planks, Gwyn led the way to one of half a dozen doors set along a passage. They were now above and to the river side of the block housing the royal apartments.

Gwyn lifted the wooden latch and stood aside for his master to enter. Though there was a hasp and staple on the doorpost, there was no lock, as apparently it was felt that there was unlikely to be anything worth stealing in a coroner's office.

'It's cooler in here, thank God,' muttered de Wolfe. He strode across the almost bare room to the window, whose shutter was propped wide open on an iron hook. Leaning on the worn timber of the unglazed frames, he stared out at the river, whose brown waters flowed sluggishly past as the tide began to ebb.

A hundred paces away, the scrubby grass shelved down to a rim of dirty gravel at the edge of the water, but John knew that in a few hours the shallow river would shrink to half its width between wide stretches of thick mud. Indeed, only half a mile upstream, it was possible for carts and horses to cross at the lowest point of the tide.

'Where's our saintly clerk? Still saying his prayers, I suppose,' grunted Gwyn, as he closed the door. The coroner turned away and sat behind his table to stare around the room. It shared one feature with their previous accommodation in Exeter – the sparsity of furniture. A bare trestle table occupied the centre, pitted and stained with years of spilt ink and aimless disfigurement with dagger points. John had a chair, a clumsy folding device with a leather back and on the opposite side of the table was a plank-like bench and two three-legged stools, which Gwyn had 'acquired' from a neighbouring empty room.

'Thomas could have shared the house with us, but

he obviously prefers the company of those monks and clerics across the road,' observed de Wolfe. He said this without sarcasm or rancour, as after three years of dismal exclusion from his beloved Church after being defrocked, John did not begrudge his clerk's delight in his recent reinstatement.

Gwyn pulled a stool over to the window and sat with his elbow on the sill, catching the slight breeze that came off the river.

'I reckon we'd be more use back in Devon that sitting on our arses up here, Crowner,' he growled. 'Not even a decent hanging to attend!'

One of the coroner's duties was attendance at all executions to record it and confiscate any property the felon might possess. But so far there had not been one hanging during the six weeks that they had been living in Westminster.

'I don't even know where the damned gallows is!' complained the Cornishman, almost plaintively.

'They've just started using a place up on the Tyburn stream, where it's crossed by the Oxford road,' replied John. 'They strung up those rebels there a couple of months ago – William Longbeard and his followers. Now it's used as much as the Smithfield elms.'

He was interrupted by a patter of feet on the boards of the passageway outside and the door opened to admit a scrawny young man with a slight hump on one shoulder. He wore a faded black cassock and his lank brown hair was shaved off the crown of his head to form a clerical tonsure. Thin and short of stature, Thomas de Peyne had a sharp nose and a receding chin, but this unprepossessing appearance hid an agile mind crammed with a compendious knowledge about all manner of subjects.

'I regret my lateness, Crowner,' he panted. 'But the archivist engaged me in a discussion about the

Venerable Bede and I could hardly detach myself from such an eminent man.'

De Wolfe grunted his indifference as Thomas hurriedly sat himself at the other side of the table. He scrabbled in his shapeless shoulder bag for his quills, ink horn and parchment, and set them on the table, ready to get on with copying the proceedings of a previous inquest on a child who had been crushed by the collapse of a wall in King Street.

'Take your time over that, little fellow,' rumbled Gwyn cynically. 'There's little else for you to write, so make it last!'

'Gwyn is right, I'm afraid,' agreed de Wolfe. 'Our duties seem very light here. I'm beginning to wonder why the king was so keen to drag us away from Exeter.'

Thomas looked up from spreading a roll of parchment on the table and weighing down the curling ends with pebbles.

'Sir, perhaps things will soon be different when the court moves away from Westminster into the shires.'

John detected a slight hint of smug satisfaction in the clerk's voice and stared at him suspiciously. Thomas was always a mine of information, which had often proved useful to the coroner.

'Going into the shires?' he demanded. 'Have you heard anything about that?'

'It is common knowledge that the old queen is expected to arrive in the near future,' answered de Peyne. 'And I did overhear a suggestion that she wishes to progress with the whole court to visit her youngest son at Gloucester.'

There was a snort of disgust from across the room. 'That bastard Lackland! Do we have to go anywhere near that treacherous swine?' Gwyn turned and spat through the window to express his feelings about Prince John, Count of Mortain.

'We must admit he's kept his head down lately,' conceded de Wolfe. 'I think Hubert Walter has got his measure after all the problems John caused our king.'

The coroner expected his outspoken officer to reply with more condemnation of the man who had tried to unseat his royal brother from the throne – but Gwyn was staring intently out of the window.

'What in hell is going on out there?' he roared suddenly, leaning across the sill and pointing with a brawny arm.

'Hey, you! Stop, you bastard, stop!' he yelled at the top of his voice, gesticulating in a frenzy of impotence.

De Wolfe skidded back his chair and strode to the window to see what had so outraged his officer. He looked down past Gwyn's shoulder at the strip of bare ground that stretched between them and the riverbank. He was just in time to see a figure racing past below them and vanishing around the corner of the building to their right.

'What happened?' demanded John, but Gwyn pushed past him and was already lumbering out of the door, shouting over his shoulder as he went.

'He stabbed some fellow on that landing stage – just a moment ago!' John craned his neck to look to the left along the bank and saw that someone lay crumpled on the planks of a small pier that projected out into the river on wooden stakes. The body was perilously near the edge, one arm and a leg hanging over the swirling brown water. John pounded after Gwyn, pushing aside a couple of men as he leapt down the stairs three at a time. At the bottom, he caught up with his officer, who seemed uncertain which way to run. They could go back to the main entrance, but that was in the opposite direction from the end of the building around which they had seen the assailant disappear.

'I'll go to the front!' yelled de Wolfe. 'See if you can

get out somewhere that way,' pointing down the dark corridor on the ground floor. Even after a few weeks, they were still unsure of the layout of the rambling collection of buildings, other than the well-trodden path to their own chamber.

Gwyn thundered off, his big feet slamming on the flagged floor, massive shoulders jostling people aside as he went. John, with a timid Thomas following behind, jogged out into the Palace Yard and doubled back around the Great Hall towards the river.

'We'd better see how that man has fared!' he panted, as he raced for the landing stage. It was not the main river approach to Westminster; this was further downstream, where an elaborate pier had been built for royalty and nobles visiting the abbey and palace. The one seen from their room was a much more modest structure used by many small boats, the wherries that ferried people across the Thames and down to the city.

De Wolfe ran towards it, but he was not the first to arrive. As he hurried the last few yards, he heard a commotion ahead and saw three men clustered on the landing stage, peering over the edge. One of them wore the long tunic and round helmet of a palace guard.

'He's gone, fell off just as we got here!' hollered the guard, pointing down at the water. The tide was now ebbing quickly and turbulent eddies swirled around the piles holding up the jetty. John looked downstream and saw a man floating face down with limbs outstretched. He was already twenty yards away and moving further away each second. The skirts of his black cassock wrapped around his legs as a sudden whirlpool in the muddy water spun the body. It submerged momentarily, then resurfaced yards away towards to the centre of the river. There was no boat anywhere near, only a couple of wherries hundreds of yards away and a distant barge moving downriver with the tide.

For a moment, John considered diving in after the man, but he was an indifferent swimmer and the treacherous-looking vortices in the river made him hesitate. The guard, a burly man with a black beard, sensed his indecision and gripped his arm.

'No point in risking yourself as well, sir! By the looks of it, he's already a corpse!'

He pointed down between his feet, where a wide stain of dark blood covered the boards, some of it dripping down the cracks into the river.

'How came he to fall in?' demanded the coroner. 'I saw him from my window and he was lying just here!'

One of the others, a fat monk in the black habit of a Benedictine, seemed in genuine anguish over what he had just witnessed. 'As I arrived, he seemed to have a spasm and rolled over into the water!' he wailed. 'There was nothing I could do to save him.'

By now, half a dozen other people had arrived, Thomas de Peyne among them. De Wolfe pulled away from the gabbling, gesticulating throng and grabbed his clerk's arm.

'Get the names of these people, so that I can question them later!' he snapped. 'See if any of them saw exactly what happened – I'm off to see if Gwyn has found the son of a whore who did this!'

He jogged off, this time going down the riverbank, with the Great Hall and then St Stephen's Chapel on his right hand. As he rounded the corner of the furthermost wing of the palace, he met his officer stamping towards him, the scowl on his face telling him that he had failed in his mission.

'Those bloody passages are like a rabbit warren,' he complained. 'By the time I found a door out to the back of the place, the fellow had long gone.'

'Did you see what he looked like?' demanded John.

Gwyn shook his head. 'I saw him for barely a few seconds. He struck the man on the pier and as he fell the assailant ran like hell down the bank. He was tall and heavily built, wearing a short tunic and breeches, both brown as I recall.'

'What about his face?'

'He had a white linen helmet on, tied under his chin, but as he ran he held a hand against his face, so as not to be recognised.'

The coroner glared around him in frustration, looking at the jumbled collection of buildings that made up this back end of the palace enclave. He had not been here before and saw that stables, wagon sheds, wash-houses and barracks filled the area between the rear of the palace and the boundary wall, beyond which was the confluence of the Tyburn stream with the river. There were a number of people about – soldiers, grooms, farriers, as well as women and children who lived in some of the small cottages that were dotted between the other buildings. None of them looked like the man Gwyn had described, though if he had pulled the white coif from his head, there would be nothing to mark him out.

'He could have slipped into the abbey – or back into the palace before I got here,' grunted the Cornishman. 'Or even gone over into the village.'

De Wolfe shrugged in disgust and turned back the way he had come. 'Let's go back to the landing stage and see if Thomas has squeezed anything out of those people.'

The little clerk had no writing materials with him, but his excellent memory had catalogued half a dozen names, including the guard, three monks and a couple of Chancery clerks who had been on their way out of the palace soon after the incident had occurred. They were still there when John returned and he set about questioning them.

'Does anyone know who the victim might have been?' he demanded, scowling around at the faces before him.

'It was one of the Steward's men,' piped up one of the clerks. 'I glimpsed his face just before he fell into the water. I don't know his name, but I've seen him around the palace.'

'I think he worked in the guest hall,' said his companion, a gangling young man whose tonsure looked strange on his bright ginger head. 'I've seen him scribing at a desk in the bottler's chamber there.'

The monks knew nothing about anything, being visitors to the abbey from their priory in Berkshire and the guard vaguely claimed to have seen the dead man from time to time.

'What about the villain who did this?' rasped de Wolfe. 'Did any of you get a good look at him? Any idea who he might be?'

There were glum looks and shaking of heads all round.

'I first noticed him only when he was running away,' proclaimed the guard. 'It was that that made me look towards this landing stage – then I saw the man lying on the boards here.'

He gave a description that was as unhelpful as Gwyn's, but added a small piece of information. 'I saw a wherry a few yards off the pier, obviously going away after having landed someone. He was well beyond hailing distance by the time I got here.'

The Thames wherries were almost as common as seagulls – flimsy craft with one oarsman, who plied their trade on a populous stretch of water, which had only one bridge, two miles downriver.

The clerks and monks looked anxious to go about

their business, so John dismissed them, warning them that they might be required to attend an inquest. Thomas quietly reminded his master that this might be difficult with no body.

'Strictly speaking, sir, we don't even know if he is dead! He might have revived and crawled out further down the riverbank.'

Gwyn gave an explosive snort of derision. 'Of course he's bloody dead! Half his lifeblood is on the timbers here and then his head was sunk under this brown shit that passes for London river water!'

De Wolfe turned to leave, telling the guard to get someone with a bucket to swill away the blood from the planks of the jetty.

'We must find someone who can tell us who the dead man was,' he growled. 'He might have a family to mourn him.'

Though the victim was apparently in holy orders, most of these were in the lower grades and were not necessarily celibate like ordained priests. They were all, however, able to claim the protection of the Church through its 'benefit of clergy' when it came to a conflict with the secular powers.

Thomas pattered along behind the two bigger men as they left the landing stage, the old phthisis of the hip that had afflicted him as a child giving him a slight limp. 'How will you discover who he might be, Crowner?' he asked. 'This place must have a couple of hundred people living and working in it.'

'Ask the damned Steward, I suppose, if those clerks reckoned he was one of his staff,' John replied abruptly.

They went back into the palace through the main entrance behind the Great Hall, the two helmeted sentries saluting de Wolfe as he marched towards the doorward's chamber just inside. Here a fat clerk sat behind a table, talking to a sergeant of the guard. This was a tall man with three golden lions *passant guardant*, the royal arms of Richard Coeur de Lion embroidered across the chest of his long grey tunic. The soldier recognised John – in fact, he remembered him from Palestine where Black John's prowess in the Crusade was almost legendary. As soon as the coroner had explained the problem, the sergeant insisted on personally conducting de Wolfe to the Steward's domain and set off ahead of the trio into the bowels of the palace, which to them was uncharted territory.

After a number of twists and turns, all on the ground floor, they came to a wide passageway, on one side of which were kitchens, full of smoke, steam, raucous voices and the clatter of pots. Opposite were store-rooms, with men trundling baskets, sacks and barrels from a wide door leading to a carter's yard at the rear.

'One of the Steward's top men lives in here, Sir John,' declared the sergeant, going to a doorless arch between two of the stores. He waved de Wolfe inside, then excused himself and strode away. John saw a cluttered room, with two desks occupied by young clerks wrestling with lists on parchment and piles of notched wooden tallies. Between them, on a slightly raised platform, was a sloped writing desk like a lectern. Behind this stood a thin, austere-looking man of late middle age, dressed in an expensive but sombre tunic that reached down to his ankles. Unlike John's collar-length black hair, the man's greying thatch was shaved up to a horizontal line around his head, in the typical Norman fashion. He stared haughtily at the visitor and enquired as to his business.

'I am Sir John de Wolfe, the king's coroner,' snapped John, who had taken an instant dislike to this man. 'And who might you be, sir?'

The official's manner softened immediately –

everyone in Westminster had heard of the appointment of the new Coroner of the Verge – a man high in the favour of both the Chief Justiciar and of King Richard himself.

'I am Hugo de Molis, the king's Chief Purveyor in England,' he said with pride. 'When the court is here at Westminster, then I offer the Steward my help in provisioning the palace.'

This sounded to John like a roundabout way of saying that he was the assistant steward, but even so, this was a responsible task. The Steward was one of the important officers of the court and always a nobleman, so this Hugo must be at least a manor-lord. His declared appointment as Chief Purveyor would make him one of the most disliked men in England, for the purveyors were those officials who went ahead of the court when it progressed around the countryside. Their task was to ensure that food and lodging were available each night for the hundreds of men, women and animals that trundled along with the monarch and his nobles. Except where they stayed at the king's own manors, the purveyors ruthlessly confiscated beds, food, fodder and everything else needed for the court's sustenance. They were constantly accused of failing to pay the market price for what they took – or not paying at all. A plague of locusts could not have been more efficient in laying waste the countryside and many folk on hearing of the approach of the court, fled into the woods with as many of their possessions as they could carry. John explained what had happened during the last half-hour.

'I am the court's coroner, charged with dealing with all fatal and serious assaults within the Verge. It seems virtually certain that this man has met a violent death and I need to know who he was, so that I can begin to deal with the matter.'

He added that two palace clerks seemed convinced that the victim was a member of the Steward's entourage, probably working in the guest chambers.

Hugo de Molis gripped the sides of his lectern and stared at the coroner. 'A man in minor orders working there?' he muttered. 'That can only be Basil of Reigate, one of my assistants!'

'We have no body to show you yet,' said de Wolfe gravely. 'But first I must be sure that this Basil is not alive and well. Can you see if he is at his usual post?'

'I know that he is not!' retorted the purveyor. 'For I myself sent him this very morning across the river to pay for vegetables and to place more orders with the farms in Kennington.'

'It seems he was attacked as he left a boat returning to this shore, which would tally with what you say,' replied de Wolfe.

'Was he robbed?'

'As we have no body and thus no purse, we cannot tell,' answered John irritably. 'Would he have been carrying much money in the course of his duties?'

Hugo de Molis shook his head. 'If he was attacked on his way back here, then he would have already paid off the farmers. Though perhaps a robber might not be aware of that.'

The coroner considered this for a moment – violent robbery was a common crime and seemed the most likely explanation.

'Tell me about this man, Basil of Reigate. It may be that I will have to identify his body if and when it is recovered downriver. And you may be required to confirm it.'

De Molis's lean, humourless face showed some distaste at the prospect. 'I am a very busy man, coroner,' he said dismissively. 'He was but a minor official, employed to serve the guest apartments on the upper floor.'

'In what way did he serve them?' persisted de Wolfe.

'His duty was to make sure that everything necessary for the accommodation and sustenance of palace guests was available to the chamberlain's men. They have their own cooks up there, so food and drink has to be supplied constantly. He was under my orders as to what was requisitioned from the main storerooms down here.'

This was of little interest to de Wolfe, who had a slaying and a vanished murderer to deal with. Further questions revealed that Basil had no family in Westminster and lived in the clerk's dormitory in the palace. The Chief Purveyor seemed more concerned at finding a replacement for the dead man than in regretting his death, but he agreed to report the matter to the Keeper of the Palace, Nicholas de Levelondes, who was ultimately in charge of the staff who saw to the running of the establishment. He also grudgingly agreed to send one of his young clerks up to the guest chambers to make certain that Basil of Reigate was not sitting there alive and well.

'What do we do now?' asked Gwyn, as they began retracing their steps through the warren that was the ground floor.

'Wait until we hear of a body being washed up on the mud somewhere,' muttered John somewhat heartlessly. 'Thomas was right, without a corpse I have no jurisdiction.'

'Are you going to report this to Hubert Walter?'

De Wolfe shook his head. 'He'll not want to hear of the killing of some obscure clerk, especially as the most likely explanation is a violent robbery.'

'What happens if we catch the villain who did it?' persisted Gwyn. Things were so different here from the straightforward routines that he was used to in Devonshire.

John thrust his fingers through the thick black hair that swept back from his forehead. 'God knows we have enough judges in this place – there's three sitting almost every day on the King's Bench in the Great Hall. I suppose Thomas will write up the details on his rolls as usual and we present the case to the justices, just as if it was an Eyre coming to Exeter.'

They reached the bottom of their staircase, familiar territory at last and began to climb to their chamber.

'But what about the abbot's jurisdiction here?' asked Thomas, always mindful of the rights of his beloved Church. 'He holds the Liberty of Westminster, which includes the abbey, the village and the palace itself. I hear from my clerical colleagues that William Postard is most jealous of his powers, worse than many a manor-lord. In fact, he is also lord of several manors in the vicinity, which he rules with an iron hand!'

Gwyn, ever cynical about anything ecclesiastical, added his pennyworth as they reached the upper corridor. 'If he's anything like the Abbot of Tavistock, he'll have his own gallows tucked away somewhere – unless he uses that one you spoke of at Tyburn.'

It was true that some of the more powerful church-men were equally as despotic as barons and earls – and many were more concerned with their estates, politics and even warfare as with the cure of souls and the propagation of the Faith. Hubert Walter himself was not only Archbishop of Canterbury, but was also the Chief Justiciar and had been at the king's right hand during the later battles of the last Crusade. It would not surprise de Wolfe if Abbot William Postard also exercised the power of life and death in his little realm of Westminster.

ChAPTER TWO

In which Crowner John disagrees
with a sheriff

Although the coroner feared that the missing corpse might be carried downriver and be lost for ever at sea, it did not in fact travel very far from Westminster.

The Thames was flowing sluggishly after several weeks of dry weather and the neap summer tides were low. By next morning, the dead man's cassock had snagged on a partly submerged tree stump in the shallows, just past the outflow of the Holbourn or Fleet stream on the northern bank, where the city wall ended.

Though corpses were found almost daily in the great river, ones with a tonsure and clerical garb were not that common and a wherryman rowing empty towards the wharf at Baynard's Castle was intrigued enough to recover the body. He hauled it aboard and had a quick look to see if the fingers bore any rings that could be looted. Disappointed, he fumbled in the leather scrip on the man's belt and was equally chagrined to find only two silver pence. He had half a mind to throw the corpse back into the water, but being so near the shore, he feared that he might be seen. Reluctantly, he rowed on to the landing stage, where a handful of citizens were waiting, augmented by some loafers who had seen the sodden body sprawled in the flimsy craft. As the cadaver looked fresh and not bloated or stinking, they helped him haul the victim out on to the wharf, where it was laid on the boards.

'It's a clerk,' declared an old man, hopping nearby on a crutch. 'May even be a priest?'

At this, a portly monk in the white habit of a Cistercian, pushed his way through the small crowd that had gathered and imperiously waved aside the nearest onlookers.

'Keep away, let me see!' he snapped. 'If it is one of my brothers, he must be treated with all respect.'

Bending over the sodden corpse, he looked at the plain cassock and noted the lack of any pectoral cross or beringed fingers. He decided that this was no archdeacon or even vicar, but merely someone in minor orders.

'What's that embroidered on his front, then?' asked the man on crutches, whose infirmity obviously did not extend to his eyesight. The Cistercian bent lower and squinted at some unobtrusive embroidery just below the left shoulder. The dark red stitching did not show up well against the soaked black fabric, but now his short-sighted eyes made out three small lions, one above the other.

'This must be a brother in the king's service!' he exclaimed, straightening up. 'Quite probably from Westminster.'

The boatman nodded sagely. 'That would fit, for he's quite fresh, even in this hot weather. So he's not come far down the river, certainly not from Windsor or Reading.'

The monk, losing interest now that the dead man was obviously not someone important in the Church hierarchy, stepped back and began moving towards the end of the landing stage, beckoning the boatman to take him across the river.

'Get the poor fellow taken to some shelter out of the sun,' he called over his shoulder. 'And tell the watch to notify the palace that it might be a royal servant.'

As he lowered himself cautiously into the wherry and was rowed off across the wide river, two large men in leather jerkins and serge breeches came striding down to the upper end of the landing stage from Thames Street, which ran along the edge of the river. They carried heavy staves and wooden truncheons hung from their wide belts. Attracted by the small crowd, these were city watchmen, employed by the mayor and aldermen to keep order in the streets. This was easier said than done, as there were only a few dozen of them to control London's thirty thousand inhabitants. Employed mainly for their brawn, rather than brains, they still managed to cope with this incident efficiently, as they frequently had to deal with 'drowners'. Taking the brief story from the onlookers, they decided to move the cadaver to the nearest church, as he appeared to be some kind of cleric. However, as they were tipping the corpse on to a barrow commandeered for the purpose, the change in posture caused blood to start leaking through the cassock. The lame onlooker, who was avidly watching the proceedings, was again the first to spot this and he gave a shout of warning.

'Look at that cut in his clothing!' he yelled. 'The man's been stabbed!'

Everyone crowded around until the watchmen shoved them roughly aside to make sure for themselves.

'God's guts, this is getting too heavy for us!' muttered the senior of the pair to his partner. 'A king's clerk, murdered and thrown into the river. This is a job for the sheriff's men!'

*

That evening, John de Wolfe decided to eat his supper in the palace, rather than eat alone in the house in Long Ditch. As usual, Thomas was supping in the abbey refectory, where he could converse with his fellow clerics, a pleasure little short of paradise for him after his years in the ecclesiastical wilderness. Gwyn, who was as fond of alehouses as the clerk was of the Church, had gone to his favourite tavern in Thieving Lane, to play dice with new cronies he had made amongst the palace guards.

In the early evening, John left his bare chamber overlooking the river and went down through the passages to the Lesser Hall, often known as the 'White Hall', on the abbey side of the main palace buildings. Although spacious, it was a quarter of the size of William Rufus's Great Hall and had a beamed ceiling, as there was another floor above it, a dormitory for palace staff. When the king was in residence, he ate there on the raised platform at one end, except when there were major feasts in the Great Hall. It was also occasionally used for meetings, including that of the King's Council, but at other times the hall provided meals for the middle echelons of the palace inhabitants – the high and mighty, like the Justiciar, Steward, Treasurer, Barons of the Exchequer and the Lord Chamberlain, either lived outside in their own houses or ate in private dining rooms upstairs, adjacent to the royal chambers.

As John pushed through the heavy curtain over the side entrance, he met a buzz of conversation, punctuated by raucous laughter and the clatter of ale pots and dishes. Unlike the refectory in the nearby abbey, there was no respectful muting of conversation and no verses from the Gospels or the Rule of St Benedict droned continually by a monk at a lectern during the meal, though a grace was always said by one of the priests present.

A servant near the door offered him a bowl of water and a towel to wash his hands before eating. He looked around at the scene. Two rows of trestle tables ran down the length of the hall and servants were scurrying back and forth from the door to the kitchens that he had seen when he had visited the Chief Purveyor earlier that day. The benches along the tables were occupied by a few score diners and the coroner slid into a vacant place. The meal had already started and grace had been said before his arrival. He found himself between a powerfully built man in a dark-red tunic and a small priest with a completely bald head.

Almost before he had sat down, a young servant boy placed a pint of ale in a pewter tankard before him and another deftly dropped a trencher on to the scrubbed boards of the table. John grunted a greeting to those on each side and nodded to a man and woman sitting opposite. The priest ignored him, continuing to mumble Latin prayers between sucking at a chicken leg with his toothless gums, but the man on his left, a handsome fellow in his late twenties responded civilly enough.

'You are Sir John de Wolfe, the new law officer, I believe? We heard that the king, God save him, had appointed someone to keep us in order!'

De Wolfe reached out to spear a large slice of roast pork with the eating knife he kept sheathed on his belt. He placed it on his trencher, along with a liberal covering of fried onions ladled from a pottery bowl.

'I am indeed, though hardly new now, for I've been here for well over a month. And I doubt I will be keeping you in order, unless you are dead or suffer severe violence!' As he attacked the meat with his fingers, his neighbour introduced himself.

'I am Ranulf of Abingdon, a knight from Berkshire. For my sins, I live in the palace as an under-marshal –

and have to endure the food in this place almost every day!'

John raised his ale pot to his new friend and wished him good health. 'I know your master William the Marshal quite well,' he added. 'I served under him in the Holy Land and we met again not long ago when he came as a judge to settle a problem we had in Devon.'

The great William Marshal, Earl of Pembroke, was a legend, both for his prowess as a warrior and his eminence in political matters under several kings.

'He has spoken of you more than once,' replied Ranulf. 'I envy the good standing you have not only with the Justiciar and the Marshal, but with the king himself.'

The man opposite leaned forward, just as John was trying to get some food into his mouth. 'You mentioned Devon, sir. I thought you had an unusual accent. I am from Blois myself, so perhaps I am more sensitive to the different dialects in England.'

They were speaking Norman-French, as did most people in the palace, above the level of servants.

'I was born in Devon, sir, so it is to be expected,' said John rather shortly. The speaker was a short middle-aged man, running to fat, dressed in a rather dandified blue tunic with ornate embroidery around the neck and cuffs. He had a sharp nose and small blue eyes, his face rimmed with a narrow beard which matched the cap of brown hair on top of his head.

'Renaud de Seigneur is Lord of Freteval in the county of Blois and has been a guest here for several weeks,' explained Ranulf, detecting some brusqueness in de Wolfe's tone and hastening to mollify it. 'Lady Hawise d'Ayncourt is his gracious wife.'

Ranulf smiled at the woman across the table and John looked at her for the first time. Until then, she had kept her head down and seemed intent on eating.

Her face had been partly obscured by the wide linen couvre-chef, or cover-chief, that veiled her head and the silken wimple that hid her temples and throat.

At Ranulf's words, she lifted her head to smile at de Wolfe and he realised that she was quite beautiful. Always having a keen eye for a pretty woman, the many weeks of celibacy had sharpened his appreciation even more. Her smooth oval face had long-lashed dark eyes, a small straight nose and lips that pouted slightly in a full Cupid's bow. What little could be seen of her hair under her head-rail was a glossy black with an almost midnight-blue sheen to it. She said nothing, but there was a look in her lovely eyes that said that she found this eagle-faced man of interest to her.

'My wife was born in England, Sir John, though her family came from Gascony,' confided Renaud de Seigneur. 'She has a brother in Gloucester and a sister married to a manor-lord near Hereford, so we are journeying there to visit them.'

'I have not seen them for eight years since Renaud married me and carried me off to France!' Hawise spoke for the first time, her husky voice matching her exotic appearance which suggested some Latin ancestry, though John detected a trace of a West Country accent similar to his own. He guessed that she was about twenty-five years of age, her husband being at least two decades older. She and her maid – a silent mousy girl who kept her eyes on her food throughout the entire meal – were the only women in the hall. Except for the families of some of the servants who lived at the back of the yards, women were not allowed in the palace, apart from the guests, who usually stayed with their husbands and tire-women in the quarters above.

Servants cleared dishes as they were emptied and brought fresh ones constantly. Herring, salt cod, eels, capon and mutton appeared, with platters of boiled beans, carrots and cabbage to bulk out the flesh. Bottler's assistants topped up their pots with ale or cider and large jugs replenished pewter cups of red wine.

Both the food and drink were of only moderate quality – especially the somewhat sour wine – but they were adequate for daily fare. John's subsistence was part of the perquisites of his appointment, but he supposed that those who were not on the palace staff had to pay for their keep, unless they were official invitees.

'Are you staying in the guest chambers here?' he asked, directing his question at Renaud, but making firm eye contact with his wife. 'I assumed that you would eat there.'

He had not the slightest interest in their arrangements, but could not resist trying to further a dialogue with such an attractive woman.

'We often do stay upstairs, but we sometimes find it more congenial here, hearing news and gossip and meeting interesting people,' said Hawise. She looked from under lowered eyelids at de Wolfe and the tip of a pink tongue appeared briefly.

Her husband seemed oblivious to her mild flirting, but Ranulf looked uneasy. 'Renaud de Seigneur and his lady are waiting for the arrival of Queen Eleanor, so that they may go with the court to Gloucester rather than risk the journey alone.'

De Wolfe cut a slice of mutton from a joint in front of him and lifted it on to his trencher. He thought of offering some to Hawise, as it was courteous for a man to supply a lady with her food, but as her husband was sitting alongside her, he thought he had best leave that duty to him, in case he was thought impertinent. Instead, he followed up Ranulf's remark.

'I had heard that the queen was coming. Do we know when? And will the whole court be moving with her?' he asked.

The knight from the Marshalsea nodded, as he waved a hand to a servant to take away the remnants of his own trencher. 'Within a couple of weeks, it is said – depending upon a fair wind from the mouth of the Seine. We have a troop of men-at-arms ready down at Portsmouth to escort her party when it arrives.' He swallowed the rest of his wine. 'And yes, within a few days of her arrival, I suspect that the grand dame will want to be on the move again, first down to Windsor, then Marlborough on the way to Gloucester.'

The eyes of the woman opposite locked with John's and a frisson of desire passed unbidden through him.

'Sir John, you are well-acquainted with the great persons of state, it seems,' she said. 'It seems strange that everyone still refers to her as "the queen" when the real queen is never mentioned!'

De Wolfe was reluctant to pursue this topic, but felt he must make some reply. 'Berengaria has never set foot in England, my lady, as I'm sure you know. She was not even at King Richard's coronation, across the yard there in the abbey.'

'I hear Eleanor is a formidable woman,' persisted Hawise. 'Have you met her yourself?'

He shook his head regretfully. 'I fear not, my lady. When I was with the king, both in Palestine and on his disastrous journey homewards, his mother was far away.'

'Didn't she go with her husband on the Second Crusade?' Hawise's eyes were wide with excitement.

'She did indeed, madam – and legend has it that she led her own company of high-born ladies dressed as Amazons!'

Hawise gasped, a hand fluttering at her neck.

'She is certainly a most extraordinary woman,' observed Renaud. 'I was in her presence once in Mortain when she visited Count John there. Though advancing in years, she is still a handsome and regal lady. I would not care to cross her!'

Nor would anyone else, de Wolfe thought. The old queen, once wife to King Louis VII of France before she married Henry II, was a powerful figure behind the Plantagenet family. Imprisoned by her husband for sixteen years for siding with their sons against him, she had later helped to save England from her youngest son's treachery when his brother was imprisoned in Germany. The conversation continued across the table for some time, mainly about the personalities in the court and the odd position of Westminster in the dual kingdom of Normandy and England.

Primarily a soldier, John had never taken that much interest in politics, though of course he knew the general situation. It was Ranulf of Abingdon who was the best informed, having been a resident here for three years.

'This is a strange place, de Wolfe,' he began, pushing back on the edge of the table with his hands. 'A royal court without a king! Since his coronation in eighty-nine, I doubt he's spent more than a few months in England – and for most of that, he was marching around the country, rather than settled in Westminster.'

Renaud de Seigneur nodded in agreement, watched intently by his wife. John had the feeling that they were avid for details of what went on in this enclave on the bank of the Thames.

'The Lionheart's true court is Rouen,' Renaud declaimed. 'Though he was born in Oxford, he is first and foremost Duke of Aquitaine and Normandy.

England is but a colony to him, a source of money and men to fight his wars.'

Blindly loyal to Richard though he was, de Wolfe could hardly deny this statement, though he was resentful to hear it fall from the lips of a Frenchman. Renaud was not even a Norman, coming as he did from the county of Blois, which had a somewhat ambiguous position between the territories of Richard and Philip of France.

'Yet there seems to be a large complement of ministers, officers, clerks and servants here, considering the sovereign never sets foot in the place?' observed Hawise, giving John another melting glance from her lovely eyes.

Uneasy that her husband might take offence at this obvious flirting under his very nose, John turned to Ranulf. 'The place always seems busy, even if we have no resident royalty.'

Flattered to be looked upon as the fount of knowledge, Ranulf launched into an explanation.

'England is now governed largely from here, even in the absence of the king,' he explained. 'The *Curia Regis*, though it mainly sits in Rouen, is also based here, in so far as decisions about England are concerned, so the major barons, bishops and other great men are constantly back and forth. This is why we maintain the guest accommodation – though the ministers of state usually have houses of their own in the neighbourhood.'

'In my father's day, I recall that Winchester seemed to be the most important place,' observed Lady Hawise.

Ranulf, who seemed to have the same appreciation of a fair lady as the coroner, nodded as he gave her his most winning smile.

'Winchester was the Saxon capital, but now almost everything has been moved up to Westminster.' He looked rather dramatically over his shoulder and lowered his voice. 'In fact, I am involved in organising the final part of the move now. The Exchequer is already here, but the remainder of the Treasury will be coming up next week, under heavy guard.'

The French baron and his wife looked suitably impressed and Renaud tapped the side of his nose conspiratorially.

'They'll hang you for giving away such state secrets to foreigners,' he joked. 'Maybe I'll hire some Welsh mercenaries and ambush you on the way!'

The under-marshal grinned and winked at Hawise, but she seemed more interested in John, who was scowling at Ranulf's indiscretion. 'Stranger things have happened,' growled de Wolfe. 'I'd not let such talk go further.'

To get away from the subject, he turned the conversation to the stabbing that had happened that day, of which the couple opposite were unaware.

'It doesn't seem to be a robbery, though we've got no body yet,' he concluded. 'So I wouldn't be too concerned about being at risk from murderous cutpurses in the palace precinct. But be careful always, Sir Renaud. Don't let your wife go out unchaperoned.'

Hawise d'Ayncourt gave him a brilliant smile at this. 'I'm sure with a Crusader on the premises, we can all sleep safely in our beds, Sir John!'

Renaud stood up rather abruptly and helped his wife to her feet, as he bade the two men goodnight. As he walked her away with her arm through his, he murmured, 'You needn't make it too obvious, lady.'

She pouted a little as they walked up the hall. 'You never know when two court officers might be useful,' she whispered.

*

The news came in mid-morning, just after Gwyn had returned from collecting their daily rations. Part of their expense allowance was in bread, candles and ale, as Thomas had his own allotment over in the abbey, in return for working in the scriptorium when not on coroner's business. Gwyn had lumbered in, clutching four barley loaves and a bundle of candles, which he dumped on the table in front of his master.

'I'll go back for the ale in a moment,' he grunted, taking a breather before he went for their daily two-gallon jar. The allowances were dispensed from a room near the entrance to the Lesser Hall. Thomas had run out of rolls to scribe and was quietly reading his precious copy of the Vulgate of St Jerome, while de Wolfe was sitting with a quart pot of yesterday's ale, morosely contemplating the floor and wondering what was happening back in Exeter.

Gwyn slumped on a stool and began cutting a thick slice from one of the loaves with his dagger, to go with a lump of cheese that had been wrapped in a cloth on a nearby shelf. He was about to offer the same to his companions, when there was a rap on the door and the warped boards creaked open to admit the head of a young page.

'Pardon me, sires, but I was sent by the doorward to give you a message,' he said hesitantly. He looked about ten years old and seemed overawed by the presence of the king's coroner.

'The Keeper of the Palace requests that you attend upon him directly, sir. It is something relating to a dead body.'

He made to withdraw, but de Wolfe roared at him and his curly head bobbed back again.

'You had better lead us to wherever he is, boy!' he snapped, his scowl frightening the lad even more.

'By Job's pustules, I don't want to spend the next hour wandering these damned passages!'

John had met the Keeper of the Palace, Nathaniel de Levelondes, several times, once in the company of Hubert Walter, the Chief Justiciar, when they first arrived, but he had no idea where he was installed in the rambling buildings. Leaving Gwyn and Thomas to enjoy their bread and cheese, he followed the nervous page along the same floor towards the royal chambers, a three-storey block built around a private cloister adjacent to the Lesser Hall. Between this and the back of the Great Hall, were the guest chambers, which de Wolfe calculated must be over the Steward's domain that they had visited the previous day. The lad, who de Wolfe guessed must be the son of a baron being placed here for eventual advancement in court, led him to a narrow stair to an upper floor, where he held aside a heavy leather curtain which did service as a door.

John went inside and found an elderly clerk writing at a table and a younger man, also with a tonsure, shuffling parchments at another. The latter jumped to his feet and ushered de Wolfe through an archway into an inner room.

'Sir, the coroner is here.'

The Keeper of the Palace was seated behind a desk, reading a parchment roll which he was unfurling with both hands. It looked as if he was one of the relatively few people not in holy orders who could read and write and John felt a pang of envy, as he had been trying to learn for almost two years, with indifferent success.

De Levelondes was an elderly man who seemed to lean forward with his head outstretched and de Wolfe noticed that his hands trembled as laid down the parchment. He had a thin, careworn face, deep grooves running down each side of his mouth. His hair was as grey as his long tunic, over which he carried a large ring of keys on a thin chain around his neck. John knew that he was not a knight or a baron, but came from an affluent Kentish family which held the post of Keeper as a hereditary gift from old King Henry. In the hierarchy of the Norman court, de Wolfe was his superior and he gave a brief nod of the head as a deferential greeting.

'I am sorry to trouble you, Sir John, but I thought I had better deliver a message to you myself, rather than depend on perhaps the garbled efforts of yet another messenger.'

His voice was slightly tremulous as he rested his quivering hands on the edge of the table for support. This was not due to anxiety, but appeared to John to be some disorder of the nerves. De Wolfe muttered a greeting in reply and waited for enlightenment.

'A lay brother from the chapel of Baynard's Castle in the city came on a donkey a short while ago, sent by the priest there to tell us that a body had been recovered from the nearby foreshore. He was apparently someone in holy orders, and had the royal device displayed upon his robe.'

John's black eyebrows rose on his forehead.

'Someone from here? Then surely it is likely to be that of the man who was stabbed on the landing stage yesterday. You heard about that?'

The Keeper nodded. 'Hugo de Molis informed me as soon as he had confirmed that Brother Basil had not returned. I understand that this probably falls within your remit as Coroner of the Verge?'

De Wolfe nodded. 'It most certainly does! My officer saw it happen and we only just missed catching the bastard who was responsible.'

Nathaniel de Levelondes sank back on his stool as if unsteady on his feet. 'The corpse is being held inside

Baynard's Castle until someone confirms it is indeed Basil of Reigate.'

John rubbed the black stubble on his face. 'I must go there at once – but I don't know this fellow from Adam!'

'No doubt Hugo de Molis can send someone with you who knew him. He will also be able to direct you to the castle.'

Glad at last to have a proper case to deal with, the coroner was eager to be off and managed to find his way down to the purveyor's chamber. Here de Molis dispatched one of the young clerks to accompany John and after gathering Gwyn and Thomas from their upstairs chamber, they collected their horses from the livery stables and set off, the clerk on a pony commandeered from another of the under-marshals who organised all transport for the palace. The coroner's trio had ridden up from Exeter five weeks earlier and John had his old destrier Odin, while Gwyn kept to his big brown mare and Thomas rode a docile palfrey.

The clerk, a cheerful young man named Edwin, was happy to have a few hours away from his tedious duties in the stores and regaled them on the way with accounts of the places they passed during the two-mile journey. They walked their steeds across the Palace Yard between the Great Hall and the wall of the abbey to reach the gateway into King Street, commonly known as 'The Royal Way'. The wide track led northward, crossing the Clowson Brook, with houses on either side.

'That lane goes down to Enedenhithe, a wharf on the river,' said Edwin, with a cheerful wave of his hand. He pointed to a short side street lined with larger stone houses, which lay on their right. 'Many of the senior court officers live there – and some of the king's ministers!' he added with almost proprietorial satisfaction.

Beyond this, the houses petered out and there were meadows, those toward the riverbank being called 'Scotland' by the clerk for some obscure reason. At the small village of Charing, the road turned to follow the curve of the river, where the Hospital of St Mary's Rounceval was placed on the bend.

From there up to the Preceptory of the Templars, with their new round church, the track followed the raised strand above the edge of the river, the clerk enthusing about some large houses, gardens and orchards that were scattered along both sides. By now the city was looming in front of them behind its great wall, as the road dipped down into the valley of the Fleet. The city was already overflowing beyond its walls, set out by the Romans in a great irregular half-circle. Each end abutted on the riverbank, the further one finishing at William the Bastard's great tower that still loomed threateningly, reminding the citizens of its royal power.

John and his two henchmen had been to London before, but the sheer size of the place never ceased to impress them. The great bulk of St Paul's stuck up brazenly, shepherded by dozens of church spires and towers across the city.

'That's Baynard's Castle there!' pointed Edwin, as they crossed the wooden bridge over the murky Fleet river to pass through Ludgate, the westernmost of the eight entrances to the city. His arm flung out towards a low fortress tucked inside the end of the city wall where it met the Thames, just beyond some busy wharves at the mouth of the Fleet.

The road was crammed with people, carts, barrows and animals coming and going through the gate. Inside, they climbed part of the slope of Ludgate Hill, then turned right to squeeze along a narrow, noisy, stinking street to the gateway of the castle. Here the two

sentries recognised a knight of some substance by
the size of his destrier, his sword and his forbidding
appearance, together with the three men who formed
his entourage. They saluted him and waved him into
the large bailey that occupied much of the space within
the walls. In the centre were several stone buildings
forming a palace and a keep, with other half-timbered
and wooden structures built against the inner walls.
There were two turrets at each end of the castellated
ramparts right on the river's edge, but John's eyes
sought out a guardhouse just within the main entrance.
With a nod of his head he sent Gwyn towards it and
the Cornishman slid from his saddle and went to seek
directions.

'The corpse is lying next to the chapel,' he
announced when he returned. The rest of them
dismounted and a pair of young grooms came running
to take charge of their horses. The chapel was a
small stone structure next to the keep and when they
approached, they saw a group of figures standing
outside a lean-to shed attached to its wall. From many
similar encounters, de Wolfe knew that this was likely to
be a primitive mortuary.

One of the three men outside was obviously a priest
and John sent Thomas ahead to greet him, as he knew
that this was often a useful tactic.

When de Wolfe reached the chapel, his clerk
introduced the priest and explained that the other
two men were sheriff's constables from the city. They
were heavily built and had the appearance of watchmen or soldiers, though they wore leather jerkins and
breeches, rather than uniforms. John thought them
surly fellows and after muttered greetings they all
turned to the open end of the shed, which seemed to
be mainly a repository for a handcart.

'I have brought someone who can definitely identify

the body, if it is who we think,' said John brusquely. He motioned Edwin forward. 'This young man is on the palace staff and knows the presumed victim.'

A still shape lay upon the cart covered with a grubby sheet of canvas. One of the sheriff's servants pulled it off and Edwin moved forward to study the dead man's face.

'There's no doubt about it, that's Basil of Reigate,' murmured the clerk, looking rather white about the gills.

The other sheriff's man, rather reluctantly deferring to a knight of the realm, wanted to know more details and Edwin described how Basil was one of the palace officers responsible for the upkeep of the guest chambers.

'I suppose you want to examine the cadaver, Crowner?' said Gwyn, moving towards the barrow. The first sheriff's officer, named William, quickly stepped forward and laid a hand on the massive arm of the Cornishman.

'What are you doing?' he demanded.

Gwyn looked enquiringly at John as he shook off the restraining hand. For a moment, de Wolfe was afraid that his henchman was going to send the other man staggering for his temerity in grasping him. He held up a restraining hand to Gwyn and glared at William.

'I need to examine the corpse! He was stabbed before going into the river.'

William glowered back at him. 'You Westminster people came to identify him, that's all! Your duty is done, for which the sheriffs will thank you.'

It was John's turn to scowl at the man. 'I am the *coroner*, fellow! I need to hold an inquest into this man's death!'

William shook his head and stood in front of the body with his arms folded in a gesture of defiance.

'You have no powers here, sir. The city of London is an independent commune and has no coroner. Our two sheriffs carry out that function, so there's no need to trouble you.'

De Wolfe glowered at the men, for the other one had moved to stand alongside William in an almost threatening manner.

He knew that the city was a place apart, fiercely jealous of its independence, arrogant by virtue of its huge commercial strength, undoubtedly greater than all other English cities put together. The aldermen, burgesses, guildsmen and merchants were extremely powerful and on occasions might even defy the king himself. John was also well aware that when Hubert Walter had instituted coroners in every county two years earlier, he had to heed a refusal from the city fathers and was forced to exclude them from the edict, allowing the two sheriffs to perform those duties.

'That may well be – for your own corpses from the city!' he protested harshly. 'But this is a royal servant who drifted down the river from the king's palace of Westminster and that falls within my jurisdiction.'

The stony face of the sheriff's man stared defiantly at de Wolfe.

'Well, he's not in Westminster now, is he? His corpse lies here in the city and that's what matters.'

The coroner felt like punching the man on his fleshy nose, but managed to restrain his short temper.

'He lies within the Verge, damn you! Twelve miles in any direction from the king's court!

The other constable, a tall, burly man, smirked. 'By Christ's bones, sir, then you've got your work cut out!' he exclaimed sarcastically. 'That encompasses the whole of London and halfway into Essex, to say nothing of Middlesex and much of Surrey!'

'Only if the deceased is connected with the court,

you damn fool!' snarled de Wolfe. In truth, he was not at all sure of the exact definition of those who should come within the jurisdiction of the Verge, but he was incensed at being sneered at by fellows who were little more than city watchmen.

William stood obstinately in front of the body. 'I know nothing of that, sir. All I know is what the sheriff ordered and that was to keep the body privy until he comes to see it and decides what to do. No doubt it will be sent back up the river to you when he's finished with it.'

De Wolfe, never known for his patience or easy temper, was fuming at the man's smug complacency. But short of starting a fight with the representatives of the city's aldermen, there was little he could do at the moment.

'And when will that be?' he demanded fiercely, glowering at the man with his arms akimbo, hands jammed into his waist. 'I need to speak to this sheriff of yours straight away. And then to the Chief Justiciar, who introduced these laws on behalf of King Richard!'

The watchman was unimpressed. 'That's nothing to do with me, coroner. The sheriff is Godard of Antioch – at least the one that's dealing with this. The other one is Robert fitz Durand, but he's away hunting in Northampton.'

'Where can I find this Godard?' demanded John.

'He must have heard you, sir,' crowed the other man, raising his eyes to look across the bailey. 'Here he is now!'

They all turned and saw a fine white horse enter the castle gate. The rider slid off and threw the reins to an ostler who dashed to meet him. Then he waddled across the open space, a fat man with a long yellow tunic reaching to his calves, slit front and back for sitting a horse. As he approached, John saw that his bulging belly was girdled by a wide belt, bearing a short riding sword. He had virtually no neck, a bulbous head rising straight from his shoulders, bristly blond hair surmounting a round, pugnacious face. John sighed and he heard Gwyn mutter.

'Another awkward bugger, by the looks of it!'

De Wolfe decided to go on the offensive right away.

'Sheriff, I am Sir John de Wolfe, the king's Coroner of the Verge! We have just identified this corpse from the river as being that of the palace clerk who was murdered in Westminster yesterday.'

Godard, who took his other name from estates his father had owned in one of the Christian kingdoms of Outremer, held up his arm in salute, but looked suspiciously at de Wolfe.

'I have heard of you, Sir John. What are you doing here?'

His tone was guarded, but not overtly hostile, as his eyes flickered from the coroner to the body on the cart and then to his pair of henchmen standing in front of it.

'This man was stabbed yesterday within the enclave of the royal palace and then fell into the river. I need to investigate his death and bring the culprit to justice.'

Godard shrugged and virtually repeated what William had said. 'This is a task for us, sir. We perform your function in this city.'

Bottling up his exasperation with difficulty, John made a further effort to reason with the man. 'I grant you that this was the situation until recently,' he grated. 'But King Richard expressly directed the appointment of a coroner to deal with all relevant deaths within the verge of the royal court, wherever it may be. He ordered the Chief Justiciar to implement his wish and I have been appointed by him to perform that function.'

He deliberately emphasized the names to convey the

importance of his office, but Godard seemed un-impressed.

'Ha, Hubert Walter! He's well out of favour in London these days, so I'd not be too ready to flaunt your warrant from him.'

De Wolfe sighed heavily. He knew Godard was referring to the harsh way in which a couple of months previously Hubert had quelled the popular revolt against taxation led by William fitz Osbert, known as 'Longbeard'. The leaders of the rebellion had been cornered in the church of St Mary le Bow, which Hubert had set on fire, driving the rebels out to be dragged to an agonising death at Tyburn. Since then, his unpopularity over the increasing burden of taxes had been worsened by accusations that he had deliberately ordered the violation of sanctuary.

'He appointed me on the orders of King Richard!' snapped de Wolfe. 'Are you challenging royal authority? That smacks of treason, sir!'

An expression of sullen obstinacy came over Godard's plain face. 'I'm challenging nothing – but the right to appoint one sheriff for London and another for Middlesex was granted by the first King Henry when he granted the city its charter. If you want to dispute that, then take the matter to the mayor, to whom I am responsible.'

'I may do just that!' rasped the coroner, his simmering anger now rising to boiling point. 'But that will take time, and in this blistering heat that cadaver will start to stink, especially as it has already spent a night in this putrid river!'

The sheriff considered this for a moment, stroking his full belly with one hand as an aid to thought.

'I'm a reasonable man, Sir John. I accept your point about the likely dissolution of the corpse in this weather,' he said mildly. 'Why do we not examine him together, then at least your mind will be assuaged about the cause of death?'

Somewhat reluctantly, de Wolfe grunted an agreement, but did not give in completely. 'What about getting the fellow back to Westminster? He is in minor orders and deserves a proper funeral before he turns green!'

'I still wish to hold my own enquiry, as is the city's right,' declared Godard pedantically. 'After that, you can do what you like with him.'

De Wolfe managed to hold his tongue until after he had had the opportunity to look at the corpse. Then he intended petitioning the Chief Justiciar to kick a few backsides in the city of London, even if Hubert was out of favour with those belligerent bastards who lived in this swarming hive on the edge of the Thames.

The sheriff began walking to the cart, his two officers reluctantly moving aside to let the coroner's team through.

Edwin once again identified the body to the sheriff, to legalise the enquiry that the Londoner was insistent upon.

'You say he was stabbed, not drowned?' demanded Godard, in his rather high-pitched voice. 'I see no blood?'

'He's been washed in the damned river for the better part of a day,' snapped John, his patience at breaking point. More calmly, he forced himself to explain the whole circumstances. 'We happened to see the culprit running away, but we had no chance to catch or even recognise him,' he added.

Almost automatically, Gwyn began to step forward to perform his usual task of removing the clothes from the body, but de Wolfe, with uncharacteristic tact, motioned him back. Instead, William stood forward and once again removed the canvas sheet.

'There should be a wound in his chest or belly,' said the coroner, as the sheriff bent closer to the corpse. After fiddling with the black garment that covered Basil of Reigate, Godard nodded his agreement. 'Here, there's a rent in the cloth, just below his breast-bone.'

John peered more closely until his hooked nose almost touched the stiff wool, the sodden cloth having dried in the sun. As the sheriff pulled the material flat, he saw a tear something over an inch in length in the midline, about two hands' breadth below the root of the neck.

William began to pull the long cassock up over Basil's head, struggling against the stiffness of death that had set in more markedly since the body had been removed from the water.

Though this intimate examination was being held in the open air, the bailey of Baynard's Castle was closed to all but those who had business there and there was no audience apart from a few curious men-at-arms who were kept at a distance by the gestures of William's fellow watchman.

When the cassock was taken off, a thin undershirt of creased, damp linen was revealed and again there was a similar slit cut in the chest area. 'Lift it up, man!' ordered Godard and a moment later, he waved a hand at the pallid skin which so far was free from even early discoloration of corruption.

'There's your injury, coroner!' He pointed a finger at the stab wound which was oozing a small amount of blood, but was careful not to touch it. De Wolfe had no such scruples and prised it apart with his two fore-fingers to look at the edges.

'Blunt at one end, so it was a blade with one sharp edge and a flat back!' he declared.

The sheriff looked at him cynically. 'And how does

that help you, sir?' he asked. 'There are probably ten thousand such knives within a mile of here.'

John ignored him and transferred his eagle-eyed inspection to the corpse's face.

'What are you looking for now?' asked Godard. 'The cause of his death is patently obvious!'

'He slipped off the landing stage while he was still bleeding,' snapped the coroner. 'Roll him over on to his face,' he ordered, forgetting his role as an invited observer. William looked at his master, but the sheriff just shrugged and the watchman hoisted up one shoulder of the corpse. As the dead clerk turned over, Gwyn and Thomas, knowing what to look for, bent to watch the face and were rewarded by a flow of pink frothy fluid from the nostrils and mouth.

'Stabbed he might have been, but he went into the river alive and drowning finished him off,' declared de Wolfe, with a note of satisfaction in his voice.

Godard of Antioch looked unimpressed. 'Any wherry-man could have told you that!' he said ungraciously. 'What difference does it make? If he'd not been stabbed, he'd not have gone into the river and died, so your mysterious assailant is still a murderer.'

'All information may be useful,' muttered John obscurely, annoyed that the sheriff was undoubtedly correct.

They checked that there were no other injuries on the body and William replaced the canvas and wheeled the cart back into the mortuary shed, where at least it would be out of the direct rays of the sun.

'Did he have a scrip on his belt?' asked de Wolfe.

'A small leather pouch with a purse inside,' answered the sheriff's watchman. 'It held but two silver pennies, so I doubt that he was killed for his wealth.'

Apart from marvelling that someone had not already stolen the coins since the corpse was recovered from the river, there was nothing else John could do and he turned to the supercilious sheriff.

'Do you still wish to continue with this matter?' he barked. 'I fail to see what you can learn here, when the crime was committed almost a couple of miles upriver.'

'I can send my men to Westminster to question you people up there,' retorted Godard stubbornly.

'I doubt the Chief Justiciar would look kindly on that, sheriff!' snapped de Wolfe. 'In fact, I strongly suspect that he will wish to have words with you and your mayor over this apparent conflict of interests.'

Godard seemed unmoved by this veiled threat. 'I will record my verdict in the usual way. After you have gone, I will assemble a jury and declare that this man Basil of Reigate was slain at Westminster on yesterday's date, by persons unknown. That will be the end of the matter.'

'Not for me, it won't!' shouted de Wolfe. 'I will investigate it properly and discover who did this foul act upon a servant of the king. You have been wasting my time, sir – and your own!'

With a face like thunder, he stalked off across the bailey towards his horse. His three companions trailed after him, leaving the sheriff and his men to their own devices. As John reached Odin and unhitched him from a rail outside the guardroom, the priest, who had remained silent throughout all the exchanges, came hurrying after them, as de Wolfe climbed into his high saddle.

'Sir John, what about the corpse? You said it must be returned to Westminster.' He was a small man, with a face lined with worry.

John looked down at him from the back of his patient destrier.

'I will speak to the Keeper and perhaps the Chief

Justiciar as soon as I return. They will arrange for the poor fellow to be collected.' He wheeled Odin around to face the gate.

'Meanwhile, keep him out of this damned sun or they'll have to collect him in a couple of buckets!'

That evening, the coroner decided to have his supper in his rented dwelling, rather than in the Lesser Hall. The attraction of the delectable Hawise d'Ayncourt was strong, but he had an uneasy feeling that he might get himself into trouble if he let matters progress too far. He could not quite understand why she still used her own name, when she was married to Renaud de Seigneur, but he decided that was something it was not profitable to pursue.

Osanna, their obese cook, told them that their meal would not be ready for another hour, so John and Gwyn adjourned to an alehouse on King Street, to quench their thirsts as the heat of the day began to lessen in the early evening. A slight breeze came up the river with the rising tide, bringing with it cooler air, scented with sewage and rotting fish.

The tavern, alongside the palace gate, had the somewhat irreverent name of 'The Deacon', perhaps to offer a weak justification or even an alibi to a number of priests and clerks who often sidled in furtively. It was an old building, built of curved crucks of trees at each pine-end and a lattice of timbers supporting panels made from hazel withies plastered with cog, all in dire need of new limewash.

There was an upper floor where rooms were let to lodgers, and above that in the loft straw mattresses were rented out at a penny a night for those who wanted cheap communal accommodation. The ground floor was a single large room where ale, cider and cheap wine were dispensed and it was here that Gwyn and his master sat to swallow a quart of a rather indifferent brew. Two stools were placed at an open window, where the shutters were thrown wide to admit the cooler air; a rough plank that acted as a sill formed a convenient shelf for their pottery mugs.

'Thank Christ you talked Osanna out of those eels,' said Gwyn with feeling. 'She says now she's got a decent bit of pork for us.'

Food and drink figured largely in the Cornishman's life, along with gambling and a good fight. De Wolfe nodded absently, his mind on other matters. 'I hadn't realised how jealous this city of London was about Westminster – though I suspect it works both ways,' he said ruminatively. 'When I spoke to the Keeper again this afternoon, you'd have thought that those across the Fleet river were as much our enemies as the bloody French!'

'What's he going to do about the corpse?' asked Gwyn, wiping ale from his drooping moustache with the back of his hand.

'He's done it by now, no doubt. Sent a cart and a couple of palace guards to fetch it back here. He says it can lie in St Stephen's Chapel tonight until it's buried in the abbey cemetery tomorrow.'

'What about an inquest – *our* inquest,' asked his officer.

'I'll have to go through the motions in the morning, I suppose,' replied John without enthusiasm. 'I've already examined the corpse, but the jury will have to see it as well.'

'Who are we going to get for the jury?'

'I trust that Thomas has some names written down. There were those people on the landing stage and the sergeant of the guard, as well as the boy Edwin. We'll have to make do with those.'

'We don't have a sheriff to inform here, not like

Exeter,' grumbled Gwyn. 'It's all so damned different. Who do you present the inquest roll to, after Thomas has written it?'

John shrugged. 'It seems to me that this Verge business was launched without much forethought. The abbot seems to think he runs everything in West- minster, so does the Keeper – and those sods over in the city claim that we're subject to the county of Middlesex!'

'So what are you going to do about it?' demanded Gwyn. 'There's no point in our sitting on our arses here, with very little to do and no one seeming to care whether we do anything or not. I wish I was back home, to tell the truth!'

He took another swallow and added, 'Especially having to put up with this horse-piss, instead of my wife's or Nesta's good ale.' The mention of his former mistress sent John into a pensive reverie. He missed the gentle Welshwoman more than he cared to admit, even though he acknowledged that she had done the right thing by marrying the stonemason. They could never have been more than lovers, skulking to meet when his wife's back was turned and with no prospect ever of a marriage between a Norman knight and a Welsh tavern keeper.

There was Hilda of Dawlish, of course, who he loved as well, but now she was on the other side of England – and Matilda, though equally distant, was still his wife, more's the pity! He was forty-one years of age and felt as lusty as ever – but unless he went whoring, he would have to put up with the frustra- tions of celibacy. This depressing thought brought the image of Hawise d'Ayncourt into his mind again and he briefly wished that he had forsaken Osanna's promise of roast pork for another meal in the Lesser Hall.

He was jerked out of his musing by Gwyn, who had been staring out of the unglazed window at the street outside.

'What's this? Here's our favourite dwarf coming.'

His affectionate slander was directed at Thomas de Peyne, who a moment later sidled into the tavern with a guilty look. Though many clerics were as fond of drink and women as the next man, Thomas was a shy, reserved little fellow, who looked on alehouses as a halfway stop to Hades. His skinny body, slight limp and hunched shoulder made him unattractive to women, except those who wanted to mother him. He was content with a world that revolved around his beloved Church and books of history and learning. His skill with pen, ink and parchment was exceptional and his insatiable curiosity had given him an encyclopaedic knowledge.

'What brings you to this den of iniquity, Thomas?' asked de Wolfe. 'Are you pining for our brilliant company or have you something to tell us?'

Gwyn reached out and dragged another stool for the clerk to sit on. 'Do you want a cup of wine, Thomas?' he asked solicitously. 'It's lousy stuff, the ale-wife says it's from the Loire, but I think she means just taken out of the river there!'

His friend shook his head, declining to compound his visit to a tavern by actually drinking there.

'I just called in to tell you something I heard about the dead man we saw today,' he said earnestly. He dropped his voice and looked covertly about the taproom, though the other patrons seemed indifferent to their conversation.

'At supper tonight in the abbey refectory, the death of Basil of Reigate was a favourite subject for conversation, as everyone knew that his body had been brought back for burial. Then afterwards, I took a turn around the cloister, as did many others to aid their digestion and gossip some more.'

'Mary, Mother of God, get to the bloody point, will you!' hissed de Wolfe, who was afraid that Thomas was getting as long-winded as Gwyn when it came to telling a story.

'Well, a novitiate that I know slightly, took me aside and said that he was very distressed, as Basil had been a close friend.' Thomas hesitated and looked a little embarrassed. 'In fact, I rather think that they might have been more than good friends, may God forgive them.'

The coroner was not interested in the morals of Westminster clerics. 'What are you trying to tell me, Thomas?' he snapped.

'This young man knew I was the coroner's clerk and said he wanted to do all he could to bring his friend's killer to justice. He told me that a few days ago, Basil had confided in him that his life might be in danger because he had overheard a seditious conversation in the palace.'

Gwyn stared at him through the ginger frizz on his lumpy face.

'What in hell is a "seditious conversation"?' he grunted.

'And why should it put this Basil in mortal danger?' added de Wolfe.

The little clerk wriggled uncomfortably. 'He was quite vague about this, Crowner,' he said apologetically. 'It seems Basil was not very forthcoming about the matter – and then the novitiate, Robin Byard by name, was also quite furtive when he told me.'

'You must know more that that!' snapped de Wolfe. 'Or why bother to tell us at all?'

Thomas almost twitched with nervousness at his master's impatience. 'It seems that during his duties in the guest chambers, Basil was behind a screen in one of the rooms, checking blankets in a chest. Two people came in and were unaware of him, but started speaking of something that would get them hanged if it was made known!'

'So what was this something?' demanded Gwyn, before John could get out the same words.

'That's the problem, Basil wouldn't tell Robin, for fear of putting him in similar jeopardy,' gabbled Thomas. 'Neither would he say who the people were.'

'So why did he bother to mention it at all?' rasped the coroner.

'He wanted help and advice, for it seems that in his anxiety to hear what was said, he tipped over the screen and the two persons saw that he had been listening,' explained the clerk. 'Basil gabbled some excuse and ran away, but they obviously knew who he was – and ever since he had been expecting to be silenced – which seems to have happened, for this killing was no robbery.'

John and Gwyn looked at each other over the rims of their ale mugs. 'Sounds a tall story, but the fact is that the fellow *was* stabbed!' said Gwyn. 'And you've no idea what this secret conversation was about?'

'We'd better have a word with this fellow Byard,' rumbled John. 'But why did Basil tell this apprentice monk, rather than someone in authority?'

'He was seeking advice, as he was his best friend,' said Thomas carefully. 'Robin Byard told him he must tell either the Guest-Master or the Purveyor – or even the Keeper of the Palace. But Basil said he was afraid he would either be disbelieved or be disciplined for eavesdropping on guests.'

'How did a clerk in the guest house come to be so friendly with a Benedictine novitiate?' asked John suspiciously.

'It seems they are both of an age and come from the same village in Surrey. This Basil had decided he wanted to enter the abbey as a novice – perhaps to be with his best friend,' Thomas added with a blush.

'What sort of secrets might justify the risks of stabbing a man in broad daylight?' queried Gwyn.

De Wolfe chewed this over in his mind for a moment. 'Unless this is all a figment of the fellow's imagination, there's some palace intrigue behind this. I've heard that the place is a hotbed of corruption, embezzlement, theft, adultery, fornication and God knows what else!'

'What about spying?' added Thomas. 'I know the king's directing his war against Philip from Rouen, but it's from here that England has to defend its coast against invasion. And the French are always trying to stir up the Scots and Welsh against us.'

'Perhaps they were planning to steal the Crown Jewels!' offered Gwyn facetiously.

'They should be safe enough in the crypt of the abbey,' replied John seriously, impervious to his officer's humour. 'Thomas, tell this new friend of yours that I want to talk to him tomorrow, before I hold the inquest. And Gwyn, in future I think I had better forsake Osanna's cooking in the evenings and eat in the palace. You never know what we might pick up there.'

With a picture of a certain lady in mind, an obvious answer came to him, but he managed to convince himself that dining in the Lesser Hall was now part of his duty.

CHAPTER THREE

*In which the coroner meets
an old comrade*

The next day, though the sun was already warming the lanes, it was still early when the coroner and his officer walked from their house to the palace. As they went from Tothill Street through the rear gate of the abbey precinct and strode across Broad Sanctuary, the sounds of chanting came from the chancel, as the monks celebrated Prime, the first office of the day.

'I suppose our clerk is amongst that lot,' said Gwyn gruffly, jerking a thumb towards Edward the Confessor's great building.

John had never managed to discover the cause of the Cornishman's disenchantment with the Church. He himself was a reluctant worshipper, especially since he no longer had his wife to drag him to devotions, but compared to his officer he was an ardent believer.

'Let him enjoy it, poor fellow,' he advised. 'There's nothing for him to do until the inquest an hour before noon.'

They passed the small church of St Margaret, built by the monks for the use of the local population, to avoid interruption of their endless devotions in the abbey. A small gate in the wall between the monastic and secular areas, led them into New Palace Yard, where already clerks, men-at-arms and members of the public were criss-crossing the wide area, dodging ox-carts and mounted men coming and going from the main gate on King Street.

Up in their chamber, Gwyn threw open the window shutter and leaned out to study the strip of scrubby grass between the base of the wall and the river's edge. Feet had worn a path of dusty earth along it, the same one along which he had chased the killer two days before. The tide was dropping now and the sullen brown water swirled downstream. Across the wide expanse, he could see more marshes and some farmland visible on the opposite bank at Lambeth, now disfigured by some large building activity.

'Too bloody flat around here for my liking,' he grumbled, determined to find fault with everywhere that was not his native West Country. Coming from the steep fishing village of Polruan in Cornwall, he missed the slopes and cliffs of his youth.

He raised his eye to the sky and frowned. 'I reckon this weather is soon going to end in a storm,' he added. 'Instead of dust, we'll have mud everywhere!'

'Jonah had nothing on you, Gwyn,' growled John, sitting behind his table. 'I think you'll soon need a trip back home to see your wife and family. I might come with you, to try to discover what this bloody wife of mine intends to do.'

His officer left the window and sat on a milking stool, which creaked ominously under his weight. 'If this whole court is going to shift itself to Gloucester when the old queen comes, maybe we'll have a chance to slip off to Exeter from there – it's nearer than this place.'

De Wolfe shrugged, doubtful if the distance would make much difference, but not wanting to dishearten Gwyn. They had spent over twenty years together away from Devon, on campaigns in Ireland, France and the

Holy Land, without being too bothered by home-sickness. However, three years back in England seemed to have softened them up. He decided to shake off this morbid mood and changed the subject.

'Thomas said he would bring this fellow Robin Byard here when they had finished singing and praying over in the abbey.'

'D'you think there could be anything in this story?' grunted Gwyn. 'Sounds a bit far-fetched to me, a clerk being afraid that he's overheard something to endanger his life!'

De Wolfe shrugged, running his hand through his over-long hair. 'Nothing would surprise me in this damned place! I know both France and our own country have a bevy of spies in each other's camps. But this might just be some petty intrigue about one man bedding someone else's wife – or even some swindle over an official selling meat from the kitchens.'

For a while there was silence in the bare chamber, as John settled down to try to re-learn some of the Latin that Thomas had written out for him in simple phrases on a roll of parchment. When in Exeter, a vicar in the cathedral had coached him until the patience of both of them had run out. Now his own clerk had taken on the task, but at his age, John's mind was too set to absorb much learning. He was a physical man, active and energetic, but lacking the concentration and willpower to apply himself to academic pursuits.

He muttered under his breath, his lips forming the unfamiliar words as his finger slowly traced out the perfect script of his clerk, while his officer perched back on the windowsill, gazing out across the Thames. A barge drifted downstream, piled with bales of raw wool, four men keeping it in the centre of the river with long oars. Above, the sky was taking on a leaden hue towards the south, and the weather lore that Gwyn had learned from his fisherman father told him that a storm was brewing.

After about an hour, the silence was broken by Thomas entering the room. He ushered in a pale young man dressed in Benedictine black, his shaven tonsure having removed most of his fair hair. Robin Byard looked nervous and ill-at-ease as he looked from the ginger giant at the window to the menacingly dark figure of the coroner sitting behind the table.

'My clerk tells me that you have something to tell us about Basil of Reigate,' began John, trying to sound affable.

To his embarrassment, Byard promptly burst into tears. 'He was my best friend, Sir John! Perhaps there was something I could have done to save him.'

The ever-sympathetic Thomas placed a reassuring hand on the young man's shoulder. 'Just tell the coroner what you know,' he advised.

'I told your clerk the little I know yesterday,' he snivelled. 'Basil was afraid for his life, in case the people he heard plotting decided to silence him.'

'Yet I'm told you have no idea either who these people were – nor what was said between them to make him so fearful?' snapped John, already forgetting his attempt at being gentle.

Robin cringed at the coroner's tone. 'He said he had no wish to drag me into danger, sir.'

'And you have no other suspicion as to who these people might be. Were they both men or a couple, for instance?'

The novice shook his head miserably. 'All he wanted was some advice as to what he should do. He was even talking about running away, back to our village.'

'And what did you advise him?'

'He worked in the guest chamber of the palace, so his immediate superior would be the Guest Master, who was one of the Lord Chamberlain's staff,' explained Byard. 'Yet he was concerned only with supplies, so he was directed mainly by the Purveyor. I told him he must confide in either of these – or go to the Keeper of the Palace himself.'

'And what did he say?' demanded the coroner. It was obvious that Basil had not spoken to the Purveyor, for that official knew nothing of it when told of the recovery of the body.

'He said he would think about it, but was reluctant in case he was not believed or thought of as causing false rumours. And that was the last time I saw him!' added Robin, bursting into tears again.

If there was anything that de Wolfe could not abide, it was weeping, especially if it came from a man. He jerked his head at Thomas to take the boy away and the soft-hearted clerk gently ushered him out of the room.

'I'll not call him at the inquest, for his evidence is not worth a bent penny,' he growled. 'And if there was any truth in what he said, there's no point in alerting these mysterious conspirators, if they exist.'

He rose from his bench and stretched his long arms.

'I've asked for an audience with our old friend Hubert Walter this morning. He's back from his parish in Kent today, so I'm told.'

He was referring to the Chief Justiciar and Gwyn guessed that John's attempt at levity about a parish concerned the Archbishop's diocese in Canterbury.

'He won't be interested in a stabbed clerk, will he?' objected Gwyn.

De Wolfe gave one of his rare grins. Hubert was effectively running England in the continued absence of King Richard and undoubtedly had more weighty matters on his mind.

'No, but I want to bend his ear about these bastards in the city,' he fretted. 'If I'm supposed to be Coroner of the Verge, then we can't have these arrogant sheriffs interfering. And what's going to happen when the court goes out into the shires? Are the county coroners going to do the same?'

He pondered for a moment. 'Mind you, if I was still Devon's coroner, I'd be hopping mad if some outsider turned up and took my cases from me, just because the court is within a dozen miles of Exeter!'

Gwyn nodded sagely, knowing his master well enough to let him blow off steam. 'When are you going to see him? That's if you can find him again in this rabbit warren.'

They had ridden up to Westminster the previous year to see the Justiciar, when they needed a special dispensation against an injustice caused to a fellow Crusader.* Gwyn recalled being led through innumerable passages to get to Hubert's chamber, but he doubted he could find it again without help.

'One of the Chancery clerks is coming to fetch me when he's ready,' replied John. 'Until then, we'll have a drop of the ale you've got hidden in that jar.'

It was the same austere chamber that they had sat in the previous year. Though as Chief Justiciar and Archbishop of Canterbury, he was the most powerful man in the country, Hubert Walter did not flaunt his power with rich robes and ostentatious jewels. A lean man with tonsured iron-grey hair, he wore a plain dark-red tunic, belted at the waist, the only sign of his ecclesiastical eminence being a small gold cross hanging by a thin chain around his neck.

In spite of the difference in their stations in life, he was a good friend of John's. They had first met in the Holy Land, when Hubert, then Bishop of Salisbury, was

* See *The Noble Outlaw*.

made chaplain to the Crusaders after Baldwin, Archbishop of Canterbury, had died before the walls of Acre. Like many bishops, Hubert was also a seasoned warrior and became the king's chief of staff, later being left behind to organise the withdrawal after Richard sailed for home on his ill-fated journey. John had been one of the royal bodyguard that had accompanied him and had suffered the same shipwreck in the Adriatic that led to the Lionheart's ill-advised attempt to reach England overland, with only a few remaining knights and squires as protection. De Wolfe still felt guilty about being away from the king's side when Richard was captured near Vienna, though the Lionheart had since airily absolved John from any fault.

'At least it's not about Richard de Revelle this time!' said the Justiciar with a smile. On the two last occasions that they had met in England, it was over problems with John's brother-in-law, the former sheriff of Devon, who had repeatedly sailed too close to the wind of treason and corruption.

'No, but his sister is causing me problems instead!' confessed John wryly. He explained the frustrating situation with his wife, who was in Polsloe Priory in Exeter, but had not committed to taking her vows nor indicating whether she would return to married life. However, his matrimonial affairs were nothing to do with his purpose today and he went on to explain in detail the confrontation with Godard of Antioch and his men.

'I must know who has precedence, Your Grace!' he ended.

Though the archbishop was an old comrade-in-arms, John was not one to ignore the formalities of address. 'If the king requires me to be his court coroner in England, then I must know where the limits of my duty lie. There's no point in having jurisdiction over the Verge, if the local officers deny me the right to investigate anything.'

The Justiciar leaned across the oak table that was half-buried in parchments. 'They delight in being awkward, those strutting city folk!' he complained. 'I'm in bad odour with them at present, over that Longbeard affair in April, so no doubt they'll take every opportunity to tweak my tail.'

He twisted a large golden ring on one of his fingers, one of the few signs of his religious primacy, for he had recently been made Papal Legate to England, the agent of the Holy Father in Rome.

'Not only that, but the Mayor, Henry fitz Ailwyn, is annoyed that I am enlarging the defences around the Tower. He says I am encroaching upon his territory, so he's trying to defy me in as many ways as possible.'

'But where does that leave me as coroner?' persisted de Wolfe. 'Am I going to face the same opposition in the shires when the court moves out into the country? If so, I may as well abandon any hope of carrying out the king's wishes.'

Hubert Walter shook his head decisively.

'I am the Chief Justiciar, responsible for law and order in England. They cannot obstruct me, much as they would wish to.'

He stood up and strode about the room, rubbing his hands together. 'As you well know, almost two years ago I instructed my judges at the Kent Eyre to appoint three knights as coroners in every county to keep the pleas of the crown. Straight away, London raised objections and the king gave in to them, wanting to keep them sweet, as they are a huge source of revenue to the Exchequer. We need every penny to pay off his ransom and to fund his wars across the Channel.'

'I understand that one of the sheriffs also acts as coroner in the county of Middlesex,' said John morosely. 'Does that mean that even Westminster comes under their jurisdiction? If so, I may as well saddle up and go home to Devon right away!'

Hubert replied by ringing a small brass bell that stood on his table.

'I'll get this settled this minute,' he promised, as one of his black-robed clerks hurried in from an adjoining room and stood waiting expectantly for instructions. 'As for Middlesex, I don't think you need worry about that. Westminster is an ancient liberty ruled by Abbot Postard, who is even more jealous of his independence than is the city. Even I as Archbishop have no say in abbey affairs, only through the Pope, but I doubt the abbot is interested in usurping the functions of a coroner.'

He turned to the elderly clerk. 'Send me in one of your scribes, Martin. I want a letter to go out to every sheriff, when you next send monthly heralds out to the counties – and a separate one to the Mayor and aldermen of London.'

He plumped himself down again on his chair and looked across at John. 'I will command them all in the king's name to allow you access and every courtesy in investigating incidents that occur within the Verge, for that is what our Lord Richard specifically desired.'

A younger clerk came in and quietly sat at a small desk to one side of the Justiciar's table, quill and parchment at the ready for dictation.

'I'll have a copy sent to you, with my personal seal attached, John. You can keep it with you and wave it under the nose of any belligerent officer who gives you trouble!'

De Wolfe recognized this as a signal to leave and rose from his seat, but as he bobbed his head in deference to the archbishop, Hubert had one last question.

'This palace servant who was stabbed in broad

daylight – have you any idea what that was all about?'

'I am holding an inquest this morning, sire, though I doubt it will achieve much. The killer seems to have vanished into thin air.'

He hesitated, unsure whether it was worth mentioning the nebulous tale offered by Robin Byard. 'There is a vague suggestion that it might have been connected with some intrigue within the palace, but I will keep you informed, if you so wish.'

Hubert nodded and waved his hand in dismissal, but just as John reached the door, he called him back.

'I almost forgot, I need you for another task this week, one for which your reputation as a safe and trusted escort fits you well.'

De Wolfe waited patiently for enlightenment, though he had misgivings about being landed with some other unenviable job.

'We have now brought almost every office of state here from Winchester, but there remain several chests of bullion which need to be safely moved to London. The Marshalsea will organise the transport, but I want you to make sure that nothing goes amiss. There are too many rogues and robbers about these days to take any chances. The under-marshals will give you all the details.'

John wondered what this had to do with being a coroner, though it was true that they could be a given a royal commission to carry out virtually any task which the monarch wished. However, he made no objection, as it sounded a welcome opportunity to get away from Westminster for a while.

As he muttered his agreement, Hubert Walter was already dictating to his clerk, so John quietly slipped away, hoping he could find his way back through the corridors of power.

*

As de Wolfe had anticipated, the inquest achieved virtually nothing, but doggedly he went through the routine, for his fervent loyalty to the Lionheart made him a stickler for keeping to the rules laid down by the king and his council.

It was held in the Great Hall. William Rufus's massive edifice was used for a variety of functions, including great feasts and accommodating the higher courts of law. The side aisles of the huge hall were divided by movable screens, set against the double row of columns that supported the roof. The court of King's Bench sat at the head of the hall, furthest from the main doors and in other areas between the pillars; various ad hoc tribunals sat as required. In other bays, lawyers were consulted by clients and some court officers used the space for their duties. There were even stalls selling parchment, pens and ink, cloth of various types and even several food booths, offering pies and pastries. These traders had their stalls near the main doors which opened on to New Palace Yard.

There was little attempt at privacy and all manner of people strode or wandered about the hall, some listening to the deliberations of the courts, often chewing on a mince pie as they did so. A babble of voices rose from all parts, but this did not appear to disconcert those who were deliberating on weighty matters. The royal judges, some being members of the Curia, sat with other Barons of the Exchequer on the King's Bench and seemed impervious to the raucous atmosphere which would have been better suited to a marketplace or town square.

Today, Gwyn had commandeered a vacant space between two of the lofty pillars halfway up on the left side, where there were a few stools and benches left by the last occupants. At noon, the small crowd that he had chivvied into attending, turned up to form the jury, these reluctant members also acting as witnesses. Normally, Gwyn would have bellowed out the coroner's summons, commanding 'All ye who have anything to do with the king's coroner for this county, to draw near and give your attendance,' but he was nonplussed by the change in circumstances and decided to leave out any mention of a county.

De Wolfe sat on a bench with his back to the massive stone wall, facing the ragged half-circle of jurymen. Thomas had a stool on his right, with another between his knees to support his roll of parchment, quill and ink flask.

Gwyn wasn't the only one confused about procedure, as John also felt uncertain about certain aspects, compared with the familiar routine back home in Devon.

Should he raise the 'Presentment of Englishry'? The dead man's relatives, if he had any, were a day's ride away in Reigate, so there was no father or brother to declare that he might be a Saxon? The inquest was supposed to be held over the corpse, but he could hardly bring a dead body on a handcart into the Great Hall, especially as it had been lying in this torrid heat for a couple of days.

'We are here to enquire into where, when and by what means Basil of Reigate came to his death,' he began in his deep, sonorous voice. 'I will hear what evidence is available, but then we must adjourn to the abbey for you to view the mortal remains, before coming to a verdict.'

The dozen men that Gwyn had mustered included the sergeant of the palace guard, the two monks from the landing stage, the Guest Master who supervised Basil, and Hugo de Molis, the Chief Purveyor, as well as a few random servants that Gwyn had summoned to make up the numbers. John had toyed with the idea of demanding that the city sheriff and his men should attend, together with the wherryman who had recovered the corpse – but he realized that his summons would be ignored, and the wherryman had doubtless vanished into the anonymity of his fellows on the river.

'We have no true First Finder of the body,' he began, glowering at the jury. 'As he appears to have drowned after being wounded, then those who tried to attend him on the wharf cannot be said to have found a corpse. The city's sheriff failed to record the boatman who dragged the body from the river near Baynard's Castle,' he added maliciously.

He turned to Hugo de Molis, who was not very pleased to have been dragged from his duties for what he considered to be a fruitless enquiry.

'Sir Hugo, can you confirm that the dead man crossed the river on the day of his death?'

Hugo de Molis grudgingly agreed that the dead man's duties had entailed him going across to Lambeth and back again.

He also agreed that though he would have had a substantial purse of money on the outward journey, his empty scrip on returning would not have provided a motive for robbery.

The coroner then enquired whether the nature of his work could have made him privy to any dangerous intelligence.

De Molis sarcastically replied that unless having advance knowledge of a rise in the price of carrots or onions was hazardous, he could not see much risk to someone who was but a lowly palace employee. 'But the Guest Master can tell you more about his duties,' he said with an air of dismissive finality.

This official was a plump sub-deacon, one of the more senior grades of those in clerical lower orders. He had an oily manner, full of smiles, which straightway caused John to distrust him. When it came to assessing people, the coroner had a profound capacity for instant likes and dislikes.

The smiles suddenly changed into doleful sorrow, with hand-wringing and sighs, when he bemoaned the sad demise of his trusted assistant, Basil of Reigate.

'What were his duties?' demanded de Wolfe. 'Did he work mainly under you or was he attached to the Purveyor's chamber?'

'He was under my direction, but his function was to ensure that all supplies for the lodging and comfort of palace guests were amply maintained without shortages. To do this, he constantly topped up necessities from the Steward's department, obtaining goods under my authority.'

De Wolfe had no interest in the internal workings of the palace and moved on impatiently. 'How much contact would he have had with the people staying there?'

The Guest Master grimaced at such an unexpected question.

'I don't really follow you, sir!' he exclaimed. 'He was in and out of the guest chambers all the time, but it was not his place to engage in conversation with the guests. He was a lowly official and sometimes we have earls, dukes and even princes staying in the palace.' He puffed himself up, as if he was responsible for attracting such nobility.

'But he would have opportunities to overhear what was being said by those guests?' persisted John.

'I suppose so, unless he was deaf!' snapped the sub-deacon. 'But a good servant must be discreet and avoid any eavesdropping. I cannot see the point of these questions, coroner!'

'That's because you are not privy to my own knowledge,' retorted de Wolfe and dismissed the man, realising that he was of no help to his enquiry. The two monks and the sergeant of the guard gave their factual evidence of the happenings on the landing-stage, then the coroner scowled around the ring of jurors and asked if anyone else had any information at all. After a resounding silence, it was obvious that nothing more was to be learned and Gwyn led the jury out of the hall and across the yard to the gate in the wall separating the palace from the abbey. With de Wolfe and Thomas walking behind, the small procession went past the chapter house and dormitory to the abbey mortuary. This was a small wooden building behind the infirmary chapel, right at the back of the abbey precinct, towards the wall that ran above the Tyburn stream.

The mortal remains of Basil of Reigate had spent a night lying before the altar in the adjacent chapel, but the effects of immersion and the hot weather had caused the abbey precentor to have it removed to the mortuary. As this was next to the latrines of the reredorter, the developing odour would not be so noticeable, but the unfortunate jurors had to come much closer, to file past the corpse while the coroner and his officer displayed the stab wound in the chest. Outside again, they stood thankfully in the fresh air while de Wolfe concluded the inquest on the spot, it not being worth trailing back to the hall.

'The cause of death is clear, being drowning after a stab wound of the chest which you have all seen,' he said grimly. 'The attack was witnessed by my officer and some of you also saw the altercation on the jetty, though regrettably no one was able to recognise the assailant. The victim would probably have died from the stabbing alone, but it caused him to fall into the river and drown.'

He glared again at the circle of faces. 'All we can do today is to come to a provisional verdict, so that he can be decently buried. If and when any further information comes to light, then I will have to reopen the inquest. But for now, I need you to return a verdict, which I cannot imagine will be anything but murder by a person unknown.'

He jabbed a finger at the sergeant. 'You can be spokesman for your fellow jurors, so now deliberate amongst yourselves and tell me what you decide.'

His tone indicated that there would be trouble if they dared to deviate from his suggestion and within half a minute the foreman announced that they fully agreed with him. The participants rapidly dispersed, all seeking their noontide dinner and de Wolfe, Gwyn and Thomas began walking through the abbey grounds back to the house in Long Ditch.

Though John had decided to go to the Lesser Hall for supper each night, they took dinner at home. Throughout the country, noon was traditionally the time for the main meal of the day, though a new-fangled habit was creeping in to the upper layers of society of having a substantial supper in the early evening – a fad subscribed to by John's snobbish wife Matilda, before she buried herself in a nunnery.

Thomas divided his eating loyalties between the abbey refectory and his master's house and today accepted de Wolfe's invitation to sample Osanna's efforts. There was not much that she could do wrong in grilling herrings and even Thomas, who normally had the appetite of a mouse, did justice to the large platter of sizzling fish that was put before them, after a bowl of vegetable broth. Followed by frumenty and washed down with ale and cider, they felt comfortably satisfied and sat talking afterwards in the downstairs room of John's lodging.

He had both rooms of the two-storeyed cottage, Aedwulf and Osanna living in a thatched hut in the backyard, where there was also the kitchen shed, a pigsty, a privy and a wash-house. They lived and ate in the lower room, into which the door to the lane opened and John slept in the smaller upper chamber, Gwyn using a pallet in the living room.

Though the circular firepit in the centre of the earthen floor held only cold ashes in this weather, they sat around it from force of habit, John in the wooden chair and the others hunched on stools.

'The Justiciar told me this morning that we have to go on a journey very shortly,' announced John, after refilling his ale-pot from a jug on the table.

'To Gloucester already?' queried Gwyn. 'But the old queen hasn't arrived yet.'

De Wolfe shook his head. 'Nothing to do with that, this is a quick jaunt to Winchester and back to escort some treasure chests. I've not got the details yet, but it looks like a five- or six-day trip. It'll make a change from this place, anyway.'

Thomas, usually very reluctant to go far on a horse, was for once keen to go with them. 'It would be pleasant to see Winchester once again, now that my circumstances have taken a turn for the better,' he said eagerly. 'Perhaps I would have a chance to see my parents.'

His elderly father was a somewhat impoverished knight who lived near the old capital and Thomas himself had attended the cathedral school there and gone on to take holy orders.

'Your last visit there was a happy one, Thomas!' observed John, referring to the joyous occasion when his clerk had gone to Winchester to be received back into the Church by the bishop, after the allegations of indecent assault had been proved false. 'But are you sure you want to wear down your backside on a horse once again?'

The little man smiled happily. 'It's much nearer here than it was from Devon, Crowner! But why exactly do they want you to accompany the treasure? It's hardly coroner's business?'

De Wolfe shrugged. 'I suspect they want someone reputable to keep a close watch on the safety of these chests while they're outside the security of Winchester Castle.'

Gwyn wiped some ale from his luxuriant moustaches and went to refill his pot. 'Where is it to be moved to in London?' he asked.

'I don't know, it's not something that's gossiped about much,' grunted John. 'No doubt we'll find out when we bring it back.'

Thomas spoke up, ever keen to air his knowledge. 'I recall that in William the Bastard's time, the royal regalia used to be kept in the Tower, but now it's locked here in the crypt of the abbey.'

'What's the royal regalia?' boomed Gwyn, proud of his ignorance of the high and mighty.

'The Crown jewels, the sacred items used at coronations, you barbarian!' snapped Thomas. 'The golden sceptre and orb and the crown of Saint Edward, God rest his soul.' He crossed himself at the mention of the kingly Confessor.

'The treasure we are collecting is nothing to do with that,' said John firmly. 'This is what's left of the gold and silver collected by the sheriffs from the county farms, as well as some treasure trove. It seems that from now on, many of them will have to make the longer journey to London.'

'Maybe someone will try to ambush us on the way back!' said Gwyn hopefully. 'I'd best sharpen my sword, I could do with a good fight, it's been an age since I blooded anyone.'

Thomas paled a little and began to regret his enthusiasm for accompanying them to Winchester, but John took pity on the timid clerk.

'He's teasing you, Thomas, I wouldn't worry. There'll be a troop of men-at-arms with us, enough to fight off half an army.'

'Maybe the French will send a whole army!' said Gwyn mischievously. 'Most of that treasure will end up in Normandy, paying for our king's troops who are fighting them, so perhaps they'll send an invasion force to steal it!'

Thomas had had enough of his big friend's efforts to frighten him and got up to leave.

'I'm going back to my tasks in the scriptorium, where there's no big Cornish idiot,' he said loftily, as he walked out into the lane.

After a few moments, when they had finished the ale jug, the coroner and his officer began walking slowly back towards the palace. It was hot and the air was still and humid, but the expected storm had not materialised, the cloud mass having drifted away to the east.

'It'll come back, mark my words,' grumbled Gwyn, unwilling to have his fisherman's forecast proved wrong. 'Probably just as we set off for Winchester, if that's going to be in the next few days.'

That evening de Wolfe ate in the palace, as he had decided that the gossip there might give some clue to the intrigues that were current and perhaps touch on the vague hints that Robin Byard had offered.

At about the sixth hour, with the sun still blazing, de Wolfe made his way to the Lesser Hall and found the place busier than on his previous visits. The two rows of tables were almost filled, but John saw that the same trio that he had talked with before were there, with a couple of empty spaces nearby. John was uncertain whether he again wanted to risk the flirtatious Hawise d'Ayncourt. He enjoyed the company of an attractive woman, but wanted to avoid both a confrontation with her husband, as well as a struggle with his own conscience. However, he told himself that seeking information was part of his duty and this salved his misgivings sufficiently for him to stride across and slide on to the bench next to the lady. Lady Hawise greeted him effusively and from beyond her, husband Renaud nodded affably. The food came to the table in regular instalments and the drink was already flowing. John tucked in with relish, as there was jugged hare, cooked in its own blood, and pork knuckles, two of his favourite dishes. As they sat close together on the benches, he felt Hawise's thigh tight against his, and suspected that the pressure she used was more than required by the lack of space.

Acting the gentleman, this time he was bold enough to cut slices of meat and slide them on to her trencher, though he was careful not to outdo her husband's duty in carrying out the same task. They made suitable small talk, though as usual in public, this was something of an effort for John, even with a beautiful woman. Everyone was complaining of the sultry heat and like Gwyn forecasting the mother and father of all thunderstorms before many days were out.

'The last time I was here, some two years ago, there was a violent summer storm and at high tide the river had risen over the banks, lapping against the very walls of the palace!'

The speaker was a heavily built priest, sitting opposite Hawise. He had a long face and a Roman nose, but his features were marred by a harelip. His speech was slightly odd, which John put down to his deformity; even so, there was a trace of accent which John recognised as coming from central France, perhaps the Auvergne. As he chewed his way through the various meats, supplemented by boiled cabbage and carrots, John gathered that the priest was known to the pair alongside him, though he could not guess whether this was from previous residence in France or merely from sitting here for meals.

So far, the coroner could not think of any way of stimulating conversation which might lead to discussion of current intrigues, but then the empty place opposite was filled by Ranulf of Abingdon. John was glad to see him, as he had enjoyed his company the other night – and possibly he might lead them into more gossip. As a servant filled his tankard with ale, Ranulf greeted John warmly and then introduced the priest sitting next to him, who it seemed was also an established friend.

'This is Bernard de Montfort, archdeacon of Saint Flour,' he announced, confirming John's guess that the man came from the Massif Central, as Saint Flour was an important town on the edge of the mountains. They exchanged some pleasantries and de Wolfe began to think he must be on the road to becoming a soft-centred expert in mouthing platitudes, instead of the hard-bitten soldier that he had been for the past twenty years.

After a few moments, the under-marshal leaned across and spoke in a low voice. 'We had better meet for a talk afterwards, I have some news for you about our trip to Winchester.'

Immediately, the sharp-eared Hawise picked up on the remark.

'What plots are you men hatching now?' she asked archly. 'Are you off on a hunting trip – or perhaps you are seeking to hunt the ladies of Winchester!'

Ranulf smiled weakly, wishing for once that she would mind her own business.

'Affairs of state, I'm afraid, nothing exciting,' he replied dismissively. He winked at John who took the hint and diverted the inquisitive woman. 'Madam, did you know this poor fellow on whom I held an inquest today? He was one of the staff in your guest quarters.'

Her husband spoke across the table before Hawise could answer.

'You mean Basil, the little fellow who made sure we all had bed linen and chamber pots?'

'He did a little more than that,' countered Ranulf. 'He also made sure that the kitchens were supplied with food for the guests and a host of other tasks to make your stay comfortable.'

'Why on earth should anyone murder such a useful fellow?' asked Hawise, fluttering her long lashes at the under-marshal, who was handsome enough in a stern sort of way. In fact, she thought, both he and the brooding Sir John alongside her, were very attractive men.

'I wish I knew, there seems no motive for it at all,' said de Wolfe. 'He was not robbed and his private life seemed too dull for him to have made enemies.'

'He was in minor orders, I understand,' cut in the archdeacon. 'More than just a servant, then?'

'He was a small, but not insignificant part of the palace administration,' replied Ranulf. 'He had to be literate and he needed to behave correctly before persons of high rank and quality – such as yourselves,' he added suavely.

Hawise preened herself at the compliment, but John had a question for her and her husband.

'On that point, did you ever notice Basil in any kind of – what shall I say – close contact with any of the guests? I mean, engaged in conversation beyond any matters relating to your accommodation?'

The couple from Blois looked at each other in mystification. 'I don't really know what you mean, Sir John,' said Renaud. 'Men like that are not noticed much – in fact, I feel that is part of their function, to remain inconspicuous. This Basil certainly went about his business quietly and discreetly, as one would expect.'

'I never noticed him whispering in corners,' declared Hawise, determined to have the last word. 'He was certainly self-effacing and discreet. Now, tell me about this mysterious journey to Winchester. I hope you are going to return before we leave for Gloucester, we need your company and your protection on our own journey!'

Ranulf managed to fob off her curiosity with adroit disclaimers and then turned the conversation around to the sightseeing and marketing the visitors had done in the city since they arrived. At the end of the meal, he managed to escape with John and they strolled out into New Palace Yard, where they were joined by Gwyn, who had come up from his supper in the soldiers' mess. They walked to the riverbank, near the landing stage where poor Basil had met his end and watched the evening sun as it dropped through a heat haze in the western sky.

'So tell me about this task we have in Winchester,' began de Wolfe. 'My officer here will be with me, as well as my clerk. The Justiciar was not very forthcoming about why he wanted me to go on this venture.'

The under-marshal hooked his thumbs into the broad leather belt that encircled a thigh-length brown tunic, below which breeches and boots were visible. He spent much of his life on a horse and rarely wore the long calf-length tunic favoured by the less-active men in the palace.

'These two chests are the last remaining in the treasury vault in Winchester Castle,' he explained. 'One is full of coin, being part of the last Exchequer collection, but I'm told that the other holds a variety of valuable objects of both gold and silver, as well as a few jewels.'

'Where did they come from?' asked John. Jewels were not common, most wealth being held in the two precious metals.

'I gather they are mostly objects recovered as treasure trove, almost all of Saxon origin. No doubt you know more about that than most folk.'

John nodded. 'We have had quite a few finds in Devon these past few years. Probably some of the contents of that chest have already passed through my hands in Exeter.'

Gwyn had been listening attentively. 'So we are to bring these safely back to Westminster. Will they be lodged in the Receipt of the Exchequer?' This was a building adjoining the front of the Great Hall, on the corner facing the river.

'I doubt it, that's only an office and counting house for clerks of the Exchequer, when the sheriffs bring their taxes up for audit. It's not very secure, so I think at first they will be housed either in the strongroom in the King's Chamber or in the abbey crypt. Some previous deliveries have been taken to the Great Tower in the city.'

'You say "at first", so are they to be moved again?' asked John, wondering how an under-marshal knew all these details of the nation's wealth.

As if reading his thoughts, Ranulf of Abingdon explained.

'I have carried out this task before, as most of the treasure has come up to London over the past year or so. Some of it gets sent on to Dover and across to Rouen via Honfleur, but the last consignment ended up in the vaults of the New Temple, a mile up the road from here.'

At John's puzzled expression, Ranulf slyly tapped

the side of his nose. 'Both old King Henry and now Richard have borrowed heavily from the Templars – I suspect that they require either some repayment or at least security for further loans.'

De Wolfe did not wish to get into a discussion about his sovereign lord's financial dealings and moved on to more practical matters.

'So what is the plan for this expedition? I'm still not clear what my role is supposed to be.'

'You are well known as the most trustworthy of Hubert Walter's knights. With so much silver and gold at risk, you are to ensure that nothing goes amiss!'

John thought cynically that if anything did go amiss, then it would be his head that would roll – perhaps literally.

'When do we leave on this mission?'

'The day after tomorrow, wet or shine! There will be twenty men-at-arms under a sergeant and three knights, including ourselves.'

'Who is the other one?' enquired de Wolfe.

'William Aubrey, who is slightly junior to myself. He will carry the writ of release for the chests to the custodian at Winchester Castle.'

A distant rumble of thunder made them glance up at the sky and they saw that a bank of almost purple clouds was rolling up rapidly from the southern horizon.

'God save us from muddy roads on Thursday!' said Ranulf fervently. 'Let's get this storm over with tonight and give it a chance to dry up tomorrow.'

They began walking back across the wide yard and the marshal went off to his quarters behind the palace, leaving the coroner and his officer to trudge towards Long Ditch Lane. As they reached their dwelling, the first big splashes of rain began falling and within minutes, a deluge dropped from the darkening sky.

They sat in the main room around the whitewashed stones of the dead firepit and drank a few pints of Osanna's ale as they listened to the rain beating on the thatch above the upper room and heard the drip of several leaks on to the table and benches below. Lightning flashed and thunder rolled for an hour until the storm passed over, but a steady drizzle of rain continued for much of the night.

John lay for a long while on his low bed, which he had shifted to avoid the drips, thinking about how his life had changed in the past couple of months. Losing Nesta was the most hurtful thing, though he fully appreciated the reasons. He fervently hoped that she was happy with her new husband, Owain the stone-mason, and had found contentment back with her own people in Gwent. For all his many amorous adventures over the years, she was the one who had tugged at his heartstrings the most and he had truly loved her – even though he had loved Hilda before her and still loved her now.

Apart from concerns over these two women, he had problems with yet another pair. Firstly, Mary, his cook-maid in Exeter was left alone in his house in Martin's Lane with only his old dog for company. Until he knew how permanent this exile to London might be – and whether or not his wife would ever return home – he could not dispose of the dwelling. He knew that Mary was unhappy with being left in an empty house with no duties except to feed herself and Brutus, and with no forecast of how long this state of affairs might last. With money not an issue, thanks to his share in a successful wool-exporting business, he could afford to keep the house on indefinitely, but it was his wife Matilda who was the fly in the honey-pot. As he tossed and turned on his hard mattress in the humid heat of the small room, he cursed again at the fate that had linked him to Matilda seventeen years earlier. Neither had a say in the marriage, forced on them by their respective parents and John had coped by staying away from his bride for most of the first fifteen years, finding campaigns, battles and then a Crusade to keep him far away. Since he had hung up his lance and shield over two years ago, living at home had only been bearable by virtue of his new job as Devon county coroner – and his liaison with Nesta. Matilda had become more and more sullen and abrasive, both because of his infidelities and by the depression caused by the disgrace of her brother Sir Richard de Revelle, who had been ejected as sheriff, mainly due to John's exposure of his malpractice. Twice she had forsaken the world and entered a nunnery, this time showing no sign of revoking her decision, and until she decided what she was going to do, Mary was left alone in the house.

With these thoughts going round and round in his head, John eventually fell asleep as the thunder rolled away over the distant Chilterns, leaving him with the half-formed decision to somehow get back to Exeter to try to resolve the problem of his resentful wife.

ChAPTER FOUR

*In which Crowner John takes
a ride into the country*

It was good to be away from the restrictive atmosphere of Westminster, riding at the head of a squadron of soldiers through the Hampshire scrubland. The storm of a few nights ago had cleared the air and though it was warm, there was a breeze with white clouds scudding through a blue sky, instead of the hazy oppression that had hung over the Thames valley.

De Wolfe trotted along contentedly on Odin's back, the heavy destrier's hairy feet thumping rhythmically on the packed earth of the high road between Farnham and Winchester. Alongside him rode Ranulf of Abingdon on a roan gelding and behind came Gwyn on his brown mare, Thomas valiantly keeping up on a dappled palfrey borrowed from the palace stables.

The score of men-at-arms rode two abreast in semi-battle order, with boiled-leather jerkins but no chain-mail. However, they all wore round iron helmets and carried either a sword or an axe at their saddle-bows. The last four in line were archers, dark mercenaries from Wales with longbows across their backs and a quiver of arrows at their knee. Bringing up the rear were the sergeant who had been at the inquest and the other under-marshal, William Aubrey, a fresh-faced young knight from Essex, who had not long obtained his spurs. He was a stocky, muscular fellow, always amiable and cheerful.

'We are making good time, John,' called Ranulf. 'At this rate we should be there well before sundown.'

'Make the most of it, as going back will be miserable, compared to this,' replied de Wolfe, never ready to be optimistic. They would be encumbered by a heavy wagon on the return journey, and even though they had been promised a horse-team, instead of the usual slower oxen, it would more than double the time spent on the road. They had slept last night at Guildford Castle, but going back would mean at least five nights on the journey.

Every few hours, they halted at a village to rest, feed and water their horses. At noon, the whole party ate the rations they carried in their saddlebags, replenished that morning at Guildford. One stop was allowed soon afterwards at a tavern in a small hamlet, where everyone, including the soldiers, downed a quart of ale.

Back on the track, they passed through interminable heathland, with bushes and small trees dotting the scrub of the sandy Hampshire soil. Only around manors and villages were there strip-fields and pasture, quite different from the greener, lush valleys that John was used to in Devon.

'Good country for an ambush,' he grunted to Ranulf, as he scanned the thickets and bushes which grew right to the edge of the narrow road. 'Though I doubt any ragged-arsed outlaws would wish to try anything on a squadron of men-at-arms.'

'And we've nothing to steal, even if they did!' replied the marshal, cheerfully. 'Coming back might be a different matter, though no one will know what we've got in our cart.'

Privately, de Wolfe doubted that, being well aware of

the rapid spread of news by word of mouth, especially in towns as important as Winchester. He wagered that half the city would know what was being hauled out of the castle before they got to the other end of the high street. Still, he had little fear of them being attacked, unless Prince John had suddenly decided to make a play for the Crown and brought the barons sympathetic to his cause with their levies. Even this was highly unlikely, as John, Count of Mortain, had been lying low lately, following the crushing defeat of his rebellion two years earlier.

These thoughts occupied John's mind as they trotted on towards the old capital of England, though his ruminations wandered once again to the women in his life – or in the case of Nesta, *out* of his life. Once again, he decided to get down to Exeter as soon as he could, to try to discover something of Matilda's intentions. He suspected that she was deliberately keeping him in the dark, though he had done nothing particularly heinous lately – one of her main grievances had been removed when Nesta had gone off to Chepstow to be married.

In the early evening, as the sun was at last dipping towards the western horizon, they came over a rise and saw the city of Winchester below them, its castle and the cathedral the prominent points within the walls.

Another half-hour saw them clattering through the eastern gate and soon they had dismounted in the outer bailey of the castle, their tired horses being led away by a dozen grooms and ostlers who were harried into activity by the castle marshal. Gwyn decided to go with the sergeant and his men to find a meal, a game of dice and eventually a bed in the barracks. Thomas was eager to seek out old friends in the abbey and said that he would sleep in the dorter there, though John knew that he would be up half the night attending the offices that began with Matins at midnight.

John and the two under-marshals sought out the Constable, who was the custodian of the royal fortress. Rufus de Longby was an elderly knight, who received them courteously and arranged for accommodation on the upper floor of the keep, as well as accompanying them to eat in the main hall.

'The officials from the Exchequer will not be here until morning,' he explained. 'But your chests will be as safe in the undercroft as the royal treasure has been these past few hundred years!' His weak humour passed over John's head.

'The undercroft? Is that a secure place?' growled the coroner, comparing it with the basement beneath the keep in Exeter's Rougemont Castle, which was little more than a temporary gaol and storage area.

'Wait until you see our undercroft,' boasted de Longby. 'It's the cellar beneath one of the gatehouse towers and would take an army to breach it.'

Soon after dawn next morning, de Wolfe was able to confirm the Constable's claim. After a breakfast of oat gruel, salt bacon and bread and cheese, they assembled in the outer bailey near the gatehouse, where the men-at-arms were already waiting. A covered four-wheel cart was standing by, with a sturdy horse waiting patiently between the shafts. Another stood in front of it, attached by traces, ready to add its strength to hauling the wagon.

Ranulf, who had carried out this task several times before, introduced John to Matthew de la Pole, the resident agent of the Exchequer, a portly manor-lord from Hampshire. De Wolfe thought him a pompous man, full of his own importance. Two cowed-looking clerks stood behind him, clutching some parchments.

'You have the document of authorisation, I trust?' snapped de la Pole, holding out a beringed hand to the coroner.

William Aubrey handed over the slim roll given him by the Keeper of Westminster, which had an impressive seal of red wax dangling from it. De la Pole, who was obviously as illiterate as de Wolfe, unrolled it and pretended to read the short instruction, then handed it to one of his clerks. This official read out in a nasal voice the standard words of release of two chests 'into the care of Sir John de Wolfe, presently Coroner of the Verge'.

John began to realise that this made him totally responsible for the safety and integrity of the treasure and wondered what the penalty would be for any mishap. It would probably cost him his neck.

Matthew de la Pole seemed to relax a little and waved a hand towards the massive tower that formed the left side of the gatehouse. 'Let's get rid of these damned boxes, then. They are the last ones and I'll be glad to see the back of them!'

Leaving Gwyn and Thomas with the soldiers, the coroner and the two marshals followed the baron and the Constable into the guardroom alongside the portcullis and then through a door, unlocked for them by one of the clerks. This led into the base of the tower, which had walls at least ten feet thick. The lower chamber at ground level was empty, but had a planked floor in which there was a central trapdoor.

'Naturally, the guardroom is manned by at least four men at all times,' explained de Longby. 'No one can get in here without authorisation – then there are those to contend with!' He pointed to a pair of massive padlocks, securing two iron bars hinged across the trapdoor. Matthew snapped his fingers at his other clerk, who came forward with a ring carrying two large keys, with which he opened the locks and threw back the bars with a clang.

Ranulf touched William Aubrey's arm and motioned him forward to help the clerk raise the heavy trapdoor by means of two iron rings. With an effort, they lifted it to one side, just as the Constable gave a piercing blast on a whistle. Immediately, the sergeant-at-arms came in with four men, two carrying a wooden ladder, the other horn lanterns. Under the direction of their sergeant, the ladder was lowered into the hole and the two lantern men clambered down. John went to the edge of the trap and peered into a bare undercroft, a dank and forbidding pit, with a damp earthen floor, well below ground level.

The other soldiers had ropes, which they lowered through the opening and amid much shouting of orders, first one, then another large chest was hauled up and placed on the wooden floor. They were of similar size, about four feet long, but one was of darker oak and had three iron bands around it, as opposed to the two on the second chest. Each had two massive metal hasps with padlocks on each.

'The darker box contains the coin, the other one is a mixture of precious objects,' declared de la Pole. He gestured briskly at one of his clerks, who proffered another roll of parchment, with three different seals of red wax dangling from it by red tape.

'This is an inventory made yesterday by myself and two other officials of the Exchequer, signed with our marks and our seals.'

He handed the roll to John. 'Now it's your problem, sir! When you deliver this roll to the Constable of the Great Tower and the Treasury officials there, they will recheck the contents of the chests with this manifest. I hope for your sake that they agree!'

He said this with a hint of malice, as if he relished

the thought of there being some fatal discrepancy.

Ranulf looked puzzled. 'I assumed that we were taking the chests to Westminster?' he said to de la Pole. The Exchequer official shook his head. 'Not this time, the treasure is urgently needed in Rouen, so it will go to the nearest place for shipment from the port of London. So make sure it gets there safely!'

'What about the keys?' said John gruffly, anxious to get away from this insolent fellow. For answer, Matthew turned again to his senior clerk and held out his hand. The subdued cleric scrabbled in the scrip on his belt and produced two more pairs of steel keys, each pair on a ring.

'These are for the locks on both chests,' he snapped. 'Normally, they are separated and one is held by myself, the other by another member of the Exchequer. I presume the same will happen in London, but that's their affair!'

As John took the large and slightly rusty keys, de la Pole offered one last barbed comment.

'They are now your responsibility, de Wolfe! Let them out of your sight at your peril!'

With that, he sailed from the chamber, his two clerks hurrying after him like a pair of chastened hounds at their master's heels.

As de Wolfe had forecast, their journey back was painfully slow. Though the two chests were heavy, the pair of horses had no difficulty in pulling the cart, especially as the road was free from the mud that could bog the wheels down in thick mire. But the beasts could do no better than a steady walking pace, and on the first day they covered a bare sixteen miles along the London road. This took them as far as Alton, where the soldiers commandeered a tithe barn to sleep in, while the three knights and Thomas battened upon the local manor-lord for hospitality. He was not all that pleased to see them, but with ill-grace gave them a meal and let them sleep on some straw mattresses in his hall.

Next day they set out earlier and rode until late so that they could reach Guildford again, where the castle was obliged to accommodate the official procession. The third day was a disappointment, as although Ranulf had hoped to get as far as Kingston, they did not even make it as far as Esher. One of the wheel-hubs cracked and they came to a halt in the middle of a forest. This failure was a well-known problem and they carried a spare wheel lashed to the tailboard, but it meant almost two hours' delay. The men-at-arms had to cut down a sapling from the adjacent woods and use it to lever up the heavy cart. Then stones and fallen wood had to be collected and used to prop up the wagon, so that the errant wheel could be removed and replaced with the spare.

That part of Surrey was covered by dense forest and villages were few and far between. By late evening, everyone was tired and fractious, so when they reached a small hamlet, John and his companions decided they had travelled far enough.

'God's guts! Where can we sleep here?' demanded Gwyn, looking around at the dozen mean huts that made up the settlement. There was no manor house, but it had a tiny church, a primitive structure of wattle-and-daub with a vestigial bell tower at one end of the tattered thatched roof. Inside the churchyard was a hut that presumably did service as the priest's dwelling.

'Go and see what your holy colleague can suggest,' said de Wolfe to Thomas, as the weary men and wearier horses stopped on the road outside. The little clerk trotted off and soon came back with a wizened man, dressed in a short smock and cross-gartered breeches. Though he looked like a hedger or a ditcher, Thomas presented him as the parish priest, proven by his shaven scalp.

'Father Aedan says that you are welcome to use his church to shelter in overnight.'

The bent old man, his remaining hair showing enough blond strands to mark him as a Saxon, had a surprisingly sweet smile.

'There are no palliasses, but it is a warm night and no doubt your soldiers are used to sleeping on the floor,' he said, exposing toothless gums behind his sunken lips. 'For you gentlemen, maybe you would prefer the luxury of a pile of hay in the barn on the other side of the church.'

John muttered his thanks, but Ranulf, who had a smoother tongue than the bluff coroner, was more fulsome in his appreciation.

'That is a very Christian gesture, father! We are tired and hungry, having been on the king's business these past three days.'

'I can do little about your hunger, sir, this is a poor and insignificant village. There is an alehouse, but I doubt the widow who runs it could provide for more than a score of men.'

In spite of the priest's misgivings, after leaving William Aubrey to organise the guarding of the wagon and the settlement of the men-at-arms, de Wolfe and Ranulf walked a little further down the track to seek the alehouse.

'This really is a dismal village,' said Ranulf, looking around in the gathering dusk at the few shacks spread along the road. Most were built of cob, a mixture of lime, dung and bracken, spread on wattle panels. One or two were dry-walled stone, but none had more than one room. All were steeply thatched, the state of the straw or reeds varying from fairly new to green disintegration, some with actual grass or weeds growing on their roofs. The alehouse proved to be almost indistinguishable from the other crofts, though a little longer from end to crumbling end. The tattered bush hanging over the door was the universal sign of a tavern and the two knights bent their heads to enter.

A frightened-looking woman appeared from behind a rickety table, apprehensive at the sudden arrival of two tall men of military appearance. Again Ranulf took the lead in reassuring the ale-wife of their good intentions.

'We are a force of soldiers on our way to London, good woman,' he said. 'We are staying in the church-yard for the night, but are seeking any food and drink that might be available.'

On learning of their numbers, the widow shook her head. 'I might have enough ale in my crocks to give you a pint apiece, sir, but as for food, there is hardly enough bread in the whole village to feed twenty-five men!'

A man sitting on a bench against the wall got up and came over to them, touching his forehead in salute. 'I killed a pig this morning, sirs, it's hanging fresh in my croft. I'd sell it for a shilling, if you wanted to roast it.'

John looked at Ranulf. 'Better than going hungry! Though it would take a few hours to roast on a spit.'

After some haggling, the crofter sold them the pig for ten pence, which Ranulf intended reclaiming from the Keeper as part of their expenses. 'Best get the men organised, if they want to eat before midnight!' advised de Wolfe.

They arranged for the ale-wife to supply all the spare drink she had, collected later by soldiers who carried the large five-gallon pottery crocks back to the churchyard. The old priest made no objection to start-ing a fire inside the ring of large stones which was used every time the village had an 'ale' for some celebration or other. The men entered into the spirit of the event, gathering fallen wood from the edge of the forest and when the gutted pig had been brought, it was turned on a makeshift spit supported on forked branches stuck into the ground.

Darkness was falling by the time the meat was cooked, making the scene look like some barbaric festival, with a circle of hungry men sitting around the fire, lit up by sizzling flares when gobs of fat dripped into the flames. As a log burnt through and fell, a shower of red sparks rose into the air, like a swarm of fireflies. When the sergeant-at-arms, who had appointed himself cook, declared the flesh ready to eat, every man, including the knights and Thomas, lined up to cut themselves slices with their eating knife or dagger. In spite of her pessimism about the amount of bread, the tavern widow had found enough coarse loaves to give every man a hunk, on which he laid his hot pork until cool enough to eat.

Together with some ale dipped from the crocks in a few pint pots and passed from mouth to mouth, the succulent meat and the comradely atmosphere satisfied everyone. By the time the hog had been reduced to a near skeleton, most of the men were ready to sleep, though four were obliged to stay awake to form the first watch to guard the treasure wagon until morning.

The rest ambled back to the little church and gratefully curled up on the earthen floor, wrapping themselves in their riding cloaks though the night was still warm.

All the horses had been watered at a stream than ran through the village and then turned out into a large meadow with a dry-stone wall around it. The cart, bereft of its draught animals, stood forlornly against the church wall, with two of the guards sitting on the driving-board and the other two crouched on the grass at the rear.

'We may as well test the softness of the priest's hay, I suppose,' suggested Ranulf, leading the way towards the small barn. Its interior was almost completely dark, but a half moon and the remains of the fire gave them enough light to see that it was almost empty. At the end of spring, most of the stored roots like turnips and carrots had been used up and it was too early for much of this year's produce to be gathered in.

'Just enough hay to lie on, I reckon,' said Gwyn, peering around in the streaks of fitful moonlight that penetrated the gaps between the rough planks that formed the walls. It was more a large shed than a proper barn, but was enough to hold the meagre tithes that such a small hamlet could produce for their priest. The five men shuffled around in the gloom and each found a corner or a nook amongst the remains of last year's crops, curling up in their mantles and ignoring the rustling of mice and rats that were their fellow guests for the night. The coroner and the two knights from the Marshalsea decided to lay where they could see the precious cart through the open doors of the barn. Gwyn and Thomas preferred a spot against the back wall.

John found it warm enough to roll up his riding cloak to use as a pillow, after he had wriggled himself into a comfortable position on a thin layer of musty-smelling hay. He had pulled off his boots and laid his belt, which carried sword, dagger and pouch, on the ground alongside him. Too tired tonight to churn his personal troubles around in his mind, he fell almost immediately into a dreamless sleep.

Hours later, when the moon had declined almost to the horizon, he suddenly awoke, with the feeling that something was wrong. As an old campaigner, used to sleeping rough where danger was ever present, he was instantly fully awake. He heard Ranulf snoring nearby, but his nose and his ears told him that they were in danger. Jerking upright, he sniffed repeatedly and then got to his feet and hurried to the door, ignoring the jabs to his bare feet from debris on the floor. As he emerged into the near darkness, there was a sudden yell of 'Fire!' from nearby and William Aubrey stumbled around the corner of the barn, clutching his breeches around his backside, his belt hanging loose.

'The thatch is on fire, come and see!' He grabbed John by the arm, pulled him to the corner and pointed up. 'I went outside for a shite and then saw flames!' he gabbled. Almost at the same time, there were sudden cries of alarm from across the churchyard, where the four sentries were guarding the wagon.

'Fire, fire!' came the dreaded yells and going further out from the barn, John coughed as a wreath of smoke drifted down from above. Due to the overhang of the eaves, he could see nothing until he ran out into the coarse grass and weeds of the churchyard. Stumbling backwards and looking up, now he could see that part of the barn's ragged thatch was alight and spreading rapidly, fanned by the slight breeze and aided by the dry state of the old straw after days without rain.

He heard shouts and running feet coming towards him, and turning saw that the soldiers from the wagon detail were racing towards the barn. A sudden thought occurred to him and he yelled at them urgently.

'Get back to your posts, damn you! That's more important than a poxy shed!'

The possibility that this could be some sort of diversion, to leave the treasure cart unattended crossed his mind, though it seemed highly unlikely. But the barn was undoubtedly on fire and John hobbled back to the entrance, cursing as small stones cut into his almost bare feet. As he went through the doorway, he was just about to start yelling 'Fire!' himself, when he dimly saw that Gwyn had risen to his feet and was starting to bellow a warning, as he pushed Thomas ahead of him to safety.

'The bloody thatch is afire!' hollered de Wolfe. 'Give that other fellow a shake, Gwyn!' he shouted, pointing at the inert shape of Ranulf, who seemed capable of sleeping through an earthquake. Scooping up his boots and his belt, John retreated to the door and hurriedly thrust his feet into his footwear and buckled on the belt. By now, the fire had reached the inside of the thatch and bits of burning straw were falling through the framework of twisted hazel withies that held it up. There was no danger to any of them, as by now Gwyn had hauled the bemused under-marshal to his feet and given him a push in the direction of the doorway, where Aubrey was tucking his shirt into his breeches and anxiously awaiting his friend.

A moment later, they were all outside and by now the men-at-arms who had been sleeping in the church had streamed out and were standing in a half-circle, staring impotently at the burning roof.

'There's no way we'll save that now!' called out the sergeant. 'There's no water here and by the time we get buckets to the stream, the place will be well alight.'

Now the crowd was strengthened by some villagers who had been attracted by the noise and the priest had emerged from his dwelling on the other side of the churchyard to witness the destruction of his property. Thomas hurried to console him, but he seemed unperturbed.

'It is the will of God!' he cried philosophically, crossing himself, content in the knowledge that the manor would have to rebuild it for him, hopefully a better one than the decrepit structure that was now burning merrily.

Ranulf, now fully awake but rubbing his eyes sleepily, decided that they themselves must have been the cause of the fire.

'Blame the damned pig!' he muttered. 'Must have been a spark that flew up from our fire that landed in the thatch and smouldered until it caught hold. I'd best give them a couple of marks in compensation – I'll get it back from the palace when we return.'

John went over to the wagon and paced around it suspiciously, under the uneasy eyes of the four sentinels. He suspected that they had all been fast asleep, as their recognition of the burning barn had been remarkably slow.

'Have you seen or heard anything untoward?' he demanded of them. They denied seeing anything out of the ordinary and when a now more wakeful Ranulf and Aubrey came across to join him, they checked the two chests and saw nothing wrong. Before long, the first streaks of dawn appeared in the eastern sky and it seemed pointless to try to settle back to sleep. When it was full light, the soldiers went off to the stream to drink and splash their sleepy faces with cold water. By then, it was time to round up the horses and prepare to continue the journey. De Wolfe was still anxious about the treasure chests and studied the locks more closely.

'No one seems to have tampered with them,' muttered Gwyn, looking over John's shoulder at the pair of large iron padlocks on each box. They were covered with a thin patina of rust, in which no fresh scratches were visible around the keyholes to suggest any attempt had been made to pick them.

Eventually satisfied that they had not been robbed,

the cavalcade moved off, leaving a village glad to see the back of them. Having had no breakfast, the troop and their officers were all pleased to reach Kingston, where they were able to eat and drink at the manor house, then set off on the last leg of the journey to London. Their slow journey kept them south of the Thames all the way to Southwark, where in the early evening their tired horses clattered over the old wooden bridge into the city. The oppressive heat had declined during the days since they had left for Hampshire and it remained pleasantly warm as they plodded the last half-mile through busy streets along the north bank to the Tower. The grim grey rectangle stood high above a confusion of construction around its base, as Hubert Walter was busy carrying out the Lionheart's orders to encircle the keep with a retaining wall and a moat. They picked their way through mounds of stone blocks and heaps of sand and lime, where masons and labourers were still working overtime to build a twenty-foot rampart, further evidence of the royal mistrust of the citizens of London.

'Our chests should be safe enough inside this lot!' jested Ranulf, as they dodged under wooden derricks and tripods hauling stones to the top of the growing wall. Once close to the Tower itself, the construction chaos ceased and they drew their cart up to an arched entrance in the north face of the cliff-like tower. Here a brace of guards with spears stood each side of the big doors which led into an undercroft, partly below ground level. The entrance to the upper floors was up a nearby flight of wooden stairs, the usual defence mechanism to prevent easy access during a siege, as the steps could be thrown down in minutes.

'Now what happens?' grunted John, tired of sitting on his horse for so many hours. As if in answer to his question, a wicket gate in the large doors opened and several men stepped out into the evening sunshine. He recognised one as Simon Basset, a senior Treasury official, for he had once sat next to him in the Lesser Hall. The other two seemed to be Tower officers, in severe military-looking tunics with the three royal lions embroidered on their surcoats. Each had a large sword swinging from a belt and baldric. John and the two other knights-marshal dismounted and went to meet the men, apologising for the delay in their arrival and explaining the problem with the cracked wheel-hub. De Wolfe thought it pointless to mention the fire, which appeared to have no relevance to their journey.

Simon Basset was a portly cleric, still a canon of Lichfield Cathedral. He had climbed the Westminster ladder during old King Henry's time and was now one of the senior administrators in the Treasury. Though he had met him only twice, John felt that Basset was an astute royal servant, as well as being a pleasant, amiable character, with a round face and pink cheeks.

'What's to be done with these damned boxes?' asked the coroner. 'We've guarded them like precious babes all the way from Winchester. I'll be glad to see them safely housed, so that we can stop looking over our shoulders at every corner!'

Simon motioned to the two gate guards to open one leaf of the heavy, studded doors. 'We'll get the chests taken inside right away, Sir John. They'll not be here more than a few days, as we are waiting for a king's ship to take them over to Rouen.'

John guessed that the sale of the gold and silver was needed to pay the Lionheart's troops and to finance the endless need for food and fodder for the large army.

The soldiers from their escort began sliding the large boxes from the wagon and carrying each between four men down the ramp into the undercroft. De

Wolfe, together with Aubrey and Ranulf, followed the Treasury official and his two companions into the gloomy basement and across to another locked door which was lit by guttering flares stuck in rings on the wall. They went along a passage to yet another heavy door, where one of the Tower officers produced a large key. He let them into a small chamber devoid of any windows or other openings, obviously deep in the bowels of the Conqueror's fortress. A soldier brought another flaring pitch-brand and by its light John could see that half a dozen other chests were lined against the walls.

'All destined for Normandy!' observed Simon Basset, as they watched the two new boxes being added to the collection.

'I presume I leave the keys with you?' growled de Wolfe, feeling in his pouch for the heavy bunches that he was only too happy to be rid of.

'What about checking the contents?' asked Ranulf. 'The inventory was certified correct when we left Winchester, but I wouldn't want any loss to be alleged while the chests were in our care.'

Simon smiled benignly. 'Very commendable, sir. I was going to do that very thing now.' He held out his hand for the four keys, which de Wolfe handed over with some relief. Now he noticed that each key had a dab of coloured paint on the ring of its stem, which corresponded with a similar blob on the face of each lock.

'I will keep the keys for one lock on each chest,' said the Treasury man, sliding two of them off the wire loop that held them. 'The other two will be given straight away to the Constable of the Tower. Neither of us – nor anyone else – can open them alone.'

Contradicting his own statement – but under the eyes of half a dozen watchers – Simon Basset used the four keys to open each of the padlocks and hoisted back the heavy lids, which were held upright by leather straps. He produced a roll of parchment from inside his black robe and held it so that the flaring light from the torch fell upon the lists written in ornate black script.

'This was sent from Winchester by a royal messenger on a swift horse after you left and arrived yesterday,' he explained. 'It is the manifest which was made immediately before the chests left the castle there.'

The two knights from the Tower garrison squatted at the side of the one of great boxes and checked the bags of money. They did not count the actual coins, but confirmed the number of bags and the fact that the red wax seal with the impression of the ring of the Exchequer official was intact. Then they turned to the smaller chest which held the gold, silver and jewelled objects. As the treasurer called out a description of each piece, they rooted around in the contents. Smaller items were wrapped in pieces of velvet or silk. Some lay in leather bags closed with purse-strings, but larger objects such as silver candlesticks, a heavy gold torc, a thick Celtic necklace and some massive silver belt-buckles, were loose amongst the other treasures.

The process of checking the items against Simon Basset's list took no longer than half an hour, at the end of which he declared himself satisfied that nothing was missing and added his signature to the bottom of the inventory from Winchester.

The chamber was re-locked, as was the outer door into the undercroft and the party moved back out into the glow of sunset outside, where Gwyn and Thomas were waiting patiently. Simon offered them all refreshment, but the Westminster contingent unanimously decided to ride back home. Now unencumbered by the wagon, the troop set off westwards and passing through the city streets and out through Ludgate, arrived thankfully at the palace less than an hour later.

Thomas hurried off to the abbey refectory and Gwyn inevitably made for the nearest alehouse for food, drink and a game of dice with his cronies. This left de Wolfe to seek supper in the Lesser Hall, accompanied by Ranulf of Abingdon and William Aubrey. The meal had begun, but they found seats opposite Renaud de Seigneur and Lady Hawise. When John slid on to his bench, he found himself next to the archdeacon, Bernard de Montfort.

'We've missed your company these past days,' offered the amiable cleric. 'We have heard that you have been on a secret mission deep into the countryside!'

John was happy to let Ranulf answer, as he was too intent on loading his trencher with a pair of grilled trout from a platter which a serving boy placed in the middle of the table.

'Nothing secret about it, merely a routine escort task for some of the king's valuables,' said the undermarshal easily.

'There will be another royal escort task soon,' commented the Lord of Blois. 'We hear that Queen Eleanor's arrival becomes ever more imminent. No doubt she is awaiting a fair wind from France.'

'Then you know more than I, sir,' replied Ranulf. 'But in any event, it will not involve us, other than to manage the horses and wagons to transport them. They will require far more august persons to attend upon her than a lowly servant of the Marshal.'

Renaud's wife answered for him.

'You are too modest, sir. I feel sure you are given assignments that would surprise us all, if you could reveal them.'

Hawise d'Ayncourt fluttered her lashes at the good-looking knight, but her eyes slid covertly towards de Wolfe, who was stolidly attacking his fish with his eating knife.

'What do you say to that, coroner?' asked Renaud, with false jocularity. 'I hear you have the ear of the Justiciar – and even of the king himself!'

John sighed inwardly, he was becoming a little tired of these mild interrogations at every meal. He would not mind bedding the delectable Hawise, but tonight he did not particularly wish to talk to her or her tiresome husband.

'The king's ear is far away in Normandy – and the archbishop's is only tuned to receiving my reports on dead bodies!' he replied rather abruptly. He lifted his ale-pot and waved at a nearby servant for a refill, hoping that the others would drop the subject. However, Hawise, tonight attired in a white gown and a light surcoat of blue silk, dextrously moved on to his private life.

'We hear that you have your own private house in the town, coroner,' she said smoothly. 'That must be very convenient for a handsome man living far from his home and family?'

The meaning of her remark was obvious from the roguish tone she used. De Wolfe was about to snub her with a cutting remark about his wife, but then thought that if that was how the land lay, then maybe he should leave the matter open. To tell the truth, he was feeling the ill-effects of a long period of celibacy since leaving Devon – and even before he left, the barren period since Nesta had abandoned him, had only twice been relieved by visits to Dawlish. If this undoubtedly handsome woman wanted to enjoy herself one evening, then why should he stand in her way?

The look he gave her from under his heavy brows

must have conveyed something of his mood, for she smiled archly at him. For her part, she thought once again that he was an attractive man, with his tall, strong body and dark brooding features. His swept-back black hair, his high-bridged nose and his full, sensuous lips gave her a quiver of anticipation. Hawise lifted her wine cup and stared over its rim at de Wolfe, already imagining those hard-muscled arms crushing her tightly against him, so different from the flabby embraces of her boring husband.

Still, at the moment that boring husband was sitting right alongside her and with a sigh she returned to her trencher of boiled salmon and her platter of beans and carrots. The conversation continued around them, and once again the lack of any progress over the murdered Basil was one of the topics.

'Probably slain by a disgruntled guest, in revenge for the poor food and service that we get upstairs!' chortled the archdeacon, an insensitive remark for one whose profession was supposed to exude compassion and respect for his fellow men.

'There should be at least one good meal on the way,' offered the cherubic William Aubrey, from further down the table. 'I hear that Hubert Walter is to hold a feast in the Great Hall when the old queen arrives, as a mark of respect for her.'

This set them chattering again about the continuing role that the ageing Eleanor still played in politics, even though she was now seventy-four years of age. She continued to champion her favourite son Richard and kept a rein on the excesses and follies of the younger John. This was undoubtedly the main reason for her impending visit, as the Count of Mortain continued to be much too friendly with Philip of France for most people's liking.

Eventually the meal ended and Hawise swayed away

behind her shorter husband, casting a longing look at John as she went.

'That dame is quite taken with you, John,' said Ranulf rather wistfully, as they went out into the twilight of the Palace Yard. 'I'd not say no to a tumble with her myself, especially as that Renaud fellow seems not to be too bothered by her wayward eye.'

De Wolfe shrugged indifferently. 'I don't want to start a diplomatic incident, even if the chance presented itself,' he countered. 'Why the hell are they here, anyway? De Seigneur is lord of some miserable place in Blois, which is not even allied to Normandy.'

Near the main gate to the palace compound, Ranulf excused himself and hurried off up King Street. 'He's off to a game of chance in one of the houses up at Scotland Yard,' confided Aubrey. 'A great one for cards and dice, is Ranulf. But when he loses badly, he's like a bull with a sore head for days!'

The under-marshal, who John felt was rather naive even for the youngest of knights, pleaded fatigue after the long day and went off to his quarters near the stables at the rear of the palace, leaving John to his own devices. He was tired as well, but decided to have a last drink with Gwyn before going to bed.

The sun had dropped well below the western horizon and the light was failing as he went into the Deacon alehouse, which seemed to have become their favourite tavern.

He found his henchman with a group of soldiers and palace guards, sitting in a circle of benches and stools, playing 'quek', an obscure game with dice and small stones, thrown on to a board upon the ground, painted with a series of squares. Money was changing hands, but he was glad to see that it seemed to be only halves and quarters of pennies. He knew that Gwyn was trying to save from his daily wage of three pence, to take money back for his wife and two small sons when they next returned to Exeter. Although John had bought the Bush inn from Nesta when she left and put in Gwyn's wife as landlady, the profits might not be much for some time, until the trade settled down after the change.

He sat with a jug of ale while waiting for the game to end and then bought Gwyn a quart of cider when the big redhead ambled across to him. 'Made seven pence tonight, Crowner! Must be the luck from all that treasure rubbing off on me.'

They sat peacefully for a while, drinking and watching the light fade in the open window space. 'Thank God that it was all intact, according to the check that the treasury man made,' said John, for Gwyn had not been in the strongroom when Simon Basset had confirmed that all was correct. 'I was worried that that fire was some kind of diversion intended to cover up an attempt to rob the wagon.'

They discussed the events of the past few days, and as usual their conversation drifted off to nostalgic longing for Devon and all the familiar things that made this exile in London seem so miserable.

'We must get ourselves back there as soon as possible, Gwyn. But this damned appearance of the dowager queen will interfere – we can't get away until her visit is over.'

'Unless we can slip away for a few days from Bristol or Gloucester?' suggested the Cornishman.

John shrugged. 'Let's see what tomorrow brings – every day seems to have some new twist.'

CHAPTER FIVE

In which Crowner John receives a welcome visitor

The new twist that arrived the next day came via the same timid page that had summoned de Wolfe the previous week. His head appeared around the door after Gwyn had yelled in answer to his gentle knock.

'Sir John, I have a message from the Justiciar's office,' he began. Taking a deep breath, the lad then rattled off a long sentence that he had obviously learned parrot fashion.

'Archbishop Walter sends his felicitations to the Coroner of the Verge and commands his attendance at noon in the Great Hall to meet various parties in regard to jurid – jurisdiction.'

He stumbled over the last unfamiliar word, then subsided into embarrassed silence, looking from one to the other of the three men in the chamber.

'Thank you, lad,' said John kindly, remembering his own days as a ten-year-old page in the service of a knight from Dartmouth. 'Do you know who else might be attending this meeting?'

'Another page has been sent across to the abbot, sir. And I know that yesterday heralds went up to the city in connection with the same matter, according to the Justiciar's chief clerk.'

The boy left, thankful for such an amiable reception and John pondered over the significance of the news.

'Hubert is either going to cave in to those arrogant louts from the city – or he's going to hold out for precedence for us,' he said pensively.

'The archbishop probably has to tread carefully at the moment,' observed Thomas, who had the best grasp of current politics. 'He is in bad odour with many of his churchmen and also with the civic authorities in London. The city is still angry with him for setting fire to one of their churches – and in knocking down so many houses to build this new wall around the Tower.'

'But that's at the direct command of the king!' bellowed Gwyn, who was as staunch a royalist as his master.

'Doesn't stop Hubert being unpopular,' said de Wolfe. 'Bloody-minded independence is virtually a way of life with the citizens of London. We're likely to have a lively meeting today, mark my words! You had both better come along, you're part of the coroner's team which is at the heart of this dispute.'

When they entered the main entrance of the Great Hall early that afternoon, they found that the meeting was to be held at the far end, on the central dais facing down the colonnade of pillars that supported the massive roof. The court of the King's Bench sat there frequently, but today it had been commandeered by Hubert Walter, who was head of the justice system – and almost everything else.

Three large chairs for the judges were placed at the back of the platform and benches were arranged at right angles in the space marked off by the bar of the court, a wooden pole which kept the public at bay. As de Wolfe and his companions arrived, so did most of the other participants, coming in from the interior of the palace through a rear door. Four palace guards preceded Hubert Walter, whose lean body was today dressed in a crimson tunic with a large golden cross hanging from a chain around his neck. His head was covered with a white linen helmet, laced under the chin and he wore gloves of thin leather.

Behind him came half-a-dozen worthies and John recognised Godard of Antioch, the sheriff with whom he'd had dealings the previous week. Another taller man with a pointed brown beard wore a massive gold chain over a robe that had fur trimming, even in this warm weather. John assumed that this was Henry fitz Ailwyn, the first Mayor of the city of London. There were several other men who were unknown to him, as well as a couple of priests, one being Hubert's personal chaplain and confessor.

Two clerks, complete with parchments and pens, sat at either side to record the proceedings. After some muted conversation and shuffling about, everyone sat themselves down, Hubert in the centre, the mayor on his right. The other chair was empty, but as the rest of the delegates arranged themselves on the benches, a new trio came marching up the main aisle and entered under the bar, lifted for them by the sergeant of the guard. These were William Postard, Abbot of Westminster, with his prior and another priest. The abbot took the vacant chair and John de Wolfe, at a sign from Hubert, perched himself on the end of one of the benches, near the door into the palace.

Gwyn and Thomas melted into the small crowd that was now gravitating to the bar and to the sides where the court was partitioned off between the first two pillars. John noticed that amongst the spectators were Renaud and his eye-catching wife, as well as Archdeacon Bernard and Ranulf of Abingdon.

The sergeant opened the proceedings by rapping the end of his pike on the platform and everyone stood while the chaplain gabbled a prayer in Latin. He made the sign of the cross in the air and everyone subsided again, as the Justiciar began speaking without any preamble.

'The issues are clear and we need not detain ourselves overlong with them,' he barked, marking his authority from the outset. 'Almost two years ago, for a variety of reasons which need not concern us now, King Richard, on the advice of his Royal Council, appointed three knights in every county to keep the pleas of the crown. The system was promulgated at the Eyre held in Rochester in September of that year and has functioned well ever since.'

There was a scornful laugh from Henry fitz Ailwyn. 'Functioned well enough for you to screw yet more money from the population!'

Hubert Walter looked with distaste at the man on his right.

'It was a natural progression of the law reforms begun by King Henry,' he said sharply. 'The royal courts are gradually replacing the confusion we inherited from Saxon times and the coroner is a vital means of servicing them.'

'The ecclesiastical courts are by no means in confusion, archbishop!' objected William Postard from his other side. The abbot was a small man, who spoke and moved quickly and rather jerkily, reminding de Wolfe of a squirrel.

'I was referring to the hotchpotch of secular courts, Lord Abbot,' answered Walter in a conciliatory tone. 'The manor courts, the hundred courts, the county courts, the forest courts – and we still have such primitive methods such as the ordeal, trial by battle and other pagan rites that have no place in a Christian realm!'

The abbot nodded, mollified by the archbishop's

exclusion of the canon law, still a sensitive subject since the murder of Thomas Becket a quarter of a century ago. 'But what is the purpose of this meeting today?' he asked.

'A matter of jurisdiction – or division of labour, if you prefer,' replied Hubert Walter. 'I have to admit that the way in which the coronial system was set up, was somewhat sketchy.'

'Damned right!' muttered de Wolfe, but kept his voice inaudible, as the Justiciar continued.

'Only one sentence, the twentieth Article of Eyre in Rochester, described the duties required by King Richard, which were to keep the pleas of the Crown. Unfortunately, these are open to various interpretations and we need to refine their meaning, especially in terms of jurisdiction.'

The mayor scowled up at the prelate. 'Say what you mean, Justiciar. We've not got all day to sit here and bandy words!'

With an effort, Hubert contained his annoyance with the man's rudeness. He looked on fitz Ailwyn as a rough tradesman, one who had made too much money too quickly and risen above his station in life, certainly from the point of view of diplomacy and social graces, in spite of being the leader of Europe's richest city.

'When the king accepted his Council's recommendation to set up coroners, he was gracious enough to also accept your protestations from London, wishing to be exempted from the provisions of Article Twenty.' He deliberately emphasised the royal element in the process.

'We have our own way of going about things,' growled the mayor. 'For centuries, the city has been self-sufficient, we need no petty rules imposed upon us from outside.'

'I trust you are not calling the king's command a

petty rule, Sir William?' said Hubert in an icy tone. This was an effective brake on the mayor's outspokenness – however much the city railed against outside interference, an outright rejection of royal writ could be construed as treason. Godard of Antioch sensed the rashness of the mayor's manner and tried to tone it down.

'Our sheriffs had always undertaken the keeping of the peace in the city,' he observed. 'We saw no need to have a system designed for the peasantry of the shires imposed upon us.'

Next to him, a swarthy man in a green tunic under a yellow surcoat joined the argument. 'And as the city has always looked after the county of Middlesex, we desire to continue to do so.' This was obviously Robert fitz Durand, the second city sheriff.

Abbot Postard jumped to his feet. 'Except for the Liberty of Westminster, sir!' he exclaimed angrily. 'The writ of the county of Middlesex does not run here, though we are embedded within its boundaries. My enclave bows its head to no one except the king – not even Canterbury!'

De Wolfe knew of the special situation of Edward the Confessor's great church and the extensive lands that it owned, which bore allegiance only to the Holy Father in Rome.

Hubert Walter held up his hands in a gesture of conciliation.

'Of course all of this is true, there is no dispute about it. But a recent case, one of murder no less, has shown that confusion and acrimony may arise when jurisdictions overlap. This has been accentuated by the king's direct command that a coroner be appointed to deal with cases that arise within the verge of the court, wherever it may be.'

He went on to expound on the problems that could

arise when an itinerant court moved through different jurisdictions. 'This produces no clash of interest when well away from London, as I have made it clear to all county sheriffs that the Coroner of the Verge has total control of incidents within the twelve mile range.'

He looked to each side to see if either the mayor or the abbot were about to raise objections, but they seemed indifferent to the problems of the rural countryside.

'The main problem lies here along the Thames,' he continued. 'Because all of London and most of Middlesex lie within the Verge when the court is here at Westminster, then theoretically, all deaths, fires, rapes and the rest of coroner's business could be considered to be within the purview of Sir John de Wolfe here.'

He waved a hand at the coroner, who sat stolidly staring at his feet.

'Then that's patently damned ridiculous!' rasped fitz Ailwyn. 'There are thirty thousand souls in the city and a few thousand more in the surrounding county.'

Hubert raised a placatory hand. 'I know, I know. We need to come to a compromise, to avoid the unpleasantness that I hear occurred last week. What seems obvious and eminently sensible, is to differentiate between types of victim and events, be they murders, accidents, rapes or serious assaults.'

'What exactly do you mean, Justiciar?' asked Godard suspiciously.

'If the victim is connected with the court or the Palace of Westminster, be they a courtier or a cook, then they fall within the coroner's ambit, irrespective of where the body lies. In the case of Westminster itself, then of course if the victim is closely connected with the abbey, be he priest or lay worker, then the Lord Abbot may deal with it, if he so wishes.'

Surprisingly, William Postard now seemed less keen to burden himself with extra duties.

'I would have no desire to waste the time of my proctors upon some drunken stabbing in a local ale-house! As long as I retain the right to decide if I need to be involved, your coroner is welcome to pursue his duties within my manor of Ide.' This was the name of the extensive lands that included and surrounded the town of Westminster.

The archbishop nodded sagely. This was at least one difficulty avoided, so he turned to the mayor – a more belligerent problem.

'Have you or your sheriffs any objection to my pro-posal, which is to concede jurisdiction to you except where the victim is clearly connected with the royal palace?'

Henry fitz Ailwyn glowered around at the faces before him, unwilling to concede anything, but feeling isolated by the common sense of the proposal and the ready acceptance already offered by the abbot. Red-faced, he leaned forward towards his two sheriffs, who sat on the bench nearby and began a muttered debate with them.

After a couple of moments, the mayor turned back to Hubert Walter. 'It depends on what is meant by being connected with the palace,' he blustered. 'Some wherryman who happened to have come from your pier, then falls into the river, is hardly a candidate for your Coroner of the Verge.'

This obviously puerile niggle caused a few covert smiles around the dais and someone down in the small crowd of onlookers gave a cackle of derision, but the insensitive fitz Ailwyn ploughed on. 'Like the abbot, we would demand the right to decide in each case, not give some blanket approval that could be flouted whenever it suited Westminster.'

The argument carried on for several more minutes, but it was apparent that by continuing to object to what were very reasonable proposals, the mayor began to look foolish. Godard and Robert fitz Durand were obviously discomfited by their leader's obdurateness and after more muttering, a grudging agreement was reached.

'But only if we retain the power to decide, Justiciar!' snapped the mayor as a parting shot, before the group broke up. The city delegates departed with ill grace, hurrying down the colonnade to find their attendants and horses, but William Postard accepted the archbishop's invitation to join him for refreshments in his chambers. As John stood with everyone else when the Justiciar and abbot rose to leave through the rear door, Hubert Walter gave John's arm a nudge. 'That should have fixed the bastards,' he whispered as he passed.

The short meeting had cut into the dinner hour and de Wolfe and Gwyn were keen to get back to the Long Ditch for their main meal of the day.

'Let's hope Osanna's not got bloody eels or salmon again,' growled Gwyn as they turned off Thieving Lane to reach their house. But as they neared it, they saw the fat housekeeper standing in the doorway, in a state of some agitation.

'You've come at last, sirs!' she gabbled. 'There are three visitors awaiting you inside!'

John looked at his officer in surprise. 'Visitors? Who the hell knows we are here?' For a moment, he wondered if Hawise d'Ayncourt had decided to force her favours upon him, but the time of day and the fact that there were three callers made that unlikely. He pushed past Osanna and peered around the gloom of the main room, dark after the sunshine outside. A man was standing in front of him and he suddenly recognised Roger Watts, the master of one of his own merchant ships. Before he could speak, Watts stood aside and there behind him was a tall, shapely woman, smiling and holding out her hands.

'Hilda! By God's bones, it's you!' He lurched forward and indifferent to spectators, threw his long arms about her and hugged her to his chest. Then he seized her by the shoulders and leaned back, so that he could get a good look at her. 'Hilda, you are a sight for my weary eyes and my lonely soul! But how came you here?'

The tall blonde took his hands in hers and beamed back at him, radiant in her happiness at seeing this dour, dark man again.

'I came with Roger on the *St Radegund*,' she said gaily. 'Far better than wearying myself on a horse for a week!'

The *St Radegund* was one of the vessels that belonged to the wool-exporting partnership of Hilda, John and Hugh de Relaga, one of Exeter's portreeves.

Roger Watts, a stocky, weather-beaten mariner, stepped forward and touched a finger to his forehead. 'Mistress Hilda persuaded me to bring her, Sir John. I took a full cargo of your wool from Topsham to Bruges, then came back to London with finished cloth from the Flanders weavers. We must sail for Exeter the day after tomorrow, I'm afraid, for your partner has another load ready there bound for the Rhine.'

'So we have a whole day tomorrow, John, for you to show me the sights!' murmured Hilda, squeezing his hands with hers.

'And two whole nights,' thought John rapturously. Her English was heavy with the accent of South Devon, music to his ears.

Gwyn loomed behind him and as soon as Hilda released John, the Cornishman seized her in a bear hug. For almost twenty years, he had watched her grow from a lanky girl into the beautiful woman she was now and he loved her himself in his avuncular way. 'It's like a breath of fresh air to have you here in this miserable place!' he boomed.

John was now aware of a smaller figure lurking behind Hilda. This was Alice, her little maid, a girl of about thirteen, one of the sailor's orphans that Hilda cared for in Dawlish. She came forward now to bob her knee, shy in the presence of this forbidding man. She knew her mistress was enamoured of him and blushed when he took her hand and bade her welcome.

'How was your journey, did you have fair weather?' John asked them, suddenly at a loss for better words.

'It was fine, far better than suffering the high roads for days on end!' said Hilda gaily. 'I voyaged so much in good weather and foul with Thorgils, that the sea holds no terrors for me – nor for Alice here, who is a true sailor's daughter.'

They were still all standing in the centre of the room, with Aedwulf peering from the back door at this lovely, elegant woman. His wife Osanna, who had been taking in this drama, suddenly bustled forward.

'Sir John, what are we thinking of! Your guests have travelled over the seas and need rest and sustenance. Sit you down and I'll get your dinner, there's enough to go round for all!'

She hurried towards the back door and yelled at her hen-pecked husband to get ale and wine for the company. The fact that Hilda by her looks and speech was obviously of Saxon blood like themselves, made them particularly hospitable.

John and Gwyn dragged stools and a bench to the table, which they all crowded around – Alice went to crouch in a corner, but the benevolent Gwyn sat her on a milking stool at the table.

As Aedwulf bustled in with ale, cider and a flask of

wine, the coroner and his officer were eager to hear news of their home city, and plied both the shipmaster and Hilda with questions, to which she had a few answers.

'When I knew I was coming to visit you, I made it my business to go to Exeter,' she said, as John placed a cup of wine before her. 'I called at the Bush and all is well, Gwyn! Your wife is busy but contented and she told me that business is excellent; she has had to take on an extra skivvy in the kitchen. The boys are well and helping her with the running of the inn. They send their love to you and hope to see you before long.'

Gwyn beamed at the news and vowed that he would visit them soon, even if he had to walk all the way to Devon!

'I have precious little news for you, I fear, John,' said Hilda more soberly. 'I called at your house in Martin's Lane and spoke to your maid Mary. She is well enough, but unhappy at the long silence, and concerned about your keeping on the empty house. She worries that eventually she will lose her job and her home. She told me to tell you that Brutus is well, though pining for you.'

To John's surprise a lump came in his throat as he heard of his old hound and his faithful housekeeper. Again he regretted the king's desire to exile him in this alien place, but there was little he could do about it for now.

'And have you heard anything of my wife?' he asked.

Hilda shook her head sadly, a lock of blonde hair escaping from under her white linen headcloth. 'I knew you would want news, John, so I went up to Polsloe Priory to see what I could learn. I managed to speak to that old nun, Dame Madge, who seems to look upon you with favour, but there was little she could tell me.'

'You did not get to meet Matilda herself?' he asked

rather ingenuously. Hilda's finely arched brows lifted in mild surprise.

'It would have been folly even to try!' she said. 'Your wife's attitude to me for many years past has not been the most cordial.' She paused to sip from her pewter cup of wine.

'No, Dame Madge told me that Matilda still refuses to talk either about you or her brother Richard and spends all her time either in prayer or helping in the infirmary.'

'Has she decided to take her vows and make her stay permanent?'

Hilda gave a delicate shrug. 'I asked the nun that and she said your wife had still not made up her mind.'

'Damn the woman,' murmured John. 'She is deliberately dangling me on a string. I cannot decide what to do about our house, in case she decides to return there at some time.'

Osanna now bustled in with wooden bowls, platters and bread, while Aedwulf shuffled behind her with a large dish of mutton stew. The housekeeper, usually indifferent and sometimes surly, seemed energised by the presence of these guests and ladled out the surprisingly good stew with exhortations to eat heartily. After the mutton, there was boiled bacon, beans and carrots and the visitors did ample justice to the food, especially after having suffered shipboard rations for over week. Thanks to Gwyn's encouragement and teasing, Alice overcame her shyness, eating and drinking weak ale with every sign of enjoyment.

There was bread, cheese and nuts to finish and conversation flowed easily. John discussed the affairs of their wool and cloth shipping business with Roger Watts and said that he would get Thomas to write a letter about it for the shipmaster to take back to their active partner, Hugh de Relaga.

'I must get back to the ship, which is berthed just below London Bridge,' said Roger when they had eaten their fill. 'There is work to be done concerning the cargoes and we must catch the noon tide the day after tomorrow. I will come for Hilda and her maid during the morning.'

He had hired a couple of rounseys for the short journey from the city, Alice sitting behind him, and now he took himself to the backyard to collect his horse, leaving the other for Hilda's use. Gwyn smiled to himself at Roger's assumption that Hilda would be staying with de Wolfe and then went on to wonder what he himself should do about it. With only two rooms in their cottage, he decided to make himself scarce for a couple of nights.

'I'll bed down with the palace guards, Crowner,' he said quietly. 'With young Alice here as well, you'll need some privacy.'

He resisted accompanying this offer with a wink, but John knew that his officer was very happy that Hilda was here to lighten the glum mood that had settled on the coroner. Though the Cornishman had been very fond of Nesta, John's previous mistress, he had realised that that the liaison was doomed in the long term. Now he trusted that his master's childhood sweetheart Hilda might be able to fill the void in de Wolfe's life – only his miserable wife stood in his way. Hilda was the daughter of the Saxon manor reeve in Holcombe, the second of the de Wolfe family's manors near Teignmouth. Though at forty-one, John was some seven years older, they had grown up together and become lovers by their teens. It would have been impossible for them to marry in those days, as Hilda was merely the daughter of a villein and John the second son of the lord of the manor, but she was now a wealthy widow, there would be no barrier to their marriage – apart from the fact that he already had a wife, albeit one skulking away in a nunnery.

As soon as Roger Watts had left, Gwyn slid away to leave the lovers in peace. Their first task was to arrange the accommodation and it was tacitly assumed by all that John and Hilda would sleep together in the upper room. Although young Alice was there as lady's maid, her role as chaperone was conveniently ignored and Osanna, rapidly summing up the situation, brought in a hay-filled pallet for the girl and set it in the corner of the main room. With the warm weather, there was no hardship in sleeping in a chamber with a dead firepit.

'I'll show you Westminster, Hilda – now the hub of government, even if the king is never here!' offered John gallantly. They set off arm in arm, with Alice trailing behind, her eyes on stalks as she looked at the grand buildings around them. De Wolfe took them into the great abbey and they stared in wonder at the many altars and side chapels and the tomb of Edward the Confessor – as a Saxon, Hilda was visibly moved by the remnants of this last monarch of her race.

As they were leaving the abbey, John caught sight of Thomas coming from the cloisters and with a great yell attracted his attention. The clerk was surprised and delighted to see someone from Devon and Hilda hugged him to her, much to his delighted embarrassment. Though he had adored Nesta, he knew Hilda from several escapades and was fond of her calm and generous nature. He joined them in their sightseeing and after looking into St Margaret's Church, the next port of call was the Great Hall of William Rufus. The lady and her maid marvelled at the dimensions of the place, gazing in wonder at the largest roof in Europe. They stood listening for a while to a session of the King's Bench, who had reclaimed the space at the end of the hall, then John took them up to the coroner's chamber to show Hilda their spartan place of exile from Devon.

'It's a miserable damned room, but the view is good,' he said, throwing open the shutters and displaying the wide panorama of the Thames. He took them to the Lesser Hall, now quiet between meals and then to the outside of the King's Chambers, which really impressed Alice, who thought of the king as only a short step down from God himself.

Their tour ended with a walk along the riverbank and back into the little town of Westminster, where Thomas left them with the excuse that he had duties in the abbey scriptorium. They wandered back to Long Ditch, where the percipient Osanna took Alice away to her kitchen in the yard, to feed her warm pastries and tell her tales of her native Essex.

Alone in his living room, John took Hilda into his arms and kissed her passionately. He had known her lips and her body for more than a score of years, but she still excited him so much that he felt dizzy when he clasped her tightly to him.

As his hands roved over her back, her buttocks and her breasts, she responded avidly and though it was barely late afternoon, they stumbled together to the ladder. A moment later, they had collapsed on to the thick feather mattress that lay on the floor of his sleeping chamber. All the pent-up frustrations of the past couple of months were released in an explosion of passion that repeated itself over and over until delicious exhaustion overtook them both. Then, satiated, they slept in each other's arms, just as they had done in a Devon hayloft, long, long ago.

If de Wolfe had been pining for more work these past weeks, the next day he fervently hoped for the opposite – that there would be no slaying, fires, ravishment

or other forms of mayhem to interrupt his time with
Hilda. Most of the day was spent sightseeing and both
Gwyn and Thomas came with them. The Cornishman
had Alice clinging behind him on his mare, as he had
become virtually a father figure to the little maid.
Thomas was his usual erudite self, surprising even John
with his detailed knowledge of London's sights and history. They jogged slowly up the Royal Way to Charing
and then along the Strand, the clerk pointing out the
great houses of bishops, magnates and barons.

'That's the new preceptory of the Knights Templar
built for the English master,' he explained, pointing
to the grand church and buildings at the top of the
slope leading down to the river's edge. Inside the city,
they marvelled at the great cathedral of St Paul,
Thomas explaining that the original church had been
established almost six hundred years earlier, when the
rest of London was an abandoned Roman ruin,
shunned by the Saxons for centuries until the great
King Alfred revitalised it.

The main thoroughfare of Cheapside and the
markets at Poultry were like a magnet to Hilda and
Alice, who spent over an hour wandering the stalls and
booths, de Wolfe walking behind them as an escort,
with that bemused look that men assume when forced
to parade past endless rolls of linen and silk, or displays
of brooches and necklets.

In Southwark, on the other side of the bridge, they
stopped for food at a large tavern in the high street,
opposite the large church of St Saviour's.

'That palace behind it belongs to the Bishop of
Winchester,' said Thomas, with an almost proprietorial
air. 'Southwark is not part of the city and actually
belongs to the bishop.' He omitted to tell her that even
the noted Southwark brothels belonged to the bishop,
who derived a useful income from them.

They stared at the Conqueror's Tower and King Richard's new fortifications around it, then after riding to Smithfield, just outside the city wall, to see the great church of St Bartholomew and its famous hospital, they made their way back to Westminster.

That evening, John decided to take Hilda to the Lesser Hall for supper, partly to show her some of the lifestyle of the palace, but also to meet a few of the people he had been describing to her. He also had a sneaking desire to show her off to them, especially Hawise d'Ayncourt. Though women were not usually present in the hall, he perversely decided that if the raven-haired beauty from Blois could be there, why not his English blonde?

No one was going to challenge the king's coroner's right to bring a guest and he was sure that Hilda would more than hold her own with any of the others in the circle that supped there.

When he told her, she delved into the large cloth bundle that she had brought from the ship and arrayed herself in a simple, but elegant, gown of pale-blue silk, under a light surcoat of white linen that matched her cover-chief and wimple. The meal had already begun when they arrived at the palace and their appearance caused a minor sensation at the table where their group habitually sat. With an awestruck Alice trailing behind as a chaperone, the men stumbled to their feet as John handed Hilda on to the end of a bench, then sat alongside her, with Alice opposite, next to Hawise's maid.

John mischievously introduced Hilda as his 'business partner from Devon' just arrived on one of their own vessels, which raised a few disbelieving eyebrows, especially from Mistress d'Ayncourt.

'Can I also join this business, if the partners are all like this exquisite lady?' asked Ranulf gallantly, earning himself a poisonous glance from Hawise.

William Aubrey, Renaud de Seigneur and even the celibate Bernard de Montfort became benign and attentive as they beamed at the delectable woman from the far west. They snapped their fingers at the serving boys to bring more food and wine and though it was John's prerogative to place the choicest morsels on her trencher, Renaud insisted on filling her wine cup from the special flask of Anjou wine that he habitually brought to the table.

When conversation began to flow, the others were intrigued by her strong Devonshire dialect.

Waspishly, though she had spoken English since infancy, Hawise addressed her in French, assuming she was some country bumpkin and she was chagrined to receive a polite reply in the same language. Though coming from a farm on the de Wolfe manor, Hilda had often travelled across the Channel with her seafaring husband and was proficient in both Norman-French and Flemish.

'Have you known our respected coroner for long, madam?' enquired Hawise haughtily, expecting to learn that the blonde was a recent acquisition of his.

'Only about three-and-thirty years,' replied Hilda calmly. 'We grew up together, you see.'

John noticed a grin spread over Renaud's face – he seemed to relish someone giving his wife as good as she gave.

William Aubrey, who seemed enthralled by the good-looking newcomer, monopolized the conversation for several minutes and Hilda, sensing that John wanted her to appear in the best light possible, adroitly avoided revealing that she was the daughter of a farm reeve and managed to let it be known that she was a widow, who had a stone-built house flanked by pillars in the Breton style.

Hawise made a last effort to gain the upper hand.

'Surely you cannot relish living out your life in a rural backwater like Devon,' she said sweetly. 'Now that you have been to the great city of London, would you not like to stay here? No doubt you could find a rich husband here to support you.'

Hilda gave her a condescending smile in return. 'I think not, as I have returned only yesterday from Antwerp, which in some ways I feel is as interesting. And as for a rich husband, I have no need of one – but would settle for a man I could love and respect.'

Glowering, Hawise retired from the debate and concentrated on her food and drink, ignoring the smirks of the archdeacon and her damned husband. As soon as she had finished eating, she hauled her maid and husband away from the table and with a last grimace at John, flounced away.

Eventually, de Wolfe prised Hilda away from the attentions of the other men on the table and they strolled back to Long Ditch in the evening sun, with Alice pattering along happily behind.

When she was safely tucked up on her bag of hay in the downstairs chamber, John and Hilda spent another night of lovemaking and slumber, tinged with sadness at the realisation that it would be the last for some time. Naked under a linen sheet in the warm summer night, they talked of many things, but never about the possibility of being wedded. In the early hours, when the blonde's regular breathing against his shoulder told him she was sound asleep, John pondered long and hard about what could be done. He was here in London, but that was not an insoluble problem. He could give up being a coroner and return home to Exeter, as, financially, it would make no difference. Coroners were obliged to remain unpaid, on pain of dismissal – and he had more than an adequate income from the wool business, as well as a share of the profits of his family's two manors at Stoke-in-Teignhead and Holcombe which his elder brother managed so efficiently. The other option would be for Hilda to come to live with him in Westminster, but he knew this would be difficult, as she was devoted to her home village, and though she might well manage the short transition to Exeter if circumstances allowed, she would never emigrate to London.

Dawn was creeping through the shutters before he fell asleep again, though a bare hour remained before they had to rise. Even this was delayed for a while by frantic valedictory passion, but soon it was time for a breakfast of oat gruel, eggs fried in butter and barley bread, before Roger Watts arrived to take Hilda back to the ship.

John, Gwyn and Thomas decided to squeeze the last drops of Hilda's company by riding back with them to the city to where the *St Radegund* was berthed just downstream from the bridge.

The forty-five-foot cog was riding high on the tide when they reached it and soon Hilda and Alice, with their belongings tied in a bundle, were climbing the plank to the deck. John saw them settled in the small cabin on the afterdeck, little more than a tiny hutch with a couple of mattresses inside.

'There's a north-easterly breeze,' declared the ship-master. 'So once we get around Kent, we should make good time to the Exe – maybe back there in four days.'

John crawled into the deckhouse to stow Hilda's bundle and took the opportunity to embrace her and kiss her lips in semi-privacy.

'I'll be back in Devon before long, by hook or by crook,' he promised. 'If we can get away during this progress of the court to Gloucester, I'll see you soon, my love. Otherwise, I'll just ride back to Devon and to hell with them.'

As soon as the tide began to ebb, the mooring ropes were cast off and the single square sail was hoisted. With Roger Watts leaning on the steering oar, the little cog drifted out into the river and began tacking downstream. John, with his officer and clerk, stood on the wharf and watched their link with Devon gradually shrink in size as it went towards the distant sea. The woman and the girl fluttered kerchiefs for a time and John waved back, but soon he turned abruptly on his heel and strode to where they had left their horses.

'Let's go, this place stinks of fish,' he growled, for the quay where the vessel had been moored was near Billingsgate. In pensive silence, he rode back through the city streets, ignoring the press of people and the raucous cries of stallholders and hawkers. In spite of the crowds, London suddenly seemed empty without Hilda of Dawlish.

CHAPTER SIX

In which Crowner John comes across a corpse

The good fate which kept John's time with Hilda free from duties, conveniently expired as soon as she sailed away.

After they reached the palace and handed over their horses to the ostlers, de Wolfe and Gwyn strolled back to their dwelling to wait for their noon dinner, whilst Thomas slid away to attend to his tasks in the abbey library. Walking up the lane at Long Ditch, they saw Aedwulf and his fat wife at the door, talking to a man who John recognised as one of the proctor's men from the abbey. There were two senior proctors in Westminster's chapter, clergy who were responsible for legal matters, discipline and order, and they were physically assisted by several lay constables, of which this was one.

'Can't be Hilda this time,' said Gwyn, recalling their similar arrival two days earlier. 'And what's going on up there?'

Much further away, beyond where the lane petered out into a path across the marshes, were several more men, tramping about in the reeds and coarse grass as if they were searching for something.

When they reached the house, the proctor's man, a

tall ginger fellow with a long staff that was his badge of office, gravely saluted de Wolfe with a hand to his forehead.

'Sir John, the prior told me to seek you out to tell you that a body has been found. Likely a murder, by the looks of it.'

De Wolfe frowned, instantly suspecting that this might throw up some problems about jurisdiction.

'Is he connected with the court? I have no power to deal with anyone else.'

The abbey constable shrugged. 'That's it, coroner. We don't yet know who he is, but the corpse is no more than a few hundred paces from here. The prior and the proctors thought it might be best if you had a look, given it's so near.' He added an incentive. 'Of course, it might turn out that he *is* from the palace, after all.'

John pointed towards the distant men trampling the boggy ground. 'Is that where he is? When was he found?'

'Not more than two hours since, sir. A shepherd came across him, face down in a reen.' This was a local word for one of the ditches that drained the marshland.

'I'll keep your dinner hot, never fear,' called Osanna from the doorway, as if she had already decided that he must go about his business. They followed the constable, who said his name was Roland, along the fast-diminishing lane by the Long Ditch and on to a track that went into a wide area of flat, soggy ground lying between the houses on King Street and distant trees that marked the Oxford Road, at least a mile away. It was poor pasture, fit only for sheep and goats – and that only in dry weather, for the many branches of the Tyburn and the Clowson Brook often overflowed and turned the land into a swamp. The path had been made over a crude causeway of brushwood to keep it above the mud, but this ended after a while and John cursed as his shoes squelched into what looked like black porridge.

'Only the men herding animals come this way, usually,' said Roland apologetically, 'but we've not far to go now.'

He shouted and waved at the four men who were scattered over the area ahead of them and they began moving back to one spot, towards which they all converged.

'Here he is, Crowner, just as he was found.' The constable used his staff to prod the back of a body lying head down in a ditch filled with brackish water. The searchers came to stand in a half-circle before them, looking with ghoulish interest at the corpse in the reen.

'Who are these people?' demanded de Wolfe.

'Two are servants I called from the abbey gardens – the others are local men who volunteered to help look for the weapon,' answered Roland. 'That one is the fellow who found the body.' He pointed to a toothless grey-haired man dressed in a tattered hessian smock and serge breeches.

De Wolfe beckoned him closer. 'Was the cadaver just like this when you found him?'

The old shepherd nodded vigorously. 'The water was bloody when I saw it, Crowner, but the flow in the reen must have washed it away. All I did was lift his head for a moment, to make sure he was dead, sir. Wish now I hadn't, the state he's in!' he added in a quavering voice.

John nodded to Gwyn who, well used to the routine, dragged the dead man's feet back until the head came up out of the water.

It was all too clearly apparent what had upset the shepherd, for across the forehead, just below a fringe of iron-grey hair, was a deep cut the width of a hand, gaping open to expose the shine of the skull, which had several radiating cracks in the depths of the wound. In addition, the face had been battered so badly that his own mother would not have recognised him. He appeared to be of middle age and wore a short belted tunic, over which was a leather apron, both now blackened by peaty water. There was some dried blood on his temples and back of the neck, but as the shepherd had pointed out, the rest had been washed away.

'That's a hell of blow, Crowner,' observed Gwyn, with professional detachment. 'What caused it, I wonder?'

De Wolfe glared around at the men standing nearby. 'You found no weapon when you searched, I take it?'

They shook their heads, but the shepherd spoke up again.

'Begging your pardon, sir, but I reckon he wasn't killed just here. He's been dragged for a bit, look at those reeds and grass.'

They all turned to look at where the ragged old man was pointing, across the rough ground away from the path and towards the outer fringes of Westminster. John now noticed a faint track of crushed and bent vegetation running intermittently towards them.

With Gwyn close behind, he strode alongside the indistinct marks, cursing as his feet either twisted between lumpy tussocks of long grass or squelched into pools of mud. The proctor's constable hurried behind them, but a few hundred paces further on, they all came to a halt.

'Can't see the trail any more,' growled Gwyn. 'The ground has risen a bit and got firmer.' As they neared the houses on the western side of the village, they had climbed a couple of feet on to what used to be Thorney Island, the gravel bank that was the very reason for Westminster's existence. By the same token, the grass became shorter and closer cropped by livestock, so that the trail vanished.

John turned around and looked back along the line they had followed, then swivelled and projected the direction ahead of them. 'The nearest houses are those,' he snapped, pointing at a row of huts and two-storeyed buildings a few hundred yards away.

'That's the top end of Duck Lane,' said Roland. 'Comes off Tothill Street, at the back of the abbey.'

'Then you had better make some enquiries there, to see if anyone's missing. Get someone to come and look at the corpse.'

They retraced their steps to the body and the constable sent the two abbey labourers back to Duck Lane as the coroner had ordered. 'What are we to do with the corpse?' he asked de Wolfe. 'You've viewed it now, so can we shift the poor fellow back to the abbey dead-house?'

John pondered the matter, aware that it was a delicate situation. If the victim was connected with the palace, then he could assume jurisdiction – and even if he was from the abbey, then Abbot Postard had more or less confirmed that he was content for such cases to be handled by the Coroner of the Verge. But if the fellow were neither of these, then those officious bastards from the city would want to elbow him out of their way.

Gwyn virtually read his mind. 'They'll never know in London that this ever happened,' he said, hopefully.

John shook his head stubbornly. 'I don't want to get mixed up in another squabble. It was only the day before yesterday that the Justiciar got the mayor and his sheriffs to compromise. We have to stick to the rules now that they've been made.'

'So what do we do with the body?' persisted the constable. 'We can hardly leave it here to rot.'

The coroner felt the heat of the noonday sun on his face and came to a decision.

'Very well, take it to the dead-house. I'll go back to the palace and make some arrangements.

A rumble from his stomach told him it was dinner-time and he took pity on his ever-hungry officer.

'You go back to the house, Gwyn, and start eating. Tell Osanna I'll be there as soon as I can.'

He began squelching his way back to the path and left the others to move the body as best they could.

'What happened, Crowner? Are we going to deal with this corpse?' asked Gwyn, looking up from gnawing on a pork knuckle he had lifted from his trencher.

De Wolfe slumped on to the bench opposite and poured himself a pint of ale from a jug on the table.

'I'm not touching it. Let those people from the city take it over. They should be here later this afternoon.'

As the landlady came in with his bowl of potage and a platter with several meaty pork bones, he explained what had happened.

'I couldn't go searching for Thomas, so I got one of the Chancery clerks to write a message for that sheriff fellow, Godard, and sent a royal messenger post-haste to the city, saying that we had a body for them.'

'What if it turns out to be a palace servant or some-one from the abbey?' objected Gwyn, who seemed reluctant to hand over their business to others. John shook his head as he dipped his spoon, carved from a cow's horn, into his soup.

'He isn't, it seems. By the time those fellows had hauled the corpse to the abbey mortuary, someone had recognised him, even with the face beaten in. His leather apron should have given us an inkling – it was covered in small burns, as he's an ironmaster and blacksmith from Duck Lane.'

Gwyn seemed faintly disappointed. 'I was hoping that we had a nice juicy assault and murder to keep us occupied!'

De Wolfe paused between spoonfuls. 'We've not made much progress with the last one yet!' he growled. 'Looks as if the palace stabbing will remain a mystery for ever, unless we get some better information.'

After they had finished everything that Osanna had produced, they refilled their ale-pots and sat back in a companionable silence. John wondered how far down the Thames estuary the *St Radegund* had reached and prayed for a safe journey for them back to Devon. The sea was a treacherous beast and each voyage was a risky adventure, which was why every ship's crew sang the traditional hymn of thanks to the Virgin Mary when they reached port safely.

Eventually, they stirred themselves from their post-prandial torpor which the returning heat had encouraged. They made their way back to the bare chamber in the palace, where they found Thomas. He was reading his Vulgate of St Jerome, his most treasured possession, which by now he must surely have known off by heart. He had already heard of the latest murder and like Gwyn he was disappointed to hear that they were not to take on the case. The Westminster grapevine must have been working overtime, as he already knew the name of the victim.

'He was called Osbert Morel and had a workshop at the back of his dwelling in Duck Lane,' he announced. 'A widower, he lived alone and was said to be a solitary, secretive sort of fellow.'

De Wolfe once again marvelled at Thomas's capacity to trawl up information in the shortest possible time.

'You don't happen to know who killed him and with what?' he asked, but the sarcasm was lost on the little priest.

'One of the proctors told me that there was blood on the ground in his yard and drips going through the gate at the back. There was still money in his scrip and his house-chest, so it can't have been a robbery.'

'Must have happened during the night,' said Gwyn. 'No one could have dragged a body covered in blood for a couple of furlongs in broad daylight.'

De Wolfe shrugged. 'It's none of my business now. He was nothing to do with the palace or the abbey, so the bloody city men are welcome to him. Let's hope they have better luck than we've had so far.'

A little later, they had a visit from Ranulf of Abingdon, who brought a welcome skin of red Loire wine to share with them.

'We need some fluid to fortify ourselves. It's as hot as hell itself over those stables,' he complained. His bachelor quarters were in the Marshalsea, the long block of wooden buildings that housed both horses and the men who were responsible for all palace transport.

When Gwyn had produced some pewter cups from a shelf, they settled to drink and gossip, which Thomas joined in again with his tale of the murder in Duck Lane. Ranulf shook his head in wonderment. 'Two mysterious killings in little more than a week,' he observed sadly. 'Apart from a few drunken brawls, I can't recall another slaying in Westminster in the whole time I've been here.'

John wondered once again why he had been saddled with being Coroner of the Verge, as there seemed little need for one, unless things were different once the court went on the move.

As if reading his mind, Ranulf came out with his own piece of news.

'A herald came up from Portsmouth today with the news that Queen Eleanor has left Rouen for Honfleur. Depending upon the weather, a king's ship is expected to arrive with her in about a week's time. We have to be prepared to be on the move soon after that.'

They discussed the arrangements as the wineskin emptied, as all this was new to John. Ranulf, as an under-marshal, was used to the perambulations of Hubert Walter's court, even though these were less frequent now that the king was abroad.

'We lodge each night at some convenient place, preferably a castle or a royal house,' he explained. 'This time it will no doubt be Windsor, Reading, Newbury, Marlborough, Chippenham and then Bristol. The old lady wants to get to Gloucester, then probably back here through Oxford, to take ship again at Portsmouth.'

De Wolfe rasped at his black stubble with his fingers. 'That journey will take a devil of a time, given all the carts with the impedimenta of the court! I doubt we'll cover more than twelve or fifteen miles a day.'

'We'll be away for a few weeks, that's for sure,' agreed Ranulf.

'If they stop at Bristol for a few days, maybe we can get away to Devon?' suggested Gwyn hopefully.

When the wine was finished, the marshal reluctantly made his way back to the stables, saying that he had better have the wagons checked for the coming long journey. After the failure of their wheel-hub on the recent trip from Winchester, de Wolfe considered this was a wise precaution. After Ranulf had left, the coroner's trio felt pleasantly drowsy, given the wine and the growing heat and Gwyn was soon snoring noisily, slumped with his head in his arms on the window ledge. Thomas continued to read, though he felt his eyelids droop, even over the sacred Latin prose of St Jerome. John managed to stay awake, though as he scraped under his fingernails with the point of his dagger, his thoughts wandered from Exeter to the image of the little ship now surely off the north coast of Kent. Then his mind's eye flew even farther away to Chepstow in Wales, where the memory of Nesta still plagued him, but inevitably returned to Exeter and the little priory of Polsloe, where Matilda was lodged like some brooding bear in a cave.

This sleepy reverie lasted another hour, until it was rudely shattered by the sound of heavy footsteps on the boards of the passage outside the chamber. A tap on the door was abruptly followed by it being flung open, the young page who had conducted the visitor being pushed aside as a large and angry man burst into the room.

As John jerked himself back to the present, he saw it was the other sheriff from the city, Robert fitz Durand, who had been at the meeting with Hubert Walter two days earlier. The wrathful look on his face accentuated the swarthiness of his skin, which almost suggested some Levantine or at least southern European blood. He offered no greeting, but launched straight into a tirade.

'De Wolfe, have you such a short memory that you already breach the spirit of our agreement, shabby though it was?' he shouted rudely.

John rose to his feet and with his knuckles on the table, glared at the newcomer. He was almost a head taller that fitz Durand, who was a wiry, but slightly built man, so he stooped to look down at the arrogant sheriff. Gwyn had also risen and lurked menacingly in the background, while the timid clerk had backed away to the wall and watched the scene with trepidation.

The coroner controlled his own quick temper with an effort.

'Why so ferocious, sheriff? The matter is in your hands. I want no part of it.'

'No part of it, be damned!' he bellowed. 'You went to

137

the corpse, you pulled it about, examined it and sent others to seek more information! Is that not interfering in a case which the Justiciar defined as none of your business?'

De Wolfe held up a hand, which though placatory, he would preferred to have slapped around the other man's face.

'Now wait a moment, fitz Durand! Firstly, I was prevailed upon by the abbey prior to view the victim as a matter of urgency. For all we knew then, this unknown man could have been from the palace – and even if he had been an abbey servant, it fell into my jurisdiction by virtue of the abbot's dispensation.'

'But he wasn't either of those, damn it!' snarled the sheriff. 'He was a villager and thus a resident of Middlesex, for which county I am responsible.'

'And how was anyone to know that, if he was face down in a ditch?' shouted John, losing patience with this blustering knight. 'As soon as I knew he was not from the palace, I went to the trouble of having a message sent to you immediately by a fast horseman. What more do you want?'

'You should mind your own business and leave such matters to those who have dealt perfectly well with such events for many years past,' snapped Robert, now with hands on hips, glaring back at de Wolfe. Thomas nervously thought that they looked like two cockerels squaring up to each other in a barnyard.

'If you have such complaints, then take them to the Chief Justiciar,' rasped John. 'And if you don't like the rules he agreed upon at the meeting in the Great Hall, then consider this – he acts upon the direct wishes of our King Richard, so if you flaunt those, then you might well be guilty of treason!'

John always liked rubbing in the royal authority and hinting at accusations of sedition.

Robert fitz Durand began protesting, but then realised he had better be careful of what he said before two witnesses, given that it was common knowledge that John de Wolfe had the ear of both the Justiciar and the king himself. His voice trailed away into a growling mumble, as John pressed home his point.

'I consider that I have acted courteously and properly, which is more than can be said for your behaviour, bursting in here in such an ill-mannered fashion! You should be grateful that I have informed you so quickly and written for you what few details I had at the time. At least I saw the corpse fresh and passed on a description of his wounds.'

He sat down again to indicate that the interview was over.

'Now I suggest that you get on with your own investigation as soon as possible, for in this weather, the cadaver will corrupt very rapidly.'

The sheriff flushed at this peremptory dismissal and stalked to the still-open door. 'The mayor shall hear of this,' he snarled as he reached it.

'I very much hope he will – and I trust you will tell him how I did my best to assist you,' replied de Wolfe, now well in control of his temper.

For answer, fitz Durand marched out into the corridor, pushing aside the page who had been eavesdropping, and disappeared without a word of thanks or farewell.

'The bastard!' was Gwyn's succinct comment. 'Are we going to have to put up with his ranting every time we get a corpse?'

De Wolfe sighed, wishing again that he was back in Devon.

'In future, I'm only going to deal with cases where we know definitely that the victim is from either the palace or the abbey. Those jealous men from the big city are welcome to any doubtful ones. Thank God we are going on tour very soon, away from the objectionable sods in London!'

In the Lesser Hall that evening, the main topic of conversation was the impending arrival of Queen Eleanor, the news of which had spread throughout the palace within minutes of its being received, thanks to the garrulous clerks in the chancery offices. As well as being Justiciar and Archbishop of Canterbury, Hubert Walter was now for all practical purposes also the Lord Chancellor, as the disgraced William Longchamp had been ejected from England almost two years earlier. Although he nominally retained the chancellorship due to the king's benevolence, Longchamp was exiled in Normandy and though Eustace, Bishop of Ely, was nominally Vice Chancellor, Hubert effectively controlled Chancery and all its business, so the news of the old queen's arrival went there first. However, after this had been gossiped over and dissected by those at the supper tables, the bloody murder on the marshes became the next topic for conversation.

'The sheriff's men have been buzzing around the abbey mortuary like flies today,' said Archdeacon Bernard. 'And judging by the smell that is starting to drift over from there, the real flies will soon be buzzing as well!'

The unpleasant images that this conjured up did not seem to discourage any of the usual group from tucking in to their food.

John had to explain why he was no longer involved in the investigation, as everyone seemed to know that he had been out in the reens to view the cadaver.

'It seems ridiculous for officers to come all the way from the city to deal with it, when we have England's premier coroner sitting right here,' effused Hawise d'Ayncourt, fluttering her eyelashes at John as she spoke.

'Perhaps an assault on a mere blacksmith is insufficient to warrant the attention of a royal coroner,' said her husband, with a trace of sarcasm in his tone.

'Was he robbed?' asked Bernard de Montfort, as he speared another grilled herring and laid it on his trencher. 'That would seem to be the most likely motive for killing a tradesman.'

De Wolfe shook his head. 'My clerk, who knows everything, says he was not. That's all I know about the matter. I am more concerned about the death of that poor fellow from the guest chambers. I suppose you have heard no other rumours from upstairs, as you are residing there?'

Renaud de Seigneur shook his head. 'We are just passing guests, we are not privy to the gossip of the servants.'

Hawise gave John a coy look, lowering her eyes as she spoke. 'All I have gathered is that Basil, if that was his name, was very friendly with a young monk across the yard. Unusually friendly, it would seem!' she added archly.

Her meaning was clear, but no one responded to her, this being a subject about which delicate ladies were supposed to remain ignorant. Adroitly changing the subject, Ranulf observed that their dining regime would almost certainly be disrupted when the queen arrived.

'This Lesser Hall was used by the king when he was in residence – as did his father Henry before him. Though usually the king ate in his chambers above, he sometimes used this for dining, as well as for large meetings and sessions of the Royal Council. I expect that Eleanor will revert to what she was used to, before her husband locked her away for sixteen years!'

De Montfort in his turn shied away from the unwelcome memory of the old king's vengeance upon Eleanor for encouraging his sons to revolt against him. 'I hear there will be an elaborate feast when she arrives. Will that be in here, I wonder?'

As usual, Ranulf was the best informed. 'I hear that it is likely to be in the Great Hall, for already the Keeper of the Palace is muttering about extra transport to bring in supplies from both the countryside and the city. I suspect that Hubert wishes to keep on the right side of the Queen Mother, for she is still a powerful force on both sides of the Channel, with great influence with her two sons.'

De Wolfe privately marvelled at the endless capacity for gossip and scandal possessed by these people at court. Most of it went over his head, as he did not know the persons involved – and did not much care about them. The talk went on as they ate their way through the stews, the roasts and the puddings, but eventually Hawise came around to John's private life.

'I suspect you are a dark horse, Sir John. I heard rumours that you were attached to a very comely Welsh woman before you came to Westminster. Just as sailors have a girl in every port, do coroners have ladies in every jurisdiction?'

Her husband gave a little snigger at this and John felt like kicking him under the table. How in God's name did she hear of Nesta? he wondered irritably. But even though Hawise annoyed him greatly, he still found her alluring, with her habit of lowering her eyes and showing those long dark lashes, before lifting them again to give him a languorous look. Perhaps his last two nights of passion had increased his amorous appetite, but he decided that he would not be averse to giving her what she obviously desired.

It was just as well that Bernard de Montfort diverted

his attention at that point, taking the conversation in a different direction.

'It seems the purpose of this forthcoming per-ambulation is to escort Queen Eleanor to Gloucester to meet her son John,' he said, folding his hands across his overfilled stomach. 'I have never met the prince, but I hear that you have had dealings with him in the past. What is he like? We hear such conflicting reports about his character.'

This was sensitive ground and de Wolfe, though he had very strong views on the subject, was not going to open his mind to a casual acquaintance, especially not knowing where such opinions might be whispered by this garrulous crowd.

'I have never been in his presence either,' he hedged. 'He was conspicuously absent from the Crusade and took advantage of his brother's misfortunes there, as is common knowledge.'

'But were you not in Ireland when he was in charge there?' persisted the archdeacon, again reveal-ing the depth of his knowledge about de Wolfe and his affairs.

John grinned wryly. 'He was not there for long and I never met him. He caused so much chaos with his irresponsible actions that King Henry soon had to recall him.'

'You do not seem overfond of the Count of Mortain,' said Renaud.

'I have good reason not to be,' growled de Wolfe. 'Several times have I been involved in defeating his schemes – though since his failed revolt against the king two years ago, he never acts directly himself, but gets others to do his dirty work!'

He was thinking of his own brother-in-law, Richard de Revelle, the former sheriff of Devon, as well as the de la Pomeroy family, to say nothing of the bishops of

Exeter and of Coventry, all of whom were eager to put John on the throne.

'Will your presence in his court in Gloucester not be an embarrassment to you?' asked Bernard de Montfort.

John shrugged. 'It might be to him, but my back is broad! I have no cause to be concerned about it.' He paused, then conceded that the prince had been quiet of late, with no more rumours of him continuing to plot against his elder brother.

Ranulf, sensing that the coroner was uneasy with the turn that the conversation had taken, adroitly steered it back to the slaying of the ironworker. 'If you have abandoned your interest in the case, John, what will happen now?'

De Wolfe noticed that the marshal's man had called him by his Christian name for the first time, and was not averse to that. Ranulf was a pleasant and intelligent person he was glad to have as a friend, even though he must have been more than a decade younger than John.

'The sheriffs have not deigned to confide in me, though I gave them all the information I could, sparse though it was,' he replied. 'I presume that they will examine the body themselves and hold some kind of inquiry.'

The archdeacon nodded. 'They were in the mortuary shed behind the abbey infirmary late this afternoon, then I saw this sheriff fellow ride off again for the city. I know the corpse is to be buried in the cemetery tomorrow, but I heard nothing about any public inquest, such as you hold.'

John gave one of his throat-clearings, a catch-all response he was fond of when he had nothing useful to say. It annoyed him to think that the self-important Robert fitz Durand seemed to be making little effort to investigate the murder and in spite of his claim to have washed his hands of the whole affair, he had an urge to find out more for himself. When the meal was finished, they all dispersed, Hawise d'Ayncourt giving him another languorous smile, as she trailed reluctantly behind her husband.

De Wolfe made straight for the Deacon alehouse, where he guessed that Gwyn would be found yarning and drinking. He beckoned to his henchman and Gwyn rather reluctantly drained the remaining pint of ale in his quart pot and followed him out into the street. It was still only early evening and there would be full daylight for several more hours.

'I have a fancy to take a look at the house where that fellow was killed,' he announced, setting off towards Tothill Street.

'I thought you had given up that matter, Crowner?' grumbled his officer. 'The body has long gone, so what are we seeking?'

De Wolfe shrugged as he loped along the street, avoiding the culvert in the middle which carried a sluggish stream of effluent.

'I don't know, but if we never look, we'll never find out!'

Still mystified as to his master's change of heart, Gwyn ambled along with him. They went partway down Tothill Street, which was behind the abbey, and then up the narrow alley of Duck Lane. The dwellings were meaner here, mostly low shacks of cob and thatch, but a few were two-storeyed and some were built of planks with shingled roofs.

'How d'you know which one it is?' asked Gwyn. 'Even our nosey little clerk didn't tell us that.'

John promptly demonstrated his method by grabbing one of the ragged urchins who were now following them and impishly imitating his long strides.

'Where did the blacksmith live, the one who was

killed?' he demanded, holding the boy by his ear. Squealing in exaggerated agony, the lad pointed up the lane, almost to the end.

'Where the sign is hanging, sir. Miserable old sod, he was, too!'

John released him with a grin and marched on to the house he indicated, with its rusty trade sign hanging over the door. It was one of the larger dwellings, with an upper storey and tightly shuttered windows facing the lane. The heavy door was similarly tight shut and Gwyn, after a futile push against it with his shoulder, looked enquiringly at the coroner. 'Now what do we do? Break in?'

'Around the back, I think! That's where Thomas said the blood was found.' He dived down a narrow alley between the house and the smaller cottage next to it and came out in a yard where a few scrawny chickens were pecking around a pile of chopped firewood. They found little sustenance there on the bare beaten earth, but the dilapidated fence allowed them to roam out on to the marshes, which stretched away into the distance. A privy, a store-shed full of iron rods and what was presumably a kitchen hut were the only structures in the yard, but near the back door was evidence of the violent crime that must have been perpetrated the previous night. A patch of earth a yard across was stained a dull red and although this had soaked into the soil, there were still a few small areas of dried blood in the centre.

'Must have lost a lot,' observed Gwyn. 'Though from what we saw of the state of the corpse, it's not surprising.'

De Wolfe grunted and turned his attention to the door. Unlike the front entrance, this was a flimsy collection of thin planks with no lock. After giving it an experimental shake, John put his eye to the crack and saw a wooden bar on the inside. He gave a nod to his officer and Gwyn almost casually lifted a large foot and with a single blow, the door flew open, the socket holding the bar flying off the doorpost.

'That bloody sheriff would probably have us both hanged for this, if he knew,' he chuckled.

'I doubt he'll ever bother to come back here,' replied John, as he went into the house. The back room was a large workshop and forge, a stone chimney going up through the roof. The furnace was cold and the large bellows silent. Although there was an anvil in the centre, much of the dead man's labours seemed to be on a smaller scale, carried out on several workbenches of grey slate.

'What sort of blacksmith was he, I wonder?' asked Gwyn. 'He doesn't seem to make ploughshares or mend wagon tyres.'

The answer came when they moved into the other room at the front of the house, which seemed to be both another workshop for finer details and a place to display and sell his wares. Several tables were littered with wrought-iron candlesticks, sconces, brackets of various types, doorhandles, locks, hinges and a host of smaller items fashioned from metal.

Gwyn picked up several and examined them closely. 'This is fine work, he seems more of an artist than an ironsmith.'

De Wolfe was looking at the confused array of objects on the workbenches. This was obviously where Osbert Morel made his masterpieces, as many were half-finished, lying amongst discarded tools and pieces of raw iron. Several vices were attached to the benches and scraps of metal and a dusting of grey filings and scurf lay over everything.

'Not a tidy craftsman, but he was seemingly a talented one,' observed John, as he picked up a few objects and laid them down again. Some were unidentifiable and he turned them over with his fingers, trying to puzzle out what they were, such as a foot-long rod, engraved with marks an inch apart. Another was a small wooden box the length of a hand, which was full of what appeared to be either soap or firm grease. He was just about to pass this to Gwyn for comment, when a voice came from the open doorway.

'Who the devil are you – and what are you doing?'

De Wolfe turned to see a man in his twenties scowling at them suspiciously. He was dressed in a plain brown tunic and breeches and John guessed that he might be a journeyman in some craft. He had sandy hair and a round, open face, though at the moment that conveyed nervous indignation.

De Wolfe countered his question with one of his own. 'And who might you be?' he snapped. 'This is the scene of a violent death.'

The younger man flushed. 'I am all too well aware of that! It was my own father who died!' Explanations followed and it became evident that the man was Simon, the only son of the slain ironmaster who had been called from the nearby village of Charing, where he lived and worked as a carpenter. Thankfully, Simon did not query why the Coroner of the Verge was involved, even though he disclosed that he had been interrogated by the city sheriff a few hours earlier.

'I returned to collect some of my father's tools and to see if there is any good clothing that I should take back to Charing. Once it is known that the house is empty and unguarded, the folk around here will soon pillage anything of value.'

Again, Simon seemed oblivious to the fact that they had burst in through the back door, presumably accepting that a royal law officer had the right to do anything he pleased.

'Have you any idea who might have wished your father harm?' asked de Wolfe.

The carpenter shook his head. 'We were not that close, since I married and went to live in Charing a few years ago. But he was just a craftsman, like myself. Who would wish to kill him?'

'I was told that he has not been robbed. Is that true?'

Simon nodded. 'When I was here earlier with the other officers, they gave me my father's money chest. It was a small thing, but had a reasonable sum in it. It was not hidden, just left in his sleeping room upstairs. Any thief would have found it in the twinkling of an eye.'

John grudgingly allowed his estimation of Sheriff Robert fitz Durand to rise, learning that he had not dipped his hand into the money chest, but restored it straight away to the family. However, this did not help him in any way to understand the motive for the crime. He waved a hand around the workshop.

'Is there anything here that is out of place or missing?' he asked. 'Though I admit it would be hard to tell, given the appearance of the place.'

Again, the son could not help, saying that he had not visited for the past month and that the workshop was always as chaotic as this. 'His living quarters are better, sir,' he added in defence of his dead father. 'There is no disorder up there.'

Nothing further could be learned from the man and with some rather gruff condolences and a promise that the house would be made secure, they watched Simon leaving, clutching some of the tools and a bundle of clothing.

John waited in the yard, morosely studying the pool of dried blood, while Gwyn found a hammer and nails amongst the litter in the workshop, which he used to roughly repair the door.

On the way back to the alehouse for a final drink, the coroner bemoaned his inability to round up the people who knew the victim and grill them for any knowledge of the man and his affairs.

'That bloody sheriff can't have made any worthwhile enquiries,' he growled. 'In the short time he was here today, he would never have been able to find any witnesses – and by the sound of it, he's not even going to hold an inquest.'

Gwyn hunched his broad shoulders in a gesture of dismissal. 'Well, although it's a mystery, it's nothing to do with us now, Crowner. We'll never hear any more of it, I reckon.'

Gwyn was not often wrong, but this was a glaring exception.

CHAPTER SEVEN

In which Crowner John comes under suspicion

The next morning brought a genuine case to the Coroner of the Verge, one that needed no consideration about involving the city or Middlesex. It was no mystery or even a crime, but had to be dealt with according to the law. A mason's labourer had been crushed to death by a large block of stone which fell from the top of the second storey of the Treasury building, on the river side of the front of the Great Hall.

This edifice had previously been wooden, but during the past few years had been progressively rebuilt in stone. The balustrade around the top, surrounding the pitched slate roof, was the last part to be completed.

'They send me idiots as workmen!' fumed the master mason, who was in charge of the construction. He was standing at the foot of the wall where the accident had taken place, with de Wolfe and his officer and clerk staring at the mess on the ground. Some of the mess was bloody, being the still shape of the dead workman, pinned under a quarter-ton block of Caen limestone imported from Normandy. Around it was a tangle of splintered timber and rope, the remains of the derrick that had been hauling up the block.

As other men prepared to lever off the stone to retrieve the body, the coroner listened to the mason's diatribe about the uselessness of his workforce, who had improperly secured the tripod on the parapet.

'The fools allowed the sheer-legs to lean out too far and overbalance with the weight of this heavy block,' he ranted. 'May the Blessed Virgin bar me from Heaven for all eternity, if I lie when I say that I have repeatedly told those men exactly what to do and how to do it!'

John allowed the fiery builder to let off steam, then told Gwyn and Thomas to organise a jury for an inquest in an hour's time, as this seemed a straightforward, if tragic event. It was obvious that the master mason felt both guilty and vulnerable to criticism, which was why he was so incensed at his men and intent on passing the blame down the line.

The inquest, held in a vacant bay of the adjacent Great Hall, was short and unremarkable, a dozen workmen being empanelled as witnesses and jurors. A few people came to the proceedings, including the Clerk of Works and the Keeper, Nathaniel de Levelondes, who was ultimately responsible for the running of the palace. Also present were several of the senior Chancery and Treasury clerks, as the building operations concerned their departments of state.

Amongst the few curious onlookers, John was rather surprised to see Renaud de Seigneur and his wife. He could only assume that having exhausted the sights of London, they seized on any diversion to fill their time until the old queen came and they could go on their way to Gloucester and Hereford.

The inevitable verdict of accident was dictated by de Wolfe to the jury. He added a comment before dismissing them.

'I see no point in declaring the errant derrick and

block of limestone as "deodands", even though they were the immediate instruments that caused death,' he boomed, glowering around at the bemused faces of the jury. 'It seems pointless to confiscate them or declare their value as a fine, when the proceeds would only go back to the Crown, who owned them in the first place!'

Leaving the Keeper to deal with any disciplinary proceedings against the master mason or his men for negligence, the inquest concluded and the participants melted away from the huge hall. Anxious to get back to Osanna's dinner, de Wolfe and his officer set out across New Palace Yard for the main gate, but were ambushed by Renaud de Seigneur and the delectable Hawise.

'That was a most effective demonstration of justice,' effused the husband. 'We do not have such a system in Blois, though of course our neighbours in Normandy have coroners.'

John felt that he was talking for the sake of making a noise, rather than from any real interest, but courtesy obliged him to stop and listen, aware that Gwyn was glowering behind him, his stomach rumbling audibly at the prospect of dinner being delayed.

John muttered a few platitudes about the advantages of Hubert Walter's importation of coroners from across the Channel, as he tried to edge away and make his escape from this clinging pair. Hawise, in an equally clinging gown of pale-blue linen, under a pelisse of cream silk, pouted as she reluctantly stood aside. 'You are always rushing away somewhere, Sir John!' she complained. 'No doubt you have important matters to attend to, but I am glad that I had the chance to see you perform today.'

As de Wolfe broke away and hurried towards the gate into King Street, Gwyn growled indignantly. 'Perform, indeed! She makes you sound like a mountebank's monkey! That woman is good for only one thing, Crowner – and she makes it bloody obvious what that is!'

John was of much the same opinion, but he held his tongue and soon the incident was forgotten in the delights of Osanna's leek soup followed by pig's liver fried with onions, with a pile of boiled carrots and parsnips. The weather had turned sultry again – hot, still and humid, with dark clouds massing on the horizon threatening another thunderstorm before nightfall. The atmosphere encouraged torpor and the two old comrades slumped at the table to end their meal with a quart of Aelfric's home brew. Soon Gwyn had rested his head on his arms and began snoring, while John lethargically mused about Hawise d'Ayncourt, wondering how her body looked under those elegant clothes. He didn't much like her, but that was no barrier to him desiring her.

As he watched Gwyn's tousled red locks quiver with each snoring breath, John sleepily analysed his love life. At forty-one, he felt as virile as he had at eighteen, but the years were passing ever more quickly and he viewed the prospect of extended celibacy with dismay, unless he patronised one of the Bishop of Winchester's stews in Southwark. Though John would forfeit his very life before being unfaithful to his king, he would be the first to admit that he was not a faithful man when it came to women. He had loved Nesta deeply enough to have rarely strayed for almost two years, but it had been an effort. He felt a similar guilt when it came to Hilda, but although he had known her for many years he had slept with other women in the lonely years of distant campaigning.

Before he also laid his head on his arms and snoozed at the table, he thought dreamily of the full lips and languorous eyes of Hawise d'Ayncourt, deciding that any reluctance for him to bed her would be on the grounds of diplomatic complications with the Lord of Blois, rather than his own moral scruples.

The under-employed coroner and his officer slept on for almost an hour before they were rudely awakened by an urgent rapping on the street door. Osanna came grumbling from the yard to answer it, but Gwyn had already yawned his way to lift the latch and peer out. It was the same young page who had brought them messages to their chamber in the palace.

'Sir John, you are required urgently at the Exchequer!' he gabbled excitedly. 'The Chief Justiciar and the barons are there already and require your presence straight away.'

'What's going on, lad?' muttered de Wolfe, rubbing the sleep from his eyes.

'I don't rightly know, sir, but two horsemen with an escort of royal guards from the Tower rode in an hour ago. Since then, there's been a great deal of bustle and commotion around the palace.'

They buckled on their sword belts and strode after the page, who was almost dancing along ahead of them in his eagerness to get them to the riverside. As they went, the coroner and Gwyn tried to guess what the emergency might be. Since they were summoned to the Receipt of the Exchequer building, from which the block of stone had fallen, John felt that it must be something connected with his inquest that morning. However, no amount of mind searching could fathom any reason for such urgency, especially involving Hubert Walter himself. They eventually decided that the most likely cause was that Queen Eleanor had surprised them all by arriving unexpectedly in the Thames, instead of at Portsmouth.

They were very wide of the mark, as they soon learned

when they arrived in New Palace Yard. There was much activity around the front of the Great Hall, with half a dozen fine horses being held by ostlers and grooms standing with a trio of soldiers in the uniform of the Tower guards. To their left, towards the riverbank, they saw Ranulf of Abingdon and William Aubrey with the sergeant of the palace guards, the one who had accompanied them on their trip to Winchester. With them were several senior clerks of the Exchequer in their black cassocks, matching the garb of Thomas de Peyne, who stood near them, looking very apprehensive.

'God's guts, what's all this about?' demanded de Wolfe of his clerk. Before Thomas could answer, one of the Exchequer officials, a grey-haired man with a large paunch, motioned John and the others towards the door to the very building which had been the scene of the fatal accident that morning.

The Receipt of the Exchequer had been built as a result of King Henry's desire to move the organs of government from Winchester to Westminster. Now the taxes were delivered here in coin by the sheriffs from every county, as well as dues from wool, tin and the many other commodities from which the king reaped an income for the pursuance of his wars.

It was built against the riverside wall of William Rufus's huge hall, in line with its front. On the opposite side, a similar edifice was being erected for the housing of the increasing number of Treasury clerks and officials.

Inside, John saw that it was a single hall, with a wide gallery all around, reached by two sets of wooden stairs. There were clerks' desks on both levels, as well as a number of large tables downstairs, which he guessed were used for the receipt of money, though the famous chequered cloths for counting the coins were not in evidence today. Two of the tables had been pushed together and behind them sat a formidable array of nobles and officials.

In the centre sat Archbishop Hubert Walter, obviously in charge of proceedings. He was flanked by some of the senior members of the *Curia Regis*, the King's Council, and a number of nobles, a few of whom John recognised as Barons of the Exchequer, the royal justices. Eustace, Bishop of Ely and Vice Chancellor was also there, as was Richard fitz Nigel, the Bishop of London and King's Treasurer.

Simon Basset, the Treasury official who had received the chests at the Tower sat with the two knights who were witnesses to the checking of the inventory. Along the sides of the tables sat the Keeper of the Palace, the Constable of the Tower, and the Deputy Marshal, Martin Stanford, who represented William Marshal, Earl of Pembroke, who was at present across the Channel, escorting Queen Eleanor.

Having taken all this in, de Wolfe knew that something was seriously amiss, to require such a panoply of senior ministers to be gathered together in such urgency. For a moment he feared that news of King Richard's death might have arrived, but such a tragic event would not have been announced in the Exchequer chamber.

A moment later, he was made uneasy when the Keeper, Nathaniel de Levelondes, abruptly motioned for de Wolfe, the two Marshalsea knights, Gwyn, Thomas and the sergeant of the guard, to stand in a line before the tables. There were no benches for them and John felt as if they were being arraigned before a panel of justices at the bar of a court.

Thankfully, it was Hubert Walter who began speaking and when he addressed de Wolfe as the most senior, his voice was grave, but in no way condemnatory.

'Sir John, most serious news has just been delivered to us from the Tower and our first line of enquiry has to be through you.'

Mystified, John racked his brains to wonder as to what prisoner might have died in custody in the grim Tower, to require the services of the coroner. The real reason never crossed his mind until the Constable of the Tower was asked to speak. Sir Herbert de Mandeville, a tall, spare man with a haggard face and slight stoop, rose to his feet and addressed de Wolfe in a sonorous voice.

'Sir John, you visited the Tower recently when you delivered certain chests from Winchester into my care. No doubt you recall the occasion?'

It was more a statement than a question, and as if struck by a lightning bolt John knew immediately that some catastrophe had occurred to that damned treasure. This was why the leaders of that expedition to Winchester were lined up like errant scholars before their magister.

'I do indeed, Constable,' he replied cautiously. 'I saw the two boxes safely placed in your strongroom in the undercroft.'

De Wolfe deliberately made the point that he had seen the chests transferred out of his custody into that of Canon Basset.

Hubert Walter now cut in on the previous speaker. 'So it would surprise you, would it not, if you were told that some very valuable items were now missing from one of the chests?'

There was murmuring along the line of apparent suspects at this. Incredulity and denial were the obvious sentiments, but the Justiciar held up his hand.

'We are accusing no one at this stage, but this is a most serious matter amounting to treason and one which we cannot keep from the king.'

'Can you tell me what is missing?' asked John.

Hubert Walter turned to one of the Treasury clerks, a wizened man with an expression like a squeezed lemon. He consulted a parchment laid on the table before him.

'According to the inventory, a pure red-gold collar with pendant breastplate of Saxon workmanship. A heavy gold torc, probably of Celtic origin, two solid gold necklaces, four thick bracelets, also of pure gold, four amber earrings, set in gold, a pair of jewelled brooches, set in fine gold – and a gold plate a hand-span in width.'

He put down the document and glared at John, as if already convinced that he was the culprit. 'These were the finest and most valuable objects in the whole delivery. I would hazard a guess that, in total, they would be worth at least nine hundred pounds!'

There were murmurs of mixed surprise and outrage at the estimate, which represented a very large sum of money, bearing in mind that most workers earned only a few pennies a day.

De Wolfe, bolstered by a perfectly clear conscience, asked more questions. 'Were the chests broken into, Your Grace? Were the guards assaulted by armed men?'

The Constable returned to the attack, defending his position as guardian of the Tower and all its contents.

'This is the whole point, de Wolfe! The boxes were unmarked and still securely locked. The doors to the strongroom and the outer chamber were also firmly locked and the guards saw nothing. If I were not convinced that evil spirits have no need of gold, I would be tempted to say that the theft was supernatural!'

Ranulf of Abingdon was emboldened to enter the dialogue.

'Tragic and heinous though this theft undoubtedly

is, sir, it certainly cannot be laid at our door.' He waved a hand along the line standing before the tables. 'We brought the shipment from Winchester with all due care and delivered it as ordered. Sir John here was most insistent that a full check of the contents against that inventory was made at the Tower before we left, to safeguard us against exactly what has transpired.'

The coroner, standing hunched in his black tunic like a large crow, nodded his agreement.

'My duty – for I readily acknowledge that the responsibility for the transfer was entirely mine – was totally discharged when I saw the chests delivered to the Tower and was assured by the Treasury clerk present, that the inventory corresponded with the contents down to the last detail. What happened after that is utterly unfortunate and reprehensible, but certainly *we* hold no responsibility for it.' He emphasised the 'we' and stared pointedly at the Constable of the Tower, whose sallow face flushed at the inference.

The Archbishop of Canterbury, wearing only his usual small pectoral cross and ring of office to denote his eminence, nodded in sad acceptance of what his old friend and comrade had said.

'We have already discussed this and have to agree that whatever happened to the treasure, it occurred after you had left it in the Tower. But for the sake of completeness and from lack of any other explanation, we had to question you as a starting point.'

His gaze swept along the line of men, from William Aubrey at one end to the sergeant at the other. 'Have any of you anything to offer on this most serious crime? Any ideas will be carefully considered.' His tone suggested that he had abandoned any suspicions of complicity amongst the delivery team.

The only volunteer was, surprisingly, Thomas de Peyne. Normally self-effacing, he piped up with a disturbing, if obvious comment that had unwelcome implications for many officials.

'The keys, Your Grace? If the chest was undamaged, then it could only have been opened in the proper manner. So who would have access to the keys?'

There was a chorus of murmuring and muttering from the seated members at the table. Hubert Walter waved a hand towards the Constable again and glowering Herbert de Mandeville again rose to his feet, leaning with both fists on the table.

'There are two complicated locks on each chest,' he snarled. 'I keep one set of two keys for these particular boxes, one for one lock on each box – though of course I have many more keys for other chests in that vault. The other pair is held by officials of the Treasury, in this case Canon Simon Basset. I trust that no one thinks that either of us is anything other than above suspicion?'

He glared around, challenging anyone to dispute what he said.

Hubert Walter fingered the small cross on his breast as he spoke. 'Let me be quite clear on this matter. You, Constable, hold a key to one padlock on this particular chest – and Canon Basset, our esteemed senior Treasury official, holds the other?'

The two men named stared at each other, almost suspiciously, then nodded. 'That is so, Archbishop,' grunted de Mandeville.

'So neither of you independently can gain access to the contents?'

Simon Basset, his rotund face pink with embarrassment, bobbed his head. 'It requires both of us to be present to open both locks at the same time.'

'And I assure Your Grace – and the rest of the company assembled here – that this never happened!' grated de Mandeville, banging the table with his fist.

'But it must have done, otherwise we would not know that anything was missing?' said the Keeper of the Palace, with deceptive mildness.

'I meant until today!' roared de Mandeville, choking back a jibe that the Keeper was an idiot.

'Why were the boxes opened today?' asked the Deputy Marshal, a straight-backed soldier with a broken nose.

'All the contents of that strongroom were given a final check, before being taken to the Tower wharf tomorrow for loading on to a warship for Honfleur,' explained Basset, with a desperate earnestness. 'It was when the manifests were checked against the contents, that the loss was discovered.' The Treasury man seemed about to burst into tears. 'This is the first time that such an irregularity has occurred in all my long service to the king!'

There was a short period of further questions and discussion, but it was obvious that nothing useful would be gained from further pestering of the team that delivered the chests from Winchester and Hubert Walter brought the proceedings to a rapid close.

'If this was not such an obvious crime of avarice, I would be tempted to add it to the list of miracles!' he proclaimed. 'There seems no rational explanation and I consider these men before us deserve nothing but praise for the way they safely conveyed the treasure to the Tower.'

There was a collective sigh of relief from the line of men, though John did not contribute to it, as he knew that no fault attached to him. But his hope that he could now walk away from the affair was soon dashed, as Hubert Walter continued to speak.

'The loss of objects worth such a considerable sum from the king's war chest cannot be tolerated – least of all by King Richard himself! The means by which they were stolen must be discovered and the culprits brought to justice, which as this amounts to treason, means by a slow and painful death!'

When it came to the king's money, Hubert Walter became very short of Christian forgiveness, for all that he was head of the Church in England.

'As the new Coroner of the Verge, Sir John de Wolfe is charged with investigating all serious crimes within the royal precincts. As he was also in charge of the transfer of this chest, it makes it all the more appropriate that he seeks out the perpetrators of this daring and outrageous act. I therefore give him a Royal Commission to enquire with all speed and diligence into the matter, and command that every one of the king's subjects, from the highest to the lowest, offer him all assistance.'

Rising to show that the session was finished, he turned to speak to the nearest members of the Curia, but before doing so, gave John a slight gesture, telling him to come to him in his chambers.

The line of highly relieved 'suspects' also broke up and filed silently out into the Palace Yard, where they mopped sweating brows and began congratulating themselves and each other that their heads were still on their shoulders.

'Thank Christ Almighty that you insisted on a check of that bloody box before we left the Tower, John!' said Ranulf. 'Otherwise we would have all been back in another small chamber there, until we all danced at the end of a rope at Smithfield or Tyburn!'

CHAPTER EIGHT

In which the coroner goes back to the Tower

At supper in the Lesser Hall that evening, even the coming visit of Queen Eleanor was eclipsed as a topic of conversation. Apart from the usual clique around de Wolfe, other diners gravitated as best they could to be within earshot of the coroner, trying glean any titbits of gossip about the notorious theft of the king's treasure. After vegetable potage and several fish dishes, including grayling, gudgeon and dace, for it was Friday, the eager questioning began. Relaxed after a stressful day by a few cups of wine, de Wolfe saw no reason not to respond, especially as he had very little to tell them.

'There is no secret about this, for every man-at-arms and kitchen scullion knows as much as I concerning the matter,' he said in answer to Archdeacon Bernard's demand.

Ranulf nodded in gloomy agreement. 'Almost everyone in London will know by now, though the king has yet to learn about it. There'll be hell to pay if it's not found before the news gets to him.'

'We heard only that a fabulous golden treasure had vanished from the Tower!' said Hawise in a suitably breathless voice.

'Valuable, but hardly fabulous,' grunted John. 'It was

part of treasure trove collected from the West Country.'

'I understand that you had a private audience with the Justiciar after that meeting in the Exchequer,' said Renaud de Seigneur. De Wolfe wondered how he knew that – the palace grapevine must have been working overtime.

'It was only to give me a parchment carrying his seal with instructions for all men to give me every assistance in the name of the king,' replied John. 'He has commissioned me as Coroner of the Verge to make enquiries as to how this crime was committed and to retrieve the stolen property.'

Hubert Walter had in fact said a great deal more than this, but John was not going to share such confidences with this nosey crowd.

'It is said that the golden objects vanished from a doubly locked chest, one whose keys were shared between two senior officials,' persisted Bernard de Montfort. 'But how could that possibly happen?'

De Wolfe shrugged. 'That's what I'm deputed to discover, God help me!'

Hawise d'Ayncourt, who was sitting opposite him, stretched her shapely leg to touch his calf, almost as if by accident.

'It seems like a miracle, Sir John,' she said, her big eyes opening even wider in pretended awe. 'Do you believe in the supernatural?'

He grinned crookedly. 'Not when nine hundred pound's worth of treasure is missing, my lady! Miracles may still occur in the religious world and if a statue of Our Lady begins to weep tears of milk, then I am prepared to accept a bishop's assurances that it is genuine. But where solid gold is concerned, I remain a confirmed unbeliever!'

Her ankle caressed his leg again and he pulled it back sharply, causing a flicker of annoyance to cloud her face. Then Ranulf, who seemed aware of what was going on beneath the table, intervened with a question.

'Do you wish for William Aubrey and myself to assist you in this venture, John? We feel as responsible as you, as we were part of the same escort that brought those damned chests to London.'

De Wolfe shook his head. 'The Justiciar instructed me to carry out this task personally, with only my officer and clerk. He wishes for everyone else to remain outside the investigation, to demonstrate that there can be no partiality, as everyone is both potentially innocent or guilty – even the Constable of the Tower, though he seems highly incensed at being included.'

'How will you go about this?' asked Ranulf.

'I must question everyone involved in the custody of the treasure in the Tower – from the Constable down to each of the guards. Even the Exchequer men like Simon Basset and Treasury clerks cannot be exempt. Anyone who seems to be suspect will be subject to arduous interrogation – even put to the torture if that seems necessary.'

His listeners heard his words in silence, impressed by the sternness of his manner. John de Wolfe was well known for his unswerving devotion to the king and it sounded as if he meant to pursue this quest with ruthless determination.

When he escaped from the inquisitive residents, John waited outside for Ranulf and William and they walked in the cooling evening across the yard at the rear of the palace towards the Marshalsea stables and accommodation where the two men lived.

'Those people from France seem to have more knowledge of this place than ourselves,' complained Ranulf. 'If this rumour about spies is true, then surely they must be the obvious candidates, always wanting to know every detail of what's going on!'

The younger marshal, William Aubrey, leaned in from the other side of Ranulf to join the debate.

'Even that priest from the Auvergne seems more concerned with palace politics and scandal than he is with the curing of souls,' he observed. 'These days, you never know who to trust.'

De Wolfe shrugged off their concerns. 'I think they are just bored and ready to feast on any bit of tittle-tattle they can find. The sooner the old queen comes, the better – then we can get this circus on the road and stop staring at our own navels!'

He said much the same thing to Gwyn and Thomas a little later, when they were sitting in the main room of the house in Long Ditch Lane. His main purpose was to discuss how they were to carry out this unwelcome commission that the Justiciar had thrust upon him.

'We have only a week or so before the court moves off, if Queen Eleanor arrives when they forecast,' he said. 'Hubert Walter will not be pleased if nothing is achieved before then.'

'We can't be blamed for that,' complained Gwyn indignantly. 'The bloody theft was nothing to do with us. We've already been cleared of any involvement, thank God.'

'I'm not so sure,' said John grimly. 'In spite of Hubert Walter extolling our good behaviour, if nothing is found before the king gets to hear of it, no one will escape his wrath – not even us.'

'But we've got a cast-iron defence against any accusations,' protested Gwyn.

'That's as may be, but I've been saddled with solving the crime, so what are we going to do about it?' grunted John, reaching for his pot of Aedwulf's ale.

'I suppose we had better visit the scene of the crime,'

offered Thomas, hesitantly. 'I presume the two chests are still there.'

'The pox-ridden guards may be at the bottom of this,' growled Gwyn. 'Surely no one could get into that chamber without a sentry seeing them? It was at the end of a passage and behind a couple of locked doors, with a sentinel outside the outer one.'

Thomas voiced what John was thinking. 'Then the thief can only be someone who had a right to be in that strongroom. I wonder how big the stolen objects were? Could they be concealed under a cloak or tunic and smuggled out?'

De Wolfe scratched his black stubble, which was due for his weekly shave.

'The plate was the largest thing. I remember it when the inventory was made in Winchester. Placed flat against a belly or chest, it could be taken out. The other treasures were small enough to be slipped into a deep pocket.'

'And they were all of gold – the less valuable silver was left behind,' added Thomas.

The three of them thought about this scenario for a moment.

'So who would have had legitimate reason to be in the chamber?' asked Gwyn.

'The Constable, Herbert de Mandeville, for one,' replied John. 'Then Simon Basset, of course, and those knights from the Tower garrison, and a couple of the guards and their sergeant.'

The sharp wits of Thomas pointed out that both the knights and the Tower guards might well be different each time the chamber was visited, as chests were presumably arriving and departing frequently, requiring inventories to be made.

'We mention Simon Basset, but there are a legion of Treasury and Exchequer barons, clerks and officials who might have reason to enter the room,' added Thomas.

John groaned. 'I'll have to talk to them all, I suppose!' he muttered. 'Though no one is going to confess, if it means hanging or disembowelling.'

'What about this key business?' asked Gwyn. 'It could only be someone who has managed to get hold of the correct two keys to the pair of locks on that chest.'

De Wolfe felt a shiver run up his spine. 'Keys which I had in my possession for only four days,' he reminded them. 'Thank Christ the Justiciar has enough faith in me to dismiss any thought of my guilt.'

'But even if you had the keys now, you had no way of getting into that chamber after the boxes were put there – and we know the contents were intact when we left,' pointed out Thomas consolingly.

The coroner swallowed the last of his ale with an almost savage gesture and slammed the empty pot on the table.

'I wish to hell I'd never had to leave Devon,' he snarled. 'We had problems enough there, God knows, but nothing like the things these slippery, scheming courtiers seem able to dream up. Sod it, I'm going to bed and hope that tomorrow will put an end to this sorry business!'

Next morning, after Thomas had finished his duties in the abbey, they rode up to the Great Tower, pushing their way through the crowded streets to the extreme eastern end of the great walled city that housed the tens of thousands of inhabitants now overflowing through the six gates into suburbs spreading into the surrounding countryside.

The brooding grey* walls, a reminder of the

* It was not called 'The White Tower' until Henry III had it painted in the thirteenth century.

Conqueror's power, glowered over them as they approached. John produced his new authority from the Justiciar and dangled the imposing red seal in front of the gate guards. Though none could read it, they unhesitatingly let the coroner inside, where the builders were energetically carrying out King Richard's order to erect new defences.

At the stables, they left their horses and an ostler took them to the steps up to the main entrance, where again a pair of sentries were impressed by John's royal warrant. They called a page and he took them up four gloomy flights of stairs built into the thickness of the massive walls. On the second floor, the Constable, who preferred to be known as 'The Keeper', had a chamber with a deeply embrasured window that looked out over the river towards Southwark and the bridge.

Herbert de Mandeville did not look pleased to see de Wolfe, as he rose from behind his table.

'I thought you would be bothering me, sooner or later,' he muttered, wiping sweat from his brow with a crumpled kerchief. It was already very hot in the room, even at the ninth hour of the morning. A tonsured clerk came in from an adjacent office dragging a folding leather chair to the front of the table. At Herbert's grudging invitation John sat down, leaving his officer and clerk to lurk behind him.

'I know this is not a welcome exercise, but it has be done,' began de Wolfe. 'You saw yesterday that I and those who went to Winchester were paraded in front of you like suspects, so it affects us all.'

The Constable unbent a little at John's tactful overture.

'It's a total mystery to me,' he snapped. 'If you can solve it, de Wolfe, then you deserve to be Chief Justiciar yourself, for I'm damned if I can fathom how it was done.'

They then went through the details of how the strongroom below the Tower was protected. De Mandeville eventually pulled out a silver chain from inside the pouch on his belt.'

'This is attached to a ring sewn inside my scrip,' he declared. 'And on the other, there is this key, which never leaves my person, except when I am in bed.'

He held up a small iron key, then rose again and went to a large cupboard fixed to one of the stone walls. It was at least five feet square, but shallow, the edges of the doors being rimmed with iron.

'This is my key store, where keys to most doors in the Tower are kept,' he announced, as he opened a padlock which secured a thick hasp, fixed to the doors by metal bolts.

When the doors were opened, John saw dozens of keys of all shapes and sizes, hanging from hooks at the back of the cupboard. Many had dabs of coloured paint on their shanks or rings, some had wooden labels attached by cords and others were identified by slips of parchment tied to them. Some of the keys were almost a foot long, but most were half that size, with complicated wards cut into the metal.

'And no one else had a key to that cupboard?' asked John. 'What happens when you are away or indisposed?'

'My chief clerk has a copy,' admitted de Mandeville, rather sheepishly. 'But I would trust him with my life. He has been here for twenty-four years. And, anyway, in respect of the Exchequer boxes, it is immaterial, as they cannot be opened with my key alone.'

John thought this system had a glaring defect as far as the keys of the Tower were concerned, but had to admit that without the other key held by the Exchequer officials, the chests seemed impregnable. After more fruitless questioning of de Mandeville, he asked to speak to the chief clerk, a white-haired old man with severe disease of his joints. His knuckles were crippled with hard swellings and he shuffled along due to painful stiffness of his hips. However, there was nothing wrong with his brain or his tongue, and he vehemently defended his trustworthiness, claiming that the key to his master's cupboard never left his person, even in bed. He had never opened the store to anyone without firm authorisation and the keys to the Treasury boxes had never been removed by anyone other than the 'Keeper' himself.

De Wolfe abandoned his interrogation and asked to be shown the scene of the crime, the chamber deep in the bowels of the Tower. De Mandeville marched ahead of them, back down the stairs and then through tortuous passages to a narrow spiral staircase that had a small portcullis and a heavy door at its bottom end.

'This is a weak spot in the defence of the Tower, should it ever be besieged,' he grunted, as he unlocked the door with a large key he brought from his chamber. 'Normally, an undercroft is quite isolated from the floors above, but maybe this could be defended by two men against an army, as it's so narrow.'

At the bottom, a man-at-arms stood on duty in the passage that led to the treasure chamber, and another man with pike and sword guarded the door through which the chests had been taken.

'I reckon it must have been a bloody miracle after all,' muttered Gwyn, as they waited for the Constable to unlock the door to the chamber. 'There's all these sentries and every damned door is locked. A flaming mouse couldn't have got in there!'

When the heavy door creaked open, the dim light from the guttering flames of small oil lamps set in niches in the passage walls seeped into the chamber. The soldier took two of these lights and held them high so that the Constable and his guests could see the contents of the room. There were now about a dozen boxes ranged against the walls, some on top of each other.

'That's the one, cursed by Satan, I reckon!' snarled de Mandeville, for his reputation, liberty and possibly his very life had been put at risk by the trouble the chest had caused.

The object of his dislike had been set slightly apart from the others since the loss had been discovered and John recognised it by the different spacing of the iron bands that encircled it. The two padlocks were firmly in place and the box looked innocent enough, in spite of the Constable's claim that it was cursed.

De Mandeville now brandished another key, which he had brought from his chamber. 'Here's mine, try it if you like – but you'll still not open the damned chest without someone from the Exchequer being present with his key.'

More out of curiosity than necessity, John took the key and inserted it into the padlock, which was as large as his hand. The mechanism operated surprisingly smoothly and the hoop of the lock hinged back easily. John withdrew it from the heavy hasp, but as expected the lid would not lift a hair's-breadth without the other lock being removed. He replaced the first one and stood up, handing the key back to the Constable.

'It's all just as you claimed, Sir Herbert,' he said sombrely. 'There's no way in which this chest could have been opened except by the use of the two keys at the same time.'

'Maybe there's a hidden trapdoor in the bottom,' rumbled Gwyn, meaning to be facetious, but raising a scowl of derision from de Mandeville. However, de Wolfe was determined to leave no possibility un-explored.

'Is there anything in the chest now?' he demanded. The Constable assured him that the remaining contents had been locked in another chest, as the security of this one was now in doubt.

'Right, let's turn it over,' he snapped, and with the Constable looking on in surprise he and Gwyn strained to turn the large box first on to its back, then right over on to its top. John carefully examined the whole surface, running his hand over it to look for cracks and tapped it for soundness. He did the same to the sides and ends, then turned it back on to its base and checked the lid. Satisfied, he stood up and smacked dirt from his fingers.

'Nothing! It had to be opened by the keys. And someone must have had both keys, unless it was a conspiracy between at least two thieves,' he announced.

De Mandeville glared at him. 'I trust you are not suggesting that I was involved, de Wolfe?' he snarled.

John shook his head. 'I am suggesting nothing. I am just stating the inevitable conclusion that this chest was opened by unlocking it.'

There was nothing more to be gained in the chamber and they retreated, the Constable securing the door and stalking ahead of them. John refused his rather stilted offer of refreshment and they were seen out of the Tower, where they collected their mounts and made their way back into the city. They went past heaving crowds around the markets at Poultry, into Cheapside and on via the great church of St Paul to Ludgate. Here, with some relief, they left the city walls behind and rode more easily along the less congested Strand to Charing and then to Westminster. Thomas hurried off to his beloved abbey and Gwyn vanished to an alehouse, leaving John to enjoy his dinner alone. The afternoon was enlivened by the coroner being called to a knife-fight between two cooks in the palace kitchens, but as neither was badly injured, John decided not to make an official case of assault, but consigned both men to the custody of the Master at Arms, instructing him to lock them up for a week.

Next day, Thomas forsook the abbey refectory and ate with de Wolfe and Gwyn in Long Ditch. Over fat bacon with onions and carrots, followed by a blancmange of almond milk and shredded chicken, flavoured with spices, Thomas enquired what the next move was in his master's investigation.

'We've talked to one key-holder, so the obvious thing is to speak to the other,' replied the coroner, digging bacon strands from between his teeth. 'I understand that Simon Basset lives in one of those houses in King Street, but first we'll see if he's in the Treasury this afternoon.'

When they had finished their dinner with maslin bread and a hunk of hard yellow cheese, washed down with cider, they walked back to the palace. The day was still hot and sultry with a distant rumble of thunder coming from the Kentish Weald. At the entrance to the Receipt of Exchequer building, the sentry saluted John with a fist across his chest, the other hand holding the shaft of a long pike. Inside it was cooler under the high ceiling, below which a dozen clerks worked at desks and tables, penning lists of accounts on a multitude of parchments.

Thomas recognised an elderly clerk sitting alone at a table facing the doorway and went across to make enquiries. After a short conversation, he came back to de Wolfe.

'Simon Basset is not here, Crowner. He was expected this morning to deal with certain matters, but has not appeared.'

'Did you learn where we might find him?'

'The chief clerk suggests that we try him at home. He

might be indisposed, which is why he did not appear,' said Thomas.

'Maybe he's quit the realm, with a bagful of gold trinkets!' suggested Gwyn, with his usual black humour. John scowled, such jokes might be too near the truth to be funny.

'Let's find the bloody man, then. We can walk that far, even in this damned heat.'

They walked across New Palace Yard to the main gate into King Street and went back along the road that they had ridden down a couple of hours earlier.

'Did that clerk give you exact directions, Thomas?'

'He said it was the last dwelling on the left side of the road, before the bridge over the Clowson Brook.' This was a branch of the Tyburn, running northwards through the abbey grounds, one of the many brooks that drained the marshes.

They passed a row of dwellings, some with shopfronts, the shutters on the downstairs windows folding down to act as display counters for merchandise – shoes, harness, candles, leather belts and a host of other things. Most of the buildings here were two-storeyed, some with upper floors projecting into the street. The little bridge was a single small arch and beyond it the houses were larger and grander, all stone-built. On the opposite side, even larger houses lined the street, where the more exalted members of the Westminster community lived.

'This must be the one, it has a Madonna over the door,' said Thomas, crossing himself at the sight of a small gaudily painted statue of the Virgin in a niche above the front entrance. The house was well kept but not ostentatiously large. It was a narrow building of whitewashed cob between heavy oak frames, roofed with stone slates. A small yard with a hitching rail for horses lay between the edge of King Street and the house. A narrow path ran around each side to the backyard, the stream being on one side in a deep culvert.

Gwyn banged on the heavy front door and soon the shaven scalp of a young man in lower holy orders appeared, looking rather nervously through the gap.

'We seek your master, is he at home?' demanded de Wolfe, after identifying himself as the Coroner of the Verge.

The door opened wider and the thin shape of the servant stood in his black tunic, rubbing his hands anxiously.

'He is not here, sir. Have you any news of him?'

John stared at the fellow. 'What do you mean? Why should I have news of him?'

Another figure appeared in the short passage behind the door, this time another cleric, but a man of early middle age and portly appearance. His fleshy face looked troubled as John explained that he was looking for Canon Basset.

'Please come inside, Sir John, I will explain.'

He led the way through a heavy leather door-drape into a comfortable, almost opulent room, where padded benches, a table and several carved chairs indicated that this was well above the usual standard of furnishing. The bareness of the whitewashed walls was relieved by fine tapestry hangings, depicting classical battle scenes and religious events. An ornate gilded crucifix was the only evidence that this was the residence of a canon of Lichfield and his entourage.

'I am Gilbert, the canon's chaplain. Please be seated, coroner.' Again, Gwyn and Thomas were left standing, but after Gilbert's instruction to the lay brother to fetch refreshments, they were invited to a brocade-covered bench against a wall and included in the offer of ale, wine and pastries.

De Wolfe suffered these formalities impatiently, then returned to his need to speak to the Exchequer official.

'I am in some difficulty over that, I fear,' replied Gilbert, anxiously. 'We have not seen him since yesterday morning. He did not return home last evening and failed to appear again today.'

A small bell of alarm began to chime in John's head. 'Is that unusual for him?' he asked.

'It is indeed, he is a man of most regular habits. He never misses a meal, as we have one of the best cooks in Westminster.'

'Where was he yesterday later on? Do you know anything of his movements?'

The chaplain shook his head. 'Martin, his steward, might be aware of those, but he is out at present – riding the roads between here and the city, in case the canon has come to some harm there.'

'The city? Was he going into London yesterday?'

Gilbert lifted his shoulders in a gesture. 'I did hear some talk of it when we came back from attending Prime at St Margaret's. But Martin would know.'

Further questions confirmed that no one in the household had any idea of where their master had gone. When the steward returned a short while later, he was unable to shed any light on the disappearance, but it was obvious that the chaplain and servants were worried about Simon Basset's vanishing act, especially if it was going to affect their comfortable life in this very desirable residence.

'There was no sign of him along the roads,' said Martin, a strongly built man with a black beard. 'He mentioned the previous evening that he might have to ride into the city sometime in the day, but he didn't say where he was going – and I'm not sure if he went or not.'

John sighed – this investigation seemed to run into the sand at every turn, like his inquest on Basil. He tried again.

'Let's get this straight! Your master went off yesterday morning, presumably by horse?'

'Yes, I saw him trotting off up the Royal Way, so I presumed he was going to the city and probably to the Great Tower, where the Treasury stores some of its valuables.'

'We were there yesterday and I am sure that the Constable would have mentioned if Canon Simon had been there, as his name was central to our discussions,' countered John. 'So it seems unlikely that he went to the Tower.'

Martin scratched his beard thoughtfully. 'Of course, he could have gone anywhere in that direction,' he mused. 'Anywhere at all in the city – or he could have turned at Charing and gone up to the Oxford Road. Or maybe he called at some religious house on the way – the Templars, even.'

'Why the Temple?'

'The king has a great partiality for the Poor Knights of the Temple of Solomon, as well as for their money, for he borrows greatly from them. The Exchequer has considerable dealings with them, my master visited them frequently to arrange or repay loans. In addition, some of the Treasury bullion is often stored in their vaults for safety.'

John knew that a steward was privy to much that went on in the household, but he seemed unusually well apprised of national finances.

'So he could have gone to the Temple?' he queried.

Martin turned up his hands in a Gallic gesture. 'Of course! But he could equally have gone to a score of places elsewhere.'

This was getting them nowhere, so the coroner drew

the questioning to a close and rose from the chair to leave.

'But in all this,' he concluded, 'the strange aspect is that the canon did not say that he might be away for a time – nor did he later send any message that he would be delayed in returning home?'

Martin and the chaplain both nodded. 'It is most unusual, which is why we are so concerned. What shall we do, Sir John? Should we inform the Lord Treasurer and the other lords of Exchequer?'

'I'll do that myself, as soon as I get back to the palace,' promised de Wolfe. 'Meanwhile, I suggest that you send to the New Temple and any other likely places, to see if Simon Basset is there or has been there in the last day. If you have any news, be sure to notify me at once, d'you hear!'

His tone made it clear that he wanted his orders carried out promptly and with that he led his pair of assistants out of the house, leaving a worried and apprehensive household behind him.

With an absentee Chancellor, as well as an absentee king, de Wolfe decided to consult the Chief Justiciar about Simon Basset's disappearance. However, he was told that Hubert Walter was across the river, inspecting the progress of his pet project. This was the building of a palace for himself in Lambeth as a London residence, as it was said that he wanted a magnificent house to spite his rival, the Bishop of London. The two major churches, one at Westminster Abbey and St Paul's Cathedral, were in competition for funds and the expression 'robbing Peter to pay Paul' had arisen from the names of their respective patron saints. Any prospect of seeing Hubert Walter that day was dashed when his clerks said that he was riding to Canterbury and would be absent for at least four days.

De Wolfe turned instead to the Keeper of the Palace, but found that Nathaniel de Levelondes was preoccupied with the coming royal visit and the move of the whole court to Gloucester.

'Report it to the Lord Treasurer,' he muttered absently. 'He's in charge of all those money-grubbers.'

Frustrated, de Wolfe went back to the Exchequer building at the other end of the palace, but the chief clerk told him that the Treasurer had gone back to his estates in Northamptonshire.

'Have you any idea where Canon Basset may have gone?' he demanded of the old clerk. 'His household have had no news of him since yesterday morning.'

Once again, enquiries were made among the other clerks sitting at their desks, but no one had any suggestions.

'Did he not have duties here each day?' demanded the coroner.

The grey-haired official shook his head. 'We are busiest when the sheriffs come to pay in their county taxes, but between times the senior officials attend only when there is something specific to be done. Canon Simon should have been here this morning to peruse and sign some documents, but they can wait until he appears.'

Cursing under his breath, John went up to his chamber facing the river, where Gwyn and Thomas were waiting. He told them of his fruitless attempts to arouse some interest in the disappearance of the man who had the only other key to the notorious treasure chest.

'I wouldn't give a damn about the fellow himself, if it weren't for the fact that I have been saddled with this commission from the Justiciar to investigate the theft,' he fumed.

'Maybe that clerk down at the front is right,' soothed

Gwyn. 'Perhaps come Monday morning, he'll turn up as usual.'

The coroner marched impatiently up and down the room, his back hunched and his head jutting forwards. The swept-back black hair, which he wore unfashionably long, bounced on the collar of his grey tunic and once again Thomas was reminded of a large crow strutting about the garden.

'Where the hell can he have gone?' he rasped. 'I've got a bad feeling about this, but short of searching every house in London, there's little we can do.'

In the afternoon, de Wolfe restlessly rode with Gwyn back to the canon's house, where still no news of him had been received by the anxious servants. Getting a description of Simon's horse – a grey mare with a white blaze on her forehead – the pair rode as far as the New Temple and made enquiries of the porter there. The man knew Canon Simon from previous visits, but was quite definite that he had not called in the past day or two.

From lack of any other inspiration, de Wolfe walked his horse around a number of byways, going up from the village of Charing to the high road which ran westward from Holbourn and then on to Tyburn, where he and his officer stopped for a few moments to look at the large elm trees that now competed with Smithfield as an execution ground. The first customer a couple of months ago had been the rebel William fitz Osbert, known as Longbeard, whose capture and hanging had brought Hubert Walter into such disfavour. But there was no sign anywhere of Simon Basset nor of his horse, so a dispirited de Wolfe followed a direct track across the marshes to where the great bulk of the abbey and palace stood up against the sultry sky.

Thankfully, that night during supper in the Lesser Hall there was no discussion about the canon, as for once, the palace gossip machine had failed to pick up the news. John was spared interrogation, but he suspected that the disappearance of someone so directly linked to the theft of the treasure would not remain a secret for long.

With a choice of boiled capon, salmon, pork ribs and a range of vegetables from leeks to parsnips, John was busy filling his stomach, but was obliged for courtesy's sake to attend to Hawise as well. She had managed to sit opposite her husband, and next to John, her hip pressed against his as he gallantly sliced pieces of chicken to put on her trencher. The Lesser Hall sported tablecloths, instead of the usual scrubbed oak boards and the large bread trenchers were placed on oblongs of wood to spare the spoiling of the linen beneath.

They had each already finished a wooden bowl of potage, a soup of vegetables in stock, thickened with oatmeal, and Hawise was gaily protesting at the amount of food John was serving her.

'You are intent upon making me fat, Sir John!' she gushed. 'I'll need a stronger horse to carry me when we ride to Gloucester!'

The warmth of her thigh moving against his distracted him so much that he dropped a chicken leg and cursed as a large stain of gravy spread on the pristine cloth. The woman giggled and briefly touched his leg under the table.

'You seem out of temper this evening, John! No doubt you're missing that blonde Saxon who shared your bed recently!' She failed to keep the jealous pique out of her voice.

The pert remark made John realize that he had not given much thought to Hilda these past few days, as the theft of the treasure and now Simon Basset's vanishing trick had fully occupied his mind. He tried to think of a suitably cutting response to Hawise, who was now resting her fingers on his thigh, as she ate with her other hand. But her husband cut in with a return to the old topic.

'Have you made any progress in finding the miscreant who stole the king's gold?' he asked in a semi-bantering tone. Archdeacon Bernard leaned forward from the other side of Ranulf, who was next to Hawise's silent maidservant. 'Give the man a chance, he's only been at the task for two days! No doubt you suspect someone in the Great Tower itself?'

'I certainly have a new path to pursue, but you will appreciate that I have to keep such matters strictly confidential,' said de Wolfe. At least I've told the truth, he thought wryly – the fact that at present his new path led nowhere, need not be voiced to these inquisitive creatures. He was finding the touch of Hawise's fingers quite pleasant, but almost reluctantly he slid his own hand under the edge of the tablecloth and gently replaced hers on her lap. As he did so, he briefly felt the warmth of her skin through the silken gown and a frisson of desire rippled through him. For her part, Lady de Seigneur gave a petulant pursing of her lips and once again John thought her husband must either be half-blind or uncaring about her flirting.

They finished the meal with a flagon of white wine from the Loire, accompanied by dried figs and apricots, then drifted out of the Lesser Hall. As Hawise was towed away by her husband towards the stairs to the guest quarters, she gave John a doleful look of longing to which he responded with a faint smile.

'She'll have the breeches off you yet, John!' murmured Ranulf, as they went out into the evening light of the Palace Yard. John had arranged to meet Gwyn in the alehouse a little later, so to pass the time, he suggested to Ranulf that they took a walk along the riverbank. Passing the stables and all the less impressive parts of the back end of the palace, they went through the gate in the wall that formed the southern limit of the enclave and crossed the small bridge across the Tyburn. The marshy flats along the edge of the Thames had dried out in the recent hot weather and sheep and goats, tended by an occasional shepherd, were dotted about the wide, flat area. They walked towards the edge of the river, where a narrow path ran above the slope down to the high-water mark, now exposing a wide shelf of mud leading to the dark water.

'Do you think she's like that with all men?' asked John ruminatively, taking up Ranulf's earlier remark.

The marshal shook his head and grinned. 'She's not set her cap at me, has she?' he countered. 'It's you that the Lady Hawise is inflamed about. I wish it was me, I'm more than a little jealous!'

The smile he gave took any rancour from his jibe.

'Even if I was inclined to oblige her,' said John. 'There's always that dumpy husband of hers to contend with.'

Ranulf stopped and stared at the sky, where thunder-clouds still massed on the far horizon. 'I get the feeling that Lord Renaud isn't all that bothered about his wife's fidelity,' he murmured. 'I'd be there like a shot if I had any encouragement.'

De Wolfe was dubious. 'Why should he have that attitude?' he asked. 'She is an uncommonly attractive woman. You'd think a plain older man like him would keep her on a short rein.'

'Unless they have hidden motives,' suggested Ranulf darkly. John came to a sudden halt on the path and turned to face his friend. 'What do you mean by that?' he demanded.

The under-marshal looked left and right as if checking that he could not be overheard, though the nearest thing on legs was a sheep a hundred yards away.

'We get to hear things at the stables, people coming and going on official business. There is a spy scare on at the moment, according to one of our men, who overheard some barons and earls he was escorting on a barge up to Windsor.'

'Spying on what? And how can that concern me and a flighty dame who should know better?'

They began to walk slowly back to the abbey and palace that loomed before them, Ranulf continuing with his tale.

'My gossip also tells me that one of the reasons for Queen Eleanor's visit is for her to impress on the Royal Council the real threat of an invasion from France – and also to dissuade her errant son John from becoming involved again in support for Philip Augustus. Naturally, the French want to know what the official reaction is and to know if military precautions are being taken along the coast of Kent and Sussex.'

'And how could that affect me? I am a coroner, I know nothing about politics or troop dispositions!'

'You have the ear of the Justiciar – and are known to be a favourite of the king himself, after the good service you gave him at the Crusade. When a spy is short of contacts, he or she latches on to the best option – and you are a good target in that respect.'

De Wolfe stared at Ranulf in disbelief. 'Are you trying to tell me that the de Seigneurs are covert agents of France?'

The marshal shrugged. 'It's a possibility. I know that warnings have been circulating for months that there are spies in England.'

'There are always spies in England – and always have been! Just as we have spies in France and every other country,' said John scornfully.

'I'm just repeating what I've heard,' answered Ranulf

mildly. 'Perhaps Renaud de Seigneur plans to catch you pleasuring his wife, so that he can blackmail you into revealing the secrets of the realm!' he added mischievously

'He'll be in for a great disappointment, then,' grunted de Wolfe. 'I've cuckolded better men than him.'

Thinking it time that he turned the talk away from himself, he delved a little into his companion's life.

'What about you, friend? You cannot be married if you live in that bachelor den over the stables.'

'I was wedded years ago, but my wife died in childbed, as did the infant.'

'Have you not remarried, then? You are still young, not yet thirty, I would guess.'

Ranulf shook his head. 'I enjoy life as it is, John. I do not lack for female company when I desire it, but enjoy men's pursuits, like gambling on dice, dog-fighting and the like. I also follow the tournaments in a modest way, though I can't yet afford to equip myself sufficiently to enter the lists in any of the great tourneys.'

John, who had also dabbled in jousting in his earlier days, knew of the passion that some men had for tourneys. Fortunes could be made – and lost – on the tourney fields, as the horses and armour of the losers were forfeited to the winners, as well as heavy wagering on the results.

'What about young William Aubrey?' asked John. 'Is he another merry bachelor?'

'He is indeed, never having married. But he is twenty-one and has little prospect of inheritance, as he is the fifth son of a manor-lord in Somerset.' He grinned as he thought of William's cheerful nature. 'He is another keen one for the girls, but he has youth on his side. Also, he shares my fondness for a wager, though ratting is his game.'

'You'll both have to be on your best behaviour when the old queen arrives,' observed de Wolfe. 'All the organisation of travel is your responsibility, I gather.'

Ranulf became serious at the prospect. 'Yes, though under the direction of William the Marshal himself, when he arrives. We have half a dozen under-marshals here and a legion of ostlers, grooms, farriers and wheel-wrights to keep the cavalcade on the road, once we leave Westminster.'

They crossed the stream and entered the gate into Old Palace Yard. Just before they parted, John told him about Simon Basset, as the under-marshal was almost as involved as himself in the matter of the stolen treasure.

'It's not common knowledge yet, but Canon Simon seems to have disappeared,' he said. 'I wanted to question him about access to the chests in the Tower, but he appears to have vanished off the face of the earth. No one in his household or in the Exchequer has any news of him.'

Ranulf's expression showed his concern. 'But along with the Constable, he's the most likely suspect, given that he has at least half the keys necessary,' he said. 'Do you think he's fled the country with a sack full of gold?'

De Wolfe shrugged. 'It seems a little unlikely that a respectable canon would give up his life in England for nine hundred pounds, though that's a lot of money. And he's left behind a valuable house and possessions, as well as a position of influence and prestige.'

'Maybe he's just having a few days and nights with a secret mistress,' suggested Ranulf. They both laughed at the thought of the portly canon indulging in some passionate affair, but as John said farewell and walked off to meet Gwyn, he wondered whether that was a possible explanation.

CHAPTER NINE

In which Crowner John visits a brothel

In an upstairs room of a house in Stinking Lane, just inside the city wall near Aldersgate, a man lay naked on a feather-filled mattress. He was not a pretty sight to begin with, having an over-rounded belly and pale, pasty limbs, but the fact that he was groaning and dry-retching into an earthenware basin, made him even less attractive to the two women who stood watching him from the doorway.

'He's been like this for the past hour,' reported Lucy, a pretty but over-painted girl of about eighteen years, with brightly dyed red hair reaching down her back. She pressed a long green brocade pelisse tightly about her body, her arms folded across her full bosom.

'Has he not done what he paid for?' demanded the older woman, a raddled former beauty, whose faded blonde hair was tucked beneath a white cover-chief.

Lucy shook her head, her eyes still on the man moaning on the pallet. 'He got as far as taking off his garments, mistress, but then suddenly fell ill.' She sounded as if it was a personal slight on her professional abilities that her client was unable to perform his duty.

'He can't stay here like this!' snapped Margery of

Edmonton, who ruled the bawdyhouse with a rod of iron. 'If he dies on us, we'll have the sheriff's men here, frightening off other patrons, as well as expecting free favours for themselves.'

The more sympathetic Lucy, who over many visits had developed a fondness for her normally amiable customer, leaned over the sufferer and tried to converse with him between bouts of retching.

'Was it something you ate, sir? Have you taken bad meat very lately?'

His eyes rolled upward and managed to focus on the face above him. 'I supped at a good inn with . . .' then his words tailed off as he tried to vomit again, though his stomach had nothing left.

His face took on a ghastly pallor and sweat appeared on his brow as a rigor shook his body. 'An apothecary – get me an apothecary!' he managed to gasp before another bout of retching started.

Lucy looked at her mistress, and then at two other girls, whose curiosity had brought them to peer into the room from the open doorway. 'Can we send for Master Justin? He usually attends us girls when we have troubles,' she asked hopefully.

The madam of the house shook her head firmly. 'I'll not have people parading through the place. If our gentlemen wish to be indisposed, they must do it elsewhere.'

'What are you going to do, then?' asked one of the girls at the door, a strange-looking strumpet with a patently false blonde wig and red dabs of rouge on her cheeks.

'Go and fetch Benedict and Luke. Tell one of them to call a chair in the street. We'll get him taken away.'

Lucy looked unhappy at this, but knew it was unwise and unprofitable to try to argue with the madam. 'Where can he be taken?' she asked.

'He's a cleric, so let him go to St Bartholomew's. They have the best hospital in London, they can surely look after one of their own.'

She waved a hand peremptorily at the other girl in the passage.

'Come and help Lucy get some clothes on the fellow! At least he can be carried decently through the streets. And then call one of the slatterns to clear up this mess.' She pointed at the bilious fluid on the floor alongside the mattress.

With much groaning and piteous wailing from the priest, the two whores managed to force the sufferer's limbs and body back into his hose, undershirt and long cassock. He seemed beyond any sensible speech now, his slack mouth dribbling saliva. The only words Lucy could distinguish as they wrestled his arms into his robe were 'Green! Green and yellow – everything is yellow.'

Now two hulking men arrived on the scene, their usual tasks being to throw out any drunken or over-perverted customers. They lifted the priest bodily from the pallet and with an ease born of long practice, carried him down the stairs to the narrow lane. It was early evening and the streets around Aldersgate were relatively quiet. One of the thugs from the brothel had sent for a litter, a crude device with a wooden chair fixed to two poles, which a pair of porters manhandled for a small fee. Margery of Edmonton had grudgingly paid the two pence demanded, taking them from the purse attached to the canon's belt, having again confirmed from Lucy that he had paid her his fee before falling ill.

She watched with relief as the two porters jogged off along Stinking Lane towards the gate, with the limp form of the sick man precariously slumped in the chair. Walking back into the house, she scowled at the three girls as if it was their fault that they had been landed with a patron who looked as if he was at death's door.

'Make sure that room is cleared up at once,' she snapped. 'And tidy yourselves as well, we're expecting some guildsmen from the Mercers within the hour!'

On Tuesday morning, de Wolfe went at an early hour up to the house in King Street to see if there was any news of Canon Basset. A very worried chaplain and steward informed him that they had heard nothing at all, in spite of having servants scour the whole neighbourhood, including Westminster, Charing and up as far as the Holbourn in a fruitless search for any sign of their master or his horse.

'I fear he has been waylaid by thieves and killed,' wailed Gilbert, the chaplain. 'There is no way in which he would have left us without word like this.'

'Did he often go off without explanation?'

The steward, Martin, shrugged. 'He is the master, he has no need to tell us what he is doing,' he answered. 'But usually he will say when he expects to be home, so that the cook knows when to be ready with his meals. The canon was very fond of his food,' he added sadly.

John, with further admonitions for them to send him a message the moment they heard from Basset, left them to their morbid fears, though privately he thought they may well be right. Unless the Exchequer official had really fled with the stolen treasure, the coroner suspected that he had met with serious trouble somewhere – though whether this was connected with the theft of the gold, he could not guess.

Back in his chamber in the palace, he was pleasantly distracted from the matter of the canon by a message which had been brought by a boatman on a wherry from Queenhithe, a wharf in the city. It was by word-of-mouth, but none the less welcome, for the man was from the crew of the *Mary and Child Jesus*, another of the cogs belonging to the consortium run by Hugh de Relaga and the two appropriately named sleeping partners, John de Wolfe and Hilda of Dawlish. In fact, it was the ship upon which Hilda's husband had been murdered with all his crew the previous year.* The *Mary* had left Topsham, a port on the estuary of the River Exe below Exeter, on the same day that the *St Radegund* had returned from London and the shipmaster had been charged with sending a message to de Wolfe to say that Mistress Hilda had arrived home safely.

Given the hazards of travel, whether by land or sea, John was greatly relieved, though it increased his desire to make a visit to Devon as soon as he could manage to get there. He had not seen his own family for some time, either: his widowed mother, elder brother and sister lived on their main manor at Stoke-in-Teignhead, a few miles south of Dawlish, which was an added incentive to get back to that part of the county.

When the boatman had gone, Thomas de Peyne arrived and in the absence of any inquest rolls to copy, he began the uphill task of teaching his master the rudiments of Latin. De Wolfe seemed to forget more than he ever learned and both were secretly relieved when they were interrupted by a page sent up by the doorward. It was not the usual fresh-faced infant, but a more scrawny, cheeky cock sparrow of a boy.

'There's a man down at the entrance, a fellow from the city,' he said pertly, his head around the door. 'He wanted to come up, but the porter wouldn't let him.'

'Where's he from? And why does he want me?' demanded John, annoyed at the boy's lack of respect. The page shrugged indifferently. 'Search me, sir! Do you want to come down and see him?'

* See *The Elixir of Death*.

The coroner suddenly decided that his lessons were more important. 'Go and see what he wants, Gwyn. If it's an angry husband, tell him I'm gone to Cathay!' he added facetiously, still pleased with the news of Hilda.

Gwyn ambled off, giving the page a playful cuff across the head for his impertinence, while John tried to concentrate on Thomas's recitation of Latin verbs. A few moments later the Cornishman returned.

'You'd better hear what this fellow has to say, straight from the horse's mouth,' he announced, leading in a rough-looking man dressed in the buff tunic and hooded leather jerkin of a city constable. With a surly gesture that John took to be a salute, the man pulled off his woollen cap and began a short recitation that he had obviously committed to memory.

'My master the sheriff says he reminds you of the agreement you all made before the Justiciar, and keeping his part he wishes to tell you that there is a dead man for you in the city.'

He said this as if it were all one long word, not pausing for breath from start to finish. De Wolfe stared up at him from his place at the table.

'Which sheriff are you talking about?' he growled.

'Sir Robert, who deals with corpses in Middlesex as well.'

'You said it was in the city?' cut in Thomas.

The constable scowled at the diminutive clerk. 'Well, Smithfield and St Bartholomew's are but a few paces outside the gates – they might just as well be in the city for all the difference it makes.'

'And why is fitz Durand handing this to me?' asked John. On past experience, the jealousies of the city men would seem to be against spontaneous gestures like this.

'The corpse is that of a holy man – and from what we hear, from Westminster.'

A premonition seized de Wolfe, a not unreasonable one given the circumstances. 'Do you know who he is?'

The sheriff's man shook his head, which seemed to grow straight out of his shoulders, without any neck. 'Not me, Crowner, I'm but a messenger. He is in the care of the hospital at the priory of St Bartholomew, that's all I know. My master says that you can do what you like, he doesn't want to know about it.'

It was soon clear that the man knew nothing more and cared even less, so de Wolfe dismissed him, with a message to take back to Robert fitz Durand. 'Tell him that I am obliged for his courtesy and will attend to the matter straight away,' he said curtly.

After the fellow had gone, John rose to his feet, eager to get some action. 'Is this going to be our missing Exchequer canon?' he asked his two assistants, as he reached for his sword belt hanging on a nearby hook.

'A holy man, that's all he said,' objected Gwyn. 'God knows there are enough of those in these parts!' He prodded Thomas playfully in the ribs, but for once the little clerk ignored his teasing.

'If he's in St Bartholomew's, perhaps he was taken ill with a palsy or a trepidation of the heart,' suggested Thomas.

'Then let's go and find out!' snapped the coroner, buckling on his belt and pulling the diagonal strap of his baldric over his right shoulder. 'Anything is better than sitting around here yawning!'

They rode around the north-western corner of the walls, not needing to enter the city to reach Smithfield, where the great priory of St Bartholomew overlooked the barren heath used for cattle and horse sales, as well as for the butchery of animals and men. Outside the priory was the execution ground for the city, the notorious Smithfield elms being used as gallows, and where burning at the stake was carried out.

'Odd place for the biggest hospital in England,' grumbled Gwyn as they tied their horses to a hitching rail under the watchful eye of a gate porter. 'Why put one outside a cattle market?'

The ever-knowing Thomas was ready with an answer. 'Because seventy years ago, the first King Henry gave the land for it, that's why.'

'Gave it to who? And why?' persisted the Cornishman. De Wolfe was not sure if his officer was thirsting for knowledge or just trying to aggravate his clerk.

'The king gave it to a Frankish monk called Rahere, who some say was previously his court jester,' pontificated Thomas. 'Rahere was an Augustinian who fell sick on pilgrimage to Rome. He swore that if he recovered from his fever, he would build a hospital in London in thankfulness.'

'So why St Bartholomew?' asked de Wolfe, as they walked towards the arched entrance into the large walled enclosure. 'Wasn't he the apostle who was flayed alive?'

Thomas nodded eagerly. 'You are indeed a learned man, master! But the monk Rahere named his hospital and priory after the island in the Tiber on which was the hospital that saved his life in Rome.'

The history lesson over, the coroner loped to the doorkeeper's lodge inside the gates and made himself known to the lay brother inside.

'The sheriff has informed me that a cleric, possibly from Westminster, was brought here and died yesterday.'

John dangled his precious piece of parchment with the impressive seal before the man's eyes. It had the desired effect, though as usual the doorkeeper was unable to read it. 'I need to see the corpse and then question whoever dealt with the poor fellow.'

The lay brother, dressed in a shapeless black habit, hastened to help the imposing visitor.

'I did hear that a priest had died, sir. No doubt his body is in the dead-house behind the hospital. I will have to enquire as to who treated him, for we have eleven monks who care for the sick, as well as four sisters of mercy.'

He rose from his table and yelled at a young boy who was squatting outside the door, scratching marks in the dust with a stick. 'Elfed, take these gentlemen over to the mortuary, then come back here.'

The coroner's trio followed the lad across the huge enclosure, where each August, England's largest cloth fair was held, with a horse fair outside on the heath. They had the impressive pile of the priory to their left, its large church towering over cloisters, dorter, refectory, chapter house and a small chapel. The usual infirmary was missing, however, as the place had been established specifically as a hospital, which lay to their right. Several stone-built wards lay at the southern end of the great yard, together with some storage and accommodation for the nursing nuns, who like the brothers, were of the Augustinian order.

As they walked, they passed or overtook a variety of people, from ones hobbling on crutches, to others being helped by relatives, some moaning and sobbing. A sister in a black habit and flowing cover-chief, tenderly held a small baby, the mother walking ashen-faced alongside. A small cart, pushed by a youth, carried a woman flat on her back, keening in pain, her anxious husband bent over her as they went.

'Cheerful place, this,' grunted Gwyn, looking askance at the plentiful evidence of pain and suffering around them.

'Thank God it exists!' countered Thomas sternly. 'Or

there would be even more distress without the efforts of these Austin monks and nuns. May Christ and all his saints bless them!'

Their barefooted guide took them past the end ward block with its stone-tiled roof and came to a small structure jutting from a low building, which from the smell must have been the reredorter, the latrines of the hospital.

'The dead-house is always in the worst possible place!' grumbled John, but he walked unhesitatingly to the door, leaving the boy to scamper back to the gatehouse. Inside, it was hot and gloomy and pervaded by the lingering smell of the thousands of corpses that had passed through it over the years.

When their eyes became accustomed to the dim light, they saw a row of four wooden biers, stretchers with handles at each end, standing on four legs. Two were empty, the other pair held shrouded bodies.

Gwyn lifted the sheet from the nearest, but replaced it quickly when he saw the face of a woman, grotesquely deformed by a great tumour that grew from the lower jaw. 'It must be the other one,' he muttered and moved to the next bier. The face that was revealed this time was familiar to them all – it was Simon Basset, one-time canon of Lichfield.

De Wolfe moved up to stand alongside his officer, with Thomas hanging well behind, fervently crossing himself and murmuring Latin blessings for the dead.

'Well, we've found our Treasury man,' said John, with melancholy satisfaction. 'Now he'll never be able to tell us anything!'

They looked down at the cadaver, whose face had a serene expression. He was dressed in a hospital shift of coarse wool, his hands crossed peacefully over his chest, with a small crucifix pressed between his fingers.

At a sign from the coroner, Gwyn pulled the sheet

right down to the corpse's feet and they studied the exposed legs, then lifted the shift and examined the belly and chest. With one powerful hand, the Cornishman turned the body on to its side, so that they could look at the back.

'He doesn't seem injured, what we can see of him,' ventured Thomas, peering round Gwyn's bulk. 'What can he have died from?'

A deep voice came from behind to answer him. 'I fear he was poisoned, brother.'

They turned and saw a tall monk standing in the doorway. He wore the black habit and scapula of an Augustinian, though over his front was a white linen apron speckled with a few spots of blood. He signed a cross in the air and Thomas responded with a genuflexion and his inevitable reflex touching of his head, heart and shoulders.

John turned to acknowledge him with a brief bowing of his head. 'I am Sir John de Wolfe, the Coroner of the Verge. I am charged with investigating the disappearance of this man – and now with his death, it seems.'

'And I am Brother Philip, one of those charged with trying to help the sick,' replied the monk, with no trace of sarcasm in mirroring the coroner's words. He had a pale, sad face under a severely cut tonsure which left little but a thin rim of fair hair around his head. 'No doubt you can tell us the identity of this poor man, for he was unable to speak after he arrived and all we know of him is that he was in holy orders, and from the royal insignia on his cassock must have been in the king's service.'

John explained who Simon Basset was and the monk's pale eyebrows rose when he learned that the dead man was a canon of a famous cathedral and a high official of the Exchequer. The coroner did not mention the matter of the missing treasure, but merely said that the priest had gone missing from home several days ago.

'This poisoning, brother. Are you quite sure about that?'

The Augustinian nodded gravely. 'I am in no doubt at all – and I know what the poison must have been, for we frequently use it as a medicament. Several of my brother physicians came to examine the patient and all agreed with me.'

'What was it, brother?' interposed Thomas, whose insatiable curiosity overcame his reluctance to stay in the dead-house.

'A common herbal remedy for dropsy and a failing heart. It was an extract of foxglove, which in small doses slows and strengthens the beating of the heart, but in excess is a potent poison.'

They all looked at the still shape on the bier, free from any sign of injury. 'How could you tell that?' asked Thomas de Peyne.

'The dramatic slowing of the pulse, which became erratic and finally ceased,' answered Brother Philip. 'And the rough fellows who brought him to the hospital, though they knew next to nothing about him, said that before his speech failed, he had been vomiting and rambling about his sight being yellow and green, which is a characteristic of foxglove poisoning.'

'Did the men who delivered him here know anything more?' asked de Wolfe. 'Where were they from?'

The Austin canon shrugged. 'I fear I do not know. I see scores of these unfortunate patients each day, but only in the wards. Unless there is a relative with them, I rarely learn anything about their circumstances. The gatekeepers might be able to give you some more information.'

The coroner considered this for a moment, then

tried another tack. 'Brother, if you are convinced that he died of poison, have you any idea how he may have taken it – or been given it?'

This final distinction was not lost on the monk.

'You mean did he swallow it himself – or was it given to him by some other person?'

When John nodded, Philip shook his head. 'I cannot tell you from a physician's point of view – all I can say is that it must have gone down his throat somehow. But as a man of God, I must surely believe that no priest would have endangered his immortal soul by deliberately swallowing a fatal dose of foxglove in order to kill himself.'

Nodding his head in fervent agreement, Thomas pursued this aspect. 'Could you tell how large a dose was taken and how long before?'

Philip pursed his lips as he considered this. 'Without knowing anything of the circumstances before he came here, it is difficult. Was he well until having his last meal, for instance, which might mean the poison was introduced into his food or drink? It must have been a large dose if the interval was short, for his symptoms were very severe.'

'How is foxglove usually given?' asked John.

'All of the plant is dangerous, the leaves, stems and roots,' explained Philip. 'Chewing those could cause symptoms, but the severity of this case suggests to me that a strong extract was used. A watery infusion is most common, unless dried and powdered plant is used. But a tincture, where an extract in spirits of wine is used, is the most potent.'

'Is this drug easily obtainable?' asked Gwyn, entering the discussion for the first time.

'At the right season, anyone wandering the country lanes could pick a sackful!' replied the monk. 'And the wise women who practise their helpful art in every village will have dried plants hanging in all their cottages. For a strong powder or a tincture, one would probably need to visit an apothecary's shop, but there's no lack of those in London.'

De Wolfe rasped his fingers over the black stubble on his cheeks as an aid to thought. 'I agree that it seems highly unlikely that a rich canon would deliberately do away with himself, so that leaves murder or accident,' he said. 'Could it have been accidental?'

Again the monk shrugged. 'As I said, it only needs a large spoonful of the strong tincture to do fatal damage to the heart. Normally, the tincture is given as a few drops. As long as the foxglove goes down the throat, it is potent – but it seems straining belief to think of any accident that could cause a person to drink it in error.'

The coroner agreed with Philip. 'So that leaves us with murder as the most likely option! Is that feasible? Does foxglove have a foul taste?'

'It is bitter, but only a small volume of the tincture is needed, which could be concealed in food or especially in wine. I have never seen a death from foxglove before, though I have had children who have unwisely chewed foxglove plants and once I saw a woman who had taken too much of her dried powder prescribed for dropsy. These people fell ill, but recovered as the dose was less than a fatal one.'

They talked around the matter for several more minutes, but it became apparent that Brother Philip had no more to tell them and he was anxious to get back to his care of the sick, a marathon task for only eleven monks and four nuns to attempt in the face of the huge population of the nearby city. They left him with thanks and a promise to notify Westminster of the death, so that Simon Basset's earthly remains could be collected for burial.

On the way out to collect their horses, they stopped

at the lodge, where John interrogated the gatekeeper. He was not the man on duty when Simon Basset was admitted, but he was soon found and had a clear recollection of the event.

'We rarely get a priest brought in a chair litter,' he observed. 'Especially from a brothel!'

'A brothel?' barked the coroner. 'How do you know that?'

'The chair men told me that they had picked him up at Margery's whorehouse in Stinking Lane. She gave them two pence to bring him here, to get rid of him, it seems.'

De Wolfe groaned – this bloody mystery was getting more complicated by the minute.

'Did they tell you anything else?' he demanded.

'Only that the fellow was puking all the way and muttering and groaning. He kept saying that his vision had gone green and yellow – they thought he was either drunk or out of his wits.'

There was nothing else to be got from the man, and after taking directions the trio set off for Stinking Lane. They trotted through some squalid lanes to nearby Aldersgate and entered the city through the stone arch in the great walls that had surrounded London since the time of the Roman Empire. Stinking Lane appeared no more foul than the other narrow streets nearby, all of which had piles of rubbish outside the houses and sewage trickling down the central gutter in the unpaved thoroughfare between the motley collection of buildings. John reined in halfway down the lane, looking around for the most likely location for a brothel.

'We're right in the city sheriff's territory now,' grunted Gwyn. 'Is he going to take kindly to us investigating on his patch, after all that damned fuss he made the other day?'

De Wolfe glowered around at the closely packed houses, some of which had upper storeys hanging over the street.

'He took the trouble to send us that messenger telling us of Basset's corpse, so it looks as if he's got no interest in it,' he replied. 'Now which of these bloody ratholes is Margery's stew?'

Thomas walked his small palfrey on a few yards, to where a cripple in rags was squatting against the wall, picking through a heap of discarded vegetables for something still edible. Surreptitiously slipping the beggar a halfpenny that he could ill-afford, the soft-hearted clerk came back with the information that Margery's brothel – not the only one in the lane – was the large house with a red door further down on the left.

Gwyn hammered on the door and a girl opened it. She looked startled at the sight of a huge man with wild red hair and moustache, assuming that he was a customer she might have to satisfy. 'You want a woman, sir? Come in, we are sure to have something to your tastes.'

Then she caught sight of the two men on horses waiting in the street. 'There are three of you? You'd best take your steeds around to the yard at the back.'

Gwyn managed to interrupt her flow of words. Grinning at the good-looking girl, who was about seventeen, he patted her paternally on her dark hair. 'We don't want your favours, lass, we want your mistress. We are law officers, seeking to discover something about a priest who was taken ill here two days ago.'

The mention of the law made the strumpet uneasy. Though it was not her problem, she knew that Margery had paid her usual bribes to the sheriff's constables to leave them in peace, but she had also heard that their regular customer Canon Simon had died in

St Bartholomew's. Opening the door wider, she stood aside.

'You need to speak to Dame Margery, then. And to Lucy, no doubt, for it was she who was with Fat Simon when he was took ill!'

By now, John de Wolfe had dismounted and had advanced to the door, leaving Thomas to guard their horses, knowing that the prim little priest would be most reluctant to enter a house of ill-repute. At the same time, the madam of the establishment had appeared, attracted by the voices.

Before she could open her red-painted mouth, John had boomed some orders.

'Take us somewhere where we can speak!' he commanded. 'I am the king's coroner and need to question you and your drabs.'

Margery of Edmonton had enough experience of both men and officials to know that here was someone who could neither be trifled with, nor bribed with money or sensuous favours. Without a word, she led the way down a short passage to a large room where there were clean rushes on the floor, several couches and chairs and a counter where a hogshead of ale and jars of cider and wine were displayed. With a flounce of her henna-stained hair, she turned to face de Wolfe.

'Where are the sheriff's men, sir? They usually deal with sad accidents such as this.'

'This was no accident, woman. The canon was murdered,' he snapped. The brothel-keeper's powdered face cracked in an expression of outraged disbelief.

'Well, he wasn't murdered here. This is a respectable house!' she added illogically, considering the nature of her business.

She sat down on a chair, but did not invite her unwelcome visitors to join her. The girl from the front door stood protectively behind her and now several other young women, all pretty and dressed in coloured silk gowns, appeared inquisitively at the doorway from the passage. De Wolfe, who in his younger days had more than a nodding acquaintance with whorehouses, recognised that this was a superior type of establishment with prices well above the stews that catered for the lower classes.

'You were aware who the dead man was?' began John, harshly.

'Father Simon, some chaplain in the king's service,' replied the madam defensively. 'We get a number of men of the cloth in here. Supposed to be celibate, I know, but that's their business, not ours.'

'He was a cathedral canon and an official of the Exchequer,' snapped the coroner. 'An important royal officer and I want to know who killed him!'

Margery, now pallid under her make-up, began protesting that he had died of bad food and that his death was nothing to do with her, but John cut across her excuses.

'Did he say where he had been before he came to relieve himself here?' he demanded.

For answer, the woman beckoned to one of the girls in the doorway. 'Lucy, you attended to the priest. Come here and tell the coroner what you know.'

Reluctantly, Lucy sidled into the room and stood before John, her eyes downcast. He thought she was too fresh and attractive to be used by any man who had four pence, though he also knew that many girls eventually found a husband amongst their clients.

'Tell me exactly what happened, Lucy,' asked de Wolfe in a more kindly tone. 'If you have done nothing wrong, you have nothing to fear.'

'He was a nice, kind man,' she said with a sniff. 'I'm sorry he's dead – but I know nothing about it. I tried to help him when he was so sick.'

'He was well enough when he arrived,' mumbled Margery, but Lucy shook her head. 'He was not his normal self even then. I noticed his brow was sweating, but thought he was excited at what was to come. Then we went up to one of the rooms upstairs and as he began taking off his clothing, he started to groan and clutch his stomach.'

'Did he say anything about where he had been?' asked de Wolfe, but Lucy wanted to tell her story at her own pace.

'He slumped down on the pallet and pulled off his hose, then apologised for not feeling well. He said it must have been something he had eaten, though he had dined with a friend at a good inn so it was surprising that there should be anything amiss with the food.'

The coroner seized upon this. 'Did he say who the friend was? Or which inn they had visited?'

To his chagrin, the girl shook her head. 'It was at that very moment that he started to vomit. From then on, his speech made no sense, he was too occupied in throwing up and groaning. I tried to comfort him and clean him up as best I could, but soon had to call the mistress, as he became so distressed.'

In spite of more questioning of Lucy, her mistress and the other whores, de Wolfe failed to extract any other useful information. It seemed clear that following a good meal at a decent hostelry in the company of a friend, Simon Basset had arrived at his favourite brothel for his regular fornication. He was unwell on arrival and rapidly deteriorated, showing all the symptoms of foxglove poisoning, according to Brother Philip. Death had occurred without him becoming rational enough to explain what had happened and once again the coroner was stuck with a mystery.

They left for the ride back to Westminster with an extra horse led on a head-rope behind Gwyn's mare, for the canon's mount had still been tethered in the yard behind the whorehouse. The crafty Margery had failed to mention it, no doubt hoping to sell the beast, until Gwyn had queried how Basset had arrived in Stinking Lane. Reluctantly, she admitted that the horse was still there and John hurried to examine it in case the saddlebag contained some further clue – for a moment he even wondered if some of the lost treasure might be there. In the event, there was nothing, but they decided to return the valuable nag to the house in King Street, when John called to give them the sad news.

During the ride back, Thomas asked what he should do about recording the investigation on his rolls and whether there was to be an inquest.

'This is a case well out of the ordinary,' mused John. 'I'll do nothing until I confer with Hubert Walter. With someone who was both a canon and a senior Treasury official, found poisoned in a brothel, I have to tread carefully, especially as he may well be involved in the theft of the king's treasure from the Tower.'

The more he thought about it, the more delicate the situation appeared. Though he himself was presently in good grace with the Justiciar and even the king, neither were men to be trifled with or offended – and there were many other powerful men, especially on the Curia, who would be happy to use de Wolfe as a scapegoat if some great scandal erupted.

Apart from that, John had no appetite for exposing the sexual inclinations of a pleasant priest through a public inquest. Though he was a stickler for applying the king's will, there were issues such as the relative immunity of those in holy orders from the secular law, which gave them 'benefit of clergy'. Especially since old King Henry's conscience-stricken surrender to Canterbury over this issue, following the murder of

Thomas Becket, one had to tread softly where priests were concerned and John was not going to put his head in a noose by doing the wrong thing.

His silent cogitations lasted for most of the journey and both Thomas and Gwyn had learned not to disturb their master when he was in this contemplative mood. At the house in King Street, one of the grooms saw them coming and recognised the canon's horse being led home riderless and drew the correct conclusions. He rushed into the house and by the time de Wolfe dismounted, Martin the steward and Chaplain Gilbert had come out to meet him, their faces full of anguished foreboding.

The coroner solemnly confirmed their fears, and taking the chaplain aside explained the circumstances of the canon's death. 'It is up to you how much you tell the rest of the household, but I would advise you holding back some of the details, at least until I have discussed it with the archbishop.'

Gilbert was a sensible man and through his grief – for it seemed that Simon had been a popular and caring master – he promised to be discreet about revealing the whole truth. He also promised to set in motion the process of retrieving the corpse from St Bartholomew's and arranging a funeral, dependent on the coroner's decision about an inquest. He would also send a messenger to Lichfield to inform the cathedral and any surviving family of the death.

Promising to keep him informed, de Wolfe left the house to the stunned residents, who were no doubt wondering when they would be thrown out into the street following the collapse of their comfortable little world.

CHAPTER TEN

In which a lady calls upon Crowner John

In the late afternoon, de Wolfe made enquiries at the Justiciar's chambers and was told that Hubert Walter was expected back that evening and would be available for audience next morning.

John had to make do with informing the most senior official he could find in the Exchequer building and he also told the Keeper of the Palace that Simon Basset was dead. He trimmed the truth by saying that the canon had been taken ill in the city and had died at St Bartholomew's Hospital, where the body was still lying.

Though the Keeper did not seem particularly interested, being swamped with work in anticipation of Queen Eleanor's visit, the news caused some consternation in the Exchequer. Apart from personal sadness at his death, Simon Basset was an important functionary and his loss appeared to cause problems in their administrative routines. John also had the impression that Simon's connection with the lost treasure made some of the other officials uneasy.

That evening, de Wolfe decided not to go to the Lesser Hall for supper, as he knew he would be besieged by questions about the death of Simon Basset. The Westminster grapevine would have easily picked up the news from the Exchequer and he knew that Bernard de Montfort and the Lord of Blois and his wife would pester him for details. He would have liked to talk over the matter with Ranulf and William Aubrey, but that could wait until the morning – meanwhile, he would settle for Gwyn's company and some of Osanna's cooking in Long Ditch Lane.

The fat Saxon did them well in providing a meal at short notice, for after a mutton broth she produced a pair of grilled trout each, stuffed with almonds. With young carrots and early peas, it was a good meal and the mazer of fresh barley and wheat bread with a new cheese that followed was washed down with ale by the contented coroner and his officer.

They discussed the events of the day until it was apparent that they could not squeeze another ounce of significance from them. Eventually, after another full quart of ale, Gwyn fell asleep at the table and to avoid his gargantuan snores John climbed up to the room above and threw himself down on his mattress to think about Hilda.

Later, as the red evening sun declined to the western horizon, Gwyn woke and called up the steps from below.

'I'm off to a game of dice in the palace barracks!' he announced. 'I'll be late home, no doubt. In fact, I may not be back at all!'

After he had left, John wondered whether he had found a woman somewhere, though he knew that some of these gambling sessions went on until the early hours of the morning. Games of chance held no attraction for de Wolfe, but it takes all sorts, he thought philosophically. After all, Ranulf and William Aubrey were very keen on gaming and Gwyn had told him that the younger knights and esquires in the palace guard played for large stakes in their quarters.

John dozed on fitfully for a while, his mind slipping in and out of slumber, wrestling with the problems of three unsolved deaths which seemed to have no obvious connection. He suddenly became aware of voices below and heard Osanna speaking to someone in the main room. Then her voice called up through the stair opening.

'Sir John, there is someone to see you!' Even at that distance, he could sense the disapproval in his landlady's voice. Reluctantly, he hauled himself up from the pallet, thrust his feet into his soft house shoes and went to the ladder, raking his dishevelled hair back with his fingers. As he descended, expecting to see some messenger from the palace, he was astonished to find Hawise d'Ayncourt standing in the centre of the room, her silent maid lurking near the door. Osanna had planted herself near the bottom of the steps, in an almost protective stance, looking dubiously at the elegant woman who had invaded her house.

'Lady d'Ayncourt, this is a surprise!' growled de Wolfe, emphasising her title to reassure Osanna that this was no local strumpet, though this should have been obvious from her bearing and rich clothing. Hawise had ventured out in the warm evening in a long gown of pale-green silk, tied with a gold cord twisted several times around her waist, the tasselled ends hanging to her knees. Over this she wore a dark-green velvet surcoat with trailing cuffs that reached almost to the ground. A necklace of pearls encircled her slim neck and a snowy linen cover-chief was held in place by a gold band around her forehead.

'My maid and I were taking a walk on this fine evening,' she explained in her husky voice. 'We found

212

ourselves in this neighbourhood and I thought I would call to satisfy my curiosity as to where you lived.'

This was a transparently false excuse, as no one in their right mind would want to come up the dismal deadend that was Long Ditch Lane. Surely the woman had not sought him out just to quiz him about the death of the Treasury canon? The alternative explanation was much more dangerous, though potentially exciting and titillating. Whatever the reason, he had common courtesies to perform.

'Please be seated, lady. You must take a cup of wine after your long walk,' he said, unwittingly sarcastic. Motioning to Osanna to put a stool in the doorway for the maid, he pulled forward the one good chair and Hawise lowered herself gracefully upon it.

'Osanna, can you find some pastries in your cook-shed?' he asked, but Hawise waved the offer away.

'Thank you, but I have not long supped in the Lesser Hall. In fact, it was because you were absent that I sought you out.'

John busied himself at the side table with cups and a skin of red wine, thankful that he and Gwyn had not drunk it all with their meal, though they usually quenched most of their thirst with ale or cider. He was not sure whether the new protocol of courtly behaviour which was now all the rage, after being encouraged by Queen Eleanor, extended to offering wine to the maid. As he handed a pewter cup to her mistress, he raised his bushy eyebrows in her direction. Hawise d'Ayncourt shook her head firmly.

'I have just realised that the evening is cooling quickly,' she said. 'I need my red brocade cape from my chamber.' Turning her head, she gave rapid instructions to her maid to return to the palace and fetch it back to Long Ditch. Silently and rather sullenly, the girl rose and vanished without a word, closing the door behind her to leave Osanna scowling at what was an obvious ploy to get rid of the chaperone.

John was also of the same opinion, but he was not going to let his landlady stand there while he talked to a guest, however uninvited she may be. He dismissed her as gently as he could and the Saxon wife shuffled out with an ill grace.

'John, don't stand hovering there like a bottler,' commanded Hawise. 'Come and sit near me.' She patted a bench that stood alongside her chair. As he lowered himself not too reluctantly, he caught the scent of her flowery perfume and came close to her full lips and glowing eyes, framed by exquisitely long lashes. He rocked back out of temptation's way, sudden images of the Lord of Blois and of Hilda of Dawlish flashing through his mind.

'Would your husband not accompany you on your walk?' he rumbled. 'The streets are not always safe places for ladies on their own.'

She laughed, a low throaty sound with seductive undertones.

'Westminster is more secure than most towns!' she countered, conveniently ignoring the fact that there had been several murders recently. 'And in the daylight, the risk is surely small.'

'But your husband?' he persisted.

'Oh, he is away, visiting some friend's estate in Surrey,' Hawise said dismissively. 'He will be away all night.'

She managed to imbue these last words with heavy invitation.

John felt the hair on his neck prickle with excitement and he raised his wine cup to cover the flushing that spread across his face. He was no stranger to seduction and over several decades had had more women than there were weeks in a year. Yet none, not even the fair

Hilda, were as exotic as this raven-haired beauty – and certainly none had exuded such blatant sexuality and availability as Hawise d'Ayncourt.

She put down her cup and placed a slim hand on his knee.

'Tell me what you have been doing lately, John. We have missed you at our pleasant suppers in the palace.'

Was she angling for information, he wondered? Would her husband burst in just as she had managed to get his breeches off and blackmail him into revealing state secrets? Yet that was a ridiculous notion, he knew nothing of any use to a foreign agent.

As the whole of Westminster would be buzzing with the news of Basset's death by tomorrow, he decided there was no reason to withhold it from Hawise, as long as he offered no details of the circumstances. He told her briefly of the event, but she did not seem very interested, except to comment that surely he was the official who had received the missing treasure into the Tower, a fact that was common knowledge. Her attitude helped to reassure him that she was there to pillage his body, rather than his mind.

'You are a famous knight, John,' she breathed. 'Tell me of some of your adventures. My husband, dear as he is to me, is a rather dull man, he spends his life in his counting house and patrolling his estates. I never hear tales of murder and battle from him.'

She held her cup for more wine and took the opportunity to pull her chair nearer to his bench until her silk-clad legs were touching his. 'And you were part of King Richard's bodyguard when he came back from the Holy Land. Tell me of that and how you tried to save him from capture in Austria!'

It was not an episode of which he was proud, as he had failed his king in Vienna, but he was flattered by having an attractive woman hanging on to his every word. Part of his mind told him that he was a silly old fool and was heading for trouble, but the humours that fuelled his masculinity overrode his common sense. Hawise next wanted to know about his exploits on many battlefields, from Ireland to Normandy and from Sicily to Palestine. Her eyes glistened at his descriptions of mayhem and carnage and when she pressed him to tell her of his work as a coroner in Devon, her pink tongue flickered over her moistened lips as he described morbid scenes of hangings, cut-throats and beheadings.

Perversely, given that he knew it was unwise to encourage her, he could not resist feeding her obvious bloodthirsty fascination with violence. Her face coloured slightly and her prominent bosom rose and fell as her breathing hastened, when he told her of his discovery of a manor-lord crucified in his own forest and his head impaled on the rood screen of Exeter Cathedral.*

Suddenly, as John rose to refill their wine-cups, Hawise jumped from her chair and pulled off her cover-chief, releasing a cascade of glossy black hair. She moved towards him and threw her arms around his neck, pressing herself against him.

'Oh God, you are a real man, John!' she gasped, almost with a groan. Although her head reached only to his chin, she stretched upwards and avidly pressed her hot mouth upon his, her tongue snaking between his lips. Surprised, but far from reluctant, de Wolfe abandoned any thoughts of restraint, as desire engulfed him. Images of Renaud de Seigneur and even Hilda of Dawlish vanished in a haze of lust. His own arms came up of their own accord and a wine cup fell uncaringly to the floor as he encircled her shoulders and waist and pulled her hard against him. They

* See *The Elixir of Death*.

returned each other's kisses as if each was trying to devour the other and he thrilled as he felt her firm breasts pressing into his chest.

'For pity's sake, John,' she whimpered. 'Take me to your bed!'

With a growl of anticipation, his one hand slid down the waterfall of shining hair, while the other crushed her firm buttocks tightly against him. Hawise kissed him again, her serpentine tongue flickering, then she pulled away and began tugging him towards the steps to the upper floor.

Then the deliciously wanton moment was shattered by a knock on the street door! A very unladylike oath spat from Hawise's pouting lips and she shrieked a command towards where she assumed her maid was waiting. 'Adele, go away, damn you! Come back in an hour!'

But she was confounded from another direction, as the inner door opened and Osanna waddled in. 'I heard a knock, sir,' she declared, but her response had been so quick that John was sure that her ear, and perhaps an eye, had been pressed against the ill-fitting boards of the inner door.

De Wolfe was inclined to roar at her to clear off, but the intensity of their passion had been spoiled and, flushed in the face, the two would-be lovers pulled apart. Hawise grabbed for her veil, which had fallen on the table and hurriedly pulled it over her head and settled the gilded band in place. Ignoring the scowls of the landlady, she stalked to the door and jerked it open.

Adele was standing on the step, uncertain whether to obey her mistress's command to vanish for an hour. Her doubts were solved when Hawise snatched the short cloak from her arm and threw it around her shoulders. 'Come, girl! We are going home.'

Her poise had returned rapidly, and as she left she turned to de Wolfe, who had followed them into the lane.

'Thank you for your hospitality, Sir John, but I think we have unfinished business!'

The Chief Justiciar of England listened gravely to the coroner's account of the events of the past few days. He had been away in Canterbury, trying to soothe the complaints of his own clergy, who were not overfond of their bishop, for they felt he was far more concerned with affairs of state than with the welfare of his diocese.

'So do you think that the murder of Simon Basset is connected with the theft from the Tower?' he asked, when John had laid all the facts before him.

'I hesitate to dismiss the possibility,' replied the coroner. 'The canon has lived and worked here for years with no problems or stains on his reputation. Then within a few days he becomes a suspect in the crime, as he is one of the only two key-holders – and then he is fatally poisoned! The coincidence is surely too great to be ignored.'

Hubert Walter sat silently for a moment, staring out through a window at the river flowing past Westminster. They sat in his first-floor chamber adjacent to the royal apartments, with the murmur of clerks percolating through the door from the next room.

'Matters are weighing ever more heavily upon me, John,' he sighed. 'The king makes increasing demands for money for his army, which becomes harder and harder to squeeze from resentful barons and merchants. This plays into the hands of the prince, who sees it as justification for his ambition to unseat Richard.'

Walter's fingers played with the small cross hanging around his neck.

'Then I have the old queen descending upon us soon, though I am partly thankful for that, as there is no doubt that she is a powerful restraining influence upon her wayward son.'

'Do you wish me to accompany the court on this journey – or remain here to continue investigating these crimes?'

Hubert shook his greying head. 'Come with us, I am sure that whoever is behind these acts is part of the court in some capacity or other. I cannot see that your staying behind can accomplish anything.'

De Wolfe was relieved by his answer, as he did not relish being marooned in an almost empty palace – and the perambulation towards the West Country held the possibility of including a quick visit to Exeter. Also, a small roguish voice in his head whispered that Hawise d'Ayncourt would be going with them.

This led his thoughts to another topic and he broached it to Hubert.

'Your Grace, I hear various rumours about spies seeking secret intelligence from the court. It may well be overimaginative gossip, though that stabbing of the young worker from the guest chambers produced an allegation that he was concerned about something of that nature.'

John explained the fears Basil had, as related by the young novice from the abbey. 'He claimed that he had overheard some seditious conversation, whatever that might have meant. It might have been something trivial or just an exaggeration by a fertile imagination. But the fact remains that he was stabbed to death a day later for no obvious reason.'

This was the first that Hubert Walter had heard of this and he took it seriously. 'We are always beset by spies, John. Every embassy that visits us has some agent attached to them whose prime purpose is to gain intelligence to take home – and to be truthful, so do we when we send deputations abroad.'

'But is there anything they can learn from just residing in the palace for a while?' said de Wolfe doubtfully.

'There is always some chance of picking up useful snippets. There are servants to be bribed and I fear that even some members of the Curia or their clerks and esquires can become loquacious after indulging in too much wine.'

'But what is there to learn?' persisted John. 'In matters of warfare, surely all the action is across the Channel, not in Westminster.'

Hubert Walter rose and paced restlessly to the window and back again. 'Not everything concerns battle, John. Our treaties and agreements with other countries are of great concern to Philip Augustus, as are matters of trade. How much silver and tin we produce relates to Richard's ability to wage war – and the current mood of potentially rebellious barons reflects on what support the French might expect if the Count of Mortain comes out of his present suspiciously good behaviour to again foster revolt.'

He sat down again and laced his fingers together over his parchment-cluttered table.

'As I said, I am glad that Eleanor is coming to add her strictures to her younger son's ambitions. You ask what secrets might be sought? Well, she has advised me privately that Philip and his son Louis favour an attack upon the south coast of England, perhaps to coincide with any move that Prince John might make to seize power. Philip still controls a stretch of coastline below Boulogne which could be a jumping-off point for an invasion, so we are making defensive plans for Kent and Sussex that would certainly be of interest to any French spy.'

He leaned forward in a confidential manner. 'In fact, that was one reason why I went to Canterbury during these past few days, spending time with various barons and commanders, to the annoyance of my brothers in the cathedral!'

Then leaning back again he abruptly changed the subject, as if he had been too indiscreet. 'Now, John, what are we going to do about this damned treasure? Is there any hope of getting it back, for I do not relish the king's temper when he discovers its loss. He covets every half-penny that could go towards financing his campaigns.'

The coroner's long face darkened into a scowl. 'At present, it defeats me, sire! But it is a point of honour for me to retrieve it somehow, for it was in my care almost up to the point when it vanished.' He angrily rasped his fingers across his bristles.

'Simon Basset is dead and he is inevitably a suspect in the theft. He cannot now be questioned or even tortured – not that the Church would allow it – so the whereabouts of the gold cannot be extracted from him. His house needs to be searched as a matter of urgency to see if there is any sign of it there – though again I am not sure if there would be some ecclesiastical prohibition on that?'

'Don't concern yourself about that, John,' said Hubert grimly. 'I know that Abbot Postard considers himself the Emperor of Westminster, but theft of the king's gold is treason and no one in England can be exempt from investigation.'

Relieved at having the Justiciar's support, John was still dubious of success. 'I doubt the treasure will be there, but there may be some clue as to his involvement, if he was guilty. But what about the Constable of the Tower, sire?'

Hubert turned up his hands in a gesture of despair.

'I really cannot see old Herbert de Mandeville as a thief, John! He has been there for many years and could have stolen before, if that was his inclination. But neither does Canon Basset fit the image of a master criminal – yet it looks as if one of them is the culprit.

'So take whatever measures you think fit to get to the bottom of this – use the king's name and warrant freely.'

The archbishop stood to indicate that the meeting was over.

'Do your best, John, I am depending upon you. We live in treacherous times and there are few such as you that the king can trust. You have proved your worth in the past and God knows that we need you again now!'

He remembered his episcopal status sufficiently to give de Wolfe a brief benediction as he left, then yelled for a clerk to come and set about the documents on his table.

With Hubert Walter's accolade and exhortation ringing in his ears, de Wolfe strode back to his chamber that Tuesday morning, determined to make progress in this apparently insoluble mystery, even if it cost him his reputation or his life.

It even drove from his mind most of the recollection of the previous evening's seductive fiasco with Hawise d'Ayncourt. He had been both relieved and frustrated, as his common sense told him that cuckolding a foreign nobleman was unwise, to put it mildly – especially as Renaud de Seigneur was living on the spot. Yet the allure of Hawise was so great that his lust was in danger of defeating his usual wisdom. Though a dour, rational man in all other respects, attractive women were John's Achilles' heel and had got him into trouble several times.

However, he now had urgent matters to distract him

and as he burst into his chamber, he almost shouted at Gwyn and Thomas to get moving. 'No need for horses, we're only going up the street! I want to turn the canon's house inside out to look for that bloody gold!'

Gwyn hurriedly swallowed the last of his ale, washing down the last mouthful of his morning bread and cheese. 'Do you want me for such a task?' asked his clerk timidly, hoping to avoid being party to such desecration of a fellow priest's domicile.

'Yes, come along and bring your bag of writing contraptions,' commanded his master. 'If we find anything, it will need to be recorded – and you are always useful where priests and chaplains are involved.'

Reluctantly, Thomas followed the two bigger men as they left the palace and went across to the gate into King Street. A few hundred yards brought them to the canon's dwelling and with a rare touch of sensitivity, de Wolfe sent his clerk in ahead to announce diplomatically that they were there to search the premises. After a couple of moments, he followed with Gwyn and was faced with the doleful faces of the chaplain and steward, who were subdued but obviously indignant at this intrusion.

'My clerk has explained that there are important issues at stake and that it is imperative that we look amongst the canon's belongings to check on certain matters,' said John, his discomfiture making him sound a little pompous.

Martin, dressed in a black tunic as a mark of mourning, nodded his understanding. 'We cannot prevent you, coroner, we were merely servants of our late master and have no status now.'

'And though nothing has been said openly,' added the chaplain, 'we know full well that this must be connected to the loss of that treasure, which is now common knowledge.'

'You'll find nothing here, sir, our master was a fine and honest man,' added the steward defiantly.

De Wolfe applauded their loyalty, but was firm in his resolve.

'That's as may be, but there might be some clue here as to what happened and I am charged specifically, in the name of our king, to leave no stone unturned in seeking the truth.'

The steward sighed, but moved back and with a gesture indicated that the house was theirs. 'I will tell the servants to give you every assistance in showing you whatever you wish to see,' he said.

John began in the chamber which Simon used as a sitting room and an office, for there was a table with numerous parchments and a sideboard carrying half a dozen books. He called Thomas in to look through all the written material, while Gwyn searched the servants' quarters, the stables and various outhouses such as the brew-shed, the laundry and the kitchen. The Cornishman poked into the privy and the pigsty, even putting his head inside the fowl-house to make sure there were no gold candlesticks hidden in the nestboxes.

John found nothing at all in the effects of the late canon, though he was again impressed by the quality and indeed opulence of most of the furniture and fittings in the house. All the floors downstairs were paved, rather than having rush-strewn earth, as was usual. The walls had costly hangings and in the bed-room upstairs there was actually glass in one of the smaller windows, an almost unheard-of luxury.

But of treasure there was no sign, apart from Simon Basset's own possessions. The documents that Thomas scanned revealed nothing suspicious – they were either detailed household accounts or letters on ecclesiastical topics from other priests, especially in Lichfield. Some of the parchments related to his duties in the Exchequer, but there was nothing to arouse the slightest suspicion of involvement in an audacious robbery.

After a last half-hearted scanning of the backyard and paths surrounding the house to see if there was any disturbed soil that might indicate something having been buried, de Wolfe admitted defeat. He made his peace with the chaplain and steward before leaving.

'There will probably be an inquest in the next day or so,' he announced. 'I will require your presence for the formalities.'

'His poor body was brought back from St Bartholomew's last evening,' said Gilbert, crossing himself, which of course set off Thomas in copying his actions. 'He now lies before a side altar in the abbey until he can be buried. In this weather, it is not practicable to take him home to Lichfield, but we have sent word by courier and in the fullness of time maybe his family or the Chapter there may wish to have his coffin translated there.'

There was nothing more to be done and the coroner's trio began walking back to the palace. Suddenly, Thomas de Peyne stopped so suddenly that Gwyn, walking behind him, stumbled against the little clerk.

'Surely there is something odd, Crowner?' said Thomas, looking quizzically at de Wolfe.

'Yes, you are bloody odd, stopping in my path like that!' complained Gwyn, but John silenced him with a gesture. He had learned long ago that any thoughts of his clerk were usually worth listening to. 'What is it?' he asked.

'We found no keys in the house. The canon still had his normal duties with the Exchequer, so where are his precious keys, including those for any chests still in the Tower?'

There was a silence while the others digested this.

'Important keys such as those should have been on his person for safe keeping,' said John. 'Just as I did when we travelled from Winchester – they never left my pouch, thank St Michael and all his archangels!'

'So where are Basset's keys?' grunted Gwyn.

John punched a fist into his other hand. 'Damn! He was dressed in a hospital gown when we saw his body. I never thought to ask for his clothing. We must get back there at once and enquire. Let's hope they've not been destroyed or given away to the poor.'

The astute brain of their clerk saw a flaw in this. 'They would hardly give a priest's cassock away nor send him back to the abbey dressed in an infirmary shroud. I'm sure the Austin canons would have more respect for one of their own and include his personal belongings when they dispatched the corpse back to Westminster.'

Gwyn slapped his diminutive friend on the back. 'Clever little sod, aren't you! Are we to try at the abbey, Crowner?'

De Wolfe had no doubt that they should and in a few minutes they were in the lofty nave of Edward the Confessor's great church. They found Simon Basset on a bier before a shrine in the north transept, still with the contented expression on his round face, confounding the common misapprehension that those who died an unnatural death had contorted features.

Tall candles burned at his head and feet and a fellow Benedictine knelt in prayer on a prie-dieu nearby.

Thomas gently interrupted him to ask where they might enquire about the canon's personal belongings and the monk directed them to a deacon who sat in an alcove near the west door. He in turn took them into the wide cloisters south of the church where a side room contained all manner of odds and ends, including broken furniture, processional banners and incense censers. The old man opened a battered chest and lifted out a cloth tied in a knot at the top. It had a scrap of parchment attached which Thomas checked, confirming that it belonged to Simon Basset.

'We are waiting to hear from his chaplain as to whether it needs to be sent to Lichfield,' explained the deacon, handing it over. John untied the knot and spread the contents on to the lid of the chest. A belt, a rosary and several kerchiefs were of no interest, but there was a bulky scrip, a leather pouch attached to the belt. John undid the small strap and buckle and tipped out the contents. There were about twenty silver pennies, a medal of St Christopher and two bunches of keys. One of these immediately caught the coroner's attention, being several large keys on an iron loop.

'Two of these have got those spots of coloured paint we saw before,' he said. 'The codes for the locks on the treasure chests.'

'Well, they would, wouldn't they,' said Gwyn gruffly. 'He's one of the key-holders, he should have them.'

'But he shouldn't have two, he should only have one,' squeaked Thomas excitedly.

'Possibly, but we can't be sure that these keys relate to the chest from which the objects were stolen.'

De Wolfe gnawed his lip in indecision. 'I need to make sure! This could either confirm or exonerate Simon Basset as the culprit. We owe it to his memory to clear any suspicion, if he is innocent.'

The other bunch was an assortment without spots and some may have been his house keys. However, John took them along with the two larger ones and left the abbey. It was now approaching noon and surrendering to the rumblings of Gwyn's stomach, he reluctantly delayed their journey to the city so that they could all eat their dinner at Long Ditch. After swallowing

Osanna's potage of vegetables and shreds of some unidentifiable meat, followed by boiled pork knuckles, they collected their horses from the marshal's stables and rode to London.

At the Great Tower, the production of his royal warrant, with the impressive seal of the Chief Justiciar dangling from it, immediately gained them admission and they were conducted at once to the Constable's chamber. Once again, Herbert de Mandeville was not pleased to see them, as a visit from the dark, gaunt Coroner of the Verge was a reminder of the failure of his responsibility as guardian of the Tower. In addition, there was the lingering suspicion of his own involvement, as one of the two key-holders.

After an abrupt greeting, John went straight to the heart of the matter. 'Have you heard yet of the death of Simon Basset?'

De Mandeville nodded. 'Only that he had some kind of seizure and died in St Bartholomew's. I suppose he was too fat and well fed for his own health.'

The coroner saw no reason not to tell the Constable the truth, though he left out the part about the brothel, as it seemed an unnecessary darkening of the canon's memory.

'He was murdered – poisoned with foxglove.' John watched Herbert keenly, to see how he took this news. The Constable's brows came together in surprise, but he seemed not too dismayed by the canon's death. 'And is this connected in any way with the theft of that treasure?' he asked evenly, giving away nothing in his manner.

The coroner reached into his scrip and produced the two large keys with the painted spots.

'This is why I am here, de Mandeville. I need to know if these keys found on Basset's person fit the locks on that damned chest.'

The older man took the keys from him and examined them.

'They carry coloured marks, like those on that box – but that is not unique, it is often done for other chests.'

'I want you to check these, either on the locks themselves or by comparing the shapes of the wards with those you keep in that secure cupboard there.' He pointed to the large flat cabinet on the wall of the chamber.

Herbert de Mandeville glared at the coroner almost triumphantly. 'Can't be done!' he declared complacently. 'The strongroom below is completely empty, for once. That chest, with what remained of its contents, was yesterday dispatched with the other boxes by ship to Normandy. It was needed to carry some additional coinage that had been in the care of the Templars – and, naturally, its keys went with it, in the care of another Treasury official.'

John glowered at the news. Now how in hell am I ever going to resolve this? he asked himself. Short of going to Rouen, there was now no way of knowing if Simon had been up to no good.

Once again, Thomas's nimble brain came to the rescue. 'Sir Herbert, when such chests arrive or depart from your keeping, are the two keys to each box always kept together on one ring?'

The other three men stared at the clerk, unsure of his reasoning.

'Of course! It would cause great confusion if they were jumbled together,' replied the puzzled Constable. 'Sometimes, after the sheriffs have delivered their county farms twice a year, I may get a dozen chests or more brought here.'

'Then what happens?' persisted the little priest.

Herbert stared at Thomas in perplexity. 'Well, after the contents are checked I separate the pair of keys.

Simon or whoever it might be, takes one and I lock up the other in that cupboard.'

'So afterwards neither you nor the Exchequer official has any reason to have two keys paired on a ring?' asked Thomas.

His reasoning was now apparent to the others, but Gwyn had an objection.

'The pair of keys might be nothing to do with the same chest. He dealt with many such boxes – maybe he just put them together for convenience.'

De Mandeville held out his hand. 'Let me see those keys for a moment.' He turned them over in his hands and peered at them short-sightedly. 'They certainly look the same size and type as the locks used on those boxes. The locks are supplied by the Treasury and I think they are all made by the same locksmith.'

He handed them back to the coroner. 'But of course, without the actual locks from that treasure chest, I cannot say if they were the keys for it.'

De Wolfe dropped them back into his scrip. 'But if the chest has now gone to Rouen, its keys have gone with it, so these cannot be the originals! Presumably you gave your key to the Treasury man who took them, but what about the other key?'

'Simon Basset handed his over as usual,' confirmed the Constable. 'He came here last week before the boxes were removed under guard to be taken down to Queenhithe to a king's ship.'

It seemed an impasse, but John had one last avenue of enquiry.

'You said the locks probably all came from the same locksmith. Do you know who he was?'

De Mandeville looked disdainfully at the coroner. 'I don't concern myself with such minor matters. But the Treasury keep a few clerks in an office downstairs, who keep records of all the comings and goings of their property. Maybe they might be able to tell you something.'

They left de Mandeville relieved at their departure and a page took them down to a gloomy archway built into the massive walls of a lower floor. Here an old man in minor orders sat with a shaven-headed youth at a couple of tables covered with parchment lists. The senior clerk scratched his scalp with a quill pen, ruining the tip until he recalled who he paid for the last batch of locks, several years earlier.

'It's Peter of Farringdon; he has a workshop on the north side of Eastcheap. We use him as he has great discretion, as it would hardly do if he divulged the secrets of the king's treasure chests. Also, he has been told that if he did, he would be burned at the stake at Smithfield!'

As they rode through the bustling city, John felt that the ramifications of this investigation were becoming too tortuous to bear. The locksmith was the last throw in this gamble to decide whether Simon Basset was or was not a villain. They found him in a small shop on the main east–west thoroughfare of the city. The shutter of the front window hinged down to form a display counter on the street, covered with metal goods such as candlesticks, sconces, hinges, locks and kitchen appliances such as trivets and spigots. These were guarded by two apprentices working at benches in the front room, who took him through to a forge at the back, where a beefy man of middle age was stripped to the waist in the torrid heat of a furnace. A small boy pumped the furnace. The man was bald, but had red whiskers to rival Gwyn's and arm muscles that were even bigger than the Cornishman's.

He was about to pull an iron bar from the white-hot coals with a pair of long tongs, but when he saw the calibre of his visitors, he thrust it back and came to meet them. John explained the problem and produced the pair of keys, whereupon Peter took them out into the open backyard, where the light was better.

'I didn't make these!' he said, within seconds of turning the keys over in his hand. 'And they are less than a few months old, maybe only weeks. I've not had an order for this sort of lock for a year or more.'

'How can you tell they're not yours?' asked John, his hopes rising once more.

'Look here, see the shanks?' he said, pointing with a finger like a pork sausage. 'They are straight, from the top right down to the wards. I always braze a ring around the lower part of the shank, to hold the wards more easily in the correct position to turn the tumblers.'

'You said they were recent?'

'Very little rust on them, the steel is still shiny. These have not gone through a wet winter like we've had this last year.'

De Wolfe nodded his understanding. 'So given that you definitely didn't make these, could they be used for opening the type of lock you supply to the Treasury?'

The smith looked closely again at the business ends of the two keys. 'All locks are generally similar, so I can't be sure. But the Exchequer was insistent upon the most secure ones they could get, so I made complicated wards and gates in the locks – and these are of that type.' He handed them back to the coroner with a gesture of finality.

'I can't swear that they must be for those locks, as other smiths are just as competent, but there's no reason why they couldn't be for the ones I supplied.'

There was no more to be gained from Peter of Farringdon and they rode off through Ludgate and back to Westminster. In their austere chamber, the heat was so intense that de Wolfe pulled off his knee-length grey tunic and sat behind the table in his linen undershirt and long black hose, which were supported by laces tied to a string belt around his waist. The fact that his nether regions were totally exposed did not in the least disconcert him, as the table shielded him from any casual visitor.

Gwyn sat in usual place on the window ledge, trying to catch any breeze from the river and Thomas, who seemed immune from overheating, sat at the end of the table, writing an account of the day's happenings for the record.

With jugs of cloudy cider before them, John went over the salient facts that they had discovered.

'The canon was murdered, there seems little doubt of that.'

'Are you quite sure it wasn't an accident or felo de se?' asked Gwyn.

'A senior member of the clergy like a canon wouldn't commit suicide,' retorted Thomas indignantly. 'Why should he jeopardize his immortal soul?'

'What about almost dying in a brothel?' objected Gwyn.

'That's not a mortal sin,' snapped the clerk impatiently. 'And as for an accident, how can anyone inadvertently swallow enough to be fatal? He wasn't out in the countryside, chewing a score of foxglove plants!'

De Wolfe held up a hand to stop the bickering. 'That raises the question, where was he before he went to the brothel? The girl said that he told her he had had a good meal in a decent inn, or words to that effect. That's where he must have been given the tincture of foxglove, given the timing, according to Brother Philip.'

'He also mentioned to her something about dining

with a friend,' added Thomas. 'Given the circumstances, that friend must have been the killer.'

'With him dead, we haven't a hope in hell of knowing who it was,' said John gloomily.

'Could we discover in which tavern it was he ate his last meal?' hazarded Thomas. 'Then we might find what friend accompanied him.'

'There must be a score of inns within a half-mile of Stinking Lane,' scoffed Gwyn. 'What chance have any of them recalling their customers from last week?'

'The canon seemed a fastidious man, rich and fond of his belly,' observed the clerk. 'He would surely go only to the best eating house – that might narrow the search a little.'

De Wolfe was doubtful. 'Perhaps so, but is that within our capabilities? In a week or so, we'll be gone away with the court.'

'What about the sheriff and his men? They would know all the good inns in that part of London. Could they not search for us?'

John made a derisory noise in his throat. 'They seem ill-disposed towards us. Although fitz Durand told us about the death of Simon, I feel he just wanted to get rid of the problem, it being a royal cleric from Westminster. I can't see him putting his strong-arm men to work for me.'

He went back to his analysis of the whole situation.

'If those keys really do fit the locks on the treasure chest, then as they cannot be the original keys, someone must have had them copied,' he mused. 'And the only person who could have done that, given that they were in his scrip, is Simon Basset himself.'

'When could he have had them copied?' asked Gwyn, to whom this was all getting a little confusing.

'He had them both in his hands in that strongroom when we delivered the boxes,' said John.

'But not before or after,' objected Thomas, who still seemed inclined to defend the honour of his fellow cleric. 'You had them until you handed them over to him, and after the checking of the inventory one key was given to the Constable to put in his cupboard. How could he have had copies made with all of us, including two knights from the Tower, watching him?'

There was a thoughtful silence for a long moment. 'He was often back and forth to the Tower and its strongroom in respect of other chests,' said de Wolfe, grimly hanging on to some hope of a solution. 'Perhaps he had the opportunity to borrow the keys then?'

Even as the words left his lips, he recognised the weakness of his argument. As the treasure chest had not been opened again until its contents were rechecked and found to be deficient, there was no way in which the key from de Mandeville's cupboard could have been handled.

'Unless the bloody Constable is also involved in the plot!' suggested Gwyn darkly. He had obviously taken against the supercilious Keeper of the Great Tower. 'If he and Simon Basset had conspired together, they could easily have taken the keys out to be copied. The city is full of smiths who could oblige for a good fee – anyway, they wouldn't know they were making keys to rob the king!'

Though John had to admit that this was a possibility, he was dubious about its probability. 'I just can't see Herbert de Mandeville risking his neck for a few hundred pounds, even though it's a great deal of money. His family have been Keepers of the Tower for generations, he surely wouldn't sully their honour in that way.'

'And he's been there for years, he could have stolen long before this,' admitted Thomas.

'Perhaps he has!' grumbled Gwyn, unwilling to abandon his dislike of the Constable.

'Well, there's no way we can accuse de Mandeville of complicity with no evidence at all,' decided John. 'And for that matter, we've no hard evidence against Simon Basset, only a suspicion based on those keys.'

'So why should someone want to kill him?' reflected Thomas. 'And why would he want to hang on to those keys, if he is guilty? Surely he would have thrown them into the Thames once the theft was completed, to get rid of any incriminating evidence.'

De Wolfe threw up his hands in despair. 'Christ Jesus alone knows! There's little I can do now, except hold a useless inquest and wait for something else to turn up, if it ever does.'

As the endless hot weather was not conducive to keeping corpses for long, the inquest had to be held early next day, before a funeral in the cemetery reserved for the clergy, which was behind the abbey. He held it in the west porch of the abbey, with the consent of the prior, William Postard's lieutenant, so that the small jury could proceed inside and view the body which still lay in the transept.

John's pessimism about the futility of the proceedings was justified, as nothing useful could come out of them. He decided not to call anyone from the brothel, to preserve the canon's reputation, even though it meant that he could not introduce any evidence about Basset's claim that he had eaten at a hostelry with a friend. The 'friend' was unknown, as was the hostelry, so there was little point in mentioning it, just as he refrained from calling Brother Philip, who he reckoned was better off healing the sick than travelling to Westminster. Instead, he called Gwyn and Thomas to say on oath that they had heard the monk explain that death was certainly due to foxglove poisoning. Martin the steward and Gilbert the chaplain both averred that Simon Basset was in good spirits when they last saw him and that he had never returned home. They vehemently denied any suggestion that he might have taken his own life and within a few minutes, after solemnly filing past the corpse on its bier, the jury of twelve men recruited from the Treasury, plus the servants from Basset's household, delivered a verdict of murder by persons unknown, which the coroner graciously accepted, though he would have instantly rejected anything else.

They attended the funeral immediately afterwards, filing with many of the abbey monks behind the prior to the large burial plot. As the coffin was lowered into the ground, John could not help wondering whether he was witnessing the final disappearance of a victim or a villain. And if Simon was the culprit, what had he done with the loot?

Walking back towards the palace, de Wolfe went over in his mind the recent cases that had come his way, none of which reflected any glory upon his office of coroner. The guest-room steward, Basil of Reigate, had been stabbed on the river pier.

Osbert Morel, the ironworker, had been bludgeoned to death on the marshes, though it was true that John had no jurisdiction over his murder. Now a high Treasury official had been poisoned – and in none of them was there any clue as to the perpetrator.

There were also hints of espionage and the undoubted theft of a large amount of royal property, yet the Coroner of the Verge seemed impotent to solve any of them. He felt again like getting on his old horse Odin and riding off back to Devon, where at least he felt that he had contributed something to keeping the king's peace.

At noon he went home with Gwyn to Long Ditch Lane for dinner, where Osanna was still giving him frosty looks after bursting in on his moment of passion with Hawise d'Ayncourt.

Whether it was because she had taken a fancy to Hilda when she had stayed there or whether she took exception to Hawise's autocratic manner, John could not tell, but from the way she banged a platter in front of him and slopped his ale into a jar, he knew that he was not in favour with her. However, her salt cod with beans, onions and last year's parsnips was palatable, as was a boiled fowl stuffed with bread and herbs. A bowl of quince and small plums was rounded off with cheese and maslin bread of wheat and rye.

As they finished eating, the sullen heat was suddenly broken by a summer storm. The black clouds that had been threatening for days, decided to accumulate overhead and abruptly unloaded torrential rain upon London, accompanied by rolling thunderclaps and flashes of lightning. Within minutes, the downpour turned the lane outside into a morass, running water even lapping against the stone slab that formed the threshold of the front door. The water began pouring off the wide expanse of marsh and the Long Ditch soon turned into a churning brown torrent.

John decided he would not bother to go back to sit idly in his chamber in the palace and announced that he was going to sleep the afternoon away. Gwyn seemed indifferent to the storm and said that he would go down to the Deacon alehouse to while away the time at dice with his cronies. He marched away through the mud, his old leather jerkin his only protection, the rain cascading off the pointed hood.

When he had gone, John climbed the steps to his room and flopped on his pallet, a lumpy hessian bag stuffed with hay, which Osanna renewed every few weeks, before it went damp and mouldy. For a short while, his mind revisited yet again the mysteries of the three killings. He lay on his back, staring up at the inside of the roof, where the irregular branches forming the rafters supported woven hazel withies holding up the thatch outside. The thunder still rolled and though the drumming of the rain was softened by the thick layer of reeds on the roof, it had a hypnotic quality that soon sent him to sleep, in spite of the drips of water that fell on his bed from above.

It was blessedly cool when he awoke a few hours later. The world seemed fresher and the birds were chirruping again, after having been driven into hiding by the storm. De Wolfe felt better than he had for days in that enervating heat and decided to celebrate by having a shave, two days earlier than his normal weekly scrape. In the backyard, Osanna gave him a few quarts of warm water in a wooden bucket and a lump of grey soap, made from goat fat, soda and wood ash. Stripped to the waist, he managed to get a meagre lather on to his black bristles and scratched at them with a small knife that he kept for the purpose, made of Saracen steel honed to a fine edge.

In his new mood of determined optimism, his thoughts turned to Hawise d'Ayncourt, the siren of Westminster. He was ambivalent about her, knowing full well that he should avoid any involvement with a woman he knew could be dangerous to him. Yet her sultry beauty and obvious availability was both an attraction and a challenge. He decided that if the opportunity was handed to him on a platter, it would be stupid and churlish to turn it down – but he also felt that he should do what he could to avoid such an opportunity arising by staying out of her way and not supping at the Lesser Hall.

This noble thought lasted less than five minutes, for

as he wiped the last of the lather from his face with a cloth, he rebelled at such craven behaviour. He enjoyed the company of Ranulf of Abingdon and young William Aubrey, so why should he, a knight, a Crusader and a royal law officer, be frightened off by a woman, attractive though she was.

With a flourish of his towel cloth, he decided to demand a clean tunic from Osanna, who did his washing as part of the bed and board that he paid her for. She was still a little surly, but was coming round and gave him a grey tunic that she had earlier thrown over an elder bush in the yard, where she dried her washing until the rain came. He dressed, then sat with a quart pot in the main room and waited for Gwyn to return. When he arrived, he had some news.

'The old queen has arrived at Portsmouth. William Aubrey has already rushed off with a troop of men-at-arms to join the escort and help organize the transport. She should be arriving at Westminster in about five days' time.'

It seemed that Ranulf had remained in the palace, rather than travel to the coast, which reinforced John's intention to take his supper in the Lesser Hall to hear the latest news. He arrived early enough to stand with a few dozen other patrons and hear a short passage from the Gospels and then a long Latin grace, this night being delivered by Archdeacon Bernard de Montfort. John was somewhat piqued to find that Hawise and her dumpy husband were not present. After having summoned up his bravado to face her after their brief but passionate embrace, he felt rather deflated at being deprived of a challenge.

Ranulf was there, with Sir Martin Stanford, the Deputy Marshal of the palace. When Bernard de Montfort came back from the lectern where he had read the lesson, he slid on to the bench next to John.

'Have to sing for my supper now and then,' he said jocularly. 'Though thank heaven there are enough clerics in this place to make it not too often.'

As they ate their supper and drank their ale and wine, the talk naturally centred around the impending arrival of Eleanor of Aquitaine, as she was still thought of by many of the older folk.

'Why have you not rushed off to Portsmouth to join her procession?' asked the archdeacon, addressing the men from the Marshalsea.

'I've just sent almost half of my contingent down there,' explained Martin Stanford. 'The rest I need for organising the move to Gloucester, which is a far bigger operation.'

He and Ranulf described the complicated procedure of trundling the whole court across the southern half of England. 'The Purveyors have already been sent out along the route,' said Stanford. 'Unwelcome though they are to the population, they have to arrange accommodation and procure food for the travellers and fodder for the livestock.'

'It'll be something to occupy Hugo de Molis – he certainly doesn't strain himself when we are here in Westminster,' observed Ranulf cynically.

John turned to the genial priest from the Auvergne. 'What about you, archdeacon? I take it you won't be travelling with us, given that you are concerned with researching the abbey's history here?'

His unfortunate harelip twisted Bernard's mouth as he smiled.

'Oh no, I'm going down to Canterbury again. I need to consult some obscure manuscripts said to be held in the scriptorium of the cathedral, so I'll make a visit there while the queen is engaged with her business at Gloucester.'

'Travelling alone can be a dangerous business, sir,'

warned Martin Stanford. 'Best go with a party of pil-grims, they leave from Southwark almost every day.'

De Montfort was benignly reassuring. 'I will have my servant Raoul with me. No doubt you have noticed that he has a frightening look about him, though in fact he is intelligent and can read and write, as well as handle a sword and mace!'

They ate their way through boiled salmon, roast duck and some slices of venison from the royal forest beyond Twickenham, finishing with a suet pudding studded with French raisins.

'Where is Renaud de Seigneur and his lovely wife tonight?' asked Ranulf innocently, as he nudged de Wolfe meaningfully beneath the table.

'I understand that Lady Hawise is suffering from some slight indisposition today, so they are keeping to their chambers upstairs,' confided Bernard de Mont-fort.

Is the woman lying low in order to avoid meeting him after their frustrated encounter? thought John. On consideration, he felt it was unlikely, given the brazen nature of Hawise. Relieved, but also disappointed at her absence, he turned the conversation back to the main topic.

'So, Ranulf, when are we setting off on this crusade to the West Country?'

'The queen is likely to arrive here at the end of this week. Give her a few days to rest, which will include Hubert Walter's welcoming feast in the Great Hall, then I expect our wagons will start rolling towards the middle of next week.'

Another week of inaction, sighed de Wolfe, but at least he now had a date to look forward to, which might lead to a quick visit to Exeter – and perhaps even to Dawlish.

*

John left the Lesser Hall after supper and strolled towards the Deacon tavern, where he was confident of finding Gwyn behind a quart pot. He was surprised to see a small figure in a black cassock lurking uneasily outside the alehouse door.

'What brings you here, Thomas? Have you taken up drink at last?'

His clerk squirmed with embarrassment, but jerked a finger at the door. 'I guessed that Cornish barbarian would be in there, Crowner. But it's you I wanted to find and Gwyn said that you would probably call in after your supper.'

The priest's pinched face was glowing with suppressed excitement at being able to once again bring his master some information. 'That secondary, Robin Byard, the one who told us about Basil's fears of overhearing some conspirators, spoke to me again in the abbey refectory tonight.'

John waited impatiently for Thomas to be more specific.

'He said that when Basil was in fear of his life, he told him that if anything happened to him, he wanted Robin to have the only book he possessed, a small copy of the Gospel of St Luke.'

De Wolfe scowled at his clerk.

'What's this got to do with anything, for God's sake?'

At the mention of the ultimate name, Thomas jerked automatically into crossing himself, but then ploughed on with his explanation. 'Robin has just found a scrap of parchment tucked behind the back cover of the book, which has worried him so much that he feels it should be shown to someone in authority.'

'What does this scrap reveal?'

Thomas turned up his hands in a gesture of ignorance. 'I've not seen it, Crowner. Robin, who is quite solicitous about my welfare, says he doesn't want to put me in any danger by involving me. But I told him he must show it to you, so he's bringing it over to our chamber in the palace tomorrow morning after Lauds.'

The expected revelation turned out to be a disappointment.

When the aspiring young priest arrived at their office next day, he was clutching a small, tattered book as if it was the Holy Grail. The illiterate coroner motioned to Thomas to have a look at it and whilst he was doing so de Wolfe had a question for Robin Byard.

'Did Basil say anything to you about this loose page in the book?'

The young fellow shook his head miserably. 'Not a word! I feel sure that he came across it after he had told me of overhearing this seditious conversation. In fact, I think he found it shortly before he was so cruelly killed.' He promptly burst into tears, to John's profound discomfiture, so the coroner turned back to his clerk.

'Well, what do you make of it?' he demanded.

'It's a well-used copy of a Gospel, one of a cheap version turned out for sale by the hundred in monastery scriptoria.'

'I don't care about the damned Gospel,' snapped John blasphemously. 'What about this message?'

Thomas held up a ragged square of parchment, the size of his palm. 'Not very exciting,' he said with a crestfallen expression.

'It has some names and numbers and a date at the top, that's about all.'

The coroner snatched it from his fingers and though he could not read the words, he could decipher the numerals written on the cured sheepskin. Even to his inexpert eyes, the inked letters seemed fresh and crisp. It was obviously not a letter or a message, the words being scattered about the page almost at random. He handed it back to Thomas.

'So what do you make of it?'

Thomas peered again at the parchment, moving it up and down until his long nose almost touched the surface.

'It was recently written, as it starts with a date. The eighteenth day of June in the seventh year of the reign of King Richard.'

John frowned. 'That suggests that whoever wrote it was not a subject of our Crown. It is usual for words such as "our Sovereign Lord King Richard" to be used.'

Thomas nodded his agreement, though privately he felt that this was not a very safe assumption in informal documents.

'It then has various words dotted around the page, as if they were written hurriedly or in difficult circumstances. They make little sense to me, but some are placenames. There is Sandwich, Dover, Rye and Saltwood. Some have numbers after them, including one-hundred, two-hundred, and one of five hundred. But after Dover there is only the word "twelve".'

'What are the other words?'

'They seem to be personal names – Arundel, de Montfort, Mowbray, fitz Gilbert.'

There was silence as they all digested these obscure facts.

'Robin, are those words written in your friend's hand?' asked de Wolfe.

The secondary immediately shook his head. Sniffing back his tears, he said, 'Nothing like it, sir. He had immaculate script, of which he was proud. These are just scribbles compared to his.'

Gwyn, with his maritime knowledge from his time as a fisherman, pointed out the obvious. 'All those places are on the coast, most of them actual ports.'

'And on the coast of Kent or Sussex,' added Thomas, not to be outdone by a Cornish barbarian. 'And the names sound as if they could be manor-lords.'

De Wolfe rubbed his chin, missing the stubble that he had recently removed. 'It's suggestive of some interest in the coast facing France,' he admitted. 'But what do the numbers mean?'

'Could they be ships of war?' said Gwyn. 'There are twelve at Dover.'

'There would hardly be five hundred ships at Rye!' objected Thomas.

'Then ships or men-at-arms,' suggested Gwyn, determined not to be bested by the priest.

The coroner ignored their banter, but agreed that this could be some form of intelligence about coastal defences. 'But where did this Basil fellow get it? And more importantly, who wrote it?'

'Given what he said to me about overhearing suspicious conversation, and the fact that he spent almost all his time in the palace guest chambers, that seems the most likely place for him to have found it,' offered Robin Byard.

As Thomas handed him back the precious Gospel, John carefully folded the piece of parchment into his scrip. 'I'll have to show this to Hubert Walter, though I'm sure he has other things on his mind at the moment.' As he did up the buckle to his pouch, another possibility occurred to him.

'And maybe I'll use it as a bluff to flush out the culprits!'

chapter eleven

In which Crowner John suffers a blow

De Wolfe was unable to consult the Chief Justiciar that day, as Hubert had gone early into the city and according to one of his secretaries, would spend the night at the Tower. John thought facetiously that he might be putting Herbert de Mandeville to the torture, to get him to confess to the theft of the treasure, but in reality he knew that Herbert was an unlikely culprit.

Late in the afternoon, as John was crossing New Palace Yard, he stopped to contemplate the small landing stage and to wonder whether he would ever discover who killed Basil of Reigate there. A moment later, he realized that a wherry was landing two familiar figures, Renaud de Seigneur and his beautiful wife.

His instinct was to walk quickly away, but he was too late as Hawise waved gaily to him and John had to stand his ground until they came up to him. In the cooler weather since the storm, she was wearing a light mantle over her gown of cream linen. Her dark hair was confined by a silver net into tight coils over each ear, over which was thrown a diaphanous veil of white samite.

He bowed his head in greeting as they approached.

'I trust you are recovered, lady,' he said stiffly. 'We heard at supper last evening that you were indisposed.'

Hawise gave him a dazzling smile, which banished any awkwardness that John had feared. 'I am quite well, Sir John, thank you. My husband has taken me on a trip on the river today, for the fresh air to banish any remnants of my problems.'

John hoped silently that for her sake they had gone upriver, as the Thames was strikingly short of fresh air where it passed through the odorous city.

Out of courtesy, he walked with them across the busy yard towards the main doors into the palace, behind the Great Hall. Renaud was full of the visit of the old queen and of their impending departure for Gloucester. Hawise walked between the two men and was able to give John sultry looks without de Seigneur noticing – or if he did, he chose to ignore them. De Wolfe remained polite but wooden-faced and when they reached the crowded main ground-floor passage, she managed to drop back a little and whisper to him.

'John, I need you! I'm desperate for your arms, we must meet!'

Thankfully, they were now at the foot of the stairs leading up to his chamber and he adroitly turned sideways on to the lower steps. 'I trust you will be in the Lesser Hall this evening,' he said in a loud voice and Renaud turned to wave at him. John could not resist winking at Hawise and was rewarded with a brilliant smile. His feet seemed lighter as he climbed the stairs, but again, that cautious voice deep within him told him not to be such a silly old fool.

At supper that evening, all the usual patrons were there, except for a few like Aubrey, who had gone off to Portsmouth. The lesson and grace were said by another priest, so Bernard de Montfort sat with them from the start. Renaud plodded in ahead of his wife, who had dressed herself with even greater care to enhance her undoubted beauty, her glossy hair encased in silvered crespines. John was sandwiched between the archdeacon and Ranulf, so she had to sit opposite with her husband, unable to press her shapely thigh against John's.

A somewhat uninspired potage of leeks, beans and oatmeal was followed by a choice of boiled fowl, roast partridge and eels to lay on their trenchers. All through the meal, Hawise covertly made 'cow's eyes' at John, raising her long lashes with her head demurely lowered, but he resolutely declined to respond and carried on with whatever conversation was in progress. Much of the talk was as usual about Eleanor's arrival, though the subject of Canon Basset's sudden demise cropped up again. Most of them knew him, as he had often supped in the hall when business kept him late at the Exchequer. They all knew the meagre facts divulged at the short inquest and were eager for more details from 'the horse's mouth', the nag in question being John de Wolfe.

'I cannot credit the fact that he was murdered,' said de Montfort. 'Though I cannot deny the verdict of your jury, Sir John, I feel sure there must be some other explanation.'

De Wolfe shook his head emphatically. 'There can be no other explanation, I fear. The canon certainly did not kill himself, both the obvious facts against that and others that I cannot divulge make suicide an impossibility. And to suggest accidental foxglove poisoning in the centre of London is equally untenable!'

'Facts you cannot divulge!' trilled Hawise excitedly. 'You are a man of mystery, coroner, but surely you can give us some hint as to what they may be?'

'Sir John is a law officer, my dear,' said Renaud. 'You must not press him further.'

De Wolfe would not have been averse to being pressed by the delectable Hawise, but this was not the time or place.

'No doubt our coroner's reticence is related to the notorious theft of that gold,' suggested the archdeacon, leaning forward to spear a small partridge and place it on the slab of bread in front of him. 'It surely can be no coincidence that after a long and blameless life, Simon Basset's death took place within days of an audacious crime, in which, inevitably, he must have been a suspect.'

There was a silence in which his listeners looked at each other uneasily. Though what Bernard had said was what all of them must have considered, no one had voiced it so outspokenly.

'We cannot even hint at guilt in such a pious and upright man,' said Renaud severely, though he could not have been acquainted with the canon for more than a few weeks.

'A hell of a coincidence, though!' muttered Ranulf, half to himself. The discussion went back and forth for a time, but covering the same ground that John and his two assistants had ploughed endlessly these past few days. Eventually, de Wolfe turned to another killing, this time intent on dropping some misinformation into the Westminster gossip machine, to see if anything was flushed out.

'Talking of murder, I have had some intelligence that throws light on the death of that unfortunate clerk in your guest chambers, de Seigneur!' he said casually. 'Again, I cannot reveal its nature, but it gives me hope of soon being able to unmask the villain who was responsible.'

This set off another round of questions and pleas for more enlightenment, which John resisted easily, as in truth he had no information to provide. The parchment which Robin Byard had found was of no use without either an interpretation of its meaning or some clue as to who wrote it. Hawise d'Ayncourt was again giving her performance of hero-worship as she gave John looks of melting adoration and, in spite of himself, he could not avoid enjoying the sensation, even with her husband sitting almost within arm's length. But wisely, he sat firmly on his bench until after Renaud had finished his meal and dragged Hawise off to their quarters, avoiding any dallying and possible embarrassment outside the hall.

He stayed on with the men from the Marshalsea and Bernard de Montfort, taking their time over the ale and remaining wine. They talked again about the imminent arrival of Queen Eleanor.

'So she should be here within a few days, you think?' asked Bernard. 'I would have thought that the Justiciar would have gone to Portsmouth to escort her here himself.'

Martin Stanford, the most senior of the marshals, shook his head. 'It was mooted, but Hubert Walter decided that he had more pressing business here – and, anyway, she will be accompanied from Normandy by William Marshal himself, who is almost the equal of the Justiciar in rank.'

The doughty old Marshal, who had already served two kings, was well known to de Wolfe, both from campaigns and even a visit to Devon not long ago. John was reminded that William's main possession was Chepstow Castle, very near where Nesta had returned with her new husband.

He pulled his attention back to the Deputy Marshal, who was still speaking. '. . . so a welcoming party will be sent out to meet the cavalcade from Portsmouth and escort it back to Westminster. Many of the members of the Royal Council will form part of it and I think

Hubert will want you included, de Wolfe, as Coroner of the Verge.'

John nodded, he was not averse to a ride in the countryside, with all the panoply of a royal procession.

'Which day will that be?' he asked.

'I have fast riders coming ahead to warn me,' replied Martin Stanford. 'Probably by Tuesday, but we will have sufficient notice to get ready.'

By now, John reckoned that Hawise and her husband would be safely lodged in their rooms upstairs, so he could leave without fear of being accosted. He had been hunted by enemies many times during his violent career, but never before by a beautiful woman. The sensation was not altogether unpleasant.

In spite of being harassed by his numerous clerks over the impending visit of his monarch's mother, Hubert Walter found time next morning to listen to de Wolfe's update on the missing treasure. Though there was not a trace of it to be found, the Justiciar agreed that the news of Simon Basset's murder was very relevant to the crime.

'It can surely be no coincidence that he is slain so soon after this infamous robbery,' he exclaimed. 'But what is the significance of it, John?' He sat behind his table and drummed his fingers on the wood, a sign of the strain that running England for the Lionheart was putting upon him. Over the previous twenty-four months to April that year, he had dispatched well over a million marks of silver to the king in Rouen, squeezed from the country by every means he could devise. Though the loss of nine hundred pounds' worth of treasure was small in comparison with this, he could ill-afford to lose a single mark, with Richard breathing down his neck for every penny.

The coroner, hunched on a chair in front of the

great man, scowled in concentration as he answered Hubert's question.

'It seems to mean one of two things, sire. Either the canon came to know or to suspect the identity of the thief and was therefore silenced before he could divulge it ... or he was implicated himself and the other conspirators disposed of him in case he was a bad risk.'

The archbishop nodded. 'And which of those do you favour, de Wolfe?'

John shrugged. 'I have no means of knowing, sire. There is no real evidence that Basset was involved, as there is no sign of the treasure at his house, after thorough searching.'

'He could have hidden it elsewhere,' objected Hubert. 'In fact, it would be more sensible than leaving incriminating evidence on his own doorstep, with the risk of the servants finding it – unless they too are guilty!'

'It is possible, though short of burying it in the marshes behind his house, I fail to see where he might have concealed it. I find it hard to contemplate a portly canon going out at dead of night to dig a hole!'

'Yet he was a surprising man, if you say that it was in a whorehouse in the city that he was taken mortally ill. I would not have expected that of him, though God knows many clerics are wont to relieve their celibacy in that way.'

De Wolfe decided to slant the subject away from the canon's morals. 'He was said to have dined with some unknown man shortly before he was poisoned. I wish I knew some way of identifying him, but given our cool relations with the city sheriffs I doubt they would be keen to offer us much help.'

'As you know, at the moment I am in bad odour with the city fathers myself,' said Hubert ruefully. 'But if this mysterious man did poison Basset's food with foxglove, as the monks claim, then we are back to the two motives you mentioned. For one reason or the other, Canon Simon had become a liability.'

John agreed, but his glum expression betrayed his frustration.

'But it doesn't help tell us which of the reasons it was. We need to catch this man and press him in the Tower to loosen his tongue.' He thought almost nostalgically of Stigand, the evil torturer back in Rougemont Castle in Exeter.

A senior Chancery clerk came to the door and hovered with a sheaf of parchments, doing his best not to glare at de Wolfe for taking up the Justiciar's valuable time. Hubert took the hint and stood up to end the audience.

'Keep at it, John! Knowing your tenacity, I'm sure you will get there in the end.'

De Wolfe rose and bowed his head politely, but had one last matter to discuss before he went to the door. He felt in his scrip and took out the scrap of parchment that Robin Byard had found in Basil's book. He held it out to the Justiciar and explained how it had come into his hands.

'Perhaps what is written upon it may make sense to someone learned in your service. It seems to refer in some way to the counties of Kent and Sussex. Given the present anxiety along that coast about a possible raid by the French, maybe it is an indication that the fears that the murdered palace officer had about his safety might have been justified.'

Hubert took the scrap and read it, his brow furrowing as he scanned the garbled words and figures. 'I will give this some thought and pass it to other barons on the council. You are nearer the gossip in the palace than I can ever get, so keep your ears open for any other titbits, John. There are persons around who bear considerable ill-will towards England.'

The coroner pondered this as he walked back towards his dwelling in Long Ditch. There were a number of guests from the continent staying in the palace, apart from those who formed their little supper group. He had met a few of them briefly, as the archdeacon had introduced him to Guy de Bretteville, a nobleman from Anjou, and Peter le Paumer, a knight from Angoulême. Before the situation arose with Hawise, her husband had presented him to a canon from the cathedral in Tours, another minor lord from Artois and an aged physician from Berri. John promptly forgot their names and where they came from.

The political situation in France was so fragmented and shifting that it was hard to know who was for the Norman confederacy or for the small, but powerful central core of France under Philip Augustus, centred on Paris. Though Richard was Duke of Aquitaine, there was constant trouble down there from rebellious barons. He had managed to wean and bribe the princes of Flanders to his side, but elsewhere, fragile truces, marriages of political convenience and untrustworthy pacts between the many small states and counties were confused even more by the battle lines that ebbed and flowed. Though the king was slowly making inroads into the Vexin, north of the Seine, recovering land that had been lost by the treachery and foolishness of his brother John, there was still a strong French presence in the north-east, which posed a danger to the southern corner of England. It was impossible to know where the sympathies of some of these cross-Channel guests lay – and even some English lords and barons held covert allegiance to John, Count of Mortain.

He continued to ponder these matters sitting silently with Gwyn, as they ate their dinner in the house.

Osanna served them rabbit stew, then salt cod with onions, carrots and cabbage, followed by bread and cheese. She seemed to have a limited range of dishes in her culinary repertoire, but both these seasoned old warriors were not that particular about what they ate, quantity often being of greater importance than quality.

The exotic dishes favoured by what John considered posturing courtiers, held no attraction for them and they were content to do without braised lark's tongues or swans stuffed with chestnuts and hard-boiled eggs.

Gwyn, used to Black John's dark moods after twenty years' companionship, made no effort to interrupt his master's reverie and devoted himself to eating and drinking. Eventually, when Osanna waddled in to remove the bowls and horn spoons, de Wolfe lifted himself from his silent contemplation and reached over the table to refill his officer's ale jar.

'We should be out of this miserable village soon, Gwyn!' he said with an almost cheerful change of mood. 'Not for long, unfortunately, but it'll be a change of scenery, especially if we manage to slip away to Exeter.'

The Cornishman's blue eyes twinkled in his ruddy face as he sucked ale from his red moustache. 'Maybe you can have a little trip down to Dawlish while we're there!' he said mischievously.

'And another up to bloody Polsloe to try to see my wife,' added John, with a scowl. 'The house in Martin's Lane worries me. Poor Mary is marooned there alone and I have no idea what to do about it. It can't stay empty for ever.'

Gwyn shifted uncomfortably on his seat. 'Are you stuck in Westminster with no hope of relief,' he asked tentatively. 'The last thing I want is to desert you after all these years, but I can't bear this place and I miss my wife and sons more than I thought.'

This was the first time that his old friend had even hinted at a possible parting of the ways and it gave John more food for thought. But there was nothing to be done about it for some time to come. The pressing matters were the solution to the theft of the treasure and the coming perambulation of the court to Gloucester.

'I spoke to the Justiciar this morning about the possible involvement of Simon Basset in the robbery,' he said, as they were leaving the table. 'I said there was no sign of the treasure in his house, but we spoke about the possibility of it being buried somewhere on the marshes behind his dwelling.'

'Do you want me to have another look around?' asked Gwyn. 'After all that rain during the storm, maybe something has been washed clear and exposed by those leats and reens. I'll have a walk up there now and poke about a bit.'

De Wolfe agreed and they parted outside the door, the coroner's officer going up the lane alongside the Long Ditch to follow the track across the marsh, which eventually led to the back of the Royal Way.

John loped back to the palace, thankful that the torrid heat had moderated to a pleasant summer's day. He found Thomas at work in his chamber, writing out some text related to his duties in the archives of the abbey, rather than anything to do with coroner's cases.

'There is nothing outstanding for me to deal with,' he explained apologetically. 'We have had so few deaths to record that I have been up to date for some time.'

'You carry on, Thomas,' said John, reassuringly. 'Maybe business will improve when we get on the road to Gloucester next week.'

He sat behind his table and half-heartedly unrolled

the parchment which carried his last lesson in Latin comprehension.

He could read and write his own name now and make some sense of the Lord's Prayer, but his attention kept wandering. He looked across at his clerk, whose thin face stared down at the document he was writing, his tongue projecting slightly from the corner of his thin lips as he concentrated on scribing perfect letters with the quill in his right hand. His lank brown hair hung down in a fringe all around the shaved circle on top of his scalp, which denoted his clerical status. John almost envied his clerk's single-minded devotion to his faith and his scholarship, the Church being the very engine of his life.

This placid scene was eventually broken by an interruption – a tap on the door heralded a young head being poked around it. It was the same cheeky page that had brought the previous message and he now had yet another.

'Sir John, a man wishes to speak to you about a matter of importance, so he says.'

'Come in and tell me properly!' snapped de Wolfe, who was used to a little more deference from messengers who were little more than children. The page slid through the door and stood before him, his tousled fair hair contrasting with the green tabard that carried the three royal lions across his breast.

'It was a man in the corridor below, sir,' he gabbled. 'He gave me a whole half-penny to bring you the message.'

'Which is what?' demanded the coroner, glaring at the mercenary young lad.

'He said if you wish to know more about a bunch of keys, you must meet him in the crypt of St Stephen's within the hour. He said you would know what he meant.'

'Is that all he said?' snapped de Wolfe.

The boy nodded rapidly. 'Just that you must come alone. Then he vanished.'

'What do you mean – vanished? Who was he, damn it?'

'It was in a crowded corridor downstairs, sire. He pressed a coin into my hand and whispered his message, then slipped away into the crowd of clerks that were jostling along there.'

'What did he look like? Have you seen him before?'

The boy shook his head again, his hair bouncing. 'Never, Sir John! He was a big man in a poor brown tunic, a short one belted over breeches. He was no nobleman, that's for sure.'

'His face, you say you had never seen it before about the palace?'

'Never, nor about the town. He was rough-featured, no beard and his hair was cropped to brown bristles. He could have been anything, a peasant or a carter.'

De Wolfe could get nothing more from the boy and he was dismissed, looking disappointed at not getting the other half of his expected penny.

'That sounds very odd, Crowner,' ventured Thomas. 'Why should a common man wish to tell you about keys?'

'The obvious reason is that he knows something about the keys to the treasure chest. No doubt he hopes to sell some information.'

'Will you go, master?' asked Thomas, with a worried look on his sharp face.

'Of course I'll go! Nothing to be lost and possibly something to be gained. Maybe it's one of a gang who carried out the theft, hoping to save his neck by turning approver.' An approver was a miscreant who sought leniency or even a pardon by betraying his fellow conspirators and it was one of a coroner's many legal duties to take confessions from such persons.

John rose from his table, pushing aside his Latin lesson with some relief. 'Don't look so worried, Thomas, whoever it is can hardly force foxglove down my throat this time.' He reached for his sword belt and baldric which hung on the wall. He did not normally wear his sword about the palace, but to be on the safe side, decided to buckle it around him this time.

'There, that should satisfy you that I shall remain safe – though it seems unlikely that I might be assassinated within the Palace of Westminster!'

As he left the chamber, Thomas murmured worriedly to himself. 'That may well have been what Basil of Reigate thought!'

There were two chapels in the palace, one in the Royal Apartments for the use of the king and his family, and another one for the use of the courtiers and their officers. This had been built by King Stephen during his disastrous reign some half-century earlier, and his small chapel was placed at right angles to the main axis of the palace, jutting out towards the Thames immediately behind the Great Hall. It had a plain nave with no separate chancel and beneath it was a pillared crypt, kept quite shallow to avoid the water table of the nearby river.

John de Wolfe knew how to reach the chapel, as he had been taken there soon after coming to Westminster, Thomas eagerly wishing to show him the religious sights of the palace. John had even attended Mass on one occasion, as although he was an unenthusiastic communicant, habits ingrained from childhood gave him a desultory desire to avoid purgatory and the fires of hell.

The entrance to the chapel was in a covered way that joined the rear of the Great Hall to the end of the

Lesser Hall, but there was also a door on each side of the chapel which led out on to the strip of land alongside the river. Within the vestibule at the entrance to the chapel, another door led down a short flight of stone steps into the crypt, which was dimly lit by small slits just above the outside ground level, as the crypt was more of an undercroft, only partly below the surface. His hand on his sword-hilt, John descended the steps into the dank space, where two lines of thick, stumpy pillars stretched ahead, supporting the chapel above. As his eyes became accustomed to the gloom, he searched ahead and to each side, where alcoves contained musty boxes and abandoned furniture, as well as devotional objects. There were some tarnished altar candlesticks, a broken plaster statue of the Virgin and a large processional cross with a bent arm. He advanced further, but saw no one waiting for him.

'Show yourself, if anyone is there!' he commanded in a loud voice, beginning to feel as if he was the victim of a hoax and that whoever had given the page a half-penny had wasted his money.

The next second, he felt a violent blow on the back of his head and he pitched forward to the damp earthen floor. De Wolfe had a thick skull and had suffered blows upon it a number of times during his violent career. He did not lose consciousness, but was rendered so groggy that he was unable to utter the stream of blasphemies and obscenities that swirled around his stunned mind. He began to recover and pushed against the ground with his hands, trying to get to his knees to wreak vengeance with his sword. However, a thin noose was whipped over his head and dragged tightly against his throat. This was new to John and was an experience he would gladly have done without, as his breath was cut off, his vision became blurred and his head felt as if it was about to burst.

He began spiralling down into unconsciousness, with a gripping fear of impending death, unable to fight back since there was a knee in the small of his back.

As his hands gave way and he fell face down on to the earth, his last thoughts were, of all things, of his old dog Brutus.

CHAPTER TWELVE

In which Crowner John goes to a feast

An hour later, de Wolfe was lying on a low bed in the abbey infirmarium, surrounded by a circle of anxious faces. He had a vague memory of being manhandled on to some kind of stretcher and of severe discomfort as he was bumped along at jogging pace across the few hundred yards of Palace Yard to the monks' hospital behind the cloisters.

His wits only fully returned when he was on this palliasse, but his return to full consciousness brought with it a burning soreness in his neck and throat. His first attempts at speech sounded like a combination of a duck and a rusty file, which prompted Gwyn to lean over him solicitously.

'Don't try to talk, Crowner! That throat of yours will need a bit of rest after the squeezing it suffered!'

Gwyn's hairy face was replaced in his field of vision by Thomas's anxious features. 'The infirmarian has sent for poultices and warmed wine with honey, which will help ease the soreness.'

John struggled to a half-sitting position and saw that in addition to his two faithful retainers, his audience consisted of a grey-haired monk, a younger novitiate, a sergeant from the palace guard, another priest who looked familiar, and Ranulf of Abingdon.

He tried to speak again, but rapidly changed it to a whisper, which seemed to come out more clearly. 'What the hell happened, for Christ's sake? Who did this to me?'

'You were ambushed, but he got away,' growled Gwyn. 'When I catch him, I'll tear his liver out with my teeth!'

The older Benedictine laid a hand gently on the coroner's shoulder. 'Don't try to talk until this bruising of your voicebox wears off, my son. We'll give you some potions to ease it, as your clerk said.'

John reached up tentatively to feel the back of his head, as he was aware of an ache there.

'Yes, you have a lump there too, John, some bastard gave you a nasty whack!' said Ranulf cheerfully. 'But it's your clerk to whom you should be grateful, he was the hero of the hour!'

De Wolfe's bloodshot eyes swivelled to look at Thomas de Peyne, though he took the advice to avoid speaking.

'The little fellow probably saved your life,' chortled Gwyn. 'That's usually my job, but he beat me to it this time.'

John risked some gargling noises which were obviously a demand for more explanation and the Cornishman began it.

'Just before I returned from a wasted search on the marshes behind the canon's house, Thomas here said he was uneasy about you going off to meet some mysterious informant, so he decided to follow you down to that chapel place.'

He nudged the priest to get him to continue and Thomas, wriggling with embarrassment, reluctantly described what happened.

'I was concerned that you went alone to meet this unknown person, Crowner, even though you took your sword. There might have been half a dozen Brabançons waiting to jump on you.'

He paused and shivered at the memory of his own desperate intervention. 'So I followed a couple of minutes later and was in time to see this evil man strike you down with a club, then slip a cord around your neck and start strangling you.'

Gwyn guffawed and slapped Thomas on the back. 'Damn me if the little devil didn't attack the assailant, though he was twice his size, according to Thomas!'

'I had to do something, didn't I?' snapped the clerk indignantly. 'I owe my life to Sir John, I couldn't just stand by and see him murdered! There was a big brass cross on a long staff leaning against a wall, so I took it and struck the man with the heavy end. I'm afraid I snapped it, though it was already bent.'

The infirmarian gave a benign smile. 'I'm sure God – and Abbot Postard – will forgive you for that! It seems appropriate that a priest like yourself should use the emblem of Our Lord to save a life!'

The other cleric – who John later discovered was Gerard, one of the two chaplains who ministered at St Stephen's – also approved of Thomas's attack with an ecclesiastical weapon. 'That was an old cross going back to Stephen's time, it was beyond repair anyway!'

John reached out and gripped Thomas's shoulder. 'Once more, I have to thank you, good friend!' he croaked, determined to show his gratitude, however painful his Adam's apple might be.

His clerk's embarrassment was mixed with happy pride in having been able to repay some of his master's kindness in giving him a job when he was destitute several years ago, but de Wolfe cut short his contentment with husky whispers.

'But did you see who the swine was, Thomas? Who did this to me?'

'I saw him clearly, Crowner, but I have no idea who he was,' Thomas bleated. 'He was a large, rough man, a labourer or perhaps a mercenary soldier. I have never seen him before – though I certainly would know him again!'

'You were fortunate that he did not turn on you as well,' said Ranulf. 'You told us he let go of the coroner's garrotte and fled.'

Thomas nodded, a rather sheepish expression on his face.

'I suspect it was the screams I made that scared him off, rather than my feeble attempts to injure him,' he admitted. 'Though I did manage to cut the back of his head when I caught him with the brass crosspiece of my weapon,' he added proudly.

The chaplain, Gerard, cut in at this point. 'I heard the yells from the entrance to the chapel above, as I was going in to prepare for the next office,' he explained. 'I shouted lustily down the steps to ask what was happening and the next thing I knew, I was being shouldered aside by this large lout, who dashed up the stairs and promptly vanished through the outside door on to the river walk.'

'And you didn't recognise him, either?' asked Ranulf.

Gerard shook his head. 'My brother Thomas's description is accurate, he was a rough-looking villain with coarse features. All I recall was that he had a hairy mole on his cheek.'

'We made a search of the palace and the yards as soon as we were told about the assault,' said the guard sergeant. 'But many minutes had passed by then and we had only a vague description of who we were seeking amongst all the crowds that come and go in the palace.'

'It was the same with that swine who knifed Basil,' growled Gwyn. 'He vanished into thin air, for this place is like a rabbit warren, with doors and passages everywhere.'

Ranulf laid a hand gently on de Wolfe's shoulder. 'Why should anyone want to murder you, John? This was a deliberate trap, luring you down to that crypt, then jumping you from behind.'

The coroner's reply was delayed by a young novice coming in with a pewter cup which he gave to the infirmarian, who held it to John's lips. It was a posset of mulled wine sweetened with honey and immediately had the effect of soothing the rawness of his throat, which had felt as if he had feasted on broken glass.

'I brought it on myself,' he whispered, in answer to Ranulf's question. 'I put it about that I was about to unmask the thieves who took the treasure and also made some hints about knowing of some foreign spies in the palace.'

The under-marshal roared with laughter, then apologised.

'Sorry, but that's rich! You put up a bluff and some-one calls it with a club and a garrotte! You should join our gaming sessions, John, you would win a fortune.'

Thomas looked far more serious. 'Do you really think it was that, master? Someone wanting to silence you?'

'It seems likely,' croaked John. 'Why else would someone want me dead?'

'Which one d'you think it was?' demanded Gwyn, ready to seek out someone and tear off his head for harming his old comrade. 'Was it over the treasure or this tale brought by Robin Byard?'

De Wolfe shrugged, finding that less painful than trying to speak, but any further discussion was ended by another young monk coming in with a steaming length of linen lying on a wooden tray. It was rolled like a large sausage and gave off a foul smell.

'All of you must leave now, if you will,' ordered the infirmarian. 'I must apply this poultice of hot clay and herbs to Sir John's neck. It will reduce the pain and swelling.'

He shooed the men out of the small cubicle and proceeded to wrap the poultice around John's neck, where an angry red line caused by the ligature had cut into the skin around its full circumference.

'It stinks!' protested de Wolfe.

'But not as much as you would stink in your grave, had not your brave clerk saved your life!' retorted the Benedictine.

It was the following afternoon before de Wolfe was allowed to return to his lodging. He had suffered repeated applications of the poultice, as well as regular doses of the herbal honeyed wine. The tyrant of an infirmarian had also taken the opportunity to bleed him and purge his bowels, so that he was more than glad to escape, even though he readily admitted that the treatment seemed to have banished most of the pain in his throat and his voice was halfway back to normal.

Gwyn and Thomas came to collect him and take him back to Long Ditch, both solicitous in their efforts to assist him. He shrugged off Gwyn's offer of an arm to lean on. 'It's my bloody head and neck that suffered, not my legs,' he growled, but leavened the rebuff with a lopsided grin.

In the house, Osanna fussed over him even more and insisted on administering a different honey posset made according to her grandmother's recipe. John accepted it with good grace, then washed it down with a pint of ale as soon her back was turned. She appeared to have forgiven him for his indiscretion with Hawise d'Ayncourt and this latest drama seemed to restore their relations to normal.

De Wolfe refused suggestions that he should take to his bed and he waited up until Osanna provided supper. She insisted that he had mostly liquid food, in the shape of a vegetable potage followed by a mutton stew in which she had shredded most of the meat so that he could swallow it more easily. The last course was a junket of rennet-curdled milk, flavoured with saffron. In fact, he was glad of her thoughtfulness, as the food slipped down easily, though he could see that poor Gwyn would have preferred using his teeth to rip apart a pork knuckle or a brisket of beef.

Thomas had gone back to the abbey for his supper and fraternal gossip with his religious friends, so after the meal the coroner and his officer sat around the dead fire-pit and drank more ale, punctuated by sporadic conversation. John wondered how many times they had done this over the last two decades – sitting together in the evening in a devastated castle or under a thorn tree, talking over the day's events, be they a bloody battle or a miserable ride across ruined French farmland or a stony desert in Outremer. His throat was improving by the hour and the desultory talk with his henchman proved no strain on his voice. The red line around his neck was still there, where the cord had dug into his skin, and a thin margin of bluish bruising had appeared alongside it, but apart from tenderness when the collar of his tunic rubbed him, he was virtually back to normal.

'What are we going to do about this, Crowner?' growled Gwyn. 'We can't let the bastards get away with attempting to kill a royal law officer!'

'We've got to find them first,' said John pragmatically. 'They'll put a foot wrong sooner or later, then we'll have them. Maybe they'll try again, but I won't be so trusting next time.'

'I'm not letting you out of my sight until this is settled!' promised Gwyn with grim determination. 'You'll not so much as go to the privy without me standing guard outside!'

De Wolfe grinned at the thought of his burly officer parading with drawn sword while he attended to his bowels, but his heart warmed to the faithful Cornishman who he knew would die for him if required.

The evening wore on, the sun still in the sky as the longest day of the year approached and it was about the eighth hour when there was a knock on the door to the lane. Osanna appeared almost instantly from the back door, like a genie from a bottle, confirming John's suspicions that she spent much of her time lurking behind it to listen to what was said in the main room.

Hurrying across to the front door, she opened it and stepped back in surprise when she saw the elegant woman on her threshold. But her indignant scowl was stillborn when she saw that behind Lady Hawise was a gentleman dressed in expensive, if rather garish clothing, with a manner and appearance that exuded nobility.

From where John was sitting, he could at first see only the woman and began to groan at being hounded once again. He rose to his feet and then saw Renaud de Seigneur, with the maid Adele sheltering behind him. For a moment, he feared that the husband had come to accuse him of trying to seduce his wife, but their expressions of friendly concern reassured him.

'Sir John, we have just heard the news, when we were at the supper table, for we were away overnight!' fluted Hawise. 'Ranulf told us that you had been viciously attacked and left for dead!'

John invited them inside and requested Osanna to fetch wine and cups. She seemed flattered to have this French lord in her house and accepted his forward wife as long as she did not throw herself again at her resident knight. Gwyn diplomatically withdrew to the nether regions with her, leaving John to entertain the guests.

The three sat at the table with the wine, the maid crouching unobtrusively in the corner, while de Wolfe regaled them with the tale of his ambush and his rescue by his clerk and the chaplain of St Stephen's. Both Renaud and Hawise seemed genuinely concerned about his health and the Lord of Blois produced a glazed pottery bottle of red wine as a gift.

'From my own vineyard in Freteval!' he said proudly. For her part, Hawise offered him a small glass jar of a salve, which she said would help to remove the sting from his abused throat.

Touched by their solicitude, de Wolfe endured their questions with patience, responding as politely as he could to their wild theorising about the reasons for this attack. Even Osanna, hovering within earshot, seemed to be mollified by Hawise's concern for John's welfare.

'It is just as well that we will all soon be on the road to Gloucester,' declared Renaud. 'Then you will be safely away from whoever wishes you ill!'

John gave one of his crooked grins. 'Unless the miscreant goes with us,' he said. 'According to the preparations for the procession described by Ranulf, it seems that almost everyone in Westminster above kitchen boy, is joining the exodus.'

Hawise fluttered a hand to her mouth in a patently false gesture of terror. 'Sweet Mary preserve us!' she gasped. 'Do you think that we might have a killer in our midst as we travel?'

De Seigneur patted her hand reassuringly. 'Calm

yourself, lady. We will have a strong escort of troops with us, for the queen's sake, if not ours.'

The cynical John felt that she was as hard as nails under that divine exterior and had little fear of being assaulted – and as for ravishment, he thought that perhaps she might welcome it as a change from the podgy Renaud.

Hawise fluttered her lashes at him again. 'And we have these doughty knights to protect us as well, Sir Ranulf and William, as well as our Crusading hero here!'

The coroner made one of his all-purpose rumbles in his throat, but found it hurt, even used as deprecation. The other pair continued to prattle on about his awful experience, then turned to ask about the other current excitements in Westminster.

'Is there any more news of who slew the poor canon?' asked Renaud, his plump face wreathed in concern. 'And has that stolen treasure turned up anywhere?'

When John had to admit to not making any progress, Hawise probed the other recent murder: 'That poor young man in our guest chambers, I still feel sad for him, though we never exchanged as much as a single word,' she said solicitously. 'It seems an injustice that he should lose his life and no one is brought to book for it.'

Although he had already raised the bluff, de Wolfe had to conceal his lack of any progress in finding a culprit for Basil's murder and muttered some vague claim about hoping to settle the matter very soon. He had heard nothing at all from the city sheriffs about the slaughtered ironworker, so that made three undetected murders of local men within a couple of weeks. Again, it made him wonder if his presence in Westminster was of any use whatsoever and, like Gwyn, strengthened his desire to go home to Devon.

When the wine was finished and the conversation was exhausted, the pair from Blois rose to leave, with renewed expressions of concern for John's health and hopes for a speedy return to full health and voice. Osanna hurried to open the door and bobbed her head obsequiously to the departing nobles.

John followed them out into Long Ditch to send them on their way and just as they were going, Hawise offered her hand to John to bow over. It was an excuse for her to whisper to him.

'You have been avoiding me, John! But our journey to Gloucester and back is a long one.'

The coroner's throat, if not his pride and temper, had improved greatly during the few days before the news was received of Queen Eleanor's impending arrival. A herald on a fast horse had been dispatched from Kingston when she arrived there, so that Westminster could be put on full alert and the next morning the welcoming party set out to meet her entourage on the high road.

Martin Stanford, the Deputy Marshal and his under-marshals, were the prime movers in organising this parade. The previous evening, their sergeants had hurried around all the personages required to take part, to ensure that they would be mounted and ready to go soon after dawn.

Gwyn had cleaned all of John's equipment, polishing up the harness of his stallion Odin, so that he was well turned out when they assembled in New Palace Yard. It was not an event that called for armour and helmet, so he wore his best grey tunic and a mottled wolfskin cloak thrown back over both shoulders. His broad leather belt and baldric carried his broadsword and his head was uncovered, his black hair sweeping back to the nape of his neck.

Twenty mounted men-at-arms formed the vanguard and rearguard of the escort, with another two-score civilians in their centre. Leading these was Hubert Walter, today in his secular mode as Chief Justiciar, rather than archbishop. He was dressed in similar fashion to de Wolfe, only in a scarlet tunic under his sword belt and a close-fitting linen helmet. Behind him were a number of earls and barons, members of the Curia, accompanied by the High Steward, the Deputy Chancellor, the Treasurer and other senior ministers. John rode in the next contingent, the middle-grade officers of the Exchequer and palace, including the Keeper and the Purveyor whilst a bevy of churchmen were led by the abbot, William Postard.

A dozen outriders, mostly esquires and knights, flanked the procession, carrying gaily coloured banners and pennants that streamed in the wind to display the arms and devices of the most prominent members of the party.

They rode out in fine style through the gates into King Street, the trumpets of the military escort blaring out as they advanced up the Royal Way towards the city, where they were to pick up the contingent provided by the Mayor and his council. A small crowd gathered along the road, always glad of some diversion in their drab lives. Some cheered or even jeered, as the cavalcade trotted past, especially when some of the horses, spooked by the trumpets, shied and skittered while their riders struggled and cursed to control them.

Once through Ludgate, the crowds were denser, as the ant-hill that was the city was penetrated by the vanguard of the troops. The mayor and some of his twenty-five aldermen were waiting at the Guildhall, with the bishop from St Paul's, his archdeacons, the two sheriffs and an escort of constables. Jealous as ever of their privileges and independence, the Mayor, Henry

fitz Ailwyn de Londonstone, led his party into the vanguard of the column from Westminster, settling them
by prior arrangement just behind the Chief Justiciar.

The augmented column set off for London Bridge,
the crowds now shouting more enthusiastically as the
leaders of their own community were seen in a favoured
position in the procession.

They crossed the bridge, the weight of the rhythmically tramping horses creating tremors in the old
wooden structure built by Peter de Colechurch twenty-
three years earlier, and causing several nervous
priests to cross themselves and commend their souls to
God. Other more hardy men looked over the side at
the nineteen new piers for the stone bridge that de
Colechurch had started.

Passing through Southwark on the south side of the
Thames, the cavalcade crossed the flat, marshy ground
to enter farmland and then patchy woodland, as the
land rose and the main track to the south-west aimed
itself towards Kingston.

A scout had been sent ahead on a fast rounsey to
warn of the arrival of the queen's party and in mid-
morning he came galloping back with the news that
there was now only a couple of miles between them.
After a consultation with the marshals, Hubert Walter
held up a gloved hand and the cavalcade came to a
halt in a large clearing with trees on either side, near
the village of Clapham.

They waited, all mounted on their steeds, some of
which were pawing the ground, shaking their heads,
neighing and snorting with impatience.

Soon there was a distant braying of trumpets and
horns, which rapidly came nearer until the Deputy
Marshal gave the order for his own trumpeters to reply.
These discordant blasts continued until the head of the
approaching cavalcade appeared through the trees, a

dozen soldiers with banners flying. John recognised the arms of William Marshal, Earl of Pembroke and then the large banner of Eleanor of Aquitaine, a single golden lion on a scarlet ground.

As they came into the clearing, they saw at last two stiffly erect forms riding side-by-side at the head of a short column of riders, which included several ladies and priests, more soldiers bringing up the rear, with outriders guarding the flanks.

They slowed their trotting steeds to a walk and spread out to face the reception party, the two main figures opposite Hubert Walter. One was a tall, stern-faced man wearing half-armour, a short chain-mail hauberk and a round helmet with a nasal guard. A large sword hung from his saddle, with a spiked mace on the other side, emphasising William Marshal's role as guardian of the queen.

Eleanor also sat as straight as a poker; her handsome face still reflected the beauty she had been in her younger days, though she was now seventy-four. The trumpets ceased and the Justiciar slid from his horse and advanced to her stirrup, going down briefly on one knee, then rising and kissing the hand that she held down to him. They were well-aquainted and spoke together for several minutes, though John was too far down the line to catch anything that was said.

Then Hubert moved across to William Marshal, who dismounted and clasped his arm. Warrior and archbishop, they were old comrades from Palestine and two of the king's most trusted servants. They moved to each side of Eleanor's white mare and took her bridle to lead her to the end of the long row of welcoming dignitaries from Westminster. This was a signal for all to slide from their saddles and stand by their horses' heads as Hubert and William led the queen slowly down the line. As she passed each one, they dropped to a knee and bowed their heads as Eleanor nodded in recognition when Walter murmured their names to her. Many she already knew well, either from her years as Henry's queen or the sixteen years as his prisoner in various places in England. It was William Marshal who was sent by Richard to effect her release when Henry died.

She did not know John de Wolfe, but had heard something of him and gave him a friendly smile when he rose from his obeisance to her, before moving on to the end of the line. Then the trumpets sounded again and everyone climbed back into their saddles, the procession soon working up into a trot and covering the few miles back to the city in good time.

At Westminster, the old queen was handed down from her horse with dignified gravity and conducted by Hubert and William Marshal to the main entrance and amidst a flurry of her ladies she went up to the royal apartments, no doubt grateful for a well-earned rest.

John made his way up to his chamber to join his officer and clerk and to wash the dust from his now-healed throat with a quart of ale. He regaled Gwyn and Thomas with a description of the journey and told them that they were invited to the great feast on the following evening, as almost everyone was included in the occasion to welcome the Queen Mother back to England. She was a popular figure, both for her proud and regal appearance, her colourful past and for being a bastion of stability in an uncertain world.

The feast next day was a triumph of organisation on the part of the Steward and Keeper and their army of servants. Tables had been set across the dais at the top of the Great Hall, where the Court of the King's Bench normally sat. These were for the high and mighty guests and were covered with linen cloths. Down the length of the hall, two long rows of bare tables accommodated the several hundred less eminent diners and in the side alcoves behind the pillars other trestles were set for the lowest orders.

When the crowd below had entered and settled in a pecking order that was checked and adjusted by the Keeper's men, who paraded up and down the lines of tables, a fanfare of trumpets from a gallery above heralded the approach of the queen. Everyone stood as the notables entered from within the palace entrance behind the dais. The chief guests came in, many splendidly dressed, and found their places around the top table, before Hubert Walter courteously escorted Eleanor to the large chair in the centre of the table, looking down the huge hall.

Still more elegant than most women half her age, she wore a gown of blue silk with heavy embroidery around the neck and a light mantle of silver brocade. Her white silk cover-chief was secured with a narrow gold crown and the dangling cuffs of her long sleeves were ornamented with gold tassels, as was the cord around her waist.

There was a roar of spontaneous cheering until the Justiciar held up his hands for silence, when William Postard, Abbot of Westminster, gave a long Latin grace and blessing to the assembly, who stood with bowed heads.

Then with a rumble of benches on the hard earthen floor, they all sat and the eating began. Immediately, a legion of servants appeared from the side doors, bearing trays of dishes and jugs of wine, ale and cider which were rapidly placed on the tables. The trenchers were already in place, though on the top tables, silver and pewter plates lay before the diners, as well as glass and pewter goblets. Two ladies stood behind Eleanor to attend to her every want, but the doughty old lady had little need of them, being well able to fend for herself.

As a courtesy – and Eleanor of Aquitaine was the queen and main inventor of courtly behaviour in Europe – Hubert and William Marshal went through the motions of helping her to the choicest morsels of the extravagant food placed before them and pouring her wine.

Compared with the usual fare in the Lesser Hall, de Wolfe decided that this was indeed a memorable feast. The top table had a surfeit of delicacies, from a roast swan which had been re-dressed in its original feathers, to several suckling pigs swimming in platters of wine-rich gravy. There were whole salmon, joints of beef and pork, numerous types of poultry and a range of puddings and sweets to follow, all washed down with the best wine that could be imported into England.

The rest of the hall also did well, if not on such a lavish scale, but no one went away unless sated with many kinds of meat, fish and sweetmeats. There were rivers of ale, cider, mead and wine, more than sufficient to send many diners reeling out of the hall at the end – or even being carried out unconscious by their friends.

John was placed a little way down one of the long trestles, as even the court's coroner had no chance of getting on to a top table filled with members of the Curia, bishops, earls and barons. He noticed, however, that Renaud de Seigneur and Hawise were seated not far from the queen, perhaps as the lady from Blois was almost the only woman present, apart from Eleanor and her ladies-in-waiting. Even amid the heady company she was with, Hawise still managed to send John a few burning glances, as he had deliberately avoided going to the Lesser Hall for the past few evenings. John saw Archdeacon Bernard a little further down the table and the two under-marshals Ranulf and William were on the next row. Thomas, as coroner's clerk, managed to slip on to a bench at the extreme bottom of the other limb of tables, but Gwyn was quite happy on a table hidden behind a pillar, together with some of his soldier friends. As long as there was ample food and drink, he did not care a toss for pomp and ceremony.

Five musicians on various instruments had been playing away manfully in the gallery. It appeared a thankless task, as no one seemed to be listening to them, even when they could be heard above the hubbub of voices. After a great deal of food had been consumed, with many a gallon of ale and wine, they were interrupted by another discordant blast of trumpets, as Hubert Walter rose to his feet and waited until more trumpeting and rapping of dagger-hilts on tables managed to bring relative silence.

The archbishop made a short, but eloquent speech of welcome to Queen Eleanor expressing delight at her return to England. When he had finished, there was more boisterous banging on tables and stamping of feet, with thunderous shouts of appreciation from the lower hall. This was a sign for more trumpets and with a radiant smile and wave at the assembled company, the Lionheart's mother allowed herself to be handed from her chair by Hubert Walter. With her ladies fussing about her, she retired through the door behind, escorted by the Justiciar, the Marshal and a number of the senior bishops and barons, no doubt to take more wine privately in the royal apartments. John noticed that Hawise and her maid also slipped away through another door, leaving Renaud de Seigneur to enjoy the rest of the evening with the men. There was still plenty of food to pick at and the drink flowed endlessly from the jugs and pitchers ferried in by the servants, so the festive evening continued until late, though it was still light when even the most hardy drinkers staggered out of the Great Hall.

John joined the people who were milling around the

tables and went over to talk for a while to Ranulf and William Aubrey, then went down to see how Gwyn and Thomas were faring. His clerk, who was no great tippler, was about to slip away to his bed in the abbey dorter, but professed that it had been a good meal and a privilege to be in the presence of the famous queen and the elite of English government, even at a distance.

Suddenly weary, John wondered whether age was catching up with him, and together with Gwyn, who was like a shadow to him since the attack in St Stephen's crypt, they went out into the summer dusk and made their way back to Long Ditch Lane.

CHAPTER THIRTEEN

In which Crowner John rides west

A court on the march was an impressive sight, even when the king himself was absent. A column a quarter of a mile long snaked through the countryside of Wiltshire, having left Newbury Castle that morning, aiming to reach Marlborough by evening, a distance of twenty miles.

A vanguard of mounted soldiers were drawn from the palace guard, augmented by troops supplied by several of the major barons who were members of the Royal Council. These provided both outriders along the length of the cavalcade and a strong rearguard at the tail. Behind the spearhead of men-at-arms came the most important people – Queen Eleanor herself, still riding stiffly erect on her white mare, with Hubert Walter, William Marshal, and the Treasurer, Richard fitz Nigel, in close attendance, her three ladies riding decorously behind. Following these was the whole column of riders of all ranks, flanked by people on foot. Colourful banners and pennants fluttered from poles and lances and when they passed a village the trumpets brayed a signal that nobility was on the march.

Unlike the journey from Portsmouth, this was a slow,

trundling affair, the horses going only at walking pace, for towards the end of the procession, a baggage train of a dozen ox-carts laboured along, piled with luggage, beds, provisions and hundreds of different items needed to keep the court viable during the next few weeks. All the lower-class staff were walking alongside, though some washerwomen and scullery maids had hitched rides on the tailboards of the carts. There were several primitive coaches, little more than curtained litters on wheels, for those ladies of the queen's entourage who preferred the bumpy ride of unsprung carriages being dragged along the rutted track.

As roads went this one was better than most, being the main highway out of London to the West Country, but it was still a rough track of pounded earth and stones, with occasional bridges of crude logs thrown across the streams. The weather had been good, so the usual quagmires of sticky mud had largely dried up, but the best the oxen could manage was about three miles an hour and often less when there was a gradient. Stops were frequent, to rest man and beast and to water and feed the horses and oxen. At midday, the whole column came to a halt for dinner and the servants hurried to the important travellers with meat and drink prepared at Newbury, whilst the rest had to cluster around the provision wagons to collect what they could.

The Coroner of the Verge was entitled to ride close behind the royal party, but John chose to stay well back with Gwyn and Thomas. Ranulf and William Aubrey were busy riding up and down the column in their role as marshals, organising matters and dealing with the endless hitches and emergencies that such a mass of men, horses and vehicles generated.

De Wolfe had kept behind partly to avoid Hawise and her husband, for he saw that the Lord of Freteval was fairly close to the queen and that Hawise, no horse-woman like Eleanor, had taken to one of the palanquin wagons. At Reading Abbey, the night before last, Hawise had sought him out after supper in the crowded guest hall, where the middle echelons had been fed. Though she had somehow managed to shake off her husband, John was so surrounded by other men that she was unable to separate him from them and had to be content with a few words and some suggestive glances, her maid standing by all the time.

Now Odin lumbered along happily, his great hairy feet rhythmically thumping the track. As a destrier, he could raise a brisk gallop over short distances on the battlefield or the tourney ground, but was not built for sustained speed. However, John knew from experience that at walking pace or even a trot, Odin could shift his half-ton of horseflesh all day without effort.

This was their fourth day on the road and with luck another two would see them at Bristol, where de Wolfe intended to tackle the Justiciar about a compassionate side-trip to Devon.

They reached Marlborough in the early evening and the cavalcade camped in the grounds of the castle, which was built on an ancient mound, in which Merlin was supposed to have been buried. Ironically, the castle had been given to Prince John by his father many years earlier, but after his treachery when Richard was imprisoned, it was removed from his grasp and reverted to a royal possession.

As before, the queen and the high officials of state were lodged in the private apartments. The other officers and clergy ate in the main hall, then slept on the floor on straw mattresses brought in from the carts. John ate a plain but adequate meal provided by the harassed servants and then decided to go for a walk to stretch his legs after a day in the saddle. Gwyn was eating in the outer bailey, where an ox was being roasted for the soldiers and the rest of the travellers, so John managed to avoid him, as he was beginning to tire of his officer's insistence on protecting him against further attempts at assassination. He went out through a small postern gate in the inner ward and across a bridge over a dry moat to a wide area kept free of trees to give an open field of fire in case of attack. It was a time of peace this far inland and no one was likely to lay siege to Marlborough that night, so John walked on, savouring the serenity and quiet after the noisy journey all day on the high road.

The sun was low but still visible in a sky studded with woolly clouds as he entered the edge of the woods that had formed the hunting park for the lords of Marlborough. There was a stream tinkling over stones a few yards into the trees and he found a fallen log to sit on, while he watched the sparkling water. It dropped into a deep pool, where small fish made circles on the surface as they snapped at the midges that flitted by. Though John was no nature lover, it reminded him of his childhood in Stoke-in-Teignhead, the de Wolfe family manor, where he used to swim in such pools and try to catch trout with a pointed stick.

He sat staring into the stream, lulled by the quiet and the peacefulness after the crowds and clamour of London, wishing again that he could return to his native land of Devon. Maybe it was a sign of getting old, he thought pensively. Then he thought of Queen Eleanor, seventy-four and still as sharp as ever, perhaps good enough for another twenty years. But she had no need to wield a sword or a lance like a knight – and a slowing warrior was soon likely to be a dead warrior.

As if to put these thoughts to the test, a pair of hands were suddenly clapped across his eyes from behind. With a roar of shocked surprise at yet another unexpected attack, he threw himself sideways and grabbed desperately at his assailant, expecting to feel the thrust of a dagger between his ribs.

They both fell full-length to the long grass behind the tree-trunk, but instead of feeling homespun cloth or a leather jerkin under his hands, they slid around smooth silk – and instead of a muttered curse from coarse lips, there was a silvery laugh.

'Why, Sir John, you seem very ardent, throwing a defenceless lady to the ground so quickly! And I thought your fondness for me had cooled!'

Shocked, but glad to be alive after his lapse of caution, he found himself lying on the soft ground, almost nose to nose with Hawise d'Ayncourt, his hands still grasping her around her slim waist.

'Where in hell did you spring from, lady?' he gasped with a distinct lack of courtesy.

For answer, she slid her arms around his neck and clamped her lips upon his in a long and passionate kiss. When he came up for air, he pulled his head away and stared at her beautiful face, only inches from his own. It was flushed with excitement, the tip of her pink tongue peeping from between her pearly teeth.

'You'll not escape me this time, John de Wolfe,' she hissed.

He loosened his hands and tried to wriggle from her limpet-like embrace, though admittedly his efforts were half-hearted.

'By Christ, woman, I'm married and have a lover who's dear to me!' he muttered, somewhat illogically. But clinging to him even more tightly, she rolled her eyes around in a parody of searching the surrounding trees.

'I see no wife or mistress, John! There's just us and the birds – and I'm sure they'll tell no tales.'

Then she returned to kissing and massaging the back

of his neck, her body squirming against his as they lay side-by-side in the soft grass. John was a sensual man who loved women – almost all women – and his self-control was very thin at the best of times. To be locked in an embrace with one of the most seductive beauties he had ever known was more than his flesh and blood could resist. With a groan of pleasure, rather than remorse, he capitulated and began returning her kisses and pulling her even more firmly against the length of his body.

In spite of the restrictions of clothing, the inevitable happened. His long tunic was slit front and back for riding his horse and each of his black hose was tied up separately to a thin underbelt. Hawise, perhaps in anticipation of the meeting, wore a flowing gown which was laced from neck to midriff and she showed a remarkable agility in undoing it and casting off the twisted silken rope that acted as her girdle.

Hawise and John were no strangers to the art of lovemaking and once committed he made the most of the opportunity. Eventually, exhaustion overtook the pair and they lay consummated and satiated, staring up at the paling sky.

De Wolfe's fevered mind gradually returned to normal as he found himself still with an arm around the woman, whose head was pillowed against his shoulder. He pulled himself to a sitting position and began restoring his clothing to a more decent arrangement. He looked down at the lady from Blois, wondering what would come of this gross indiscretion. At least her husband had not appeared on the scene, to blackmail him into giving away state secrets, as he once had feared.

'This is a fine situation, madam!' he growled. 'The man is supposed to seduce the woman, not the other way around!'

She smiled lazily up at him. 'If I were to wait for you, I'd wait for ever, John!'

She held out a hand for him to pull her up and began re-lacing the bodice of her green silk gown, which thankfully – or perhaps by design – would not show any stains from the lush grass.

'Don't fret, Sir Crowner, I'll not petition the Pope to seek an annulment and then insist that you marry me!' she said archly. 'We've had a pleasant diversion, that's all – and there's no reason that we should not have several more, before I'm dragged back to a dull existence as a dutiful wife in Freteval.'

John had his own ideas about that, but he thought that this was not the time or place to fall out with her. He had enjoyed their 'diversion' immensely, but he had no intention of making it a habit, there were too many potential complications for that.

'How did you come to find me here?' he asked, after they were both dressed decently again.

'I always have my eye set upon you, John,' she said earnestly. 'I saw you slip away without that hulking great fellow that guards you like a wet nurse, so I followed.'

'What about your husband and your maid?'

'Renaud is safely drinking with his fellow lords in the guest chamber. I feigned a headache and then got rid of Adele for an hour with a two-penny bribe.'

John stood up and lifted her to her feet with a strong hand.

'You had best go back alone, but I'll watch you from the edge of the trees to see you safely to the postern gate,' he said gallantly. Hawise reached up and as a farewell put her arms around his neck again and kissed him on the lips. Not so passionately this time, but it was a warm and comforting embrace. As she walked off, with a girlish wave of her fingers, he thought that in different circumstances, free from all the other baggage that his life had accumulated, he could love that woman – and certainly enjoy his nights with her.

When he had seen her safely across the open field to the castle, he returned to his fallen log and looked down at the crumpled grass behind it. Another memory for his old age, if he ever lived to see it!

He sat and delved into his feelings, to see what remorse and shame were welling up there. He ticked off the positive factors first – the husband did not know about this and Hawise seemed quite relaxed about the adultery. She was not going to scream 'rape' or make him marry her. Then Gwyn knew nothing of this escapade, so would not be making reproachful hints about his master's infidelity. On the down side, his own conscience was the main problem. He had no scruples where Matilda was concerned, as she had made it abundantly clear that her marriage to him was a penance and she wished she had stayed a spinster. Thank God they had had no children, though this would have been a physical impossibility during the past dozen years, unless she managed another virgin birth. Nesta was no longer a factor, as she had taken herself off to be married. It was Hilda who was the problem, and she was the reason for the devilish imp that sat on his shoulder and hissed the mantra of his conscience into his ear.

Yet even she had not had him exclusively, as when her husband, Thorgils the Boatman, was alive, John had only sporadic access to Hilda when the shipmaster was away on voyages, so he had to vent his amorous energy elsewhere. Even when he was with Nesta, he had occasional flings with Hilda – and the blonde woman knew that he was not faithful to her either, for there had been a sprightly widow in Sidmouth who gave him favours, until she went off to marry a butcher.

As he sat on his log, he chided himself for his wanton behaviour and vowed that in future he would be faithful to Hilda. He convinced himself that this episode tonight was an aberration, verging on a rape of himself by Hawise. He felt he was hardly to blame, as it was more than any man could have stood, to be wrestled on the ground by such an ardent beauty. He dismissed the devil of conscience with a promise that henceforth he would be a model of fidelity and chasteness except where Hilda was concerned. He had one mental eye on his excursion to Devon in a few days' time and wanted to appear in Dawlish as pure as the driven snow – so Hawise would henceforth be strictly out of bounds!

Inadvertently, the Chief Justiciar helped de Wolfe to maintain his celibacy, as John was able to leave the procession early and so remove himself from the temptation offered by Hawise d'Ayncourt. He had originally intended waiting until they reached Bristol before seeking Hubert Walter's consent to leave for Devon, but on the night after his escapade with Hawise, they stopped at Chippenham, the last stage before Bristol. By chance, the Justiciar turned his horse as soon as they arrived at one of the royal manors and rode back down the line, greeting many he knew and enquiring if all was well after a day on the march. When he came to de Wolfe, the coroner took the opportunity to broach the matter of going to Devon to settle his family affairs, since so far there had not been a single incident that required the attention of the Coroner of the Verge. After some thought, Hubert agreed and suggested that he may as well leave in the morning, rather than go on to Bristol.

John made sure that he remained invisible to Hawise for the rest of the night and at dawn he set off across country with Gwyn and Thomas de Peyne. The route that led through Shepton Mallet and Ilminster to Honiton and thence to Exeter took them two nights and three long days of hard riding, which taxed Thomas and his rounsey to the utmost. During the journey, John had plenty of time to reflect on many aspects of his present situation and also to revisit the unsolved mysteries in London. They seemed a world away, here in the rural fastnesses of western England, but he knew this was only a respite from the problems that would still confront him when he returned to Westminster. Was there some French subversive seeking to ferret out secrets of Kent's defences? And had he murdered Basil, a potential threat to his identity, as Robin Byard had claimed?

And where was this damned treasure hidden away? Was Simon Basset involved and if not, why should anyone wish to poison him?

As they rode the last miles towards Exeter, de Wolfe sighed and consigned these problems to the future, knowing that he had other more immediate problems to deal with when he reached the city. Soon the tops of the great twin towers of the cathedral were visible as they trotted along Magdalene Street, the country road to the south of Exeter where the gallows tree stood. They reached the South Gate just before it closed at curfew and turned up through the Serge Market and the Shambles, where in the mornings beasts were slaughtered in the road. At the top was Carfoix, the crossing of the main streets from the four gates which had been there since Roman times. Here they parted, as Gwyn and the clerk were going down to the Bush Inn, where his wife was now landlady, and where Thomas would lodge during their short stay.

John turned right into High Street and a tired Odin plodded up past the Guildhall, his nostrils twitching as he picked up the old familiar odours of the livery stables where he used to live. This was in Martin's Lane, a narrow alley that led down into the cathedral precinct and was virtually opposite John's house.

Andrew the farrier was happy to see both Sir John and his stallion and when John had seen Odin fed and watered, he crossed the lane to the front door of his tall, narrow house, one of only two in the lane. As always, the door was unbarred and he pushed inside to the vestibule, where boots and cloaks were kept. The door to the hall, the main room of the house, was on his right and to the left a covered way went around the corner of the building to the backyard. The front door had barely slammed behind him when a large brown hound loped around that corner, as fast as his old legs could carry him. With a yelp of pleasure and a great wagging of his tail, Brutus rushed upon John, slobbering a welcome into his hand.

Close behind him came a handsome, dark-haired woman who gave a less demonstrative, but equally warm welcome. John hugged Mary to him and gave her a long kiss, not passionate, but full of warmth. They had had furtive tumbles in her cook-shed or laundry in the past, but when his wife had taken on a nosey French maid several years earlier, Mary had decided that her job was worth more than tumbles with her master. Now that Matilda was no longer there, matters could have been different, but John's new state of virtue put that out of his mind.

'This is a surprise, Sir Crowner,' said Mary, her voice rich with the Devon dialect. 'I had a message from that shipman, Roger Watts, to say that you hoped to get home some time, but I did not expect you this soon.'

As he had done for years past when he wanted a gossip and a decent meal, he went around to the yard and sat with Mary in her kitchen hut, where she also lived and slept. Producing good ale and a platter of

savoury pastries, she promised him a full meal as soon
as she could prepare it. He sat on a milking stool and
told her all his news, though avoiding any mention of
Hawise d'Ayncourt. While she stoked up her fire and
put the makings of a mutton stew into an iron pot
hanging on a trivet, Mary told him of events in the city,
though there seemed little enough to relate.

'Your brother-in-law still has his town house in North
Street and Lucille is still in service with his wife,' she
announced. Lucille had been his wife's handmaid, but
she had been shunted off to Eleanor de Revelle when
Matilda took herself to the nunnery. This brought
them to the vexed question of his wife.

'Have you heard anything of her, Mary?'

'Nothing, apart from the fact that she is still at Polsloe
and presumably is in rude health,' she answered. 'I wish
to God and all his angels that I knew what was to
become of me and this house, for it seems wasteful for it
to stand empty with me living here like a hermit.'

'I will go to Polsloe first thing in the morning, good
girl,' he promised. 'This matter must be settled one way
or the other.'

While Mary finished cooking for him, he stripped
to his hose in the yard and with a leather bucket of
water from the well, washed the grime of many days
travelling from his body. He did not go so far as to
shave, but finding a clean tunic still in his chest up in
the solar at the back of the house, he felt refreshed and
sat to enjoy his meal all the more. Though it was now
dusk, he walked down through the lower town to the
Bush, savouring the sights and smells of Exeter that
were so different from those of London. It was strange
to enter the tavern in Idle Lane without Nesta being
there to greet him and a wave of sad nostalgia engulfed
him for a moment. However, the welcome from Gwyn's
buxom wife and a quart of excellent ale soon restored

his spirits, as he greeted many old acquaintances among the patrons. Gwyn was beaming with pleasure at being home, his two small sons clinging to his breeches as he helped his wife to serve the customers. Old Edwin, the one-eyed potman, was still there and cackled a greeting to John as if the coroner had been gone only a couple of days.

Thomas had vanished down to the cathedral to meet his ecclesiastical friends and no doubt would spend half the night and most of next day at the many services that dominated the clergy's day. De Wolfe was soon brought up to date on all the local gossip, though nothing of great importance seemed to have happened in the few months since he had left.

'The new coroner is well liked – he seems a fair man,' said a master mason, who John had known for years. 'But I hear that he is fretting somewhat at having to spend too much time away from his manor down west.'

Sir Nicholas de Arundell had been persuaded into taking the coronership when de Wolfe left and John suspected that he had done so mainly out of gratitude for his help in rescuing him from a life as an outlaw on Dartmoor and restoring him to possession of his manor of Hempston Arundell.*

Gwyn's wife Martha persuaded him to eat another meal, in spite of having had Mary's mutton stew; and after a few more quarts of ale, it was growing dark when he finally tore himself away from the familiar and hospitable inn and made his way home to Martin's Lane. After kissing Mary goodnight, he wearily climbed the outside stairs to the solar, built up against the back wall of the house and gratefully slid into bed, a large mattress on a low plinth on the floor of the bare room,

* See *The Noble Outlaw.*

where he had spent so many lonely nights, with Matilda snoring on the other side.

De Wolfe could only afford to spend a couple of nights in Exeter before setting off again for Gloucester, where he had promised to return to Hubert Walter's company. He decided that there would be no time for him to go down to Stoke-in-Teignhead to visit his family, as this would take at least an extra day.

As he had promised Mary, his first task was to try to make some decision about his wife's future and an hour after dawn he was back in Odin's saddle and on his way to Polsloe. He had told Gwyn and Thomas to make the most of their time on their own affairs, so he rode alone for the mile or so from the East Gate to the small Benedictine priory. Here seven nuns lived and provided medical care to the women of the area. John knew the prioress well enough, but his main contact there was a formidable nun, Dame Madge. She was a tall gaunt woman, with a specialist knowledge of women's ailments and the hazards of childbirth. She had been of considerable help to John when he was county coroner, in cases involving rape or miscarriage.

It was Dame Madge that he sought out when he reached Polsloe and, after leaving his horse with the gatekeeper, a novice took her a message. As men were not particularly welcome inside the building, he waited in the porch of the west range until she arrived. Dressed in her black habit, tall and slightly stooped, she was almost a female counterpart to himself and in spite of her often stern, abrupt manner, they got on well.

'I have come from Westminster, sister, in the hope of seeing my wife and learning of her intentions,' he began.

The old nun gave a grim smile and shook her head. 'We have been over this ground before, have we not, Sir John? This must be the fourth time you have sought to see your wife here.'

'Is it not natural, sister?' he grunted. 'For better or worse, we were joined by the Church in matrimony and now she rejects me – or at least, I assume she has, for she refuses to say anything, one way or the other. I need to get on with my life.'

Dame Madge nodded sympathetically and they talked for a while, as he explained how his situation had been so radically altered on the orders of King Richard. For her part, the nun could only repeat that Matilda had given firm instructions that she was not to be contacted by any of her previous friends or relatives, especially her husband.

'But that must have been some time ago, as she cannot know that I was to come here today,' urged John. 'Can we not try once more, to see if her resolution has weakened?'

Dame Madge again shook her head sadly. 'I very much doubt her opinion has changed, for she is a very strong-willed woman. But we can speak to the prioress, to see what she thinks.'

They went into the building and upstairs to the prioress's parlour, a comfortable room where a small, rather plump woman sat behind her table studying the monthly accounts of the little establishment. She received John graciously and given that the hour was too early for wine sent for some damson cordial and pastries. After hearing of the same old problem, she asked Dame Madge to go down and speak to Sister Matilda, to see whether she would receive her husband to speak of the future. When the older nun had left, John asked the prioress how his wife was faring in this solitary life.

'She is very devout, Sir John,' she answered frankly. 'Almost too devout in some ways, as she is inflexible and intolerant of any straying from the path of right-eousness. I sense that she is saddened by life and constantly angry that she can do little to alter it.'

De Wolfe was not sure what she meant, but it sounded typical of the old Matilda that he knew all too well.

'I never wished to cause her such discontent and sadness,' he admitted. 'But I of necessity was away from her for most of our married life.'

'I do not think that you are the sole cause of her disillusionment,' said the prioress thoughtfully. 'It is her brother's misbehaviour and fall from grace that is a major factor – but, of course, she blames you for being the instrument of his downfall.'

Dame Madge returned with the not unexpected news that Matilda had flatly refused to see her husband.

'She is adamant and would not even discuss the reasons with me,' said the nun. 'I fear it is hopeless trying to pursue the matter, Sir John.'

He sighed. 'What am I to do? I have a house in the city and cannot either use it or sell it, in case she decides to return. I have a maid living there, discontented and worried. It is no secret that I have a liaison with another lady, but I cannot do anything about that. Archdeacon John de Alençon has advised me that even if Matilda takes her full vows, that will not dissolve the marriage and leave me free to take another wife.'

He turned up his hands in despair. 'She has found the most exquisite method of punishing me, worse than the thumbscrews or the torments of the Ordeal!'

The two women were sympathetic, but impotent to help. The prioress pressed more cordial upon him and they began talking about his new life in London. For celibate ladies who had chosen largely to cut themselves off from the outside world, they were intensely curious about Westminster, the court and the personalities that John knew. He regaled them with a description of the palace and the abbey and of the huge city that lay a couple of miles down the Thames. He told them of Queen Eleanor and the pomp of her arrival from Portsmouth with the Archbishop and the Marshal, then the procession of the court across England to meet Prince John. They listened avidly and he guessed that they would have plenty of material to gossip about with the other sisters at the supper table that night.

When he had exhausted his fund of stories about his life as Coroner of the Verge, he took his leave, despondent but not surprised at the complete failure of his mission. As Dame Madge saw him off at the porch, she left him with a sliver of hope for some resolution to his problem.

'It will be many months yet before she has to decide whether or not to finally take her vows and make her position here irrevocable,' she said. 'Perhaps before then, she may again change her mind, as she did before when she came to Polsloe.'

With this tiny crumb of comfort, he rode back to Exeter and went up the familiar hill to the castle, known universally as 'Rougemont', from the colour of the local red sandstone from which it had been built by William the Bastard in the northern angle of the old Roman walls. In the keep, built inside the inner bailey, he found his old friend the sheriff, Henry de Furnellis, sitting in his chamber off the main hall, struggling as usual with the documents and accounts that his chief clerk incessantly placed before him. Glad of an excuse to escape the bureaucracy, he called for ale and they sat chatting for an hour. John learned that the new coroner was competent and efficient, but that his heart was not in the job.

'He's not like you, John, you were like a terrier, worrying away at a case until you got the answer,' said Henry, an even older Crusader than John, having been persuaded into taking the shrievalty of Devon when Richard de Revelle fell from grace.

They were joined by Ralph Morin, the castle constable, another old friend and John had to repeat his description of life at Westminster for their benefit. The sheriff's bushy grey eyebrows rose at some parts of the tale.

'You lost part of the king's treasure from the Tower itself!' he boomed incredulously. 'And have suffered an attempt on your own life? Trust you, John, you always seem to attract disaster!'

When he left the keep, he called on a few more old friends, including Sergeant Gabriel, who headed the garrison's men-at-arms, and Brother Roger, the amiable chaplain of Rougemont.

The coroner was away at his manor, so he could not enquire of him how he was coping with his new appointment, but as he left the castle, he felt sad that he had to leave the next day and be deprived of all the comradeship that he had built up here over the past years.

'But I'll not be deprived of the company of one particular person today!' he averred, as he trotted Odin down to the West Gate, where he forded the river and set off at a canter for the ten miles to Dawlish.

CHAPTER FOURTEEN

In which Crowner John returns to Westminster

John spent an idyllic afternoon, evening and night in Hilda's house in Dawlish, a small fishing port built around a tidal creek. He arrived in time for dinner and left at dawn next day, spending much of the time in Hilda's bed, a high French one that her late husband had brought back from St Malo.

Surprised and delighted to see him, the slender blonde woman firmly relegated her maid Alice to the small room she occupied downstairs and kept John almost prisoner in the two spacious chambers on the first floor of the fine stone house.

Though it was not many weeks since Hilda had made her adventurous voyage up to London to visit him, their affection and passion was undimmed. John managed to convince himself that the brief interlude with Madame d'Ayncourt was an aberration forced on him by Hawise and was able to put it out of his mind as he revelled in Hilda's company. For her part, though she was a devout woman who regularly attended Mass and did much charitable work in the parish, she accepted his adultery as a technical problem due to Matilda's intransigence in entering a nunnery and leaving the poor man in matrimonial limbo.

During one of the brief periods when they were dressed and in her living chamber, they talked at length about his visit to Polsloe that morning. Hilda had been down to her kitchen shed to order some food, which the part-time cook, a sailor's widow from the village, prepared and sent upstairs with Alice.

As they sat eating at her table, de Wolfe related Matilda's continued obdurateness about revealing her intentions.

'After all these months, John, surely she is now intending to take her final vows and stay on at Polsloe for the rest of her life?'

'And where does that leave us, my dearest lady?' he asked despondently. 'We have been lovers since I first grew stubble on my chin.'

'It leaves you far away in Westminster, John,' she reminded him gently. 'If you were here, then we could be together as often as you would wish.'

'Can you not come to London, Hilda? There we could live together far more discreetly than in a tongue-wagging place like Exeter – or far worse, your own village of Dawlish.'

She shook her head sadly. 'Do not ask me to do that, John. I would be like a fish out of water. I am a country girl, I have my fine house and my share of your business. I still have my family a few miles away in Holford, I love the Devon countryside and have so many widows and children dependent upon me since their men died at sea serving Thorgils, God bless his soul.'

John nodded sadly; he had anticipated that this would be her answer. 'Then let's make the most of today, my love!' he said, reviving and seizing her once again in his arms.

The coroner's trio rode into Gloucester on the last day of July, weary after their long ride from Exeter.

Knowing that the court cavalcade would have long left Bristol, they bypassed the city and went up the edge of the Severn to Gloucester. The castle, near the river in the south-western part of the city, was not large and the descent of Queen Eleanor with her large entourage stretched it to its limits. Prince John was staying there, though it did not belong to him, as the king had wisely retained it as a royal possession when he returned his treacherous brother's lands to him after he foolishly forgave him for his abortive rebellion two years earlier.

Though the most important people were accommodated in the castle, the rest were distributed all over the city and the lower echelons of the Westminster contingent had to camp out in the castle grounds and surrounding fields. The Purveyor and his staff had worked strenuously to find places for the middle ranks, filling every inn, lodging house and even confiscating private houses.

By the time John de Wolfe and his clerk and officer arrived some days later, there was no room anywhere within the bulging city. At first, he viewed this with some relief, as lodging at a distance meant that he could avoid Hawise, until he recalled that she and her husband had gone on to visit her relatives in Hereford, a day's ride away. Thomas de Peyne, using his priestly connections, managed to find a pallet in a corner of the great abbey, but John and Gwyn rode a mile or two to the east where, in the village of Brockworth, they found room in a crowded inn, each sleeping on a bag of hay in the loft.

On the first morning after they arrived, John presented himself at the castle to tell the Justiciar's clerks that he was back. Thankfully, they informed him that there had been nothing that required his attention during his absence, but that Hubert Walter wished to speak to him. An audience was fixed for the middle of the afternoon and at the appointed time John was called into a chamber in the gatehouse.

He found the Justiciar and William Marshal there, together with Richard fitz Nigel, the Bishop of London. The King's Treasurer was a florid man in the evening of his life, one of a line of fitz Nigels who had rebuilt the Exchequer after the anarchy of Stephen many years before.

The three men sat easily with goblets of wine around a small table and John was relieved to find that he was not being arraigned before a tribunal. In fact, he was invited to sit in a vacant chair and given wine by a servant, who then withdrew.

'I am glad to see you back safely, de Wolfe,' said Hubert. 'I trust your visit to Devon was satisfactory.'

John thought about Dawlish and considered the visit very satisfactory indeed, but he forbore to trouble Hubert with the continuing problem of his wife and merely thanked him for allowing him to go. What was this all about, he wondered, looking around at the faces of the three great men?

The Justiciar soon enlightened him.

'The Marshal was recently with the king until he came across the sea with Queen Eleanor. Before he left Rouen, my dispatches, which recorded the theft from the Tower, had arrived.' He stopped and looked at the long, stern face of William Marshal, then invited him to continue.

'As was to be expected, King Richard was most concerned,' rasped the Earl of Pembroke. His long face cracked into a wry smile. 'You will know from personal experience, de Wolfe, that our beloved Richard is prone to outbursts of extreme temper, like his father before him. He was not amused by this theft of his precious funds, which are so desperately needed for his army.'

John nodded his heartfelt agreement, as he well knew of his volatile moods. But he failed to see where this was leading, until Richard fitz Nigel took up the tale, voice quavering a little.

'Not to beat about the bush, the king wants his money back and the thieves hanged! No effort is to be spared in achieving this.'

The Marshal came back in a more conciliatory mood. 'The king realises that no fault attaches to you, de Wolfe. This audacious robbery took place after you had delivered the treasure safely to its destination. But he wants the matter settled quickly and commands that you use every means to effect this. He wishes me to tell you that he has every confidence in your ability to do this.'

There was an undercurrent of meaning in the Marshal's voice that suggested that old friendships would count for little if he failed. Hubert Walter threw back the rest of his wine in a gesture that said that the interview was almost over. 'John, I think it best if you go straight back to London and get on with this vital task. The court is returning through Oxford and will not be back at Westminster for at least ten days. There seems little point in your staying on here, given that there seems to be no call upon your services.'

He stood up and de Wolfe hurriedly emptied his own cup and got to his feet, backing towards the door. As he bowed to the others and declared that he would do his very best to solve the mystery and bring the miscreants to justice, the Justiciar reminded him of the authority he had been given.

'Remember, de Wolfe, you already have the king's writ, carrying my seal. You may go wherever you wish, interrogate anyone and summon any aid whatsoever. So take no nonsense from those sheriffs in the city. You can put the Mayor of London himself to the torture if you think it will help!'

With these rousing words echoing in his ears, John withdrew and closed the door. He had mixed feelings about what had just been said – on the one hand, he was flattered by the trust that was being put in him, yet daunted by the task which had so far been like kicking uselessly at a stone wall. And the price of failure was not to be contemplated.

Whatever the problems and possible penalties looming over him, de Wolfe saw one immediate advantage in cutting and running from the royal cavalcade – he would not have to dodge the seductive temptations of Hawise d'Ayncourt. Hopefully, she and her husband would be travelling back to France in the queen's retinue and apart from a night or two when passing through Westminster, he would be safe from her beguiling charms. Though he had admittedly enjoyed his romp with her in Marlborough very much, his day with Hilda had brought it home to him how fond he was of the Saxon woman.

Early on the morning after his ultimatum from the Justiciar, Marshal and Treasurer, de Wolfe and Gwyn were joined by Thomas at Brockworth, the little clerk rather sulky at being so prematurely wrenched from the great abbey of Gloucester, where he could have indulged himself for far longer in the liturgy and offices of such a famous religious house.

They set off for London by the most direct route, across the Cotswolds to Witney and then on to Oxford and Wycombe.

The magic document with Hubert's seal dangling from it readily got them bed and board at royal castles and manors for the four nights that they were on their journey and at the end of the fifth day's riding, they arrived in King Street, with the abbey and the irregular outline of the palace looming over the Thames.

Much as John preferred his native Devon, Westminster was a welcome sight after all those weary miles and Osanna's hurried meal of oatcakes, boiled bacon and eggs was like nectar.

With Thomas safely in the abbey dorter, he and Gwyn crawled to their palliasses and slept like logs until morning.

When their clerk arrived after his early duties in the abbey the next day, the coroner's team held a council of war, as John had told them of the direct order from the king to bring this crime to a rapid conclusion.

'He wants his money back and the perpetrators dangling from the elms at Tyburn!' said de Wolfe. 'So we had better come up with some ideas or it may be our own necks that get stretched!'

They spent an hour discussing every aspect of the matter, but it seemed an intractable problem. As often happened, it was the nimble brain of Thomas de Peyne that had the first original thought.

'Crowner, do you still have those two keys that we found amongst the possessions of Simon Basset?'

John stared at his clerk, wondering what tortuous thoughts were going through his mind. 'I do indeed, but we have stared at them long enough before this. We don't even know if they were for the locks on that damned chest, as it has gone off to Rouen. What else could be seen upon them?'

'Perhaps not *seen* upon them, master,' answered Thomas cryptically. 'But could I handle them once more, with your leave?'

De Wolfe groped under his table, where a shelf lay beneath the oaken top. Amongst oddments which included a broken knife, two part-used candles and an old leather belt, he found the two keys, put aside as being of no further use to their investigation.

'What do you expect to find after all this time?' he grunted, as he handed them to his clerk. To his surprise, Thomas hardly looked at them, but rubbed them between his fingers, then held them to his thin, pointed nose where he sniffed at them like a hound on the scent.

Gwyn gave one of his booming laughs, laced with derision. 'What in hell are you doing, man? Are you going to track down the robbers by their smell?'

Unfazed, the little priest nodded. 'Maybe I will, as something is tickling my memory.'

He handed the keys back to the coroner. 'Feel those again, sire, do they not seem greasy to you? And there is an odour which I have smelt somewhere before.'

John did as he was bid and then handed the keys on to Gwyn, who made a great performance of sticking them under his huge moustache and sniffing loudly.

'There is something,' agreed John cautiously. 'But what use is that to us?'

Thomas stood up. 'I think that we should go again to that ironmaster's house in Duck Lane.'

The dwelling and workshop was still empty when they arrived half an hour later. John was prepared to wave his royal warrant at anyone who questioned their right to be there, but it all seemed deserted. Going around to the back, they saw that weeds were already reclaiming the muddied yard, and someone had broken into the house by smashing the temporary repairs that Gwyn had made to the back door. They went in and looked around the gloomy workshop and at the confusion of bits of metal that lay on the dusty benches and earthen floor.

'If there was anything useful here, it's been stolen by

now,' Gwyn growled. 'Good job that the son took away all the tools.'

'What are we looking for, Thomas?' demanded de Wolfe.

The clerk scanned the rough shelves above the workplaces and then looked on the floor under the benches. He bent down and picked up something, then reached up to a shelf and took down a rusty metal pot. He sniffed both these unprepossessing objects, then handed them to the coroner.

'How do these compare with those keys, Crowner?'

John obediently put his nose to them, then passed them to Gwyn.

'It's the same smell, like beeswax and turpentine, at a guess.'

The Cornishman grudgingly agreed. 'So what does it mean?' he asked.

The clerk held out the object from the floor. 'I think you noticed this last time we were here, Crowner. A little wooden box, half-filled with the stuff from this pot. It's a soft wax, that could be used for taking impressions, so that a metal copy could be made by a competent craftsman.'

'But then it would be the originals that stank of the wax, not the copies!' objected Gwyn.

Thomas smiled smugly. 'I feel sure that the copies would have to be repeatedly matched to the wax impression, while the blank wards were being filed down to make sure they were an exact fit.'

Light dawned on de Wolfe. 'So Canon Basset could have pressed the keys of the chest into the wax, then brought it here for this man Osbert Morel to make copies?'

Thomas nodded energetically. 'Certainly! The only problem is when would he have access to both keys to allow him to do that?'

They all thought about that for a moment. 'Both keys are only together when the chest is actually being opened in that deep chamber in the Tower,' said Gwyn. 'But the Keeper is always there then, having brought his own key.'

John shrugged. 'I wonder if he stays all the time when men from the Exchequer are checking and rechecking the contents?' he said. 'I suspect old Herbert de Mandeville would have often gone back to his chamber upstairs and left Simon to get on with his boring tasks.'

'Unless he was in conspiracy with the canon himself,' suggested Thomas.

John cautiously dipped his finger into the brownish substance in the pot and found it to be as firm as a pat of good butter. His fingertip sank into the surface and left a perfect impression. He repeated the process with the smaller amount in the little box, with the same result.

'That's how it was done, then!' he said with satisfaction. 'Simon Basset, man of God or not, is our culprit. He managed to copy both keys and then when he was in the Tower on one of his legitimate visits to check other boxes, he somehow opened the treasure chest without being seen.'

Gwyn leaned back against a table, making it creak alarmingly.

'How would he manage that? There was always a guard with him, surely?'

'Basset was very well known there; he was a senior member of the Exchequer and came regularly to deal with the inventories,' countered Thomas. 'I doubt the guards would be watching him like a hawk all the time he was there. They weren't to know that he wasn't supposed to open that particular chest.'

De Wolfe nodded. 'It happened, so that's how it

must have been done, for lack of any other explanation. He could have slid some gold objects under his wide cassock while he was pretending to count the items. Maybe it was done over several sessions, not all at once.'

Back in their chamber in the palace, John put their trophies of the wax box and pot of mixture on his table and regarded them solemnly.

'There is one big problem with all this,' he said sadly. 'If Simon Basset was the perpetrator, why was he murdered?'

There was a silence as the other two contemplated this recurring riddle.

'He must have had an accomplice,' said Gwyn. 'Otherwise, who killed the ironmaster? I can't see a fat canon committing murder on the marshes, even though it was not far from his house.'

'And where is the stolen treasure now?' asked Thomas. 'There is no trace of it in the canon's house, so presumably this unknown accomplice has it in his keeping – and perhaps eliminated Simon Basset to avoid having to give him his share.'

De Wolfe peered into the wax pot as if he could find the answer in its rusty depths.

'Clever though you have been, Thomas – and I give you full credit for it – we are no nearer solving the mystery because of it. We need this second villain – and most of all we need to recover that gold, or we'll have the wrath of the king and his Council upon us.'

For lack of any other inspiration, the next day John rode into the city to question Herbert de Mandeville about the keys. Gwyn stuck with him like the shadow he had become, but no assailant leapt from a side street to attack him. The Constable of the Tower was not pleased to see the coroner yet again, but given the

Justiciar's overriding authority, he had no choice. The interview was fruitless, as the Constable vehemently denied ever leaving Simon Basset alone with the chests in the strongroom. John did not believe him, as there was something in his voice that was too defensive and it was patently obvious that he could never have admitted to being in dereliction of the rules for opening the boxes. In fact, at first de Mandeville refused to accept that the canon was involved in the theft at all and tried to denigrate John's evidence that the keys from Simon's pouch had been pressed into wax for nefarious purposes.

There was nothing to be gained by arguing and de Wolfe left the Tower, unsure of what to do next. As they walked their horses slowly through the crowded, smelly streets, Gwyn ruminated on the litany of events that had brought them to this stage in the investigation, if it could be called that with so little progress.

'Surely this mystery man is the key – the one who ate with Basset before he was taken ill in the bawdy house,' he called to the coroner, pushing aside a ragged fellow who ran alongside his mare, trying to sell him a handful of bruised-looking plums.

De Wolfe moved Odin nearer, as there was a hideous racket coming from a quartet of musician-beggars who were performing at the side of the street on pipe and tabor, rebec and bagpipes.

'So he might be!' he yelled at his officer. 'But how are we to find him after all this time?' They moved on to a less noisome part of Cheapside, riding knee to knee to make conversation easier.

'What about trying to get the sheriff's help, now that we have direct orders from the king himself?'

They were within a short distance of the Guildhall and John felt that there was no time like the present. They left Cheapside and turned into a side street to

reach the building that housed the city's administration, an impressive stone edifice that had been built
only two years after St Bartholomew's Hospital, which
also figured in the dead canon's epic.

Leaving Gwyn holding the horses, he went inside
and demanded to see one of the two sheriffs. After a
cool reception from a clerk sitting in an anteroom, he
produced his warrant, which he now carried rolled in
an inner pocket of his short riding mantle. The sight of
the three royal lions and the dangling red seal, which
was large enough to cover the bottom of a pint ale-pot,
immediately changed the surly attitude of the official,
who led him to an upstairs chamber where Godard
of Antioch was sitting at a table on a low platform,
directing the activities of a trio of clerks busy scribing at
desks below him.

The fleshy sheriff was no more pleased to see him
than the Constable of the Tower had been, but again
the sight of John's warrant made him listen to what the
coroner had to say.

'I have now had direct and urgent orders from the
king himself, to pursue this matter of the theft of royal
revenue,' said de Wolfe, in a decisive tone that made it
clear that he was in no mood for prevarication.

'What do you expect me to do about it?' growled
Godard, who like everyone in London knew of the theft
from the Tower.

John explained the canon's involvement in the
crime.

'But it is clear that there must have been at least
one other involved, possibly more. One of these must
have been responsible for his poisoning and I need to
know who it was who ate with him shortly before he was
taken mortally ill.'

'And how by St Peter's cods, do you think I can help
you with that?' grumbled the sheriff.

312

John patiently explained the need to find the tavern where they had eaten and to try to trace the other man. Godard was scathing in his response, but John's persistence and his tapping of the Lionheart's warrant, eventually persuaded the sheriff to give his grudging agreement.

'You are wasting my time, de Wolfe, you must know that!' he sneered. 'How in hell's name do you expect me to find a fellow, description unknown, several weeks after eating at an unknown tavern in an unknown part of England's greatest city? Hey?'

Privately, John found it hard to disagree with him, but he was getting desperate.

'Your constables know the city like the backs of their hands – the eating place cannot be far from Stinking Lane, as the canon walked there, according to the girl in the brothel. A fat canon may well be remembered by a skivvy or a potboy, especially if a reward is offered. I am sure the Exchequer would gladly pay a few shillings for useful information.'

After more grumbling and a grudging acceptance, the sheriff agreed to set some of his men on to the task, as long as it did not interfere with their other duties. Unconvinced that Godard would put himself to much trouble over this, John rolled up his royal parchment and put it away inside his cloak, then thanked the sheriff and went out of the building to his patient officer waiting in the street.

With no other leads to follow up, they made their way back to Westminster where, somewhat to John's surprise, a case was waiting for him. The sergeant of the guard accosted him as soon as they entered and told him his services were needed at the back of the palace.

'One of the laundry girls claims she has been ravished, sir,' he announced. 'We have a man already chained in a cell, but I'm told that this now comes under your jurisdiction.'

John sent Gwyn to collect Thomas from their chamber upstairs and the three of them followed the sergeant around to the large open area at the back of the palace, where the stables and servants' lodgings were situated. The place was quiet, as the majority of the people and horses were far away in Gloucestershire. The laundry was a large wooden hut, steam billowing out from iron cauldrons set in stone fireplaces. Behind were several lean-to rooms where the women lived and in one cubicle a girl of about sixteen was lying moaning on a mattress laid on the floor. Two older women were tending her solicitously and raised outraged faces to the coroner as he walked in.

'The poor wretch has been shamefully abused, sir,' said one forcefully. Middle-aged and shabby, she held a cup of weak ale to the girl's lips. 'The bastard should be flayed alive, the dirty swine!'

John's task was to confirm that the victim had indeed been raped and to record the facts for submission to the justices, which in this case would be the barons sitting on the King's Bench in the Great Hall. However, he was no physician and needed some advice on the state of the girl, so a midwife was sent for, one of those who practised in the village. While they waited for her, he extracted the story from those who appeared to know what had happened. The girl herself was too shaken to speak coherently, her teeth chattering as she lay hunched beneath a tattered blanket, the younger woman holding her hand and making soothing noises to her.

The older woman was more than forthcoming with her evidence.

'That evil bastard Edward Mody did it, Crowner,' she snapped. 'I more or less saw it happen – heard it, at any rate. He took her in this very room while I was dollying sheets in the main hut!'

'Mody's an ostler from the stables,' explained the sergeant. 'He's the man we've got locked up.'

'Always sniffing around young Maud here, he was. Wanted to walk out with her, but she turned him down and quite right too. He's a pig of a fellow, smells like one and acts it, too.'

The midwife came, a wheezy old woman who walked with the aid of two sticks. How she managed to deliver babies in her state of health, John failed to imagine, but he left her to her task whilst he went to see the suspected man, locked in one of the cells that acted as the palace gaol, yet another shed attached to the back of the stable block. The sergeant opened the door and John went in to find Edward Mody, a coarse-looking man of about thirty, chained by an ankle fetter to a massive iron ring set in the wall. He was crouched on the floor, which was covered in dirty straw that looked as if it had already been used in the stables.

'I didn't do anything wrong, sir. She was quite willing, I swear!' he yelled as soon as de Wolfe entered. The rest of the interview was a loud declamation that she was his girlfriend and that she had changed her mind about allowing their sexual congress after the deed was done.

John had heard similar stories many times before and he suspected that probably some of them were true. However, it was not his duty to judge the matter, only to record all that was said and present it on his rolls to the judges. He came out within a few minutes and told Thomas that he would dictate his statement when they got back to their chamber. Going back to the laundry, he saw the old crone with the walking sticks, who gave him a piece of rag stained with blood.

'You'll need that to show the justices as proof,

Crowner,' she cackled. 'The poor girl's been ravished right enough and her a virgin, too! Bruised and battered, she is, around her vital parts. Still bleeding a little, as that cloth testifies.'

He gave her a penny and she stumbled off, quite satisfied with her fee. As she left, the gaunt figure of the Keeper appeared, having heard that there had been trouble in his palace, breaking the welcome quiet that the exodus with Queen Eleanor had brought him. Anything untoward that happened in the precinct came within his notice and Nathaniel de Levelondes was still concerned that one of his guest-chamber clerks had been murdered and no one had yet been arrested for it, as well as the coroner himself being half-strangled in St Stephen's crypt.

He heard from de Wolfe that this was a genuine rape that had happened on his premises.

'I'll see that the girl gets a few days free from her duties in the laundry,' he said magnanimously. 'And the miscreant can appear before the justices in the morning – we can get him hanged by nightfall.' They went on to talk about the stabbing of Basil of Reigate and John had to admit that he had made no progress in finding the killer.

'My officer had a brief glimpse of him as he ran past our chamber, but then he vanished,' he said in his defence. 'This palace is too large and full of passages and doors to catch anyone unless you are right on their heels.'

The Keeper grunted his agreement. 'There are plenty of louts in the village, to say nothing of the city, who would murder their own mother for half a mark!'

'I wonder if it was the same lout that had me by the throat under the chapel the other day,' growled de Wolfe. 'The problem with this place is that half the population of England seem to wander in and out as they please.'

De Levelondes shrugged. 'What else can we do but let them in? It is a court of law, where all sorts of folk, criminals, witnesses and jurors have to attend. We have merchants in the hall, and traders bringing supplies to us, pilgrims by the hundred coming to the abbey – Westminster is at the crossroads of the world!'

John then brought up the vague hint offered by Robin Byard about Basil being afraid of the consequences of overhearing some seditious talk in the guest chambers.

'Do you think that is a feasible possibility?' he asked. 'There have been rumours of King Philip sending spies to England.'

The Keeper gave a cynical laugh and repeated the Justiciar's opinion on the matter.

'There have always been spies here and no doubt the palace shelters more than its share of them. We have a constant stream of visitors from across the Channel and God knows where the sympathies of some of them may lie.'

John went back to his chamber and when Thomas had written the short account dictated by the coroner on to his rolls for the use of the court next day, they settled back into their usual inertia, as de Wolfe could think of no way to push forward any of their investigations, in spite of the stern admonitions of Hubert Walter. That evening, he went to the Lesser Hall for his supper, where the patrons were few in number now that the court was absent. At least he did not have to dodge Hawise, as the certainty had strengthened within him that Hilda was his true love and that he must remain as faithful to her as his poor weak nature would allow.

The two under-marshals were also absent and he

found himself sitting opposite Archdeacon Bernard de Montfort, who had remained in Westminster to continue his researches in the abbey archives. With him were the two other nobles from across the Channel, to whom Bernard had introduced him some time ago, Guy de Bretteville and Peter le Paumer.

'My work is coming to an end soon, so I shall take myself back to the Auvergne,' he said, with his usual slight lisp due to his distorted lip. 'I have another trip down to Canterbury to search for one more ancient document which I think is in the scriptorium of the cathedral.'

He was an amiable companion, with a massive appetite that demolished each new dish that the servants placed on the table.

John asked him about his research, more for politeness' sake than any real understanding of his obsession with the saintliness of Edward, last king of the Saxons. De Montfort readily obliged and chattered on happily, with John giving monosyllabic replies, more concerned with getting his share of the roast pigeon and the boiled bacon.

By the time the puddings, figs, nuts and cheese appeared, de Bretteville and Peter le Paumer had engaged de Montfort in an obscure debate about the criteria that Rome employed to elevate worthy men and women to sainthood and John's attention had wandered. De Montfort must have sensed that he was being left out of the conversation and brought him back into the fold by asking him how his own investigations were progressing. John felt some sympathy for physicians and apothecaries, who must suffer like coroners, when their friends pester them about their own illnesses, as he often was about his efforts at detection.

'There is something to report about the robbery at

the Tower, I'm pleased to say. The king himself has charged me, through the Chief Justiciar, with discovering who stole his treasure, and I am making rapid progress towards catching the thieves.'

He uttered this bare-faced untruth with no compunction at all, as it was his only hope, faint as it was, of scaring the culprits out of cover.

The archdeacon nodded as he swallowed the last spoonful of his cherry torte. 'And what about this rumour we heard of spies in the palace being connected to that poor clerk who served us so well in the guest chambers?'

Again John concealed his total ignorance of who might responsible. Bernard de Montfort was an inveterate gossip and there was no better way of spreading John's false optimism, than telling the archdeacon.

'Ah, there I am also most optimistic!' he replied. 'I hope to lay my hands on Basil's murderer before the week is out. There are certain pieces of the riddle still to fall into place, but I shall soon have them, never fear!'

If he had been Thomas de Peyne, the coroner would certainly have made the Sign of the Cross and murmured a prayer for forgiveness for his blatant lies.

CHAPTER FIFTEEN

In which Crowner John goes hunting

The next few days passed without incident until the palace began to murmur with anticipation at the return of the court from Gloucester. A herald rode in with the news that they were at Oxford and would probably arrive in Westminster in three days' time. This meant a great deal of work for those who would have to deal with the sudden influx of several hundred hungry souls, horses and oxen. The Keeper was seen to be striding around with an even more woebegone face than usual, harrying his staff into greater preparedness.

For the Coroner of the Verge, there was little to do. The only event that concerned him was a fire in Thieving Lane, where sparks had set the thatch of a house alight. Neighbours and lay brothers from the abbey managed to limit the damage by rushing for ladders and pulling clumps of smoking straw down into the street, but John still had to attend the scene and get Thomas to write a short report for the abbot and the justices, as fires in towns were a serious hazard which could destroy acres of closely packed buildings.

Two days before the queen and her entourage were due to return, John had an invitation from Bernard de Montfort to join him and some others in a hunting trip to one of the abbey manors. Unusually for a knight, John was not addicted to hunting, perhaps because he had spent so many years in campaigns and battles, where the hunting was usually of two-legged beasts. Most of his fellow Normans saw hunting the boar, the stag and the wolf as both a sport and a means of keeping them in practice for war, by honing their skills with horse, bow and lance.

However, he had little else to divert him and he agreed to go with them to the forests around Greenford, one of Abbot Postard's manors, about twelve miles to the west. He took Gwyn with him as his esquire, as the Cornishman was still adamant that he was not going to let him out of his sight until his would-be assassin was dealt with. They left Westminster in the afternoon and rode out with Bernard de Montfort, Guy de Bretteville, Peter le Paumer and half a dozen others, including the prior and the precentor of the abbey, both keen hunters and Gerald, the chaplain of the palace chapel.

John had borrowed a couple of 'coursers' from the Marshalsea, as Odin and Gwyn's heavy mare would be of little use for rapid sprints in woodland. The stay in the manor house at Greenford was pleasant enough, with a good meal and plenty of ale, cider and wine to lubricate the conversation. Early next morning, they rode out from the stockade around the house into the surrounding farmland, then into the park. This was a few hundred acres of forest that had been surrounded by a deer-proof fence to keep in the game and discourage those who might risk the inevitable death penalty for poaching. At intervals around this fence, there were deer traps, a deep ditch on the inner side to prevent the animals from escaping, but a grassy ramp on the outside to allow any wild beasts to enter. Attracted by hinds in season, males would jump in, but were unable to get out again and so increased the manor's stock.

The hunting party, about a dozen in number, assembled on their horses and waited whilst the hunt-master and his assistants marshalled their hounds. The different types of dog had different functions – the scent-pursuing lymer, the running-dog for stamina and the greyhound for the speed needed once the quarry was sighted. The hunters carried a variety of weapons, some with short bows, others with crossbows. A few preferred the short lance and most carried clubs hanging from their saddle-bows. A platoon of servants ran beside them when they began to move, some holding hounds on the leash, others beating the trees and yelling to drive the quarry out of hiding. Several green-clad hunt-masters and their assistants were mounted and kept in touch by blasts on their horns.

Soon the party broke up into smaller groups, most with a hound or two out ahead, being controlled by a handler running behind. John cantered down a path between the trees and then turned to follow the sudden urgent sound of horns, somewhere away to his right. Gwyn came close behind, with Bernard de Montfort, dressed in a very un-clerical brown tunic and breeches, his silent manservant Raoul close behind on foot. The path narrowed and then petered out so that they had to go forward between the trees and saplings at a walk, their horses brushing aside leafy branches and bushes.

'This is getting us nowhere, de Wolfe!' called the archdeacon from behind. 'Best to go back and work our way around on the main track.'

John, brought up against what seemed to be an impenetrable thicket of ash and hazel, had to agree and pulled his courser's head around to face back down the path of crushed vegetation that they had just made. As he did so, there was a distinct and chillingly familiar twanging sound from beyond the bushes and John de Wolfe jerked in his saddle as a crossbow bolt hit him in the chest.

'I'm all right, Gwyn! You get the bastard!' roared John, who rather to his surprise was still alive and apparently uninjured.

He looked down at the tear in his grey riding cloak, which now overlaid a smarting bruise over his ribs, but nothing else.

Gwyn, ignoring his master's command, hastily came back and slid from his saddle, with de Montfort close behind. John looked down and saw a bolt on the ground nearby, with some odd red fragments scattered around it. The Cornishman insisted on feeling around de Wolfe's chest to see if there was any wound or bleeding. Both he and de Montfort took some convincing that he was not seriously hurt, but again he yelled at his officer to pursue whoever had loosed off the crossbow at him. With a roar of rage, the Cornishman set off on foot, crashing through the bushes towards where the bolt must have come from.

'My man has already gone after him, he's quick on his feet,' bellowed the archdeacon. 'But you, Sir John, what about you? How could you survive that bolt?'

The coroner, still in the saddle, had been investigating his chest, pulling aside his cloak over the painful bruise that was now smarting like fury. He gave a shout of surprised astonishment.

'Hubert Walter saved my life! By God's guts, that's incredible!'

He opened his short cloak and showed Bernard de Montfort a torn parchment in a ripped inside pocket. Pulling it out, a shower of brittle red fragments fell from where a length of pink tape carried the sparse remnants of a thick wax seal.

'But a crossbow bolt would go through that easily!' protested the priest, unable to believe his eyes.

'It must have been a glancing blow and it skidded off sideways! Thanks be to the Virgin and all her saints!' he added fervently. 'Now let's get after your servant and my officer; we need to catch this murdering swine and find out who he is.'

Shocked by his miraculous escape, but too hardened to admit it, he kicked his horse into action and heedless of branches and brambles tearing at him, charged off down the path to the main track, with de Montfort struggling to keep up with him. He turned left in the direction that Gwyn and Raoul must have taken, pounding along, shouting for his officer to say where he was. Suddenly, the trees thinned and they found themselves almost at the edge of the forest, with the park fence ahead of them.

'There he is, at the deer-leap!' shouted Bernard and true enough three figures were seen in the pit beneath the sheer wall of the trap. John slid from his horse, wincing at the pain in his chest and stumbled down the steep slope which formed part of the one-way system for the deer.

Gwyn and Raoul were bending over a still shape that lay at the foot of the ten-foot drop from the outer side of the leap.

'The sod is dead, blast it!' yelled Gwyn, incensed beyond measure. 'I wanted the joy of twisting his head off myself, but he's beaten me to it!'

'Damn that!' stormed de Wolfe. 'I wanted him alive so that I could discover who's behind this.'

'How did this happen, Raoul?' demanded the archdeacon of his servant.

The powerfully built Raoul looked sullen at this condemnation of his efforts. 'He was dead by the time I got here, sire!' he growled. 'He was well ahead of me when I heard him crashing through the bushes. Then he streaked down here and started to climb the leap, as the fence is too high elsewhere. He almost got to the top, then fell back and must have broken his neck.'

The angry coroner looked at the low man-made cliff that fronted the grassy ramp on the other side. It was made of earth and rocks, partly colonised by clumps of coarse grass and weeds.

The dead man lay crumpled on the ground at its foot, his head bent at an unnatural angle. A few large stones lay tumbled nearby as if they had fallen out of the cliff face when he attempted to climb up.

'Turn him over, Gwyn, let's have a look at the bastard,' commanded de Wolfe. He did so and the sightless face of a rough-looking man in a brown smock and serge trousers stared up at the sky. He had a tight wide belt carrying a long dagger and wore wooden-soled shoes on his feet.

'Anyone recognise the bastard?' asked Gwyn. 'I've never seen him before.'

None of the others admitted to knowing him and by this time one of the Greenford hound-masters had joined them, as his dogs had run to this unusual gathering as they passed by on the main track. He was told of the failed crossbow attack and after some strenuous blasts on his horn, others of the hunting party came to join them. The prior was one of them and he was aghast at yet another attempt on the life of the palace coroner.

'You must have made some persistent enemies, Sir John,' was his comment, as he studied the features of the dead man. The face of the corpse was dirty and coarse-skinned, with heavy brows and a lantern jaw. He had no beard or moustache, but a raised dark brown mole, the size of a thumbnail and covered in coarse hairs, sat on his right cheek amongst the cow-pox scars.

'I seem to recall this fellow's face and that hairy tumour on his cheek. I have seen him about Westminster, though I have no idea who he is.'

More hunters gravitated to the leap and soon almost all the party was there, commiserating with John and making sure that he did not need the services of an apothecary. They all clustered around the corpse and one of the lay brothers that came with the abbey precentor also recognised the man.

'He is a ruffian I have seen about the town,' he said confidently. 'I remember that disfiguring mole and once saw him staggering drunk out of the Crown alehouse in Tothill Street and starting a fight with another man.'

John, remarkably composed for one who had escaped death by a miracle, thought it very significant that the failed assassin was from Westminster, a dozen miles from home. It confirmed that whoever had employed him – for he was obviously a hired killer – must also be from there. Though he had no recollection of the man who had attacked him in the crypt of St Stephen's Chapel, he felt it likely that this was the same man.

This was rapidly confirmed when another of the hunting party came forward to view the cadaver.

'That is the man I saw running out of the passage outside the chapel!' declared Gerard, the chaplain who had tried to come to John's aid at that time.

In spite of the drama, the hunters had come to hunt and even such a startling episode as this did not put them off. De Wolfe and Gwyn decided that they had had enough excitement for one day and after the rest had regrouped to go back into the forest for their entertainment, they trotted back to the manor house, leaving some of the manor servants to carry the corpse back to the stables. As Greenford was just outside John's jurisdiction, he was not bothered about any legal formalities. If the bailiff wished to report the matter to the sheriffs who acted as coroners, it was up to him and John for once had no enthusiasm for seeing that the law was followed to the letter.

Gwyn fussed over his master like a hen with a single chick, but all John wanted before they made their way back home was to sit down in the hall with a quart or two of ale and something to eat. This was readily provided on the orders of the house steward, who had heard of the incident in the forest and was eager to do all he could for the king's coroner. As they sat eating and drinking at a table in the hall, Gwyn wondered aloud what was provoking these murderous attacks on his master.

'Is it because of the treasure or this tale about spies that Byard spun us?' he said. 'For someone is trying to shut your mouth for ever!'

De Wolfe put down his mug and gave a wry grin. 'I may have been asking for it, in a way. Several times now, I've deliberately boasted about being on the verge of making an arrest for both the crimes. I hoped that it might provoke either culprit into taking flight or giving away something that would show their guilt.'

Gwyn smoothed down the ends of his drooping moustaches.

'Instead of that, they tried to strangle you and then shoot your giblets out of your chest!' he exclaimed. 'But we don't know which crime it was for.'

'No, but both attacks were by the same man, so it was for the same crime. It would be too much of a co-incidence if the same lout was hired by two different parties.'

None of this told them which party it was and eventually they rode home being none the wiser – and now John would have to go the Justiciar's office when

Hubert returned, to get a new seal placed on his most useful warrant.

'Maybe you should ask for one made of iron,' suggested Gwyn, facetiously. 'Next time, perhaps sealing wax won't be as effective!'

The royal procession returned with somewhat less pomp and glamour than when they had left several weeks earlier. The banners still waved and the trumpets still blew, but in the late afternoon of a hot day, everyone was tired, dusty and limp, apart from Eleanor of Aquitaine and William Marshal, who still rode stiffly upright in their saddles. They came in from Windsor and after the major figures had been escorted into the royal apartments and the chambers above and around the Lesser Hall, all the others rapidly dispersed. Grooms and ostlers ran to take care of the horses and the ox-wagons came to a halt in Old Palace Yard behind the stores' entrances. Ranulf and William Aubrey had plenty to occupy themselves in sorting out the confusion of animals and carts, and John did not see them until the evening, as he kept well out of the way in his chamber facing the river. He wanted to keep out of sight of Hawise for the time being, though he realised he would have to face her sooner or later. Thankfully, she and her husband would soon be leaving with the queen, as Eleanor would be departing for one of the channel ports within a few days.

He was not all that keen on meeting Hubert Walter either, given what little progress had been made over recovering the treasure, though at least he could confidently report now that Simon Basset was almost certainly the man who had stolen it from the Tower.

A new decision was fermenting in de Wolfe's mind, stemming from his abject failure to solve either the theft of the king's gold or the murder of Basil, which seemed linked to some espionage activity. He was considering asking the Justiciar to release him from this appointment as Coroner of the Verge, given that he was patently unfitted for the task. He would have to leave with his tail between his legs, but at least he could go back to Devon and live out his life in quiet obscurity. Gwyn would no doubt revel in becoming landlord of the Bush Inn and Thomas would be happy to go back to his duties in Exeter Cathedral.

It would mean a serious loss of face for him as a knight, especially as the king himself had insisted on the appointment. Creeping back to Exeter to lick the wounds of failure would be a bitter pill to swallow, but life in Westminster seemed too artificial to be borne. The advantages of life in Devon would be some compensation – except that he already anticipated the gleeful crowing of his hated brother-in-law, Richard de Revelle, when he heard of John's fall from grace.

But while de Wolfe was gloomily rehearsing the plans for his own professional suicide, things were happening nearby that were likely to alter the whole scenario.

In spite of his earlier reluctance to face Hawise d'Ayncourt, John's Crusader spirit rose sufficiently for him to damn the power that women held over him and to declare himself master of his own soul. At about the seventh hour by the abbey bell, he went to the Lesser Hall and took his usual place on a bench with his acquaintances. Bernard de Montfort was there, as ready as ever to shovel good food into himself, as well as Guy de Bretteville and the physician from Berri. John was pleased to see William Aubrey and Ranulf of Abingdon back safely and in apparent good health. They greeted each other warmly, though John thought that Ranulf was somewhat reluctant to meet his eye as he sat down next to him on the bench.

Opposite were Renaud de Seigneur and the ever-lovely Hawise. De Wolfe was girding himself to be polite but distant if she began using her cow's eyes on him and making her usual suggestive and flirtatious remarks. Thus he was surprised when she responded to his civil greeting with a frosty nod and then proceeded to ignore him. John was rather piqued as well as surprised, for though he had decided to be firm in his avoidance of any further dallying with her, it was galling to know that his attraction for her suddenly seemed to have evaporated.

He also came to realise that her husband was not his usual cheerful self, as Renaud sat silently picking at his food, darting glances now and then at the row of men sitting opposite. Archdeacon Bernard seemed oblivious of any such tension and chattered away, telling the company of the coroner's miraculous escape from a murderous crossbow assassin and invoking the divine protection of God and King Richard in placing the stout warrant seal between the crossbow bolt and John's vitals.

Hawise affected to take no notice and though Ranulf and William showed concern, John thought that the marshal from Abingdon had only half his mind on the escapade. It soon became obvious what was going on as John began to intercept covert glances between Hawise and Ranulf and though they spoke not a single word to each other he knew with certainty that they had already become lovers.

He felt relief, tempered by a little jealousy, that the younger and undoubtedly handsome under-marshal had now taken the problem off his hands. Ranulf had no wife, as he had once told him that she had died, so Ranulf had no impediment to taking Hawise either as a mistress or a wife, if the complication of having Renaud de Seigneur as husband could be overcome.

Anyway, he thought, it was no business of his and he felt as if a weight had been lifted from his mind, no longer having to avoid the woman or make stern refusals of her future favours.

As soon as Renaud had finished his meal – not that he had eaten much – he rose abruptly and almost dragged his wife away, murmuring a bare goodnight. Accompanied by her maid, Hawise followed reluctantly, giving Ranulf a soulful glance and a covert flutter of her fingers as she trailed after Renaud towards the doors.

While de Montfort prattled on to Guy de Bretteville on his other side, John prodded Ranulf gently in the ribs with his elbow and leaned over to speak to him in a low voice.

'Well done, sir knight! I see how the land lies between you and the fair Hawise,' he murmured. 'But watch your step, the husband looked none too pleased, I doubt he's ignorant of what's going on.'

Ranulf gave a sheepish grin, but John sensed that he was both excited and agitated beneath his efforts to keep a calm exterior. De Wolfe hoped that Hawise had restrained herself from boasting to the under-marshal about Marlborough. She wouldn't disillusion the younger man by flaunting her promiscuity, he thought.

He let the subject lie and they talked of other things, including the return journey through Oxford and the fortitude of the old queen and William Marshal on such a long and gruelling ride.

John had hoped for a walk along the riverbank with Ranulf, to catch up on the events of the return from Gloucester and to tell him more details of his own recent brush with death. But the younger knight seemed abstracted and excused himself straight after the supper, taking Aubrey away in a rather abrupt fashion. John wondered if Hawise had in fact told him of her previous passionate episode with him and this had made Ranulf embarrassed. John shrugged it off, he had more pressing matters to think of, mainly how he was to tell Hubert Walter that the investigation had stalled and that he wanted to resign as coroner.

For some exercise to settle the meal in his stomach, he walked into the abbey precinct and across Broad Sanctuary to come out in Thieving Lane. He loped back towards the main gate of the palace and the Deacon tavern. This route took him past the Crown alehouse, a low-class drinking den of which the man who had assaulted John had been a patron. On impulse, he turned into the inn and pushed his way past the drinkers standing almost shoulder-to-shoulder in the low-ceilinged taproom.

The place reeked of sweat, spilt ale and urine – both human and animal. The floor rushes looked as if they had not been changed since before the Conquest and several cats and dogs scratched through the litter for mice, rats and scraps of fallen food. Compared with this hovel, the Deacon was as much a palace as the one across the road.

De Wolfe pushed to the back of the room, where several casks were propped up on wedges and racks. A landlord almost as big as Gwyn stood truculently in front of the kegs, his hands on his hips. He had a large cudgel propped against a barrel, ready to deal with the frequent fights that broke out. The man wore a stained leather apron over his bare chest, his lower half encased in serge breeches. He glared at de Wolfe, who was obviously not one of his usual class of customers.

Thinking it politic to act like one, he asked for a quart of ale and gave a quarter-segment of a penny in exchange. Rather cautiously, he took a sip and to his surprise found it of better quality than that on offer in any of the other Westminster taverns. He complimented the landlord on the taste and received a grunt in reply, but persisted in his quest. This was no place to flash his royal warrant, especially without its impressive seal.

'I met a man recently who recommended your brew,' he lied. 'A big fellow, with a curious brown mole on his cheek.'

The publican stared at him suspiciously.

'Then you'll not meet him again, for I hear he's dead. Fell down and broke his neck.'

Obviously the instant news network of Westminster was not confined to the upper echelons of the palace and abbey.

'Indeed, that's a pity,' said John insincerely. 'What was his name?'

'Jordan the ratcatcher, that's who he was.' The dead man had obviously not plied his trade in this alehouse, by the state of the place, but that was no concern of John's.

'And you are the coroner, sir – so why are you asking these questions?' growled the landlord suspiciously. It was hardly surprising that he had been recognised, as de Wolfe was a striking figure, stalking around in black or grey, well known to most as the king's new coroner. Deprived of anonymity, he thought he might as well be frank.

'This Jordan tried to kill me, probably more than once,' he growled. 'Is it known that he took on such tasks, as well as killing vermin?'

The landlord, summing up the coroner's demeanour and the size of the sword he carried, forbore to say that he thought that royal officials were just another class of vermin.

'Jordan was a violent man, sir. Many a time I've had to deal with his brawling in here.' He looked down at the heavy club propped against a barrel. 'But I wouldn't know about any other troubles he might have got into.'

'You never saw him in the company of clergymen, I suppose.'

John was thinking of the possibility that Canon Simon might have had some nefarious dealings with the man, though as he was already dead at the time of the two attacks on John, he could not have been involved in those. But perhaps the silencing of the iron-master might have been ordered by him or his partner, the mysterious man in the city tavern.

The innkeeper gave a derisive laugh. 'Jordan? I doubt he's been to Mass or confession since he was a lad. And the clergy, for all their sins and corruption, never come into the Crown, it's way too rough for them.'

John looked around the room at the suspicious stares that the patrons were directing at him. He knew he would never get any information from them, even if some knew of Jordan's exploits. He decided to send Gwyn to see if he could pick up any useful information, as alehouses were his forte, just as abbey dorters and refectories were happy hunting-grounds for Thomas de Peyne.

Sinking the rest of his quart, which he admitted he enjoyed very much, John went out into the far fresher air of the street and walked home to his bed, frustrated again by a failure to make any progress.

Next day, de Wolfe awoke with a sense of foreboding, for this might well be the day he would be called to account before Hubert Walter. If no summons came that morning, he would have to take the bull by the horns and seek an audience, confessing that he had failed and that he wished to resign and slink home to Devon.

But fate had other ideas for that day. Soon after the eighth hour, Thomas arrived in the coroner's chamber from attending Prime in the abbey. They had just begun their second breakfast of bread, cheese and cider provided as usual by the ever-ravenous Gwyn, even though he and his master had had Osanna's gruel and boiled eggs soon after dawn.

An imperious rap on the door heralded an unusual visitor, in the shape of Martin Stanford, the Deputy Marshal, who had never before sought out the coroner.

The three residents rose to their feet, for Stanford was a knight of greater seniority than even de Wolfe. He was one of the deputies to William Marshal himself, though to be fair, he never gave himself any great airs. A stocky man in his late fifties, he had a short neck and a red face, his brown hair cropped to a mat on top of his head in the old Norman style. He looked agitated and began speaking without any preamble.

'De Wolfe, you supped in the Lesser Hall last evening, I understand? Were two of my under-marshals there with you?'

John waved an invitation for Martin to be seated, where Thomas had hastily vacated the bench, but the marshal ignored this and waited impatiently for an answer to his strange question.

'Yes, they usually eat there. Ranulf of Abingdon and William Aubrey kept me company, as they often do. Why do you ask?'

'Because they've both damned well disappeared!' snapped Stanford. 'Of all times, when I need every man in the Marshalsea to start preparing for Queen Eleanor's departure to Portsmouth tomorrow.'

'They said nothing to me about going away when I spoke to them last night,' replied John. 'Is there no sign of them in their quarters?'

Stanford strode to the open window and slapped the

sill angrily with his riding gloves. 'There's nothing left there – they've taken their personal belongings and vanished! It seems that they left before dawn, for only a stable boy saw them both saddle up and ride away. Are you sure they said nothing about leaving?'

John shook his head. 'Not a word! I must say that Ranulf seemed somewhat distant, compared to his usual talkative self, but there was no mention of leaving Westminster.'

Martin Stanford's rather small eyes stared suspiciously at the coroner. 'What d'you mean, he was somewhat distant?' he demanded.

De Wolfe felt trapped, as he had no wish to start gossip that might prove unfounded. 'There might have been a reason, but it was a very personal one and as I'm only guessing, it would not be fair for me to repeat it.'

Stanford glowered at him. 'Damn it all, de Wolfe, this is a serious matter! If you know or even suspect something, I need to know. They were two of my most senior assistants.'

John wavered until he decided that he had better divulge his suspicions about Ranulf and Hawise, but he was saved from this awkward position by yet another interruption. This time there was no knock on the door, it was flung back with a crash to admit Renaud de Seigneur, followed by a worried-looking Keeper of the Palace and an even more distraught Guest Master.

'Sir John, do you know where my wife has gone to?' he demanded in his shrill voice. For a moment, de Wolfe feared that he was going to denounce John as an adulterer and accuse him of adultery with his wife, but thankfully he had a different target for his anger.

'You were in the supper hall last evening – did that bloody man Ranulf say anything to you about her?' he almost shrieked.

Before John could again deny being told anything by

the under-marshal, Nathaniel de Levelondes laid a restraining hand on the Lord of Freteval's shoulder and tried to placate him.

'De Seigneur, I'm sure there must be some innocent explanation. Let us begin a search of the palace, for perhaps your lady has had some temporary loss of her mind and is wandering the passages and rooms.'

Renaud twisted away and red-faced, began to shout again. 'Loss of mind be damned! She has gone off with that devil of a horseman! Left her maid and almost all her clothes behind, just taken her jewels!' he yelled.

Stanford turned to stare at the coroner. 'Is that what is behind this, de Wolfe? Is that what you were going to tell me?'

John shrugged. 'I know nothing definite, believe me. It's just that at the table last night, I thought I detected – well, a situation between the Lady Hawise and Ranulf.'

'By God's bones, you certainly did!' snapped Renaud. 'I saw what was developing during the week it took to come back from Gloucester. I regret to say that my young wife has a weakness for handsome men.' He did not look at de Wolfe when he said this and John was unsure whether to be relieved or insulted.

'Then last night, she said she wanted to petition for an annulment, ridiculous though that may sound. She has had many a flutter with other men, but has never gone as far as that before.'

It was now clear to the other men in the room what had happened before dawn broke that morning.

De Levelondes summed up the situation. 'So we must assume that the Lady Hawise has eloped with Ranulf of Abingdon. This must surely be some passing infatuation, Lord Renaud. She will come to her senses very quickly.'

Stanford soon picked upon a flaw in his optimism. 'For a knight in the king's service to suddenly abandon his career is a major disaster for him, so if he has fled with a lady, then he must be very confident of her fidelity to him.'

He stopped and slapped his head. 'And why in the name of God has William Aubrey gone with them? She cannot be infatuated with them both!'

This pronouncement suddenly ignited a train of thought in de Wolfe's mind. Ranulf and William Aubrey, fleeing and abandoning their careers? What would they live on now? Was it possible? He began to think the unthinkable.

'We need to hurry to the stables and speak to anyone else who knows these two men,' he said decisively and without waiting for anyone's reaction, he motioned to Gwyn and headed for the door.

Within the hour, an urgent meeting had been convened in the Justiciar's chambers. Hubert Walter presided, sitting grave-faced at his table, with William Marshal on his right hand. Nathaniel de Levelondes, the Keeper of the Palace, Martin Stanford, the Deputy Marshal, William fitz Hamon, one of the Barons of the Exchequer, John de Wolfe and Renaud de Seigneur were sitting or standing around the table. At the back of the room, between two palace guards and looking very apprehensive, were Hawise's maid, a stable-boy and two of the esquires from the Marshalsea.

The pressing nature of this most high-level congress was not because an under-marshal had run off with a young woman, even though she was the wife of a minor noble from Blois. It was because of what John de Wolfe had postulated back in his chamber – the coincidence that the two under-marshals who had escorted the treasure chest back from Winchester, were the same ones who had cut and run, without any apparent funds.

All that was so far known about the emergency had already been given to Hubert Walter by the Deputy Marshal and by the coroner and now the Justiciar wanted to harden up the available evidence.

'What do we know about this Ranulf that might be relevant?' he demanded. Martin Stanford beckoned to the two esquires, who reluctantly came nearer.

'These men knew him best, as they shared accommodation,' he began. 'For my part, I know that Ranulf of Abingdon was a most competent and reliable man when it came to his duties.'

'Your tone suggests that there was another side to his character,' snapped Hubert.

'He was a young and energetic fellow,' said Stanford. 'He was fond of women, as many of us were at his age. But he was also keen to the point of obsession on gambling, both at dice, cards and in the wider sense, as well as chancing his luck at tournaments, where he was a skilful fighter.'

He prodded one of the squires, a young man of about twenty, who looked frightened to death in this august company.

'Elias, you knew him best, for you sometimes acted as his squire in the tournaments and melees. What can you tell us?'

'He was certainly devoted to jousting, sir, mainly because of the prize money and the forfeits of horse and armour of those he defeated.'

'Has he said anything of suddenly leaving the king's employ?'

Elias shook his blond head. 'No, but he often boasted that one day he would take himself abroad and make his fortune going around the tournaments in Germany and Flanders. He said that the restrictions in

England made it hardly worth the trouble of entering for the jousts.'

John knew it was true that, though King Richard had relaxed the rules, his father Henry had been against knights killing themselves for money, so many went across the Channel for their sport.

'What about this lady?' demanded William Marshal. He almost said 'this bloody woman', but realised that her husband was present. 'Did he say anything about her?'

Elias reddened. 'I was not with him on the progress to Gloucester and back, my lord. But since he has been back, he spoke of little else other than a new paramour, though he would not name her.'

'But you must have known who it was!' barked the Keeper.

'Indeed, it was obvious that it was the Lady Hawise,' admitted the squire.

'And you say you had no idea that he was going to vanish so precipitately like this?' growled Hubert.

'None at all, Your Grace! He has seemed excited these past few days, but I put that down to his latest romance. He has had quite a few of those; I knew the signs.'

Renaud de Seigneur made a gargling noise at this exposure of the nature of his wife's lover, but the Justiciar overrode him.

'Have you any idea of where he might have gone? And what of the other man, this Aubrey?'

'He gave no indication at all, sire! I cannot understand it, but Gilbert here knew William Aubrey better than I.'

The other young man, a muscular red-headed fellow, was pulled forward by the Deputy Marshal.

'Do you know anything that throws light on this unfortunate affair?' he rasped.

'William said nothing to me, though like Ranulf, he seemed very excited these past days. He, too, was a keen gambler and I know that both of them were deeply in debt during the past few months.'

'How so?' demanded de Wolfe, venturing a question for the first time, as money seemed at the root of this debacle.

'He and Ranulf had been several times to the Jews for loans. They had lost heavily at a tournament in Wilton last winter and they had visited several money-lenders, paying off debts owed to one with borrowings from another – a recipe for disaster in the long run.'

'Maybe they have run away to escape repaying these debts,' suggested William fitz Hamon, a judge from the King's Bench.

Gilbert turned up his hands. 'Perhaps, my lord. For some time, they were very anxious about their debts, but, recently, they no longer spoke of them and I got the impression that somehow they had come by substantial funds once again. I assumed one or the other had made a big winning at dice or cards, as they have not been jousting for some time.'

William Marshal spoke again. 'Have you any idea where they might have gone?'

'As Elias has said, Ranulf was always talking about going to Flanders and Germany to make their fortunes in the big tournaments that are held there. I have no other suggestion, my lord.'

The questioning and discussion went on for a time, with no concrete conclusions being made. By then, the Lord of Freteval was almost jumping up and down with impatience, demanding that something be done to 'rescue' his wife, though most of those present felt that Hawise failed to look upon it as an abduction.

Hubert Walter eventually stood up to terminate the meeting.

'All that we can do is pursue these men, both for the sake of the lady and her husband – and because there are possibly other issues at stake.'

'And where are we to seek them, Your Grace?' asked the Deputy Marshal. 'It sounds as if they might make for the Continent, but at which port? Dover is the nearest for Flanders, but there are a dozen havens from Portsmouth round to the Thames or even up to Essex and Suffolk that would do as well.'

Another discussion began and it was decided that the Deputy Marshal would send out a number of small search parties to the most likely ports on the Kent and Sussex coasts, each with a knight or squire and a couple of men-at-arms. As the fugitives already had a number of hours' start and their destination was unknown, it seemed a forlorn hope, but it was all that could be done.

As the meeting dispersed, John went to speak to the Justiciar and William Marshal.

'I have a bad feeling about this, sirs!' he began. 'Those two would not suddenly abandon their positions here and streak for foreign parts if they were not well provided with money or the means to obtain it. From being deeply in debt to the moneyers, suddenly they seem to have ample funds to throw away their careers and seek a new life abroad.'

The Justiciar nodded. 'I know very well what you are suggesting, John. Have these two benefited in some way from the theft of the gold from the Tower? I thought you had pinned the blame on Canon Simon?'

'He was certainly involved, but he was murdered and that suggests that he had at least one accomplice who may have wanted to silence him.'

'Then how was it done, de Wolfe?' demanded William Marshal. 'By Job's pustules, I fail to see how they could have got hold of the keys to the chest in the Tower.'

John was beginning to have his own ideas about that, but this was not the time to go into it. Instead, he asked permission to join the hunt for the two men.

'Each search party needs to know what they look like and I certainly do,' he said. 'I would like to take my officer and begin nearer home, in case they are seeking a ship along the Thames.'

Hubert nodded his agreement, exasperated that all this trouble had arisen on the day before the queen was leaving, when the Marshalsea would be at its busiest.

'If you do find the bastards, drag them to the Tower straight away. There are ample means in the dungeons there to get the truth out of them!'

Another hour saw de Wolfe and Gwyn cantering past Charing on a pair of fast rounseys from the stables, on their way into the city. John had decided to leave Thomas behind, as he was an impediment to swift travel and he thought speed may be of the essence if the fugitives were intent on leaving by ship. However, Gwyn pointed out that the tide was almost at the ebb, so no vessel would be leaving for another six hours.

'Are we going to search all along the wharves?' called the Cornishman as they clipped along the Strand towards the Temple. 'There are many of them, both in the Fleet river, the city and beyond it past St Katherine's, where ships also berth.'

'We need only vessels bound for a Channel crossing or directly across to the mouth of the Rhine,' shouted John. 'No need to concern ourselves with those who are going up the east coast or around to the west.'

As they passed through Ludgate, the magnitude of

their task came home to the coroner. They needed some help in deciding where along the seething banks of the river to make their search.

There was no evidence that Ranulf, William and the woman were even in the city, for they may have crossed the bridge and be on their way to Dover or Ramsgate by now. As they reached the end of Cheapside, John was uncertain whether to continue or turn down Watling Street to the bridge. Then he decided to seek some help, if it was forthcoming.

'Let's go to see that damned sheriff again,' he declared and turned up towards the Guildhall. He had no impressive warrant to show this time, but the clerk recognised him and moments later he was again in Godard of Antioch's chamber.

'The Justiciar needs some information of a different nature this time,' he began. 'About vessels along your wharves.'

The sheriff scowled and held up a hand. 'God's teeth, you are a persistent fellow, de Wolfe. You've not had the result of your last request yet.'

John stared at him. 'You mean that you've discovered something about the man who was with that murdered canon?'

Godard nodded with smug satisfaction. 'My men traced the tavern where he ate.'

'Why didn't you let me know?' snapped John. 'It was vitally important.'

'It must have slipped my mind,' said Godard casually. 'But I'm telling you now. One of my men asked around the streets and it seems that this fat priest that died in Bartholomew's was well known in an eating house in St Martin's Lane, leading up to Aldersgate. He probably went there every time before he vented his lust in the Stinking Lane brothel.'

'Did they say there was another man eating with

him?' demanded John urgently. 'And whether they knew him, too?'

The sheriff held up a hand to stem the flow of questions. 'For hell's sake, what do you expect from us, coroner? The tavern keeper only recalls this canon because he was a regular customer. He can't be expected to do more than that!'

De Wolfe calmed down and after he had obtained the name of the inn, he thanked Godard and left, almost at a run.

'I know the eating house where Basset ate,' he yelled at Gwyn, as he swung himself into the saddle. 'It's worth seeing if Ranulf was the second man.'

St Martin's Lane, sounding so similar to John's address in Exeter, was only a few yards away and within minutes they saw the Falcon, a large and respectable-looking tavern fronting directly on to the busy thoroughfare that led up to Aldersgate. It had two storeys, with shuttered windows on either side of the large central door. There was a side lane which led around to a yard containing stables and various out-buildings. As they could not leave their horses in the road, John led the way around to the back, where a snivelling barefoot boy took their steeds and hitched them to a rail.

'There's a door to the taproom there, sirs, to save you going round to the street again,' said the lad, as John gave him a half-penny.

'Let's see if the landlord recalls who might have dined with our lecherous priest,' said John, pushing open the back door that the urchin had pointed out. Through a short passage, half-filled with casks and crates, was an arch into the main room, crowded with drinkers even at mid-morning. They either stood in groups or sat on benches around the walls. There was a cacophony of chatter, some drunken singing and in a corner the twanging of someone playing a lute. There were several harlots with painted lips and cheeks plying their trade, dressed in striped gowns and wearing bright-red wigs, the uniform of London whores. A pair of hounds were wrestling playfully on the rushes, watched at a distance by several wary cats.

Drink was being served from barrels behind a table, from which a potboy and a wench were selling pint jugs of ale. De Wolfe pushed his way to them through the uncaring throng.

'Where's your master, the landlord?'

'Still at Smithfield, buying meat,' said the girl. 'But the missus is in the eating hall, through there.' She flipped a hand towards another arch which led into the other half of the ground floor.

John, with Gwyn close behind, went through into a room with one long table and several small ones, where people were beginning to settle on benches for their early pre-noon dinner. A large woman in a long linen apron was carrying in baskets of bread and John moved to intercept her with his questions, when he received a hard nudge in the back from Gwyn.

'Just look who's over there, Crowner!' he hissed, jerking his head. John followed his gesture and saw that, at a table in the far corner, were two men and a woman – the very ones they were seeking.

CHAPTER SIXTEEN

In which Crowner John draws his dagger

Almost at the same moment, William Aubrey noticed them standing inside the entrance. He blanched and leaned forward to whisper to Ranulf and Hawise, who were sitting with their backs towards the newcomers. Their heads shot around and in any other circumstances the expressions of surprise on their faces would have been comical. William sat transfixed, but Ranulf recovered his poise almost immediately, rising to his feet and coming across to John and his officer with a smile on his face.

'Great God, John, how came you here? Do you seek me or the Lady Hawise?'

De Wolfe was not sure if there was some innuendo in his remark, but that was not his main concern. 'I think you have some explaining to do, Ranulf of Abingdon,' he said harshly, moving towards the corner table.

The young marshal turned up his hands in a parody of supplication. 'You have caught me red-handed, sir! What can I say, other than love is blind and will not be denied, even by common sense?'

John hesitated. Was the dashing young knight only involved in a foolish elopement, running away from a jealous husband? Perhaps his other suspicions were unfounded, after all.

'I can well understand that the fair lady may have captivated your heart, Ranulf,' he growled. 'But what of William there?'

He jabbed a finger towards Aubrey, who was stuck half-risen from his bench, apparently paralysed by indecision. 'Does this lady's power over men extend to more than one at a time?'

He had not meant to be offensive, but the silent Hawise turned her head to give him a poisonous glare.

'My good friend William has decided to join me in our new life, Crowner!' replied Ranulf, almost light-heartedly. 'We have tired of being superior stable boys at Westminster. There are fortunes to be made in the tourney grounds of Germany.'

He waved a hand at their table, where food was half-consumed. 'Join us for a meal, you and your good man Gwyn.'

De Wolfe shook his head, still suspicious of the situation.

'I need some answers from you and Aubrey. Why did you choose this tavern to hide away, presumably to wait for a ship for Flanders?'

Ranulf stared at him. This was a question he had not expected.

'Because I know it well, it has the best roast beef in London and clean beds upstairs. We need a decent night's lodging, so where else but the Falcon?'

De Wolfe fixed him with a steely eye, his brooding hawk's face searching the man's features for the truth.

'And not because you know it well from your visits here with Canon Simon Basset?' he snapped.

Ranulf stared back at him guilelessly. 'By Christ's wounds, sir, you speak in riddles! We are merely waiting here until a cog is due to sail for Antwerp on tomorrow's tide.'

The coroner looked across at William Aubrey, who remained as if turned to stone, only his frightened eyes watching every move. Then John moved to stand over Hawise d'Ayncourt, who looked at him as if he was something scraped from the midden in the inn's backyard.

'Your husband will be overjoyed to know that you are safe after your abduction, lady,' he said sarcastically.

She glared up at him. 'Abduction be damned! I have left that fat pig, the dullest man in Christendom!'

She was not to know that lifting her head to speak was the trigger for mayhem.

As she raised her chin defiantly, John saw a glint of gold appear above the neck of the pale-cream gown that she wore. Careless of any courtesy to a lady, he plunged his fingers into the space between the linen and her soft skin. Paying no heed to her scream of outrage, he pulled out a heavy necklace of solid gold, embellished with intricate designs typical of Saxon craftsmanship.

'I think the last time I saw this, it was in the strong-room of the Great Tower!' he roared at Ranulf. 'So where's the rest of it, you thieving bastard?'

Three men on the next table had leapt to their feet when they heard the scream and saw the bosom of a fine lady apparently being violated, but they backed away rapidly when Ranulf whipped out a long dagger from his belt and advanced on the coroner, waving it dangerously close to his face. Simultaneously, William Aubrey unsheathed a short sword and, with his dagger in the other hand, leapt over the table to stand back-to-back with his friend, facing the somewhat astonished Gwyn. The room went into pandemonium, as the other diners fell over themselves in haste, to get out of range of what looked like a fight to the death.

De Wolfe and Gwyn had left their long swords in their saddle-sheaths, as they had entered the tavern expecting only to search for information, so both had to grab for their own daggers, which never left their belts.

'You stupid cow!' roared Ranulf at his mistress. 'I told you not to wear that damned thing until we left the country!'

At the same time, he lunged at John, who stepped back sharply and knocked over a fat dame who was desperately trying to get to the safety of the other side of the room.

'You cannot escape the city, Ranulf!' snarled de Wolfe. 'You may as well surrender and put yourselves at the mercy of the court.'

For reply, Ranulf slashed out again at John, this time slicing into the sleeve of his grey tunic. 'What mercy will we get?' he yelled. 'The choice between hanging or flaying alive?'

Behind him William Aubrey was challenging the big Cornishman and it became obvious that both these younger men, strong, fit and well trained from their frequent practice on the tourney fields, were expert fighters.

But the coroner and his officer, though more than a dozen years older, were crafty and experienced.

As Aubrey advanced on Gwyn, the ginger giant swept up a stool with one hand and swung it like a scythe, knocking the sword from the other man's hand. As it flew across the room, there were redoubled screams from the unfortunate patrons of the Falcon, who were struggling to get out of the doorway.

Ranulf and John circled each other, knife hands outstretched, each making feints and retreats, knocking over benches and stools as they glared into each other's eyes, watching to anticipate every new move. Hawise shrunk back on her bench, her face contorted partly by fear and partly by the thrill of having four reckless men fighting over her.

Aubrey, having lost his sword, was now on equal terms with Gwyn but arrogantly thought that he would easily dispatch this lumpish oaf from Cornwall. He made a sudden thrust, but the big man was not where he expected him to be – on the point of his dagger. Gwyn had stepped sideways and in a flash sunk his own knife deep into William's belly. He dragged it upwards under his ribs and a scream from the younger man was almost instantly staunched as a gout of blood erupted from his mouth.

As he pulled out his dagger, his opponent crashed to the floor, to the accompaniment of more shouts, curses and screams from the remaining bemused and frightened patrons.

'Settled this sod, Crowner!' yelled Gwyn. Moving towards the coroner and his adversary, he hesitated, wondering when to intervene and bring this fracas to a speedy end.

'Don't kill this bastard as well!' hollered de Wolfe. 'Or we'll never know what happened.'

But Ranulf had other ideas in his desperate situation. Suddenly stepping back from the coroner, he threw an arm around Hawise's waist and hoisted her to her feet, putting the point of his knife against her throat.

'Now back off, both of you!' he screamed, pressing the dagger so that a drop of blood appeared on the woman's white skin. 'Let us through and out into the yard, or she'll die!'

De Wolfe was outraged at his lack of chivalry. 'Is this what you won your spurs for, damn you? To shelter behind a woman's skirts?'

His contempt was far outmatched by Hawise. She screamed some obscenities that no high-born lady should have known as she wriggled in his grasp, but the knife bit even deeper and she subsided.

'I thought you were enamoured of this woman!' raged John. 'Now you are prepared to kill her!'

The knight gave a twisted grin. 'She is a demon in bed, for which I give thanks. But if it is a matter of her life or mine, then mine wins every time!'

Frustrated, but afraid that Ranulf would keep his promise and drive the knife deeper into her neck, John could only stand impotently while the other man began to pull her towards the door.

'Shall I have him, Crowner?' shouted Gwyn, waving his dagger hopefully. John shook his head. 'The swine is mad enough to slay her. Leave it, he can't get far.'

In fact, he got nowhere at all.

Suddenly, a glazed look came over Ranulf's face and he slid down Hawise's body to a crumpled heap on the floor. Astonished, John and his officer looked down at him, and saw that his eyes were open and his arms were flailing weakly, though the dagger had dropped from his fingers. Hawise was still on her feet, also looking down with a hand to her mouth in surprised consternation.

'She's stabbed the sod!' hissed Gwyn. 'There's a little knife sticking out of his back.'

An onlooker, in butcher's tunic and apron, gaped at the victim.

'He's been pithed!' he shouted, with professional expertise. 'The blade has gone into his backbone, between the chops.'

By now, the landlord had returned from market, to find his dining chamber resembling the shambles at Smithfield that he had just left. A corpse lay on the floor, covered in blood and another man had fallen, partly paralysed, against one of his tables. Now that the violent action had ceased, the room was a babble of excited talk, some of which apprised the landlord of what had happened. John went across to him as Gwyn and the butcher knelt by Ranulf's side.

'Good man, I am the king's coroner and that is my officer. We came across these two men who are urgently wanted by the Chief Justiciar for most serious crimes. They resisted and one is dead. The other seems badly wounded and we need to find a physician to attend to him.'

John was afraid that Ranulf would die before he could discover what had happened, and the landlord said that he would get some men to carry him to St Bartholomew's, this being the only place nearby with reputable medical care.

As he went off to organise this, John went over to the fallen marshal, who was slumped forwards, murmuring indistinctly.

Gwyn had kicked his dagger away for safety, but there seemed little chance of Ranulf becoming a danger ever again. Hawise was sitting weeping on her bench, but when John placed a consoling hand on her shoulder, she looked up defiantly.

'Have I killed him? He was going to murder me, after all we've been to each other these past two weeks.'

John looked down at the small ivory-handled knife, still sticking out from the centre of the man's back, below the shoulder blades. 'That was your eating knife?' he asked gently.

She nodded, wiping her eyes angrily with the hem of her sleeve.

'He was stabbing my neck, I could feel the blood running.' She lifted her chin to prove it. 'I thought he was going to kill me there and then, so I reached behind me to the table and grabbed the knife. I thrust it at the nearest part of him I could reach, to make him stop hurting me!'

She burst into tears again and he patted her shoulder awkwardly. Crying women frightened him more than a horde of Saracens.

'We'll get you taken back to Westminster as soon as we can arrange it. But you had better let me have that necklace, it would be better for you not to be seen wearing it.'

As she took it off, he made sure that she was not in possession of any more of the looted treasure. 'It's all in his saddlebag in the chamber upstairs,' she confessed. 'He said we would be rich when it was sold in Germany and that he'd win even more in the great tournaments.'

Gwyn came up and muttered in his ear. 'I reckon this fellow's going to die. If you want to get him to talk, we'd better look sharp about it.'

As if they had heard him, two servants pushed their way into the chamber with a door unhinged from one of the bedrooms.

They laid it alongside the injured man, then looked at John.

'We can't lie him down with that knife in his spine. Shall I pull it out?'

De Wolfe looked at Ranulf's back, where a thin stream of blood was running from around the knife blade staining the green cloth of his tunic. He shook his head.

'It might kill him, for all I know, stuck in his backbone like that. Put him face down, with his head turned to the side.'

As they jogged off up the road, John had a grim memory of Canon Simon being carted off to the same hospital in much the same fashion.

'You are going to die, my son, do you understand?'

These solemn words were uttered by Brother Philip,

the same Augustinian monk that had attended the poisoned canon.

Ranulf nodded weakly. 'I need to confess and be shrived, father,' he said. With the knife now removed, he lay on his back on a mattress on the floor of a cubicle in the hospital.

The monk-physician had earlier told John and Gwyn that there was no hope for the younger knight. 'The point has not only cut the vital pith that runs inside the backbone, but the amount of bleeding both outside and under the flesh, shows that some major vessel has been punctured. It is only a matter of time before he dies.'

'How long has he got?' asked Gwyn.

The monk turned up his palms. 'Impossible to say. It could be minutes, if the bleeding increases. Or it may be weeks, but he has lost the use of his bladder as well as his legs and that usually means that corruption of the kidneys will come sooner or later.'

He stopped and crossed himself. 'It would be better that a fit young man like that dies soon, rather than suffer the distress and indignity of his paralysed condition.'

'I had best speak with him right away,' said de Wolfe. 'He has committed heinous crimes against both the king and his fellow men. I suspect he was the one who poisoned the canon you treated some time ago.'

They went back into the small ward and John crouched alongside Ranulf of Abingdon.

'William Aubrey is dead and I fear that you will be joining him before long. You now have nothing to lose and perhaps by full confession, your soul will have something to gain in purgatory. Do you understand?'

The under-marshal nodded, tears in his eyes as he realised that his legs would never move again, even for the short time he was expected to survive. Brother

Philip pressed a crucifix into his hands and murmured a prayer.

'Tell me all about it, Ranulf,' urged de Wolfe. 'Simon Basset was another of your conspirators, eh?'

'Yes, it was his idea from the start,' muttered Ranulf, fumbling with the rosary attached to the cross. 'He was overfond of the good life. You have seen his house, his rich furnishings, his love of the best food and wine – especially his fondness for whoring. Well, he has an even grander house in Lichfield and he was always in need of money to buy more luxuries and to pay his debts for the ones he had.'

'So he came to you with a plan? But how did you come to conspire with a canon?'

'As marshals, we have several times brought treasure boxes from Winchester, which were received by Simon as a senior Exchequer official. He also was fond of secret gaming, and we came to know him well from that. He said that if we could get an impression of both keys of one of the money chests, he could manage to steal from the strongroom and we could share the proceeds.'

'So when the special box of treasure trove was to be moved, you decided to act? But how did you get the keys, I had them all the time?'

The dying man smiled weakly. 'Not all the time, Sir John. Remember the fire in the barn? We set that deliberately.'

De Wolfe was still mystified. 'But how could that benefit you?'

'William Aubrey pretended to go out for a shite at the back of the barn. He took a brand from the remains of the fire and set the thatch alight. When it was going well enough, he raised the alarm, but I pretended to sleep on. You rushed out in your bare feet, but left your belt with your pouch behind, next to where I made sure I was lying.'

'You bastard!' said John, forgetting for a moment that he was speaking to a dying man. 'But I was gone only a moment or two. I suspected it might be a diversion to rob the chests on the cart, so I rushed back again.'

'It was but the work of a few seconds to take the keys and press them into that box of wax which I held ready under my blanket.'

John shook his head in amazement at the sheer nerve of the thieves and the risk they had taken.

'But how could you know that we were going to be forced to stop at that village, where there was a convenient barn to set alight?'

'We didn't! It was a fortunate chance which we took on the spur of the moment. Originally, we were going to creep up on you at night and strike your head to knock your wits out, then take an impression of the keys as well as stealing the contents of your purse to make it look like a casual robbery.'

De Wolfe was aghast at the casual way the man spoke of an assault which might well have killed him.

'How did Canon Basset spirit away the gold?' he demanded.

'I do not know the details. I did not want to know them!' whispered Ranulf. 'I presume he managed to be left alone with the chests in the Tower for long enough to stuff some of the better trophies under his cassock.'

'Then what happened to them?'

The knight looked towards the Augustinian. 'Am I really going to die, Father?'

The monk nodded. 'You cannot survive this, my son. After you have made your legal confession to the coroner, we will take another for the sake of your soul.'

Ranulf sighed and held the crucifix to his lips for a moment.

'I did not fully trust Simon Basset. He used to cheat

at cards, which is a bad sign as to a man's true character. At first, he did not want to tell William and myself where he had hidden the treasure, but we threatened to expose him and then run away ourselves, so he gave in. He had placed them in a pottery jar concealed behind a loose stone in the abutment of the bridge next to his house – the one where the Royal Way crosses the Clowson Brook.'

Gwyn groaned. 'We would never have found that hiding place, if we looked until Doomsday!'

Ranulf sank back weakly, the cross falling from his fingers.

The monk looked at him with some concern and reached out a hand to feel his pulse. 'His breathing is becoming very shallow. I think that perhaps the blood in his spine is rising towards his brain.'

'What about that ironmaster?' asked John, urgently. 'I am sure he was the one who made the copies of the keys?'

'Yes, we were afraid that he might betray us, as he was asking for a larger reward, so Simon said he had to go.'

'And you did it?' rasped the coroner.

'Yes, God forgive me. He was too much of a risk.'

His face was very pale now and his lips were taking on a violet hue, so John hurried on. 'And the canon, what of his death?'

'He said that as he had taken all the risks in taking the treasure from the Tower, he also should have a greater share. We had agreed to split it three ways, but he wanted a half share. Aubrey and I decided that if there were going to be half shares, we should have one each. I arranged to meet him at the Falcon and I slipped a large dose of foxglove into his food.'

'Where did you get that?' demanded Gwyn.

Ranulf managed a slight shrug. 'William got it somewhere. Any shady apothecary will sell you anything, if the price is right. I think he told the man he wanted to get rid of a sick dog.'

John looked across at Gwyn and they both shook their heads in wonder. The cunning, deviousness and lack of honour shown by two knights of the realm and an ordained canon was beyond belief. All for the love of money and the things it could buy.

'Have you done with your questions, Sir John?' asked the monk. 'I think this man, evil though he has been, has had enough for the moment.'

Ranulf certainly looked as if he was at death's door; rising, John had one last question.

'You were prepared to attack me to get the keys – so was it you who tried to strangle me in the chapel crypt and then fell me with an arrow at Greenford?'

Even in his failing condition, Ranulf managed to look astonished. 'Why should I want to do that? I know nothing of those incidents, Sir John, as God is my judge.'

Though John would not now have believed anything the rogue said, there was ring of sincerity about the denial.

'God soon will be your judge, Ranulf! You have caused deaths, a great deal of distress and besmirched the name of the knighthood you hold. I hope that you have sufficient remorse to allow God in heaven to show you some compassion.'

He walked out with Gwyn behind him, into the sunlight of the large precinct around the hospital. Then he stopped and looked down sadly at the ground between his feet.

'I have not come out of this well, Gwyn! I was given charge of those bloody keys and I failed, even though it was but for a few moments. Those cunning bastards outmanoeuvred me and once again I have betrayed my king.'

Gwyn began to demur, but de Wolfe raised a hand to silence him. 'This makes me all the more determined in what I had planned to do,' he declared obscurely. 'I need to see Hubert Walter as soon as possible, tell him how this business has turned out – and then tell him I no longer feel able to keep the post of coroner.'

Three mornings later, the dust had settled on the hectic events that had involved the Coroner of the Verge. The palace was relatively quiet, as Queen Eleanor had ridden off for Portsmouth two days earlier with William Marshal and her retinue.

John sat in his chamber overlooking the Thames, with Gwyn perched on the window-ledge and Thomas at his usual place at the table. A few sheets of parchment now lay completed in front of the clerk, as he had just finished writing the account John had given him of the past few days, to be placed in the Chancery records.

'So the Lady Hawise is now safely restored to her husband,' said Thomas reflectively.

'When we got back to Westminster, I sought out Renaud de Seigneur, who was prowling the palace like a man possessed,' said John. 'I think he was more angry at being cuckolded than at the loss of his wife, but when I told him that she was in the city, left in the care of the wife of the landlord of the Falcon, he yelled for his servants and galloped away to fetch her.'

'I saw them returning some time later,' reported Gwyn, relishing the memory. 'She was riding pillion behind him and neither looked very pleased with each other. He almost dragged her away into the guest quarters and she looked far from happy at being reunited with her husband.'

'They went off with Queen Eleanor's procession, so by next week they'll be back in Blois. God knows what will become of them then, they are hardly a pair of lovebirds!'

'She'll no doubt find some good-looking knight to amuse herself with,' prophesied Gwyn, with a guileless look at his master, who was heartily relieved at the departure of the feckless beauty.

John was still smarting at the news that Hubert Walter had given him when he reported the success of his mission to find Ranulf and William Aubrey. His visit to the Justiciar's chambers was made even sweeter when he was able to dump a saddlebag on the floor and produce all the golden objects that had been stolen from the Tower, including the heavy Saxon necklet that he had retrieved from around Hawise's neck. But this triumph was somewhat dampened when he told Hubert of his suspicions that the lady and her husband may have been spies for Philip of France and his regret that they had left before he had the chance to expose them.

Instead of expressing concern, the archbishop let out a loud guffaw and slapped his hand on the table in a gesture of good humour.

'Don't fret about that, John! They were indeed spies – but for me, not the French! Renaud de Seigneur came across to report what he had recently picked up in Blois and neighbouring counties about Philip Augustus's intentions in that area.'

The coroner was mortified. 'Did his wife know about this?'

Hubert grinned roguishly at his old comrade. 'John, the old dog used Hawise and her insatiable appetite for younger men, to gather intelligence wherever it might be found – often in some large French bed, no doubt!'

De Wolfe felt sullied by the knowledge, though later he consoled himself with the thought that at least she had wanted him for his body, rather than to worm French secrets from him.

It also deepened the mystery of who had ordered the two attacks upon his life, as several times he had falsely claimed in the presence of the de Seigneurs, that he was on the point of unmasking some foreign spies. But if they were on the side of England, this ruled them out as the instigators of the assaults.

Since his interview with the Justiciar, he had had news of Ranulf's death in the Hospital of St Bartholomew. Though the man was a murderous rogue, John felt a twinge of sadness for both him and William Aubrey. They had been amiable companions, even though their duplicity was unforgivable.

Gwyn had felt no compunction or guilt about so effectively dispatching the younger marshal, as his philosophy was 'kill or be killed' and anyone who drew a sword or knife upon him was fair game for fatal retaliation. Now he hauled himself off the windowsill and stretched his hairy arms above his head in a lazy movement.

'Are we really going to get out of this miserable place and go home to God's own land?' he asked.

De Wolfe nodded, almost afraid to tempt fate by parading his good fortune. 'I have promised to wait until next week, until other arrangements are made,' he said. 'Hubert Walter has committed himself, though I still have concerns about what King Richard might have to say.'

After settling the affair of the treasure with the Chief Justiciar, John had stood squarely before Hubert's table and, after a few preliminary throat clearances to cover his nervousness, launched into his plea.

'Your Grace, though this matter has ended satisfactorily, in that the gold has been recovered intact and the miscreants have paid the ultimate penalty, I feel that I have failed you and the king. I was charged with the safe keeping of that treasure and, as I have explained, I was tricked into losing possession of the keys, albeit for a brief few moments.'

He paused for breath, but Hubert sat with his fingers interlaced and did not interrupt.

'Once before I failed in my duty to my king and I consider that I should no longer hold this position of trust as Coroner of the Verge. I have to say that the problems of jurisdiction and the dearth of work here, also make me feel redundant. I humbly seek your consent to my release, so that I may return to Devon and live out my years quietly.'

He swallowed hard, partly from emotion and partly from the effort of making an unusually long speech, then waited anxiously for the Justiciar's response.

'By St Peter's cods, John, that's bloody nonsense!' said Hubert, in most un-ecclesiastical language. 'The king himself absolved you from any blame over the Vienna capture. If anything, it was his own fault for being so rash! And as for this present escapade, you brought it to a successful conclusion single-handedly, apart from the help of that great ginger fellow and that remarkable little clerk of yours.'

De Wolfe opened his mouth to repeat his confession of failure, but Hubert held up his hand.

'No, John, you were duped by clever and un-scrupulous men, and no blame can be attached to you. The king will be well satisfied that the gold has been recovered and the perpetrators dealt with in a summary fashion, with no jeering tales to be bandied about.'

'I still feel unable to continue as Coroner of the Verge, sire,' said John stubbornly. 'I am sure you can find some knight or baron more suited to the life of the court to take my place – the duties are far from arduous.'

After some more contrary argument by Hubert, he eventually gave in.

'If you are really set upon this – and I suspect it is as much your wishing to return to your beloved Devon as eschewing the duties here – then so be it. I will have to concoct some tale for the king when I see him in Rouen next month, but I trust that he will agree, as a reward for your recovering his precious gold!'

There the matter was left, but now John was able to confirm to his two assistants that in a week or so they would be back on the road to Exeter.

'I will be happy enough helping my wife in the Bush,' boomed Gwyn cheerfully. 'And playing with my lads and drinking half the profits of the tavern!'

'And the archivist in the cathedral invited me to return there to help him at any time,' added Thomas. 'I'm sure I can eventually find a living somewhere, perhaps in some remote parish.' He sounded a little wistful at that, as at heart he was an academic priest, rather than one who would be content to tend his flock in a rural village.

'But what about you, Crowner?' asked Gwyn solicitously. 'You and I are too old to go campaigning abroad, seeking new battles – our sword arms are getting tired. What will you do with yourself?'

John grinned crookedly. 'I have this partnership with Hugh de Relaga, so I can take a more active interest in it, as it brings me sufficient to live on. And no doubt I will be taking the road to Dawlish quite often!'

His smile faded. 'Though God knows how this matter of my wife will be resolved – I am neither married nor a bachelor these days.'

After their dinner at the dwelling in Long Ditch Lane, where Aedwulf and Osanna received with equanimity the news that their tenants were leaving, de Wolfe and his officer walked back to the chamber in the palace. They were resigned to another afternoon of boredom, as no palace resident had been murdered, raped or battered.

As usual, Gwyn stared out of the window at the ever-changing river, the boats plying up and down and the muddy banks being covered and exposed twice a day by the tide. John sat at his table, his Latin exercises lying ignored before him, while he thought dark thoughts about Matilda's continued obdurateness. When he went back to Exeter, something must be done to resolve the problem, though for the life of him he could not imagine what. His mood lightened when his mind moved on to his house and his dog, with images of himself sitting before his hearth in the coming autumn, with a quart of ale and old Brutus's head on his lap. And the journeys to Dawlish and the company of the delectable Hilda were the pinnacle of his wandering thoughts.

They were shattered when Thomas came through the door, out of breath and obviously in a state of great excitement.

'Crowner, you remember that novice I brought to you, Robin Byard, who told us that tale about Basil of Reigate?'

De Wolfe sat up straight and glared at his clerk. 'What of him? Has he been slain too?'

'No, it's not him, but another novitiate that Robin brought to see me after dinner in the abbey refectory just now. He was also a friend of Basil's.' Thomas reddened slightly. 'Another very good friend, if you know what I mean.'

'For the Virgin's sake, get to the point, Thomas! You're as bad as Gwyn for spinning out a tale!'

'This young man, Alfred, has been away for some weeks at the chapel in Windsor, for he is a particularly sweet chanter.' Thomas caught the impatient glint in John's eye and hurried on.

'So he knew nothing of Basil's death nor what Basil had told Robin Byard about overhearing some treason. But today he learned from Robin – who is also his very good friend indeed – what Basil told him of his fears.'

'What the hell's all this about, dwarf?' grumbled Gwyn, who was getting confused.

'Basil had also told Alfred that he overheard sedition in the guest chambers – but he knows who it was that was speaking, for Basil had told him!'

The coroner rammed his fists against his table and levered himself up to tower over his clerk. 'Who was it, Thomas? Don't tell me that after all, it was that fat lord from Blois?'

Thomas shook his head emphatically. 'Not at all, Crowner! It was the archdeacon from the Auvergne, Bernard de Montfort. He was giving a parchment roll to another guest, a chaplain from some priory in Ponthieu. Basil heard him say, in Latin, that he must get it to Paris, as it listed the manor-lords of Kent and Sussex who were favourable to Prince John and also the disposition of garrisons along the coast. The archdeacon said it was the result of a month's work on his part and not to fail him in its delivery. Then the screen fell down and the two men saw Basil crouching there.'

That was all Thomas's news, but it was more than enough. De Wolfe was blazing with anger, as not only had the archdeacon brought about the death of the innocent guest-chamber clerk, but he must have instigated the two attacks upon John, fearful of the truth of John's boasts about soon unmasking the spy.

'How did he manage it, Crowner?' asked Gwyn. 'That fat priest was not fit enough to go stabbing, strangling and shooting crossbows! He must have employed that ratcatching villain who died in the forest in Greenwood.'

'A very convenient death, too!' snapped John. 'I always thought that falling a bare dozen feet from that deer-trap was unlikely to have broken his neck. Now we know, for it was de Montfort's servant who chased him and happily found him dead, so that he could not confess as to who had hired him. That Raoul must have deliberately broken his neck before we got there!'

'So who stabbed Basil on the river pier?' queried Thomas.

De Wolfe looked at Gwyn. 'The man you saw running past that window – could it have been this Jordan fellow?'

Gwyn shrugged. 'Just a big fellow, no way of telling.'

He paused, his brows furrowed. 'So what are you going to do about the archdeacon, Crowner? He went off with the queen's party and is in Portsmouth by now.'

John paced up and down the chamber in indecision. 'I'll have to tell the Justiciar, obviously. It's now probably too late to chase them to the Channel, but that's up to Hubert to decide. Get that fellow Alfred over here, Thomas – and Robin Byard too. Hubert Walter must be informed of this, but he's so devious in his ways, that for all I know, Bernard de Montfort might be one of his agents as well, giving false information to the French. If the stakes were high enough, that wouldn't stop them from killing a clerk or even a lowly coroner in order to keep their secrets safe!'

By the end of that day, John had done all he could by delivering this latest news to the Keeper, Nathaniel de Levelondes, as Hubert had gone off to Lambeth to view his new palace. What they did about it was no longer his concern, he was tired of Westminster and all its intrigues. The sooner he could get home to Devon, the better he would be pleased.

He trudged home with Gwyn at about the sixth hour, in the warmth of a pleasant summer evening, as the oppressive heat of previous weeks had moderated. Thomas had gone off to the abbey and the two old campaigners walked in companionable silence down Thieving Lane towards the Long Ditch. Both had the feeling that another phase of their life was coming to a close and were wondering what lay before them back in Exeter. For each of them, things would be very different. Gwyn would be living with his wife and running an alehouse, a very different life from being a coroner's officer.

John would no longer be that coroner, so would time hang heavily on his hands? How was this new liaison with Hilda going to work out? She had made it clear that she was not willing to give up her fine house and life in Dawlish. He still had the responsibility of his dwelling in Martin's Lane and of Mary, to say nothing of the embarrassment of a stubborn wife hiding in Polsloe Priory.

They turned into Long Ditch Lane and ambled up towards their lodging, but as they neared it, the globular figure of Osanna came out of the door and stood waiting for them, hands on her hips.

'What's she want now?' growled Gwyn. 'To tell us it's eels again for supper?'

Her news was quite different. 'There's a lady arrived to visit you, Sir John. With a mortal lot of possessions.'

His face lit up, trusting that Hilda had again come on one of their ships to the Thames. Did a great deal of luggage mean that she had decided to come and live with him?

He hurried inside and stopped as if he had run into a stone wall.

Sitting on a stool, surrounded by bags and bundles, was Matilda!

Arrayed in dusty travelling clothes, she glared at him, her mouth a hard, disapproving line in her square face.

'Matilda!' he groaned. 'How came you here?'

'With a party of pilgrims on their way to Canterbury,' she snapped in her gravelly voice. 'I have decided that it is not seemly that the coroner to the king's own court should live without his wife.'

She meticulously rearranged her skirts across her knees. 'The prioress and Dame Madge told me of your tales of the grandeur of Westminster and all the eminent nobles and prelates with whom you associate. It is only right that I should be by your side.'

John threw back his head and gazed at the ceiling, wishing it would fall upon him and put him out of his sudden misery.

Where all his attempts at coaxing her out of Polsloe had failed, her unbridled snobbery and mania for social advancement had succeeded. All that remained was for him to gather the courage to tell her that they would be returning to Exeter within the week and that he would shortly be neither the Royal Coroner of the Verge – nor any sort of coroner at all!

POCKET
BOOKS

Bernard Knight
The Elixir of Death

1195. Prince John still plots to seize the throne from his
brother, Richard the Lionheart – and in his wicked
schemes he is supported by Philip of France. The French
king offers to help John financially by sending him a
mysterious alchemist, a Mohammedan named Nizam,
who claims to be able to turn base metals into gold.

But the ship which was transporting Nizam and his
retainers is found wrecked off the south Devon coast,
its crew savagely slaughtered.

Shortly afterwards, a Norman knight named Philip le
Calve is foully murdered, his severed head stuck on the
rood screen of Exeter cathedral.

It's up to Sir John de Wolfe, the county coroner, to find a
motive and connection between the killings. And just
what is his unscrupulous brother-in-law, the disgraced
ex-sheriff and Prince John-sympathiser, Richard de
Revelle, trying to hide?

'Packed with the sights, sounds and smells of medieval
England, the Crowner John series is a national treasure'
Mike Ripley, *Birmingham Post*

ISBN 978-0-74349-215-7
PRICE £6.99

POCKET
BOOKS

Bernard Knight
Figure of Hate

October, 1195. High-spirited young knights, drunken squires, pickpockets and horse thieves are pouring into Exeter for a one-day jousting tournament. Not even the discovery of a naked corpse in the River Exe can spoil the excitement.

During the tournament there's a serious altercation between Hugo Peverel, a manor lord from Tiverton, and a Frenchman by the name of Reginald de Charterai. When, two days later, Sir Hugo's bloodsoaked body is found in a barn on his estate, de Charterai would seem the obvious culprit.

But there's no shortage of people who wished the hated Hugo dead. All three of his brothers have a motive; as do his stepmother and attractive young widow. The manor reeve, Warin Fishacre, had his own reasons to loathe his lord and master.

With so many suspects, Sir John de Wolfe, the county coroner, hardly knows where to begin. And just what is the connection between Sir Hugo's murder and the battered body in the River Exe?

ISBN 978-0-74349-214-0
PRICE £6.99

POCKET
BOOKS

Bernard Knight
The Witch Hunter

Exeter, 1195. When a prominent burgess and
guild-master falls dead across his horse, Crowner
John declines to hold an inquest as the man had
been complaining of chest pains and shows no
sign of injury.

Events take a sinister turn, however, when a straw-
dolly is discovered hidden under the man's saddle,
a spike through its heart. The victim's strident wife
declares her husband's death to have been the result
of an evil spell, cast at the behest of a rival mill-owner
who wants to acquire his business. Enlisting the help
of her cousin, a cathedral canon with an eye to
ecclesiastical advancement, the widow begins a
campaign in the name of the Church against witchcraft
and the so-called 'cunning women' who practise it.
This escalates until Exeter is divided into two camps
and a climate of fear predominates. Still the coroner
refuses to get involved – until his beloved mistress
accused of witchcraft.

Can Crowner John unearth the real culprit and save
Nesta from the hangman's noose?

ISBN 978-0-74344-989-2
PRICE £6.99

POCKET
BOOKS

Bernard Knight
The Noble Outlaw

Exeter, 1195. Renovations at the new school in Smythen
Street are disrupted by the shocking discovery of a
partially mummified corpse hidden in the rafters – and
Sir John de Wolfe, the county coroner, is summoned
to investigate.

Richard de Revelle, Sir John's brother-in-law and
founder of the school, immediately tries to blame
Nicholas de Arundell, a young outlawed knight living
rough on Dartmoor. As Sir John discovers, Nicholas has
good reason to bear a grudge against the unscrupulous
de Revelle.

But is he really a killer? With the victim's identity
unknown and the motive a mystery, the murder
remains unsolved. Then comes news of a second violent
death – and Sir John is forced to track down the noble
outlaw in order to find the answers . . .

ISBN 978-1-41652-593-6
PRICE £6.99

POCKET
BOOKS

Bernard Knight
The Manor of Death

April, 1196. When an unidentified body is discovered in the harbour town of Axmouth, twenty miles from Exeter, Sir John de Wolfe, the county coroner, is summoned to investigate. The manner of the young man's death is a matter of some dispute. But, as Sir John discovers, it was no accident. The victim did not drown, as the manor reeve alleges, but was strangled to death.

The ensuing murder enquiry is frustrated by what appears to be a conspiracy of silence among the seamen and townsfolk. Just what is the local population trying to hide?

In order to root out the truth, Sir John hatches a cunning plan. But is he playing with fire? There are those who would go to any lengths to ensure the shocking truth remains hidden, and Crowner John must draw on all his resources of courage and ingenuity if he is to escape from Axmouth with his life.

ISBN 978-1-41652-594-3
PRICE £6.99

**POCKET
BOOKS**

This book and other **Bernard Knight** titles are available from your bookshop or can be ordered direct from the publisher.

978-1-84739-328-9	**Crowner Royal**	£6.99
978-1-41652-594-3	**The Manor of Death**	£6.99
978-1-41652-593-6	**The Noble Outlaw**	£6.99
978-0-74349-215-7	**The Elixir of Death**	£6.99
978-0-74349-214-0	**Figure of Hate**	£6.99
978-0-74344-989-2	**The Witch Hunter**	£6.99
978-0-74344-990-8	**Fear in the Forest**	£6.99
978-0-67102-967-8	**The Grim Reaper**	£6.99

Please send cheque or postal order for the value
of the book, **free postage and packing within
the UK**, to SIMON & SCHUSTER CASH SALES
PO Box 29, Douglas Isle of Man, IM99 1BQ
Tel: 01624 677237, Fax: 01624 670923
E-mail: bookpost@enterprise.co.uk
www.bookpost.co.uk

Please allow 14 days for delivery. Prices and availability
subject to change without notice